BROKEN

NOWHERE TO TURN
BOOK 1

STACEY UPTON

MIKE KRAUS

MUONIC
PRESS

BROKEN
Nowhere to Turn
Book 1

By
Stacey Upton
Mike Kraus

© 2023 Muonic Press Inc
www.muonic.com

———————

www.eatwriteplay.com

———————

www.MikeKrausBooks.com
hello@mikeKrausBooks.com
www.facebook.com/MikeKrausBooks

CONTENTS

WANT MORE AWESOME BOOKS?

Find more fantastic tales right here, at books.to/readmorepa.

If you're new to reading Mike Kraus, consider visiting his website at MikeKrausBooks.com and signing up for his free newsletter. You'll receive several free books and a sample of his audiobooks, too, just for signing up, you can unsubscribe at any time and you will receive absolutely *no* spam.

You can also stay updated on Stacey Upton's books by visiting her website at eatwriteplay.com or on her instagram at instagram.com/staceyuptonbracey.

SPECIAL THANKS

Special thanks to my awesome beta team, without whom this book
wouldn't be nearly as great.

Thank you!

READ THE NEXT BOOK IN THE SERIES

Nowhere to Turn Book 2

Available Here
books.to/KcKMO

CHAPTER ONE

The Guy-Greenbriar Fault

Addison Howell stepped onto his back deck, the thick air popping beads of sweat on his bare chest the moment he left the cool of the double wide. He rested his coffee cup on the peeling paint of the rail, rubbed his eyes and stretched, then scratched his belly as he listened to the peaceful drone of the insects out in the tall grass. A few neighbors had lights on, but for the moment, it was just him and the bugs and the press of midsummer heat outdoors in the predawn. A breeze tried to stir the air and momentarily moved the big old cottonwoods on the edge of the trailer park where it dipped by the stream, dark movement against the greying sky. Then the breeze gave up, leaving behind the sense of a breath held in its absence.

The screen door squeaked, and Darcie's hands snaked around his torso as she hugged him from behind, the solid baby bump of kid number three nestling in just under his waistline. "Earthquake weather," she commented.

"No such thing as earthquake weather." He brought her around in front of him and planted a kiss on the top of her head, snugging her tighter to him. "Wish I could go with you to see the doc."

1

She shrugged. "Better that you're working again. I packed your lunch. Two PB and J's and some corn chips. You want a Ho-Ho too?"

"Packing me a kiddie lunch," he said grumpily as he followed her back inside and snagged his neatly pressed work shirt off of the kitchen chair. "And yes to the Ho-Ho."

Darcie was too quiet as she handed him his hard hat and lunchbox. He touched her arm gently. "What's wrong?"

"I just wish they'd never decided to reopen those gas wells."

Addison tapped the frown line that had appeared between her eyebrows. "Stop worrying. They've run the equipment all week with no problems to get to the lower layer, and today we go horizontal."

"Well, have fun getting past the picketers. Janell says she's rounded up another twenty people to protest."

"That's what my four by four is for," he joked. "To move 'em aside." He dodged her playful slap and headed out the door.

Addison drove his truck along the county road just ahead of the sunrise. He turned onto Main with its two stoplights and four churches, then continued west to the fracking site in the long, low hills outside of town. Sure enough, Janell and her protester friends blocked the gate to the fracking site as they waved signs and chanted, "We said no!" Addison slowed his vehicle to a crawl and rolled down the window to talk to their neighbor.

"Janell, don't you have better things to do?"

The thin woman put a hand on his door and gripped it as if she could forcibly stop his truck from moving forward. "Don't go in there and start it up, Add. It's not safe. You know we had all those cluster quakes before."

"Janell don't start that fearmongering with me. It's bad enough you've got Darcie all twisted up."

"I'm serious, Add. I wouldn't be out here if I wasn't. You know I'm right!"

"What I know is that you're in my way."

Up ahead, the foreman and several guards pushed aside protesters and the car line started to move. Addison pointed ahead. "I'm going in there so I can feed my family, Janell." He buzzed up the window and kept pace with the other vehicles, rolling his eyes at the sound of

Janell's fists as they banged on his truck. She could protest until the cows came home; it wouldn't stop him from doing his job.

The men were gathered into the common room after they'd clocked in. The packed room was like a reunion of sorts, holding men he knew from church and even a few other defensive linemen from his high school football team. The suits from the gas company were up in front, along with a couple of science guys in white coats who droned on about how it was a big day for the community, how safe things were and how the microquakes were nothing to fear. Addison shifted from one foot to the other, impatient for the yammering to stop so he could get to work. It'd been nine months since he'd been laid off from the long hauls and he was done with Darcie being the only one who brought home a paycheck.

Finally, the bosses were done talking and Addison joined the flow of men as they walked outside into the dull glare of an overcast sky. He threaded through a maze of low pipes as he strode toward the tall drilling rig and the three giant fluid waste containers that squatted behind it. Addison reached his fracking fluid truck and did a quick check that the outflow valves were positioned where they needed to be, then climbed in the cab and cranked up the air-conditioning before he toggled his walkie.

"Fluid truck five, good to roll."

Addison flapped up his shirt, so his belly got a good blast of the cold air. His sigh of pleasure turned into a grunt as the big compressors started up, their low rumble combining with the brain-splitting high whine of the drill bearing down in the old well as it reached for the gas rich layer eight thousand feet below. He winced and clapped on his ear protectors as he cursed himself for not getting them on sooner.

The shaking came through the bottom of his boots first, then encompassed the whole cab. Addison gripped the wheel of the truck when the odd vibrations grew stronger. Movement above him caught his eye as the big three-story drill rig started to sway side to side, the top arcing a good fifteen degrees each way from vertical. A clutch of fear grabbed Addison's gut at the sight, which redoubled at the sound of sloshing water in the tank behind him as his truck yawed side to side, the agitated contents pounding the sides of its container. It'd tip if it kept up much longer.

A sharp jolt bounced him in his seat, followed by two more in quick succession. The ear protectors flew off and his teeth snapped down and bit into his tongue. Addison swore as he spat the blood onto his jeans and grabbed the door handle, his muscles tensed and ready to run, but then the motion eased. The tower shuddered back to center as puffs of disturbed earth swirled along the ground.

Addison blew out a long breath, then jumped as his walkie sparked to life with a series of squawks. The foreman's voice shouted to shut things down. In moments, the whine on the drill dimmed to silence while the compressors continued their hum for a few seconds more. As they slowed, the sway returned for a heart-stopping moment, then the earth settled to solid, the way it was supposed to be.

"Whew." Addison puffed out a sigh of relief. He flipped down his visor to see how much of a hole his teeth had put into his tongue, wiping away the blood with the back of his hand. He released a shaky laugh, then shook his head. Darcie would be telling him she'd been right about the earthquake weather for the next month, maybe even for the next year. He turned up the air to its highest level and leaned back in his seat to wait for his heart to resume its normal beat again.

A barely noticeable rumble along with vibration under his boots made him sit upright. Alarm zinged through Addison as the vibration became a sound like a freight train headed straight at him, growing in intensity as it turned from sound to violent vertical shaking in a matter of moments. Addison bounced hard in his seat, his head smacking the top of the cab before he was flung sideways against the door. The earth under his truck cracked in half, elevating the passenger side of the truck. The up and down movement intensified while Addison grappled with the door handle, his sweaty fingers slipping on the metal. The crack in the earth that had opened up beneath him continued to grow outward even as it widened from a few feet to several yards in the space of his indrawn breath.

The crack swept under the footing of the big drill, causing the scaffolding to jerk upwards as its bolts popped from the concrete.

They flew through the air, the hardware turned into deadly missiles. One snapped through his windshield, shattering it as it punched clear through the seat next to him to lodge in the back of the cab. Addison flinched but couldn't take his eyes off of the three-story tower that danced on its tiptoes for a moment before the whole edifice twisted sideways, then tipped, the main portion falling straight toward him. Addison scrabbled frantically to pop the door open, tumbling out seconds before a red-painted steel beam crushed the roof of the truck and the water container. The sweep of air and dust from the fallen tower choked him as he scrambled to his feet.

The buckling ground beneath him heaved as if he were on an angry ocean rather than land as he ran from the opening maw of the earth. One of the men near him teetered sideways, captured by one of the widening cracks that multiplied like living things. The man's arms flailed, and he loosed a terrible scream as he fell into the chasm just before Addison could reach him.

Three huge bangs like giant drums being beaten made him turn to look just as a flood of water knocked Addison forward onto his hands and knees. Momentarily submerged, he heaved up from the foul wastewater, choking and spitting as the vile stuff streamed over his shoulders and head, washing him along the ground as if he were no more than a bug. In the ebb of it, Addison got back to his feet but only managed two or three steps forward before staggering sideways as the up and down jolting continued. The motion was so violent that it shook the two-story main building in front of him to bits, its red brick pulverized into clouds of dust. Addison's throat hurt from screaming, but all he could hear was the violent tearing of the earth and the screech of metal grinding on metal as the pipes surrounding him burst and erupted. His throat raw, he gasped to breathe in the middle of the murk of upflung dirt and debris as he staggered toward the parking lot. A waft of clear air revealed a chaotic scatter of vehicles, some on fire and belching black smoke, others dropped sideways, or on their roofs as if they were tiny toys flung by an angry child.

He changed direction and aimed to exit the epicenter of chaos through the front gates, other men running beside him as the earth continued to open in ever-widening cracks. He leapt over a crevice that appeared in front of him, kept his legs churning. A bright spear of fire erupted a hundred yards away and then the aftermath of the explosion hit with a wave of superheated air and gouts of fiery gas. Addison threw himself to the ground as a fireball ripped past him then exploded into the line of trees beyond the fence line like a mortar, making the dry woods leap into flames.

The heaving continued, the earth groaning as it was rendered into smaller and smaller pieces, whole sections liquified into a slurry that swallowed anything that rested upon it. Addison was forced to slew his trajectory sideways as the biggest crack widened even more. Ten yards across, it raced due east toward the town as if it had waited a thousand years to be freed.

Addison kept moving forward as more explosions from the yard sounded and the broiling heat from the inferno scorched the back of his neck. Ahead, the earth rolled like a quilt lofted onto a bed, the wave of it carrying the burning trees and then the buildings of the town up, then down. He cried out in dismay as the church steeples rose high in the sky, then toppled one after another, bells clanging in protest. The dust from downtown's destruction clouded the air as more and more buildings collapsed. Bangs, then sparks from blown transformers went off in a weird parody of the Fourth of July as fire erupted along the main street's wooden storefronts.

Addison screamed his wife's name as the destruction continued to roll in front of him, headed straight toward their home. A sharp jolt jammed the earth upward in front of him, catching him in an awkward mid-step and his ankle snapped, sending a bolt of agony along his leg. Addison crashed to the ground as he clutched at the ruined limb. An odd crackling sound filled the air, the sound a wave makes as it pulls back from a rocky shore, then the hard ground soft-ened beneath his back. Terror gripped him and he tried to roll away from the spot, but it was too late. Addison's final scream was engulfed by a wave of earth and rock that swallowed him whole.

The fault arrowed through the town, moving fast as it destroyed the small trailer park on the far side, reducing the poorly built struc-tures to rubble in seconds. The quake raced outward, travelling both west and east as ancient plates slipped for the first time in a millennium. The grind of their sideways passage thousands of feet below the surface of the earth created more vibration as new pathways formed and shook more dormant faults to life, all eager to find a new shape and relief from long constraint, utterly indifferent to the awful destruction their release rendered atop the crust of the earth.

CHAPTER TWO

The New Madrid Fault

Deb Varden sighed as she pulled her short pony tail through the back of her baseball cap and looked at her sports watch again. The apartment elevator was taking its own sweet time getting down to the ground floor, so there'd be no easy stroll up Washington Avenue today to get her legs warmed up. Even if she ran flat-out she'd still be late meeting up with Katie and Janell for their morning run.

She adjusted her full water bottle on the belt around her waist, cinching it tight so it wouldn't bounce on her hip. As soon as the clunky elevator opened its doors, Deb pulled out her cell phone and punched in Katie's number while she pushed out of the apartment complex doors into the sticky Memphis heat. The phone rang as she headed toward the Mississippi river at a quick pace.

Katie answered, the humor bubbling through her stern words. "You're late again, aren't you?"

"Yeah, about seven minutes away. Sorry. We had a bunch come in to the hospital last night, so I had to do overtime." At least there weren't many people out to get in her way, so Deb let her sturdy legs stretch out as she paced along the sidewalk. The rising sun elongated her shadow in front of her, turning her into a running giant.

"Girl, I know you were just swilling some down on Beale, don't give me that."

Deb chuckled. "That was you, Katie. Hey, make Janell do stretches or something, so she doesn't get mad."

"Janell isn't mad," Deb's other friend shouted from a distance to Katie's phone. "But I'm going to make us do those heavy rope things if you're not here in five minutes."

"You hear that?" Katie asked. "She's got her serious face on. Hurry up."

Deb smiled as she tucked her cell into the pocket of her running shorts and zipped it up as she took the cutoff through the little park in front of the sheriff's office onto BB King. The park wasn't that far away, and her legs didn't feel too bad, even if she was pushing her cadence. She hated doing the ropes as much as Katie did, and Janell would make good on her threat, too. Deb inhaled the rich, moist air from the river less than half a mile away. The good feeling of her body moving and the promise of friends waiting for an early morning run and the clear air elevated her mood. Deb took the left onto Poplar and upped her pace just because she could. Mud Island Park was two short blocks ahead, where the street came to a T intersection. Then she just had to cross the street to a two-story parking garage whose stairs would let her descend to the green beltway where Janell and Katie waited. She'd beat the five-minute limit and save them from the dreaded rope workout for sure.

A huge flock of starlings winged above, giving her momentary shade as they went by. They flew silently as if they were on a desperate mission, their flight arrowing straight east instead of their usual meandering stop and start. Deb's skin was already slick with sweat as she passed the squat Presbyterian church, and then the loftier Methodist one on the same block. An odd tremor vibrated under her feet as if a heavy truck had passed by, but the street only had a few parked cars on it along with one or two others making their way to the same running paths as she was. The bell tower at the front of the Methodist church swayed a bit, the bell gently hitting its clapper with a soft bong.

Her phone rang, and she fished it out as she approached the tall office buildings that fronted the Mississippi. "Nearly there," she told Katie.

"Did you feel that?"

"Little earthquake, I think. See ya in a minute."

Deb snapped her phone shut just as the street jolted violently. Deb staggered as she tried to keep upright, her bright blue running shoes doing an intricate dance as the sidewalk lifted, then rolled. Terrible cracking and grinding noises followed the roll, and the shaking continued to build. A car slid in front of her, crashing into the building on her left, the terrified face of the driver peered out at her just before the airbags went off. Across the street, the giant metal sculpture in front of the performing arts center heaved on its four legs, a silver monster come to life as another sharp jolt, then several in succession knocked her to the ground. The huge glass walls of the arts center shattered, sending shards flying outward straight toward her. Deb screamed and whirled away into a protective crouch, covering her face with her hands just in time as the glass cascaded down, the glass pattering on her hat, its sharp edges nicking her bare arms and shoulders. Above her, the government building teetered, the windows snapping outward as the big building moved with the earth in undulating waves that got larger with each successive one. Deb scrambled to her feet, intent on getting to an open space and away from the office buildings which surrounded her.

Deb ran full out toward the parking lot for Mud Island. If she could get there, she might be safe, away from the buildings that seemed ready to topple on her at any moment. The roll beneath her feet grew even more pronounced as she dashed forward. Just steps before she reached it, the top of the two-story parking garage in front of her shuddered, then dropped, the cars on its upper level hopping into the air a couple of feet as if they wanted to take flight before they slammed to the surface, then dropped again as the entire structure pancaked onto the lower level. A gigantic plume of dust rose, and car alarms added to the cacophony of grinding concrete and smashing glass. Deb screamed as she scrambled backwards, her retreat stopped by a wall.

She pinned herself against it, legs wide to brace herself, hands plastered to the surface on either side of her, trying to stay upright. Deb had a desperate hope that if she stayed close enough to the wall, she'd be protected on at least one side from more cascading glass or the cars that continued to slip and slide on the street beside her. The ground continued jolting and sliding, the movement never ending, creating billows of dust as buildings toppled on each side of the river. To her right, the iconic giant pyramid on the banks of the Mississippi lifted up and down, then the glass sides exploded outward, the panes sparkling madly as they spun in the early morning sun.

Directly in front of her the massive bridge that carried six lanes of Interstate 40 across the river moved as well. The double arches quivered as the whole stretch of it undulated from the Arkansas side to the Tennessee side, like a ribbon on the staff of a rhythmic gymnast. Two eighteen wheelers coming toward downtown Memphis were midway across the bridge when the movement hit them. At first they rolled with the motion, but then they both tipped on their sides and slid in awful coordination as they smashed through the guard rails and dove cab-first into the river like a pair of divers at the Olympics. The bridge continued to twist and bend, metal stanchions popping, the cars that had been on it flung off into the churning river below. The river itself, normally a steady flow of brown heaved with waves and crashed against the banks as the mighty bridge fell.

The water surged outward as the ground beneath the river shuddered as it pushed the water up to overflow the banks and the park where her friends had been waiting for her, the flow so fast and strong that it knocked over everything in its path. Deb cried out as she thought she saw the bright pink hat that Katie always wore cast upward in the giant wave that continued up and out over land. Deb fled from her spot, back up the street she'd run along just a minute before as relentless water cannoned into the narrow defiles of the Memphis streets. A long roaring sound followed by an immense crash alerted her that the office building she'd been next to had crumbled. A huge gust of debris and dust swirled around her and beyond in curling shapes as Deb ran east, away from the surging river. The Methodist church succumbed to the ongoing shaking, letting its tall, lean structure go with a final shimmy, the stone raining down. Deb skirted away from the blocks of crashing stone and kept going.

First Presbyterian's church bell clanged as the tower fell, but the main structure seemed to be holding, Deb ran for the sanctuary, lifting her knees high as she splashed through the filthy mix of river water, debris, and glass that threatened to knock her down as the surge built and pursued her. The cars that had been parked along the street and on top of the parking garage caromed past her in the rush of water, knocking over streetlights as the surge swept them forward. There were a few other people running as well, all of them coated in dust, so that they looked like running statues. Deb focused on her feet as they splashed through the fetid, cold water that swirled around her knees, knowing that if she fell she was lost. She flung herself up the five stone stairs to the big red doors of the Presbyterian church, praying that they would open, but they were shut tight. Trapped, she stood beneath the stone lintel of the door as the rocking continued to build, and the Mississippi river poured from its banks, the water splashing between the buildings like it had become some sort of water park adventure ride.

Numb, unable to move backward or forward as the river ascended toward her step by step and surrounded the church, a disembodied sense of peace washed over Deb, replacing the terror that had driven her. She folded her bloodied, dust-covered arms and shivered despite the heat, grateful for the solid church doors behind her and allowed herself to dissolve into a state of calm as the destruction unfolded in front of her. It was the same calm that often rolled over her as she worked in the ER at Saint Francis, as if she were the eye of some vast storm, simply doing the next possible thing in the midst of pain and suffering and terror. Deb kept her knees bent and rolled with the earth as it continued to heave.

The city Deb had lived in for the past ten years crumbled, and dead bodies that had fallen or been crushed tumbled in the frothy dark water that swept inland. Office buildings collapsed or stood, the pattern random, the rumble as they fell adding to the incredible noise that filled every inch of air. Sirens wailed in the distance as the shuddering earth began to settle and the water which had lapped the bottom of her shoes as she stood a good five feet above street level subsided as the flow slowed. An enormous dead catfish, its mouth agape and whiskers torn off of one side of its face floated toward her. Repulsed, she kicked it away.

Deb blinked as she tried to make sense of the ruined landscape around her. Cars floated down Poplar, their metal bodies banged and smashed, carried from the parking lots that lined the Mississippi. Entire trees eddied in the slowing waters as well, spinning as the river reversed course and began to seek its old pathway again. Just as she was thinking it all might be over, another jolt and shudder hit, and with it, another roll. She pushed her hands against the stone of the entryway to stay steady as the federal building just across the street, whose courtyard she'd cut across just ten minutes before lost its battle with gravity and the steel and concrete tumbled into the street to the south. Deb had a moment to feel grateful that it had fallen away from her, as she would have been crushed if it had fallen the other way, but moments later, she gasped as a wall of water pushed from the fall hurtled toward her. Deb turned her back to it, grasped the long metal door handle of the church with both hands and forearms and held her breath. The water pushed up to her waist and crested above her head as she clung like a limpet, resisting the suck of the wave as it receded.

Shaking, Deb looked at her watch, stunned to realize that only four minutes had passed since the first tremor. Desperately thirsty, she took a long drink from her water bottle, then leaned her head against the stout wooden door to shut out the horror around her. Deb tried to think of what she should do next. Her friends were gone, she was sure of it to her core, there was no way they could have survived that initial wave of water that had poured from the Mississippi. She'd be gone too if she had been on time to meet them. A jagged bolt of grief ripped through her, matching another shake of the earth.

Ash and debris choked the air, blotting out the sun as the rolling eased. An acrid, mechanical stench accompanied it similar to the scent of brakes burned through on a car. Deb used her water bottle to wet the bottom of her shirt before she pulled it over her nose and mouth to use as a makeshift mask and made herself turn and survey her surroundings.

She'd walked or run the street hundreds of times, but she barely recognized it after the barrage of destruction. Nearly all of the buildings in the immediate vicinity had fallen, leaving stumps of the few left sticking up like broken teeth in diseased gums. Fine, particulate dust swirled through the air, giving everything a coating of dull grey. The river had slowed its outward rush, and instead pulled back in an ever-increasing speed, its waters filled with destruction and scraps of humanity. A rocking chair floated by, along with many bodies, all broken in horrible ways. Bits of paper and plastic bobbed beside bottles and cans, lampshades, wood laths, broken furniture, and artwork in the rushing flow.

Deb looked to the east, hoping to see her own tall apartment building still standing but the dust was too thick. If it wasn't there, her hospital was twelve miles away to the east. Perhaps it had escaped the violence that had happened at what Deb suspected was the epicenter of the massive quake.

Deb pulled out her phone to call her sister and let her know she was safe for the moment. She pushed the contact for Mara, but there was no signal.

"Help! Help us!"

The sound snapped her head up as she shoved her phone into her sports bra. A car floated toward her, its windows broken out, the front end crumpled, cries of terror coming from the woman in the driver's seat. Deb waded into the cold, disgusting water, angling up against the current. She stumbled and her ankle rolled as she stepped on a chunk of debris and something soft bumped against her legs beneath the murky water. She shuddered as a half-submerged hand brushed her lower calf like a lover, swallowing hard against the bile and refocusing on the car's occupant.

The young woman screeched as she waved her hands. "I'm stuck, take my girl!"

Deb grabbed the door handle of the car as the woman tried to pass a little girl out over the steering wheel, her movement limited by the crushed interior space.

"Hold on to the nice lady, Mattie." The child, eyes wild, backed away, shrieking. Despair washed over the woman's face as she broke into weeping. "Please, baby, go to her."

The car stuck on something beneath the surface, and Deb used the momentary pause to pull hard on the door, but it wouldn't budge. The woman's torso was jammed, her chest smashed between the steering wheel and the seat back. Praying she was right about a possible solution, Deb leaned all the way into the car and scrabbled on the side of the driver seat, finding the lever that would ratchet the seat backwards. She found it and yanked, but that only gained a couple of inches. It would have to be enough, as the car tilted sideways, and water rushed into the passenger side window, threatening to submerge the whole car in the next few moments.

"You have to get out," Deb ordered. "I don't care if it hurts. Do it for your kid."

Deb bent her knees as she grabbed the woman under her armpits and pulled, leaning backwards, letting the action of the car caught in the current help her pull the woman out. The woman screamed as Deb ripped her out of the car to splash belly down in the river. Whatever had stopped the car beneath the water let it go, and it drifted away, filling quickly as the shrieking child called out for her mom. Deb let go of the mother to pursue the car before it got too far away and got to it in five stumbling strides, then reached in and snatched at the child as the child clambered out of the window.

"Hold on to me, I'm taking you to your mom."

She turned and waded at an angle back to where the sobbing woman struggled to stand against the moving water. Deb braced her leg so she could rise, then passed the child over. Seeing she needed to assist further, Deb moved upstream and steadied the mother by grasping her arm. "Get to the church steps!"

They made it to the relative safety of the steps as the woman alternately gave her thanks in a hitching voice and hushed the little girl. Deb nodded as she caught her breath and assessed the situation with a critical nurses' eye. The woman probably had several broken ribs, though the child looked to be unhurt, her own arms were cut up, her right shin bled from a gash and her twisted ankle had begun to swell despite the cold water that had surrounded it. So they were in a bit of trouble, but they could still move.

Deb frowned at the water. It was rising to their position again, up a whole step in just a few moments and coming closer with every second. She peered into the gloom at a clump of cars that had drifted together and formed a wedge that was pushing up against the rubble of the fallen buildings, effectively forming a dam just up the street.

"We can't stay here. St. Jude isn't far, let's get you some help there," Deb told the woman.

"I'm Jenny, and this is Mattie. Thank you."

Deb nodded, then addressed the little girl, who was sucking her thumb. "Mattie, I'm going to carry you. Your mom's hurt so she can't carry you, but she's going to be right next to us."

The little girl looked at her with her big blue eyes, sniffed, and clambered over, her round soft weight settling on Deb's hip.

After her experience feeling dead things touching her in the water, Deb was reluctant to get back into it, but there was no other way. She grabbed a passing tree limb and gave it to Jenny, and snagged another one for herself.

"Use it to sweep in front of you, there's all sorts of debris under the water." Deb didn't elaborate but she could see the comprehension on Jenny's face.

They waded slowly as Deb peered ahead through dust, looking for the tall white building with the red lettering, but couldn't see it. Swishing their makeshift poles in front of them, they got to the next block and what used to be the Catholic church, but was just rubble now. Their way was blocked by the collapse of both the church and the highway which used to stretch above the street, leaving no way through it.

The little girl who Deb guessed might be around four, whimpered as Deb swung her to her other hip. "We'll have to go further east, down to Danny Thomas Boulevard." Hopeful that the hospital still stood, she took one careful step, and then another through the black river water as Jenny followed behind her.

It took them nearly an hour, but they made it to St Jude's campus. Deb was relieved to see that part of it still stood intact, including the statue of St Jude in front of the entrance. A few other survivors were making an approach also, two helping a third who appeared to have a broken leg, a man carrying a little boy with a head wound. Deb stepped through the revolving door into the glory of air conditioning, the prickling cold a relief and proof that the hospital still had power.

"Praise be." Jenny was weeping again. "Thank you, Deb."

A harried-looking Filipino woman in green scrubs with a pattern of little pink dancing unicorns approached them with a clipboard and package of wet wipes, which she handed to Jenny. "Names?'

"Jenny and Mattie Delacroix."

"Deb Varden. I think Jenny has broken ribs. I'm an ER nurse at Saint Francis," Deb added. "I can help if you need it."

The woman nodded gratefully and pointed. "Great. The locker rooms are down there, so you can get cleaned up and into scrubs. Jenny and Mattie, go down that hall, there's juice and cookies there, and we'll get to you as soon as we can."

The shower was barely a trickle and not warm. Deb took her phone out of her jog bra and left it on the counter, then stepped straight into the shower with all her dirty clothes, opened her mouth and drank. She washed the coating of grime and blood off of herself and her clothing with the liquid soap inside the shower, being careful to thoroughly clean the cuts on her arms and shoulders and the gash on her shin. After toweling off, she used supplies in the first aid cabinet to tend to herself, hissing at the sting of the alcohol wipes on her wounds, then got into the same green-with-unicorns scrubs the other nurse had been wearing. She found a couple of pairs of dry socks in the lost and found box, and took the time to tape her feet against developing blisters from her still-wet shoes. She wrapped a pressure bandage around her ankle, then swallowed some ibuprofen down with a swig from the faucet. She took another moment to refill her water bottle, then belted it back around her waist.

Deb pulled her damp hair back from her face and secured it with her scrunchie before she looked at her phone once more to see if she had any service, but no bars showed. Transferring her wallet and phone to the pockets of her scrubs, she contemplated her clothes for a moment. She didn't want to give them up, so she put her damp shorts, shirt, socks, and hat into a plastic bag. After a momentary hesitation, she put a handful of Band-Aids, a tube of antibiotic ointment, alcohol wipes, another pressure wrap and a bottle of painkillers into a second bag along with a ratty towel and slung the whole thing on top of the lockers so she could retrieve what might be her only possessions in the world after she was done helping here. The supplies could be a payment for the services she was about to provide.

She took a moment to look in the mirror before she left the locker room. Her long face with its pointed chin, straight nose, light brown eyes, and brown hair all looked the same as they had two hours ago when she'd left her house for a morning run with her friends, the marks of the terrible day not yet visible aside from a few cuts on the surface. Her outsides didn't match the pit of anger and grief she carried on the inside, that much was certain.

Deb squared her shoulders and moved through the door to see who she could help.

CHAPTER THREE

The Blacksburg-Pembroke Fault.

Mara Padgett tied her apron around her waist as she eyed the neat row of six glass quart jars arrayed on the solid old kitchen table in front of her and the round basket of tomatoes next to them. If everything went according to plan, by the end of the morning, the jars would have home-grown tomato sauce properly sealed inside of them, and she'd have taken the first steps at mastering a new skill.

"Are you sure it takes three pounds of tomatoes to fill one quart jar?" Mara asked her stepdaughter Caroline, who was perched on a high stool next to the counter.

The sulky teen sighed as if she'd asked her to do quadratic equations. She shook her long, currently blue hair back from her face and looked up from her focus on her cuticles. "Yes." Caroline's tone was long-suffering, and the eye roll that went with the single word expressive as she recrossed her long, tan legs and kicked at the leg of the table with her flip-flop.

Mara fought down her frustration and smiled instead. "Great. So think I have everything. I have my big pot, with the thing in it—"

"Trivet," interrupted Caroline, accentuating the t's in a clipped tone that helped convey her disdain. "It's called a trivet. You still need citric acid, though. That's what my mom always used."

"Okay, I know where that is." Mara walked to their walk-in pantry and pulled the white powder from its place on the seasonings shelf. "So, now I boil the water in the pot with the trivet, and start another pot of water to blanch the tomatoes, and while that heats up, we prep the tomatoes."

Mara didn't miss the tightening of the girl's shoulders at the word 'we.' It was disappointing to see, and it hurt that nearly a year after Mara had become her stepmother, Caroline still acted like she didn't like her at all. Caroline's dismissiveness wasn't just feigned or ordinary teen drama, either. There'd been plenty of teen drama with her own son, Ethan, who was just a year older than her new stepdaughter, she knew what it looked like. Mara took a deep breath and soldiered on. All she could do was continue to be patient, and engage the teen in tiny, daily activities, and try to at least be her friend. She wanted her newly blended family to work, and if it was going to take ninety percent effort on her part, and only ten on Caroline's, that was just the way it was.

Her attention was broken by the whirlwind of gangly limbs and curly brown hair that was eight-year-old Will as he dashed through the kitchen in his usual attire of jeans, baseball cap, and a t-shirt. The boy was followed by one of her personal additions to their family, a cock-eared black and tan Beauceron-Shepherd mix named Gretel, the dog's toenails clicking loudly on the linoleum floor as she followed her favorite human to the screen door.

"Will! Chickens and Goats!" Mara called after her stepson to remind him of his chores.

"Got it!" He waved his hand in acknowledgement as he held the back screen door open for Gretel, then let it slap behind them with an accompanying screech of the hinges. Mara made a mental note that she'd have to remember to get out some WD40 and get after those later. She chuckled to herself as she remembered that just a few weeks ago, she'd been grateful school had let out, so she'd have some more time to herself instead of spending eight hours a day as the high school librarian. The old farmhouse clearly had different ideas about that, as there was always something to be done or needed to be fixed.

Mara moved the big pot into the deep farmhouse sink and turned on the tap to fill it with water, then turned once more to the old recipe book that she'd found at a used book store. Mara tapped her finger down the yellowed page that outlined how to do simple canning. It didn't seem to be particularly difficult if you went step by step, and she was glad to make her first efforts in the art of canning with the seemingly endless amounts of tomatoes that poured off the vines in their garden. If she was successful with the current batch, then she'd be able to restock their cellar, which had grown a bit lean in the past few months. Mara had done a careful inventory, and there were plenty of empty quart and pint jars she could use with the purchase of new lids and seals if the batch proved to be successful, and she didn't blow anyone up during the process.

As the pot filled, Mara looked out of the big window above the sink at the vegetable garden that stretched behind the house. It had sprouted, then exploded with growth in the past few weeks, a blessing of abundance that only required an hour or two a day of her care to flourish. The eggplants had their pretty purple flowers, the zucchini their yellow ones, but she also appreciated the healthy deep green tops of the beets, carrots, and potatoes. The broccoli and cabbage were coming on nicely next to the line of poles that supported green beans, snap peas, and a variety of peppers. The strawberry patch she'd planted with sweet Earliglow strawberries were earmarked for homemade ice cream, and to be put up as jam later.

The next rows held her tomato ladders with the sprawl of the cucumbers beneath them, and the herb patch with parsley, basil, lemon balm, peppermint, echinacea, and two big rosemary bushes. Further back in the yard were the 'three sisters' mounds, the corn supporting pole beans and squash, along with the vibrant yellow-petaled burst from the fourth sister of sunflowers, all growing adjacent to their farm pond, which Logan had stocked with carp. Beyond that, their apple, plum, pawpaw, and peach trees flourished, along with a huge patch of blackberries on the far fence. They'd added two extra hives of bees recently, bringing the total to six with no issues, the inhabitants settling in easily to the little paradise that was their homestead. If only her integration into Logan's family had been so smooth.

Mara sighed as she glanced at her watch. It was nearly eight in the morning and the summer heat was building fast, but her favorite pastime of tending the gardening would just have to wait until her first attempt at canning was completed. She tensed her muscles to lift the full pot out of the sink and onto the big gas stovetop. The flame lit with a satisfying pop, then she put the lid on the pot to bring the water to a slow simmer before crossing back to the table to start scoring the bottoms of the tomatoes, her thoughts of the garden meshing peacefully with her current chore.

"OMG!" Caroline exclaimed.

Startled at the outburst from the normally quiet girl, Mara moved past the table through the open space between the big kitchen and their living room. Her stepdaughter's gaze was riveted on the television, which was tuned to the local morning news channel. The red chryon scroll above the newscaster's head had one simple phrase: Massive Earthquake in Memphis.

Mara gasped. Her older sister, Deb, worked in Memphis. She whipped out her phone to dial her number as she listened to the newscaster. "An estimated nine-point-seven earthquake hit the New Madrid fault line just minutes ago. It's too early to tell just how much damage has been done, but our affiliate at ABC24 News reports that most of the city near the river has been leveled, and that more cities along the fault line have also been hit."

Chills raced up Mara's spine when her cell phone said that the call could not go through as dialed. She stared at the device while her heartbeat raced as images of her sister lying dead in the street, crushed by a building, or somehow worse, that she was trapped and unable to get out of the rubble, dying slowly of thirst and pain filled her mind. Following both deep instinct, and the need to force the terrible images out of her mind, Mara quickly dialed Logan.

"Hey babe," the comforting rumble of her husband's voice was a relief. "You caught me just in time. We're at Love Field, about to take off."

"There was an earthquake in Memphis, a bad one!" Her words tumbled out.

His tone changed. "Is your sister okay?"

"I can't get through." Mara fought to keep her voice even.

"If the cell towers were knocked down, that would explain it. I'm sure Deb is fine. She's a rock." Logan assured her. "You and the kids doing all right?"

"Yes, we're good—"

The call dropped suddenly, the cell screen zapping to black before she could complete her sentence. Her unease mounting, Mara dialed Logan again, but her phone was unresponsive, even though she'd charged it fully last night. Mara reluctantly tucked the phone into the pocket of her cargo pants and wiped her sweaty palms on her apron as she moved next to Caroline, who stood mesmerized by the ongoing broadcast.

The newscaster stopped speaking; her face showed genuine fear as she paused with her hand to her earpiece and nodded her head. She licked her lips and nodded a second time before clearing her throat and continuing in a shaken voice. "We are also hearing that there was a prior nine point three earthquake on the Richter scale in Arkansas that leveled multiple towns along an east-west corridor centered near Searcy." The woman stumbled on the name. "And we are also getting reports of another line of massive quakes centered on the Rough Creek fault line which have reportedly struck Cincinnati." The newscaster's voice trailed off as she clutched the news desk with both hands, looking around frantically.

Two big lights on the set of the newscast crashed behind her as the studio swayed. The camera angle bounced away from the woman as she screamed, then the image on their television screen fizzled and went dark.

Caroline and Mara shared a wide-eyed look just as their own floor jiggled, causing the glass jars on the table to vibrate, clinking together as they stuttered toward the edge of the table. A violent upward heave threw her and Caroline and the glassware a good foot into the air, the jars smashing to the ground along with the plops of tomatoes falling to the floor. Caroline screamed as they landed on their hands and knees and Gretel began barking furiously, alerting to danger above a loud grinding sound that rose to a crescendo as another jolt hit and an ongoing rumble built in volume.

"Get under the kitchen table!" Mara shouted at Caroline as she scrambled to her feet and dashed for the back door, intent on getting Will and Gretel to the relative safety that the table provided. She was knocked sideways on the porch, and grabbed for the railing to stay upright as Gretel continued to bark, the dog's attention on Will, who stood stock still between the henhouse and the shed on the left side of the backyard, his horrified gaze riveted on a giant crack in the ground that dissolved all in its path as it raced across the yard toward the chicken coop and himself.

"Will!" Mara ran to the young boy, who had frozen in place. She snatched him up, grunting at his solid weight as she grabbed him away from the crack that had widened in the moments it had taken her to get to her stepson, swallowing part of the chicken run and moving on. A trio of trees that stood in the crack's path swayed and tipped along the wave of earth, while the hives toppled, and the pond water sloshed. The ground moved in a series of ripples beneath her feet, tossing them to and fro, as if they were popcorn kernels in hot oil. Mara fell to her knees twice, but didn't let go of Will as she staggered up the porch steps and into the house.

"Gretel, come!" The dog ran to her and followed them inside. Mara skittered across the kitchen as the crockery and pots and pans crashed around her. The pot of hot water jostled its way to the edge of the stove and crashed onto the floor, flooding it with steaming water. She pushed Will under the table, taking a moment to snap off the gas on the stove. Her feet slid in the hot water as she half-fell, half-dove under the massive kitchen table where Caroline huddled with her brother and Gretel whined next to them. Mara grabbed two legs of the bouncing table, and hung on, praying that the sturdy furniture would protect them as the kitchen floor rolled and heaved, splashing them with hot water.

The noise of it was incredible and got louder the longer the shaking went on until it sounded like they were in the path of a jumbo jet taking off. Added to that were the bangs and crashes of furniture tipping, dishes smashing, and the house itself creaking and moaning. The pantry door burst open as a cascade of cans and containers fell from their shelving. The television flipped off of its stand and somersaulted in the air as if it had become a trained gymnast before landing on the couch, which then slid into the oak china cabinet, and caused all the Royal Dolton dishware inside to fall and shatter.

The house tipped sideways like they were in the fun shack at the county fair, then jolted several more times before steadying into an even roll that diminished to tremors, which finally quieted. A few late-falling things smashed, then there was utter silence except for the diminishing rumble Mara guessed was the earthquake rolling on into the distance.

"You think it's over?" Caroline whispered, as if she was scared the sound of her voice would call the quake back.

Mara shook her head. "No idea. I didn't even know our area got earthquakes, I thought those only happened in California and Alaska." She looked carefully at both the children, examining them for cuts and injuries. "Are you okay?"

"I think so," Caroline said, pulling away from Mara.

"Yes." Will said, but his voice was shaky. "Did you see that ginormous crack out there? I think it ate the henhouse!"

Mara wanted to pull him to her, but he stayed glued to Caroline. Instead, Mara petted Gretel, who trembled and panted anxiously, her ears laid back and her tail tucked between her legs. Mara pulled the phone from her pocket, hoping to reach her sister or Logan, but the screen remained black, and punching buttons did nothing to change it.

Mara didn't want to leave the safety the big kitchen table had provided, but hauled herself up anyway and surveyed the mess in the kitchen. Her feet crunched over broken glass and pottery and the contents of what the vessels had held. She picked up the dog's water bowl from where it had overturned and rolled next to the refrigerator and filled it for their pet, grateful that their water still flowed, at least for the moment.

"Careful as you come out, there's glass everywhere. I think, before we do anything else, we should grab containers and fill them with water. We don't know what damage the earthquake did to the underground pipes."

"We have the pond, and a well." Caroline said as she gingerly crawled out from under the table, followed by Will. Her voice was back to the irritated tone she generally used with Mara, which oddly, was rather comforting.

"Right, I forgot. But our well needs a pump, right? So if the electricity goes out—"

"Mara. We have solar panels and a gas generator. We'll be fine."

"Okay, great. Good. Then let's put on some dry clothes, and then get gloves, and get started cleaning this mess up."

"Where's Ethan? He should help," Will piped up.

Mara's breath caught at the simple sentence, gut punched at the realization that she'd been so caught up in the immediacy of the earthquake that she'd forgotten about Ethan and that her son had gone on an early morning trail run. Mara checked her watch, dismay filling her when she saw the time, and realized her son had been gone for at least three hours, which was much longer than Ethan normally ran. A thousand terrible scenarios about what could have happened to him out in the woods before or during the quake vied for dominance in her imagination with her self-recrimination.

"Caroline, did he say where he was going on his run?"

Caroline shook her head. "He was out before I got up. Maybe up to the Star? I think that's his favorite." Her voice held a tinge of worry.

Mara nodded and struggled to keep her voice calm. "Caroline, I'm going to ask you to take charge of the cleanup, and Will you help her? Keep Gretel inside, and if it starts shaking again, get back under the table, okay? Just start in the kitchen, and when I get back with Ethan, we'll help you."

Caroline nodded her agreement. "You should take the ATV."

Mara gave her a smile, and even though it had been her intention to do just that, she gave the girl the hat-tip. "Good thinking, I'll just go get changed."

A small tremor had her grabbing the kitchen sink, but it subsided after only a few seconds. She made her way across the kitchen floor to the narrow staircase that led up to what used to be the attic of the one story farmhouse. Logan had converted it into an airy bedroom and sitting room combination, and had even run pipes up from the kitchen area to create a small bathroom. It afforded them privacy, while also allowing each of the kids to have a bedroom downstairs along with a shared bath.

The stairway remained solid and unaffected by the jostling the house had just endured, just letting out the usual creaks and moans the old hickory wood normally made as she ascended. Their bedroom was another matter, the contents of her bookshelf scattered on the floor, both of the side tables and their lamps toppled, while the queen bed had translocated across half the floor to rest at a cockamamie angle against the back window. The glass had huge cracks running through it, but it had held together in the frame instead of breaking. Mara wanted to tape it, but that was one more thing that would have to wait until after she found Ethan, as would an examination of the cellar and its contents. Mara winced as she thought about the mess that might lurk in the basement of their home with all those storage jars on tall shelves. With a sigh, she hurried to strip off her wet clothing, her hands shaking a bit as she draped the clothes on the edge of the tub, then quickly changed into heavy jeans, thick socks, and a long-sleeved shirt. She took a moment to braid her long blonde hair on both sides to accommodate the helmet she was going to put on and slicked on some Chapstick.

Mara came back down just as the kids emerged from their rooms, having changed out of their own wet clothes. "I'm sorry to leave you with the cleanup, but I'll be back as soon as I can."

Will still seemed shaken as his gaze flowed over the destruction inside the house. Hoping activity would help him recover, she touched his arm. "Will, can you go get some of those thick gardening gloves from the shed for you and your sister? And a few of the cardboard boxes we have in there, too." Mara grabbed Gretel's collar so the dog wouldn't follow him outside.

As soon as Will was out of the door, Mara purposefully moved to Caroline and took her by both shoulders. She waited until Caroline's hazel eyes looked into her own, and was once again struck by how similar they were to Logan's. "If I'm not back by dark, or if there's an aftershock, I want you to take Will and Gretel and go to either the McKinney's house or to Lloyd and Eva's place. Just as a Plan B. It's always good to have a Plan B." She'd spoken confidently, but the worried look on Caroline's face deepened. Still, to her credit, Caroline nodded that she understood.

Mara fished out one of the go-bags they kept stashed in the pantry, brushing glass off of its surface and took the time to check the contents, although she knew what was in each bag. First aid supplies, some cash, a NOAA battery-powered radio, a rain jacket, a headlamp and a flashlight, a solar-powered cell charger, a multi-tool, compass and maps, packets of tuna and nuts, energy bars, and bottles of water. She took out the pet supplies it held and put in an extra bottle of water.

The clicking of Gretel's nails on the wide wooden planking of the kitchen floor alerted her just as the dog nosed under her arm, giving it a hard nudge, her signal that she wanted to be petted. Mara placed her own forehead against the dog's as she scratched her pet behind the ears, and around her chin, and found comfort in the moment of bonding. A gentle lick on her fingertips as she withdrew from the connection let her know that Gretel had needed the brief exchange as much as she had.

After lacing on her hiking boots and a final pat for Gretel, Mara slung the backpack over one shoulder and strode out of the house with a wave to Will, who was just emerging from the garden shed, holding boxes and gloves. The porch steps wobbled alarmingly as Mara stepped down them, another thing that they'd have to fix, before her feet hit the gravel path that led to their garage. Logan had converted the tobacco barn that had stood on that spot for nearly a hundred years into a combination garage and storage area. It seemed to have gotten through the quake unaffected, the sturdy old hickory wood standing strong against both the test of time and the disaster. There were faint tremors coming up through the soles of Mara's boots as she walked and the trees still swayed, although there was not a breath of a breeze. There was a lot of dust in the air as well, and in the distance, she could hear sirens going off in town.

Mara opened the barn door to expose their Ford pickup truck as well as the mowing equipment they stored here. She glanced at the bicycle rack, hoping to see Ethan's ride still lodged there, but the grey road bike was gone, which would mean her search for him would widen considerably. Next, she checked their thirty-gallon containers of fuel, relieved that the red containers had remained upright and in place before she turned to the ATV. A tap on the tank gave back the reassuringly solid sound that it was fully fueled. Looking outside at the swirling dust that had already begun to dim the morning sun, Mara pulled out an N95 mask from a storage cabinet along with some leather gloves, donning both before she grabbed her helmet and her husband's denim jacket off of their wooden pegs. She took a deep inhale of the jacket and got a comforting sense of Logan's presence before she buttoned it up and drove outside, leaving the engine running while she shut the barn door and strapped on the helmet.

Mara took off down their short driveway, slowing as she intersected with the county road to go around a big section of their privacy fencing that had fallen down at the top of the driveway. As she edged around it, the wheels of her ATV clearing the thick wooden posts that lay across the yard and onto the main road, there were more obstacles. Huge sections of the road had heaved upward, creating an uneven surface. As much as she wanted to hit the road at high speed, Mara resigned herself to keeping a moderate pace so that she wouldn't hit anything as she made the right turn toward the mountain trails where she hoped to find her son.

CHAPTER FOUR

The Big D Fault, Dallas Texas

Logan Padgett settled into his window seat and tucked his backpack under the chair in front of him before buckling in. He looked up as the last few passengers were herded onto the plane by the flight attendants and winced when a familiar man waved his pudgy hand at him.

"Hello Jasper," he said politely to the short man with big glasses when the man stopped at his row. "Great job on your presentation about community involvement with your high school yesterday."

"I do my best, everyone expects a good presentation from me," Jasper responded, hefting his stuffed carry-on into the overhead bin with a grunt and a hop on his toes to reach it. He turned around and wagged his finger in the officious way he had. "Your ideas about getting low-performing kids actively involved in homesteading and teaching them science and reading that way were...unique."

Logan could tell that his fellow high school principal had reservations about his presentation by the way he goggled his eyes at Logan after his pronouncement. "Sometimes they have to see why they're learning what they're learning," he responded evenly. Jasper Collins was not someone to make an enemy of, the man had a long memory for supposed affronts, and an even sharper tongue he'd used on some of their other colleagues, joyfully cutting to shreds their ideas on how to make schooling better in front of anyone who'd listen.

"The cynical would say you're just brokering free labor for the homesteaders, and that could lead to a mighty slippery slope."

"The kids take home a share of the food they help produce. It seems to make everyone happy, and hey, teenagers are actually eating vegetables, too." Logan kept his tone jovial and light against the criticism, but Jasper gave him a single shoulder shrug that fell somewhere between agreement and skepticism before he sat down two rows back.

Logan had run into the response several times when he was setting up the program, but after the first year with the significant gains in grades and general improvement in teen attitude that they'd seen with the participants, the naysayers at his school had been placated. Sharing the findings at the yearly conference had been a big goal, one he'd hoped would make a difference in other regions of the US, but he was relieved it was done, and eager to get home to Mara and the kids. Logan glanced at his simple wind-up watch Mara had gotten him as a wedding present. Just four more hours and he'd be walking in his own front door and breathing the fresh mountain breezes that kicked up in the afternoons in the western part of Virginia, not the canned air that already smelled stale on the plane.

He moved his elbow from the middle armrest so the woman next to him could have it. She'd pulled out her e-book to read and gave him a grateful glance. Up at the front of the plane and just behind him near the emergency row, the attendants stood in the aisle giving their spiel about emergency exits and oxygen masks, and as usual, no one was paying much attention to them. Logan looked out of the oval airplane window to beyond the end of the upturned wing of the aircraft, and felt a pang of compassion for the men with their little orange sticks who waved the big plane out of the gate as they wiped sweat off of their foreheads and then walked briskly beside it as it continued outward.

He'd endured that heat when he'd gone for a pre-dawn run in

anticipation of being trapped on an airplane for several hours. Even at four in the morning, the temperature had been ninety-two degrees, the night having done nothing to take the edge off of it within the confines of the concrete and glass city of Dallas and he'd cut his run short because it had been so unpleasant. With the sun having risen the heat was even more intense, and could be seen in the air above the tarmac as it rippled with the kind of waves that look like the promise of an oasis of cool water to men dying of thirst in the desert. Logan shook his head at the sight. While it got hot during the four months of summer in rural Virginia, it didn't hold a candle to the heat Dallas sweltered under in mid-July, even so early in the morning.

Logan pulled his shade down to block the bright light as they taxied out to the runway. At least once they took off, and the plane climbed above ten thousand feet, the air outside would cool. He toed his backpack to him and pulled out his paperback, looking forward to continuing his action adventure read, but was interrupted by the silent vibration of his phone in his jacket pocket. He smiled when the readout said it was Mara, although his conscience pricked him that he'd neglected to put the device into airplane mode.

"Hey Babe, you caught me just in time. We're at Love Field, about to take off." His wife's scared voice sent pinpricks down his spine as he listened to her frantically describing a series of earthquakes that were occurring, trying to reassure her about her sister's safety, but the conversation cut off in the middle of her sentence. He quickly redialed, but the message flashed that the call could not go through as dialed.

A crew member approached, a frown on his face. "Sir, you need to put your phone in airplane mode and put it up now."

Logan shut off the device reluctantly and tucked it into his jacket, wishing he could have reached Mara so they could complete their conversation, his powerlessness grating on him as the anxiety caused by the call roiled in his gut. Logan shoved the book into the seat pocket in front of him, his taste for reading eclipsed by worry.

The plane inched forward past the terminal and made a slow turn to get onto the takeoff runway, squaring up as the flight attendants took their seats. Suddenly, the plane bounced, and the seatbelt cut hard across his lap as it prevented his rise into the air. The woman next to him gasped and clutched her book to her chest with a worried look, and the big man in the aisle seat of their row shifted anxiously.

Mutters filled the cabin and a few young children started crying as Logan pushed up his window blind to see if they'd perhaps hit something on the tarmac. His focus was immediately pulled by movement to the southeast horizon, where the structures of downtown Dallas swayed side to side. The tallest glass tower gained momentum, and on its third sway, it did a slow, almost graceful tumble into the building next to it. Another structure with what appeared to be a keyhole at the top of it stood firm for a moment longer before collapsing, trailed by a third towering one with a spherical globe atop it, both of them tumbling to the ground. The devastation flowed out from those initial falls. Other shorter buildings tumbled in an ever-widening line that arrowed toward the airport, the vision of it preceding the rumble of sound as the enormous buildings crashed to the ground just as the flash of a lightning bolt comes before the crash of thunder. Screams and shouts filled the plane as others with windows viewed and then heard the same horrific destruction.

Stunned speechless by the unbelievable sight of the giant buildings toppling so quickly, their cascade to the ground accompanied by mountains of billowing smoke and dust, Logan's logical mind scrambled to understand what was happening as he put together the dreadful view in front of him with what Mara had told him about the violent quakes that had just happened in Memphis. But Memphis was several hundred miles away, so the earthquake he was experiencing surely couldn't be the same one.

"It's all coming down," the woman in the middle seat said in a hoarse voice, looking past him at the sight of downtown Dallas falling.

The big man who sat on the aisle in their row unbelted his seatbelt and leapt out of his chair. "Let me off the plane!"

Several others joined him, shouting that they had to get off, that they needed to get back to their families. The attendants barked at them to take their seats, to calm down, but it was too late for words to control the panic. Chaos erupted as people tried to force their way into the aisle, their goal being to reach the emergency doors behind Logan in the middle of the plane, people scrambling over seats as they screamed at the people in the middle aisles to pull the levers on the emergency exits so they could get out.

The plane's captain was saying something on the intercom, but Logan couldn't hear it above the screams and shouts of the passengers and the attempts of the crew overtopping them as they tried to make them settle. The plane jolted again, harder than before, tumbling the people standing in the walkway into the laps of seated passengers and into the narrow strip of aisle.

Logan's head smacked into the window with a sharp snap while the screams of his fellow travelers grew in volume. Holding his hand to the injury he was staggered at the sight of the low buildings lining the runway vibrating violently as the other planes that were still parked at the terminal staggered and slid back and forth as if they were bad ice skaters trying to reach the rail. A plane wing smashed into the glass of the waiting area, shattering it, while other aircraft slid into each other, and the chutes that funneled people onto the planes ripped away from the terminal building, falling heavily. The big new parking garage just behind the airport shook vigorously, then slewed to one side, causing the cars on the upper deck to cascade off of it like a waterfall made of metal, along with several human bodies making the same unintended fall.

Just then, their plane rolled and tilted sideways, the wingtip on Logan's side of the aircraft brushing the surface with a grind of sparks before rolling back the other way as the earth beneath it undulated in ever-increasing waves. The jet accelerated after it stabilized from the roll, the aircraft groaning and bouncing as it moved forward on the suddenly uneven runway, but gaining speed, until they lifted off in a steep climb. Logan was pressed back into his seat as if a giant invisible hand pushed him. The plane continued to build velocity as the nose tilted upward at a steep pitch, causing the people who were still out of their seats to tumble backward with shrieks and cries. Only a few were quick enough to grip the backs of seats and brace their feet to stay upright as the plane continued its climb at an extreme angle, away from the trembling earth.

Logan remained glued to the view out of his window as it telescoped into a bird's-eye view in mere moments, witnessing with crystal clarity the cracking and expanding of the ground as it wended its way in an ever-growing maw from downtown through the established neighborhoods toward Love Field. Many parts of the earth along the cracks appeared to simply dissolve, and the houses and streets that stood upon the cracking sections dropped several feet straight down before losing their integral structure and utterly collapsing. The long row of car lots that stretched down a major road near the airport were folded together within one of those dissolving stretches like an invisible giant was closing two ends of a book, the cars on the lots smashing together before dropping into the earth. Other sections shook violently as if the buildings were fighting to stand, but they quickly lost their battles. He gasped as Parkland Hospital, with its distinctive architecture that looked like shipping containers stacked on top of each other, tumbled apart and crashed into the earth, obliterating the long line of cars on the street that ran next to it.

The plane continued in a steep upward climb, its engines screaming as it hurtled past the fallen buildings of downtown, and the high-flying exchanges of the stacked multiple freeways which were packed with bumper to bumper traffic in the morning commute. Logan's heart pounded as the overpass bridges collapsed one after the other, the cars, vans, buses, trucks, and people below them crushed in moments. The plane kept turning to the right as it angled away from downtown and the awful destruction, but not before the three bridges that crossed the Trinity river dropped into the defile below them as the banks they were anchored to crumbled. Dust and debris rose in huge swirls of grey and white and black to block out the terrible view as the plane rose higher, and higher yet until they finally passed through a few clouds and calm, brilliant blue sunshine, ascending into heaven from the depths of hell in the space of only seconds.

The plane leveled from its steep ascent and the people who'd been out of their seats struggled to stand again, moans coming from the ones who had been hurt and the babble of frightened conversation started up. The woman next to him was crying silently, huge teardrops pattering onto her lap. Logan reached his hand over and grasped hers to offer some sort of comfort.

The voice of the airplane captain crackled to life as the aircraft leveled out and the first bits of frost gathered on the corners of the window, indicating they had reached a high altitude. "This is Captain Beresford. As soon as I know anything about what just happened in Dallas, I'll relay it to you. For now, listen to the crew, and get back in your seats. We're all safe for the moment."

There was a subdued hum of talking as shaken passengers made their way back to their seats or tried to make calls. Logan flipped out his own phone again, but the line still wouldn't connect, so he put it away. The big man on the aisle of their row was beet red, his seatbelt undone, and his shirt half pulled out so that his hairy belly showed. "Should've let us off the plane. Don't know what he was thinking."

"That pilot saved our lives," Logan snapped. "It's a miracle he was able to take off during that earthquake, so stop your complaining."

The man appeared as though he wanted to snarl back, but Logan kept his gaze steady until the man looked away, grumbling under his breath. Logan could read the signs of personal fear that could turn into aggression, as he'd broken up plenty of teen fights during his teaching years, and the man had all the hallmarks of being someone who'd easily get riled up and start something.

Once the passengers had been reseated, the crew passed through the cabin with a first aid kit attending to them, guiding a man with a broken arm to the front row of the plane so they could help care for him more easily. Logan admired the professionalism of the three women and one man as they reassured passengers, particularly after the near-riot had broken out during takeoff. "Captain Beresford is one of the best pilots we know," he overheard one of them say to the people a few rows behind him. "He'll let us know what is happening soon."

The woman beside him had dug out a tissue from her purse and blew her nose, her breath evening as she found a space of calm for herself. She glanced out of the window next to Logan. "I can't believe that happened to Dallas."

"It happened in Memphis too," he told her. "My wife's sister is there. That was what she was calling me about a few minutes ago, before the call dropped."

"My heavens, that's terrible."

Terrible. Awful. The words didn't come close to describing the utter catastrophe that he'd just borne witness to, the hundreds of thousands of people who'd died in moments in the buildings and on the streets of Dallas and Memphis. Logan found himself at a loss to imagine what the full impact of the destruction of at least two major midwestern cities might mean, not only for the people who had lived there, but the entire country. Catastrophes like Ike and Katrina or the Twin Towers or the ninety-four earthquake in Los Angeles had caused terrible losses of life and had also sent the American economy reeling, even though they had been relatively localized. Multiple earthquakes in major cities, though? He couldn't imagine how that wouldn't dwarf every other disaster that had come before.

After a long lull, the woman spoke again. "They're close, your wife and her sister?"

She seemed to need some sort of semi-normal conversation, so Logan rallied his scattered thoughts to respond. "Yes, they are. When they were young, their parents were killed were in a car accident, and they ended up being raised by an aunt and uncle." He didn't add that the aunt and uncle had been elderly and not the sort of people suited to raise two young girls with love and care.

The woman made a concerned humming sound before nodding. "Oh, my, I can understand how that would make them close. I don't have any sisters or brothers, but I always wanted them."

"I don't have any either. I definitely wanted an older brother when I was being picked on when I was going through my geek phase in middle school." Logan managed to smile at her and offered his hand. "I'm Logan Padgett from Roanoke, Virginia."

The woman shook, her hand soft and delicate. "Myrna Goenka, originally from Mumbai, but now living in the suburbs of Atlanta. Your part of the world is beautiful. My husband and I drove up the

Shenandoah Valley several years ago on the way to DC and stopped to tour a few Civil War battlefields. We both love history."

"Yes, there's a lot of history there." Logan's words sounded stilted as they dropped out of his mouth in a dull tone that was unlike his usual speaking voice, but it was his best attempt at normal conversation considering what they'd just witnessed.

Her attention drifted to the aisle where two members of the cabin crew had arrived with the drinks cart, as if it were an ordinary flight. "Can I have an orange juice, please?"

"Ya got any booze?" The lout in the end seat asked.

"Sorry sir, the card readers aren't working, so we aren't offering liquor at this time."

"You should just give it to us for free after what just happened."

"Sir, the last thing we want on the plane are intoxicated people after what just happened. Water, coffee, juice, or soda?"

"I'll take a Sprite," he grumbled. "And a cup with extra ice."

"Can I have a Coke in the can, but please, don't open it." Logan requested. After the flight attendant handed it to him along with a tiny bag of pretzels, he bent and stashed both in his backpack. He didn't know what would happen once they landed, but having a few extra calories on hand was never a bad idea.

"Hey, Logan." He turned to face Jasper. The man leaned into the aisle from his seat. "Did I hear you say there was an earthquake in Memphis?"

"Yeah, my wife heard it on the news and called me."

"The guy next to me says St. Louis and Cincinnati were hit, too, right before we took off."

"Maybe that New Madrid Fault line went off, and it triggered all these other ones." Myrna spoke up. "You know, the one that runs up the Mississippi river?"

"I've heard of it," Logan said.

"I was just reading about it the other day," she went on. "It last went off a couple hundred years ago, right when the area was first being settled, a pretty big quake that made the river flow backwards, and there were reports of the bells in Boston ringing. So it could be possible that fault line going off was big enough that it triggered others."

"Buncha hooey." The man in the end seat spoke aggressively. "I work in oil and gas. There ain't no way one earthquake triggers more. Flat out none. Talk like that's for nutbags and conspiracy theorists."

"She's just stating her opinion." Logan was compelled to defend Myrna when she shrank away from the big man.

"Well, her opinion is wrong. One hundred percent wrong." The big man glared at both of them before turning away and guzzling his Sprite in long gulps, then crushing the can in a decisive motion.

Logan bit back a retort as he could tell the man was itching for a confrontation, and the flight attendant had been correct, the last thing they all needed in a small space was an altercation. Seeking calm, he looked out of the window. There were the normal puffy clouds floating beneath the plane, but below that was a solid blanket of dirty grey that formed a sort of floor between themselves and the ground, created by particulate dust that had been thrown up by the violence of the earthquake.

The loudspeakers clicked back on. "This is Captain Beresford. Folks, we've had word that we have been re-routed to Minnesota. There's been a series of earthquakes up the Mississippi river, so all the planes currently in the air in the center and east of the country have been diverted to airfields in Iowa, North Dakota, and Minnesota."

Gasps of dismay filled the cabin, along with some stifled screams. The captain went on speaking. "We have enough fuel to get us there, and you have my promise I will land our plane in a safe area. Just keep calm and stay in your seats if you can, and let the crew have an easy job. We're going to need them when we land in about two hours and twenty minutes."

"Safe area? What does that mean?"

Logan turned from the window to his seatmate. "I think it means that the airports may be full of planes trying to land if those are the only airfields available, so he may need to use an alternate."

"An alternate?"

He nodded. "Either a smaller airstrip, or if the plane is too big for that, a highway, or a field, maybe. I guess we'll know in a couple of hours."

"Oh, my." Myrna looked physically ill, but there was nothing he could say that would improve their situation.

With nothing to see out of the windows except high blue sky in front of him, and a dingy blanket of grey below, Logan attempted to return to his paperback, but he just kept reading the same paragraph over and over until he gave it up and leaned back in his seat and shut his eyes to rest. That proved to be fruitless as well, as the images of Dallas crumbling into dust were on repeat, so in order to channel his thoughts into less nightmarish paths, he forced himself to think about what he would do after Captain Beresford got the plane on the ground.

Mentally, he went through the backpack at his feet, the modified go-bag he carried when he travelled. At the bottom were six MREs and three water bottles he'd filled after moving through security at the airport. He'd packed some toiletries and a spare shirt, a space blanket, a rain poncho, his first aid kit, a compass, and a small solar-powered LED flashlight and solar recharger that could also charge his phone. He'd had to leave out his multi-tool because of security restrictions, but had stocked the space with some packets of dried fruit.

Logan rubbed his chest as it was struck by a pang of longing with the memory of Mara handing him a coil of paracord to add to the pack as she quoted Sam Gamgee from one of her favorite books. "What about a bit of rope? You'll want it if you haven't got it." Well, he did have it if he needed it, thanks to her thoughtfulness, and he was prepared in a small way to sustain himself for a few days if it came to that after they landed.

He pondered his attire, relieved that he chose to don his running shoes and jeans along with a cotton button-down shirt on the flight instead of the formal dress shoes and clothes he had been sporting during the conference's previous three days. His lined dress jacket wasn't ideal for any heavy work or travelling much distance on foot, but would at least provide an extra layer of warmth and protection at night, and it had deep pockets, which were always handy. They might need to leave their suitcases behind, for a few days at the minimum, if the plane was going to make a landing outside of the normal confines of an airport, but he could make do with what he had on board with him in his carry-on.

Logan pulled out his phone and tried dialing Mara again, but his device might as well have been a matchbox for all the good that did. He returned it to his pocket slowly, troubled that he'd spent the past twelve years creating a homestead that would keep his family secure, but now that the trouble he'd been preparing for had come, he wasn't there. All he could do for the moment was hope that Mara, Caroline, Will, and Ethan hadn't been affected, and that the reason the call had been dropped when he was talking to his wife was due to cell towers getting knocked down, not because his family and home had been hit with an earthquake. Logan had no idea if the homestead was on a fault line, but he couldn't recall any tremblers since he'd been on the land. Earth science just wasn't his area of expertise, and when it came right down to it, he'd never had any concern that the earth beneath his feet was anything other than solid. His only worry before now had been how to best amend the clay-ridden soil so that his vegetable garden could be more productive and less likely to break the tiller blades.

Both he and the people they'd left behind on the fickle ground had been shown a different reality, revealing that what they'd thought of as endlessly stable had been an illusion. It was sobering to contemplate, aside from the loss of life, what kind of damage had been done to the infrastructure of those zones hit by the quakes. He'd seen first-hand what had happened to the bridges and roads and buildings on the surface in Dallas, but beyond that were the pipes that carried water and sewage, the power lines and cell towers that had been wrenched apart or knocked down, and the subsequent fires that would break out. It would likely be months or even years before those places came back to what they were like before the earthquakes.

The overwhelming logistics of rebuilding entire cities flowed through his mind, but he focused on something he might have some type of control over if he did some pre-emptive planning. Logan guessed at the likely place where they might land, doing a quick math calculation in his head. If they ended up ,somewhere in Minnesota, that would be at least a thousand miles he'd have to travel to get home. That travel might well be impeded by no bridges and heavily damaged roads that wouldn't be traversable by a car or train. Flying would be ideal of course, but the pilot had made no mention of landing the plane at much closer airports to Dallas that weren't on the fault Myrna had mentioned, the New Madrid, like Nashville, or Atlanta or Charlotte, which meant he had to consider the possibility that there was more destruction than the passengers knew about. The pilot, despite his promise to let them know more, had been silent, and they wouldn't have known about Memphis or St. Louis or Cincinnati, except for a few last phone calls that had gotten through before Dallas was hit by the earthquake.

Logan frowned as he put a few pieces of what was surely a much bigger puzzle together. There was a strong chance that sitting in a somewhat comfortable chair, flying high above all the destruction below, breathing clean air, with food and drink and a bathroom available were luxuries that would soon be out of his reach, and there were resources available to him that he should take advantage of before they were ripped away.

Logan unbuckled and indicated he needed to move to Myrna and the oil and gas man. They both moved out of his way, she politely, he with a grumble and a lot of puffing. Progressing down the cramped aisle to the rear of the plane, Logan entered one of the small bathrooms. He used the facilities, and after washing up, he took a good handful of paper towels, tucking them into his jean pockets. They'd be useful not only as napkins but also as fire starters in a pinch.

"You don't have anything sweet, do you?" He asked the female crew member who stood in the galley after he exited the bathroom.

"I think we have a few biscotti cookies," she replied.

"Can I have a handful? I have a row of cranky people."

"Tell me about it." She said in a dry tone as she handed him a huge handful of foil-wrapped cookies.

He stuffed them into his coat pockets. "May I have some tea bags, too? And a can of coke?"

42

She sighed, but gave him the items. "Anything else?"

"I promise I won't ask you for another thing. Thank you."

He paused by Jasper's seat on the way back, but the man had a sleep mask on, his chair tilted, his shoes off and his tiny hands clasped neatly across his chest, so Logan didn't bother him. Maybe getting rest was a good idea, but he didn't know how the guy had managed it..

He made his way back to his row where the big man was punching his phone angrily and waited for him to lumber out of the way. "No luck getting through?"

"Nothing. Doesn't make sense that the cell towers would be out a hundred miles north of Dallas, too. I don't like it."

The man had a point. Logan handed him a packet of cookies. "Here, I sweet-talked some of these from the flight attendant."

The man's grumpy nature didn't miraculously change, but he did seem slightly happier as he took the cookies. "Thanks."

Once he was back in his seat, Logan put the paper towels, cookies, and pretzel bags into his backpack, keeping out a couple of packets of Biscotti. He offered one to Myrna.

"I don't eat sweets," she said.

"You might need the energy," Logan advised in a hushed voice, pressing them to her. She regarded him with a crease of worry between her big brown eyes before accepting, then looked down at his backpack.

"You're expecting trouble?"

"I don't know what to expect," he told her truthfully. "But I'm trying to be prepared for anything."

Logan ate a packet of cookies and drank his coke, following his own advice to fuel up in what he had realized was a temporary lull in what might prove to be a very long storm.

CHAPTER FIVE

Central Virginia Seismic Zone and The Stafford Fault System

Ripley Baxter hurried down the central hallway of the White House. The temporary badge that had been issued to her five minutes ago bounced on its blue lanyard and threatened to become permanently tangled with her long necklace of amber beads. She wore her only good black jacket over a white collared shirt and black pants along with her black sneakers which she'd thrown on only an hour before when she'd been awakened by a call from her boss at the US Geological Survey office that someone needed to brief the President of the United States on fault lines, and she was who was available.

"I look like a waiter," she muttered as she made an effort to keep up with the long-legged aide who hurried in front of her, turning every once in a while with an impatient look on his face. She slowed her pace as they came to a flight of stairs, leaving the beautiful décor behind them.

Ripley's breath hitched as she called out to the aide. "Wait, why are we going downstairs?"

The aide looked at her as if she'd grown an extra head. "That's where the secure conference room is." Without waiting for any sort of response, he clicked down the stairs in his polished shoes, the tails of his suit jacket flapping as he trotted down them. She had no recourse but to follow, so Ripley used her trick of counting steps to help her get past her innate fear of enclosed spaces.

Twenty-seven steps later, they reached the base of the stairs. They entered a low-ceilinged corridor painted in battleship grey that boasted the kind of linoleum she associated with high school hallways, along with the peculiar lemon scent of disinfectant. After a stretch of empty wall, a stout wooden door turned up as a bit of a surprise. It had a stenciled name on the wavy glass of the windows, as if it belonged to a PI in an old noir film, and after a long section of nothing there was a second one, but they both seemed abandoned, with no lights shining through. The tight confines made her skin prickle, but Ripley gamely moved on in the aide's wake.

To her dismay, the corridor led to yet another flight of stairs that headed even more deeply into the bowels of the earth. Ripley gripped the handrail tightly and counted as they descended, conscious of the weight of both buildings and ground that stretched a good forty feet above her head. She'd heard the stories, just like every other government worker, of the array of both walkable and drivable tunnels that lay beneath the White House and the other buildings that made up the Federal District of Washington D.C., but never expected to have to walk through them, and certainly hadn't ever wanted to descend a total of fifty stairs to reach them.

Her guide kept going, taking turns as the hallway branched, and the corridor turned into a simple, narrow passageway with no rooms leading off it. Ripley gave up trying to coordinate their path with the terrain on the surface. At her side, she clutched the brown accordion binder, which carried the seismic maps that she hoped would help shed some light on the ongoing activity that had engulfed the United States over the past hour.

"How deep is the conference room you're taking me to?"

The aide seemed to be surprised she'd spoken. "We're nearly there. You'll be briefing President Ordway, both the Deputy Administrator and the Chief of Staff of FEMA, the director of External

Affairs, the head of Homeland Security, and the Directors of Emergency Management and Emergency Operations, and I believe the Chief of Staff and our Press Secretary. The head of the Joint Chiefs will be there as well." The young man clipped off the titles at a pace that nearly matched his stride down the long corridor. He stopped in front of a single oak door at the end of the corridor which had cameras mounted above it and an electronic keypad beside it. The aide raised his hand to punch in a code.

"I gotta take a breath." Ripley's heart thundered from her contained fear as she held up a hand to stop him. She had to control something immediately, so she grabbed her long bunch of braids and gave them a twist to knot them at the nape of her neck and secured it with a pencil she pulled from the binder. Trickles of sweat that were a combination of the brisk pace and her jangled nerves trickled down from her scalp, which she wiped away with her hand, drying it on her pants leg. She sucked in a deep breath of air and then nodded to her guide to go ahead and get her inside the room.

She entered just behind the aide, shuffling to his left when he stopped after a single step into the large, blank-walled conference room. It was outfitted simply with recessed lighting and a large wooden table with ten armchairs spaced around it, nine of them filled with serious-looking men. Two men in the ubiquitous dark suits she associated with the Secret Service were stationed at the corners of the room to the rear of the man at the head of the table, whom she recognized immediately as the President of the United States.

President Blake Ordway glanced up at their entrance, his hands on his hips with his shirt sleeves rolled up over tanned forearms, the collar open. No wonder people compared him to JFK with his youthful vigor, handsome features, broad shoulders, and vibrant charisma, for even in a room full of what she was sure were powerful men, he stood out from the rest as a natural leader. To quell the burst of nerves that the single glance from the President had created, Ripley reminded herself she was present because she was an expert in seismology. *And because everyone else was at the USGS conference in Philly*, a nagging interior voice intruded.

"I don't have time for you right now," Ripley said softly to herself, to quell the unhelpful inner chatter as her mental health counselor had advised her to do when it tried to subvert her confidence. The aide gave her a stern look as he patted his hand in the universal signal to pipe down and to keep her attention on what was going on in front of her.

President Ordway addressed a middle-aged Asian man sitting halfway down the long conference table. "Are our sat phones still operational, Daniel?"

"Currently, yes, sir."

"Why just currently?"

"The collapse of buildings throughout the Midwest has generated significant dust and debris, which is now reaching the troposphere. That debris is beginning to block our ability to connect with the satellites as it thickens, but it should clear in a few days after the quakes stop, but as of right now, we have approximately another hour of patchy communication before our line-of-sight with our satellites is lost."

"What if the quakes don't stop?" The President's question landed with a thud and was followed by a long silence.

"Well, of course they're going to stop, sir." A lean black man with a tight buzz cut and a sleek blue suit spoke up. "Earthquakes don't just... go on."

Ripley twitched at his words. The tall aide noticed her movement and with a raised finger caught the eye of a man with a pronounced widow's peak and bushy grey eyebrows who sat to the right of the President. The gentleman gave a faint acknowledgement to the aide before turning his bright blue eyes on her. His mouth sagged downward as if what he was seeing disappointed him, then in a surprisingly high tenor voice he cut through the buzz in the room full of people agreeing that earthquakes didn't just keep going.

"Sir, we have the person who can answer that question. Ms. Baxter, who has just joined us, has been called in from the USGS office. She has a Master's of Applied Geophysics and the confidence of the Director of the US Geological Survey."

The hubbub stopped and all the people at the conference table looked at Ripley at the same time, as if they'd been turned into a single mechanized unit. She clutched her binder to her chest as she nodded her head. "Gentlemen. Mr. President."

"Applied Geophysics, huh? Where'd you get your degree?" The question was from a thin man with an unfortunate combover who sat nearest them and the door. She caught a whiff of strong aftershave as he turned around to look at her, his long aquiline nose leading the way.

"The Colorado School of Mines." Ripley didn't put a sir at the end of the sentence. She'd been briefed that she should only use it when addressing the President.

President Ordway walked around the table toward her with his hand out. Ripley sank her weight into her heels so her legs wouldn't tremble and reached her own to shake it, the brief touch strong and warm. He took her by the elbow and guided her along the length of the table. "Come on up next to me, Ms. Baxter," the President said. "Jerry, scoot over to that empty chair, will you?"

The man with the widow's peak who'd introduced her got up with alacrity and held the chair he'd just vacated for Ripley as she sat in the warm spot he'd left behind. He then moved down two chairs. With her seated, the table was full, and all eyes were on her. The President sat as well, steepling his fingers in front of him. "So, is Thaddeus, our Director of Homeland Security, correct in his assessment that 'earthquakes just don't go on?'"

Ripley wished he'd started with an easier question, but plunged in. "I don't know, sir," she began. The men around the table gave each other surreptitious looks, but she'd expected the dismissiveness. She'd dealt with being underestimated and written off before she said a word many times in her chosen profession, which had few women in it, and even fewer women of color. With her short stature, flawless skin, and long braids, she was fully aware she looked like she was barely out of high school.

"However, before today, if you'd asked ten geologists if this many seismic events could go off, one after another in sequence, all ten of them would have said no." She kept her remarks directed to the President, but had her voice pitched so that everyone in the room could easily hear her. "While the Cascadia and San Andreas faults on our west coast have exhibited this propensity to sync up or trigger each other, we're in new territory with these, sir, but I will do my best to give you the information you need to prepare a response and a recovery."

The President nodded thoughtfully. "What can you tell us, Ms. Baxter?" He paused and added, "And please keep the explanation simple; the rest of us don't have a Seismic Master's degree."

Ripley undid the brown binder, then stood as she pulled out the analog map she'd brought of the United States with all the fault lines and seismic zones marked on it and laid it out in front of the President. The west coast looked like a child had taken red, black, and yellow crayons and simply scribbled all over it. There was another thick red and yellow mark that travelled in a north-south direction roughly following the path of the Mississippi river, as well as huge cross-hatched swaths that stretched down the Atlantic coast from Wilmington to Savannah, and along the southern coast of the United States east of New Orleans to Brownsville, Texas, with a sizeable finger stretching up the I35 to Dallas.

Ripley pointed at the red mark in the middle part of the map. "This is the New Madrid fault line, which we've considered to be a moderate to low risk for activity for many years. Today that fault line was triggered, and the shaking was so violent that it appears to have set off fault lines that stretch east to the Atlantic coast, and also west, into Texas and Oklahoma, as well as ones further north."

"What do you mean, 'triggered?'" The pointy-nosed comb-over man at the end of the table interrupted.

Ripley had hoped not to answer that question so early, either. Her theory was controversial, but like it or not, it was on the table. "I believe that this morning's catastrophic earthquake in Searcy, Arkansas, twenty-two seconds prior to the New Madrid fault was the proverbial straw that broke the camel's back. We know that vibrational waves at 200 Hertz at a depth of eight thousand feet, travel underground at a speed of five miles per second, and Memphis is one hundred and ten miles from the fracking site that started horizontal drilling operations at seven thirty this morning. The Memphis quake started exactly twenty-two seconds after the one in Searcy. That timing lines up exactly with—"

"Don't tell me you think fracking is responsible for this mess?" It was the Director of Homeland Security who said what she assumed most of the table was thinking. Thaddeus glared at her as if he wanted to incinerate her with his eyes.

"It is a viable, mathematically provable theory," Ripley replied, using her most proper voice, and fighting not to swallow and give away her nerves.

"Let's not get sidetracked, Thaddeus," the President interjected. "There'll be time for finger pointing later." He pointed at the map. "What are all those scribbles on the west coast?"

"Those are the fault lines most of America has heard of. The San Andreas, the Cascade subduction zone, and most worrying, the Hayward Fault by San Francisco, since it's overdue for a large quake by about three hundred years." She glanced at her watch. If she was right, they'd be hearing about those faults going off in the next five minutes, as well as the ones under DC itself and the Ramapo fault that would strike through the heart of New York City and up the east coast.

"And what about this crosshatching, and why is there a patch of red over Charleston, South Carolina?" President Ordway gestured to the map. "And this stuff all along the Gulf Coast?"

"The first is the Charleston liquefaction zone, and the fault that lies underneath it, and the second is the area where the earth has decoupled from the crust." She risked a glance at his serious face and the way his head tilted slightly in query. "The first one is very bad, the second one is an arena we don't know much about."

"Stop beating around the bush, Miss. What does 'very bad' mean?" Thaddeus asked in an aggressive tone which set her back up, along with his dismissive use of Miss.

"It means that if these earthquakes are triggering each other, which again, ten out of ten geologists would tell you is not even a remote possibility, except that it seems to be the only explanation for what is currently happening." Ripley put a bit of a bite into her words. "Then the 'bad part' is that the area in the liquefaction zone—"

and there are more of them scattered throughout the country—is made of a type of earth that will, when hit with something like an earthquake, will turn into a liquid like substance, and all the buildings on it will fall, without fail. It happened in several sections of Studio City and the San Fernando Valley in the 1994 Northridge Quake in California. Buildings on liquefaction sections fell while other buildings, some literally next door, remained standing because they were not built on a liquefaction zone."

The President took in her words. "So from Wilmington to Savannah is all that kind of earth?"

"And Charleston is built on top of an active fault line, yes sir, which is why it's so bad." Ripley couldn't help but put a slight emphasis on the last part of her sentence while she looked at the scowling Head of Homeland Security. "If the liquefaction happens, as it is likely to in any quake of six point eight or above, then the ocean will also become part of the problem." She looked at her watch again.

"And I thought learning about the aliens was bad," the President quipped, his face a bit pale, though Ripley couldn't tell if he was joking to alleviate the tension in the room or not.

"You're inferring the ocean will sweep inland with a tsunami effect?" Thaddeus stood as he spoke with disbelief tingeing the words, then added impatiently, "Ms. Baxter, why do you keep looking at your watch?"

Ripley stood as straight as she could to bring authority to her statement, expecting further derision and disbelief. "If I'm right about my theory, the seismic zones we've been discussing will trigger in the next three minutes, set off by a series of faults that cross the USA." She indicated the appropriate red marks on the map, her finger crossing the plains in Oklahoma, stretching up through the Rockies, until the faults intersected with the ones in California.

President Ordway nodded, his face grim, but maintained his demeanor of calm. "So we could be looking at a nation-wide catastrophe, not just localized disaster areas." He dropped his head in thought for a few seconds, and when he raised it again, there was a determined gleam in his eyes.

"Okay, Daniel, have your communications staff hop on the sat phones while they're still functional. Let's get the planes out of the air, somewhere, anywhere. The last thing we need on top of everything else is chunks of metal falling out of the sky with hundreds of people aboard because they've got nowhere solid to land." He turned to Ripley. "Any places that won't be affected if you're right?"

The response that Ripley had prepped in the car on the way to the White House flowed out. "The basalt under Iowa, North Dakota, and Minnesota should remain stable. There's also a solid section in the Four Corners region in the desert southwest." Just as she finished speaking, the water glasses on the big table vibrated and whatever comments that had been about to come out stopped as the men all stared at the vibrating glasses. A Secret Service man was the first to react as he stepped to Ordway's elbow. "We should get you to a more secure position, sir."

"If you can't translocate me to Iowa, North Dakota, or Minnesota, I doubt it's going to make a difference. Is that right, Ms. Baxter?"

Before she could respond, a sharp jolt bounced the glasses on the table, sending them tumbling and a crack which appeared in the ceiling above them let loose a patter of plaster onto the wide oak surface. "What the hell was that?" One of the men exclaimed.

"The Central Stafford fault zone," Ripley supplied as more dust sifted from the cracked ceiling, her fear making words tumble from her lips. "It's an upthrust fault. You can see part of it in a fenced off section at the National Zoo. Sir, we need to get topside. Structural failure down here would mean..." As if to emphasize her point, the ceiling cracked further along its length.

President Ordway gave her a wry look, already on the move to the door. "Hard to disagree with you, Ms. Baxter." Ripley gathered up her folder and map and followed him and the other men back into the long tunnel, everyone walking at a quick pace as they followed its zigs and zags.

The Secret Service man hustled next to them. "Sir, we're going to evac you and the others to Cheyenne Mountain."

Ordway looked at Ripley. "Yay or nay to that?"

"I'd advise against it, sir. If you're going to go anywhere, I'd recommend either the Four Corners or Iowa. Anywhere underground isn't a good idea." Her breath came in short puffs as she hustled to keep up with the running crowd, ongoing tremors vibrating the floor.

"As opposed to Minnesota or North Dakota?"

"It's warmer in the winter down south," Ripley said succinctly, bracing herself against the wall as a violent shudder hit. "There's no telling what the landscape of the United States will look like when this first activity subsides, if it subsides."

"You mean you think it will go on?"

As if answering him, the ground bounced hard, knocking several of the men down. It took every ounce of grit Ripley possessed to stay next to the President, rather than taking off down the hallway to get to the stairs and out of the enclosed space so deep underground.

"Looks like your theory has some legs," the President said to Ripley as the rolling eased after several seconds. "Let's all get a move on, Ms. Baxter, stay with me, please." Ripley followed closely behind him as the two Secret Service converged next to the man. As they moved along the narrow passageway, President Ordway continued to snap out orders as the rest of his leadership team flowed with them at a fast trot, some puffing harder than others.

"Daniel, I know you're a runner. Go on, get those planes down, send 'em to airfields where Ms. Baxter recommended. I don't have any idea what's out in that Four Corners region, but the Secretary of the Interior will be informed about that." The man nodded and set off at a sprint.

They reached the top of the stairs and progressed through the long hallway that smelled like lemon disinfectant. President Ordway turned to another man, one who had medals stretched across his narrow chest. "Chester, get the message to the rest of the Joint Chiefs and contact all our bases to let them know the plan for the aircraft, and to be prepared to assist the people on those planes as they land."

"Yes, sir—"

Another violent upthrust hit, the strongest yet. Ripley fell to her hands and knees and dropped her binder of maps, gasping as hands grasped her around the waist and hauled her back onto her feet with a scent of strong aftershave.

Pointy-nose gave her a quick once over before waving his hand to follow him. "Let's go!"

"Keep moving!" The Secret Service Men gripped the President by both elbows and ran for the second set of stairs double time, their long legs making short work of the corridor while Ripley followed with the rest at a dead run. The long corridor creaked and moaned, the walls bowing as the President and his escort hit the long stair.

Then the overhead lighting snapped off, plunging them all into utter darkness. Ripley thought there was a momentary gleam of light from the top of the stairs, but then that winked out as well. Shouts from the men still in the corridor with her increased in volume as they blindly crashed into each other and into walls as the tremor continued, making it impossible for them to keep moving in a straight line.

A series of sharp cracks made her scream, unable to contain her long-held terror at being so far underground and in the pitch black. The jolting got worse as she tried to stand, knocking her into a person next to her who shoved her away. In an attempt to keep moving forward, Ripley crawled on hands and knees, but someone tripped over her, painfully bruising her ribs, and cracking her face against the floor. Her nose broke with a decisive snap, followed by a sharp pain and a gush of blood. Whoever had tripped over her kicked her again in the midsection as they tried to get to their feet, but she was beyond shouting at them. Instead, Ripley gathered her wits and focused on crawling in a forward direction. She'd been so close to the stairs, not more than twenty feet away, if she just kept going, she'd find that last, long set of stairs and count her way up them to the blessed surface.

Her head hit a wall, sending a new wave of pain pulsing through her body and a fresh patter of blood from her nose. Ripley shook it off as she reached her hand to the solid surface and used it to help her stand. Another shock popped along the corridor and chunks of ceiling crashed around her. "Find a wall, and follow it to the stairs," she called out, choking on bits of dust and debris that must be swirling through the air. "There are twenty-seven steps!"

"Can't see anything," a voice moaned in the dark.

"Find a wall and use it," Ripley repeated. She shuffled her feet forward as quickly as she could, pushing small chunks of debris out of the way. Each push forward with her foot would equal about six inches, she told herself. So two pushes forward would be one foot, which made forty pushes to reach the stairs so she could escape. The calculations calmed her shrieking panic, and she kept moving but stopped when her fingers encountered a gap. For a moment, her heart leapt, thinking she'd found the stairs, but as she patted it, she discovered a ripple of a cool, smooth surface, and as she hunted lower, her hand brushed round, cold metal. It was one of the two doors that she'd observed earlier in the hall. Ripley swiped her face clear, breathing through her mouth as she fought to remember if one of them had been near the bottom of the set of stairs. Racking her brain, she focused back to just a few minutes ago when she'd practically run along the corridor after the young aide, and visualized those images. No, the offices hadn't started right away because it had surprised her to see one as they'd trotted by.

She'd been headed in the wrong direction. Ripley fought back tears, her breath hitching as she turned in a deliberate half circle and prepared to shuffle back the other way. "You did thirty pushes this way, so you've got seventy to get to the stairs." She squared her shoulders and started the count again, but had only reached five when the next wave of ground movement forced her to cling to the wall. The floor jumped and then tilted sideways, and her shoulder rammed into the wall, but she kept both her feet and her count moving, counting aloud over the ongoing rumble of the quake as it continued to jolt in sudden pops.

"Twenty-two, twenty-three—" She broke off with a startled gasp as a hand wrapped around her ankle, nearly pitching her to the floor.

"Help me."

Ripley squatted down but kept one hand on the wall as she moved her other hand along the person's arm, feeling her way along until she was above his elbow and got a good grasp on the man. "I'm going to haul on three, but you have to do most of the work, you understand?"

"On three, yeah."

They did the count, and she hauled, but the man barely budged. Frustration and fear surged through Ripley as a distant but growing rumble signaled that another shock was coming. "I can't pick you up, mister. You've got to stand or crawl right now!"

A moan filtered through the growing roar of tormented earth and rock as whoever the person was used her like a ladder to haul themselves up as she braced herself against the wall. "I think my leg's broken," they said.

"Well, the rest of you is going to be broken and dead unless we get up the stairs. Move with me and help me count. Focus on the count, we need to get to seventy!" Ripley moved forward, forcing the man to follow suit. He grunted with pain but counted with her.

The next shock threw them to the side, and more debris tumbled onto them from above, crashing all around them. "Faster!" Ripley cried out as the chunks from the ceiling kept coming down. "The roof's not going to hold!"

The man slung his arm around her neck and gritted out the numbers with her. "Sixty-two!"

On step sixty-five, they ran into a fallen person who blocked their path. The fragrance of aftershave drifted up, the man who'd both sneered at her in the conference room and helped her up when she'd first fallen. She urged the man she was assisting to lean against the wall while she stretched her fingers to touch the body. Her hands encountered chunks of debris, sticky liquid, and the ruins of what used to be a face. She couldn't feel breath or a heartbeat.

"He's gone," she said, grimly wiping her hand on her slacks. "Five more steps."

They stepped over the body and kept going, her panic rising as they hit seventy, and then two more beyond it.

"I thought you said seventy," the man next to her groused, but she could hear the real fear that matched her own.

"It's not an exact science," she said, stepping forward, gazing ahead with straining eyes, hoping to see something more than pure darkness..

Her toes rammed into something solid. Leaning forward, Ripley felt the rise of stairs in front of her just as another shake ripped through the building.

"Switch sides with me. You can use the handrail and my shoulder to hop up these stairs," she shouted above the noise of both the quake and smashing walls behind them. "Double time for twenty-seven steps!"

He jumped, and she stepped upward in unison, their feet sliding under the grit of fallen debris, twice shaken, and falling, twice getting back up, sweat pouring off of them with the effort of ascending as the building continued to heave around them.

"Twenty, nearly there!"

"Why can't we see anything yet?"

Ripley clamped her lips shut, not wanting to guess at the answer, but it came all too soon. When they got to the twenty-fifth step, the free hand she'd been holding in front of her smacked into hard stone. Shaking, she explored further, felt sharp edges of concrete, and snapped wood. Ripley sank to her knees, her ears full of a roaring as more of the hall behind them fell, more choking dust rising. The reason no light had filtered down to them as they climbed the stairs was because their escape path had been blocked by fallen debris and rubble, leaving them with no way out.

CHAPTER SIX

The Blacksburg-Pembroke Fault

Mara was glad she was wearing the N95 mask as she weaved in and out of fallen debris on what used to be a well-paved two-lane road as she made her way to the third place Ethan went to run, on the packed dirt trails of Read Mountain Preserve. The air was thick with particulate matter that had been thrown up by the quake, and the two aftershocks that had followed during the past few hours and her arms were coated with a fine layer of dust that floated in the air. The artificial cloud created by the dirt had done nothing to mitigate the heat, though. It was getting brutally hot as the day moved past noon, even at the higher elevation.

She slowed her ATV as she came across a sedan that had been tipped over by the sudden rise of one side of the road, and the opening of a crack on the other, the left wheels sunk into the crevasse. Mara geared down and took the ATV around the blockage onto the downslope, driving below the driver's side door, which hung partially open. It was a relief to see that the car was empty, as she didn't know if she would have stopped to render aid or followed the incessant pull to block out anyone and anything until she found

Ethan. Her son would've come home after the initial earthquake if he'd been mobile, which meant he was injured or unconscious, or—she blocked herself from any other imaginings.

Mara grimly clutched the handgrips on the vehicle as she made the turn onto Crumpacker Road and into the subdivision where the trailhead for Read Mountain was, muttering prayers to stave off her growing anxiety. The suburban neighborhood was active, as people picked up after the earthquake. Chainsaws buzzed as they cut the branches of fallen trees, swept up fragmented glass, nailed up plywood over shattered windows, and hauled broken furniture and dishes from inside their homes curbside, the people focused on their work, trying to regain normalcy. Mara bit down on the pang of jealousy that rose watching them do the tedious tasks, and wished fervently that she were at home doing the same things instead of seeking her lost child, her worry mounting with each failed search.

The trailhead parking lot was a mess with fallen trees tumbled over it, the picnic table flipped over and the single portapotty tipped onto its side, its putrid contents spilled into a large puddle. Mara's hopes dropped as she scanned the area for any sign of her son's bike, but didn't spot it. Disappointment flooded through her, and tears rose, threatening to overwhelm her. Defeated, she drove to the edge of the area, as far away from the stink as she could get, into the blessed shade of the big trees before she turned the engine off and removed her helmet. The air was a bit clearer, so she removed her mask with a sigh of relief. Mara swung her backpack off to get a drink of water and a bite to eat to keep fueled for her search while she tucked the keys and the driving gloves inside it.

"Where are you, baby?" She murmured as she took tiny sips of water, holding them in her mouth before she swallowed, as Logan had taught her to do on one of their very first dates. There was the other worry, her husband's whereabouts, although she had complete confidence in his abilities to survive anything thrown in his path. She pulled out her cell phone for the hundredth time, and tried to call both him and her sister to no avail. She sighed deeply, feeling her throat grow thick and her eyes prickle with suppressed emotion. Crying wouldn't help matters at all, and there was nothing she could do about her husband or her sister at the moment. Ethan needed her to find him, and her son was the only person she should focus on. Mara contemplated her next moves as she moved into the wooded area. She'd try the Star Trail next, the one that Caroline had suggested, although that would mean navigating either through or a great distance around downtown Roanoke to reach the popular hiking spot. She'd seen multiple black coils of smoke coming from the city, which didn't bode well for going through it, that was for certain.

The greens and browns of the steep forested trail that rose from the parking lot mocked her with its emptiness when what she yearned to see was the mop-haired, gangly limbed boy that held her heart as he descended the dirt path. She studied the front part of the trail, which climbed up steadily before it branched. Sometimes Ethan didn't bother to lock his bike up at the trailhead, instead preferring to stash it in some underbrush, along with his bike helmet. They'd had arguments over the behavior multiple times as she'd parented him as a single mother through his early teen years, but it was a bad habit he'd stubbornly retained.

The natural area of the mountain held a substantial scattering of fallen tree branches, but little else to mark the disaster that had hit so hard below. Perhaps the underlying stone of the mountain had something to do with it, or the give of the trees themselves. Mara shook her head, leaving the geology questions for another time, after Ethan and her husband were both safely home. She focused on the bushy undergrowth and fallen branches near the trail, She took a page from her son's book and tucked her bike helmet behind a large tree so that it was out of sight. She started to hunt, ranging several yards on either side of the trailhead, looking for her son's dull grey bike. Too bad he hadn't picked a neon green or brilliant blue for the frame that would've stood out easily against the deadfall. She hiked up a good hundred yards seeking for a sign of his bike, and even pushed a little further upward, far past where he'd have stashed it, but found nothing, so turned around and headed back down.

As she descended, her heart grew heavier with each step, and she had the nagging feeling she'd made a huge mistake by choosing to leave, or maybe she just didn't want the challenge of getting to the Star trail. Whatever the reason, her feet dragged as she traversed the last few yards of the trail. Birdsong trilled from the bushes to her left, a happy, almost defiant song against the murky grey heat that blanketed everything. Mara turned her head to see what kind of bird it was and found the bike.

A large, fully leafed limb had fallen on top of it, wholly obscuring it from any view other than from the exact spot where she stood above it, the silver of its bent front spokes gleaming a bit in the gloom. Her hands flew to her heart in grateful prayer as she hauled the big branch away from Ethan's bike and found his helmet tucked beneath it. She burst into loud sobs and collapsed to the ground as she heaved tears of sheer relief. Mara composed herself together after a minute, then hauled herself up and double-timed it up the trail. She tried to study the ground for footprints as she went, but she wasn't a tracker. It all looked like a confused path of imprints to her.

"Ethan!" she called at the top of her lungs at intervals, then stood still to listen for a response, but there was nothing but the sigh of a breeze through the trees and a bit of birdsong, the tranquility of it mocking her inner fears that had returned after the momentary relief of knowing she was on the right trail. Quelling the idea that Ethan was so badly hurt that he couldn't respond, Mara continued to hike upward along the narrow path, keeping a sharp lookout for scuffs on the edge of the trail where it plummeted down at a steep pitch. As violent as the main quake had been, it would have been all too easy for him to have missed a step and taken a tumble down the steep incline.

Two hours passed as she hunted, pausing only to call for her son, or to take a sip of water. She was nearly at the top of the third trail she'd tried, and her legs and lower back screamed for her to stop and rest. With a sigh, she leaned against a large pine tree and let out a long breath that was close to a sob. She wouldn't give up on him; not now, not ever.

She gathered her voice and called again, "Ethan!"

"Mom." The single word had never sounded sweeter to her. It

came from below the path she was currently on, from the steep downslope to her left.

"Ethan!" Mara scrambled to peer over the edge. Some twenty feet below the lip of the trail, her son was sprawled on a forty-five degree slope covered with low scrub and pine trees. Beyond him, she could see dislodged dirt and leaves where he'd struggled and hauled himself upward over the past few hours.

"Are you hurt?" She knew he was, but the words popped out of her.

He nodded his head and gestured to his left leg. "Yeah, I think my lower leg's busted, that same one I broke in gymnastics."

Mara sucked in air at the memory. That had been a month in a cast that had stretched all the way up to his hip, and then another month in a short cast that went to his knee. "Okay, do you have water?"

"Not anymore. I lost my bottle." His voice sounded faint. "And I dropped my phone somewhere."

"The phone can be replaced. I'm going to lower a water bottle to you while we figure out how to get you up top."

Blessing the hank of paracord inside her pack, she tied a water bottle to it and lowered it to her son. "Not too much at once, okay?"

"Yeah, yeah."

The slightly annoyed tone gave her a bloom of hope, and she stifled the sob that rose unexpectedly from her throat. If he had enough energy to be annoyed at the reminder, then he could get back up onto the trail, and they could make their way back down the mountain. She just needed to figure out how to help him get up to where she was. Mara eyed the end of the paracord she still held, and compared her relatively small body mass to the sturdy six feet two inches of Ethan and frowned. No matter how much adrenaline flowed through her, she wasn't going to be able to haul him up by herself, but going for help from the neighborhood below wasn't likely to work, either. Everyone there was dealing with their own problems, and as for professional help, emergency services were bound to be overwhelmed by the disaster.

The 550 paracord in her hands was fifty feet long, and the fir tree she'd rested against near the edge of the trail might do the trick if Ethan could move about a few feet to his left to line up with it. The paracord was rated to hold five hundred and fifty pounds of static weight and her son weighed a touch over two hundred pounds, so it should hold and allow him to make his way up the steep incline as long as he didn't make any sharp movements, or the earth didn't decide to jolt some more.

"Ethan, untie the water bottle. I'm going to tie the cord off on a tree and we'll use it to get you back to the trail."

"Okay, but do you have any food?"

A laugh burbled from deep inside her. Of course he wanted food, he was a growing teenager. "I'll send it down in my rain jacket, along with some painkillers. I know you've got to be hurting."

"You can say that again."

"I know you've got to be hurting," she repeated as a joke, even though her heart was breaking, knowing how true the statement was.

"Mom, really?"

She allowed their banter to settle her nerves. After she'd sent down her remaining protein bars, tuna packets, and medicine, she moved to the tree, and tied the cord around it with a good bowline knot. "The rabbit comes up out of the hole, runs around the tree and back down its hole." She chanted the instructions for the king of knots as she secured the paracord to the stout trunk of the pine, happy to see the U-shape appear that showed she'd done it correctly.

"Ethan, I'm going to throw down the line, but it'll be about ten feet to your left, okay?"

She weighted the line with her driving gloves, then laid on her stomach to watch his pained progress crabbing sideways on the slippery slope to reach the cord and the gloves.

"Just go hand over hand, as slow as you need to, and I'll pull at the same time. You lead the way with the timing."

"Okay." The line tightened as her son pulled on it and used his good leg to inch his way up to her. His grimace revealed he was in terrible pain, but he doggedly kept going as she continued to encourage him.

Finally, nearly a half an hour later, he crested the edge of the path.

Mara cradled her boy in her arms and cried with him as they sat on the rim of the trail. Then they shared her final water bottle to prepare for the long journey down.

"Lay back, let me look at your leg."

He had other scrapes on his face and arms, but the leg was by far the worst of his injuries. The area around his left shin and ankle was swollen and purple, but Mara saw with relief that the bone wasn't sticking through the skin, so at least the threat of infection was diminished.

"Ok, the first thing we're going to do is splint your leg before we head down."

"You going to give me a mile and a half piggyback ride?" He asked her with a little smile.

Mara gave him a look. "You wish. Those days are long gone, son. Rest for a minute. I'll find something we can use for your splint and a crutch."

Ethan gave her one of his patented long looks. "Let me guess. You went down a rabbit hole looking something up for a student, and learned how to make one from a book."

She chuckled. "Close. It was an on-purpose rabbit hole, for a paper Will was assigned. We watched a video."

Mara hunted up good, thick tree limbs, then used her all-in-one tool to shape them. She took off Ethan's T-shirt, turning it into five thick strips that she'd use to bind his leg into the final part of the makeshift splint she was about to construct. In a seated position, Ethan helped her to first wrap her long-sleeved shirt around his leg as a bit of a cushion, then to maneuver the rain jacket under his leg, after they piled a thick layer of soft, dead leaves between the shirt and the jacket as cushioning and brought the hood of the jacket up over his foot to help stabilize it. They went above his knee and tied two lengths of the portioned t-shirt with an extra surgeon's twist in each, so that they would remain stable.

Mara used a box tie below his foot and bow ties around his ankle, and one just below his knee. Finally, she cut four lengths off of the paracord and bound long, stout sticks on either side of the now-padded leg, again using two around his thigh, and two lower down, by his ankle. Then she fashioned a crutch using the remaining paracord to lash a stout foot-long branch onto the longer length of branch she'd found into a T-shape. She wound the last bit of cord around the top of the T to function as cushioning for his armpit and then made him put on Logan's jean jacket.

"It's too hot," he complained.

"It's a mile and a half to the base of the trail, the skin under your arms would become one raw, gaping wound by the time we got down to the ATV. You'll put on the jacket, and you'll wear the bike gloves, too." She refrained from buttoning it onto him like he was a four-year-old.

"You're using your mom voice." The complaint was mild, and he said it with a smile.

"It's the only one I've got." She took a moment and looked at her son; his soft, grey-blue eyes fringed with thick, dark lashes, the angular face with a strong, pointed chin that had a hint of beard and moustache starting up, and his sandy blonde curls that were always messy, even when he'd brushed it moments before. She pulled a few errant pine needles that had tangled in those curls before she cupped his cheek with her hand and said the words she'd secretly worried she'd never be able to say to him again.

"I love you, son."

"I love you too, mom. Thanks for the save." He said the words easily, the product of nearly fifteen years of life when it had just been the pair of them against the world.

"Anytime. Let's get going and find you a doctor." Mara placed herself to his right in case he needed to grab her shoulder for balance.

Their slow progress down the hill took a deep toll on Mara's energy. Twice they had to drop to the ground as aftershocks rattled the mountainside, their backs braced against the biggest trees they could find to wait out the tremblers as branches fell and rocks tumbled around them. Later, when they had to navigate a huge tree which had fallen completely over their path that hadn't been there on the way up, Mara swallowed hard and blessed their luck so far at not being crushed by nature. After a difficult scramble over the wide trunk, they used it as a resting place, while she checked her phone to see if there was service, but it remained inert. They were forced to inch down the final steep pitch a half step at a time until they reached the place Ethan had stashed his bicycle.

"Oh man, my bike is trashed," Ethan spoke mournfully as Mara retrieved both his helmet and her own from the brush.

They'd talked about the best way for him to ride on the ATV during the descent, and arranged themselves with Ethan seated sideways on the widest section of the seat, his broken leg to the inside, the makeshift crutch wedged on the outside to keep it as still as possible. Mara rode in front of him on the narrow part of the saddle and wore the backpack on her front as a windbreak while Ethan kept on the jacket.

"I wish I'd thought to bring a mask for you," she fretted as they maneuvered into position. "The air is even worse than it was a few hours ago."

"I'll keep my head ducked down, I guess. I'm ready, mom, let's go."

Mara started the engine and pulled out as slowly as possible, angling around the overturned portapotty to get out of the parking lot, wincing at each crack in the road. She'd mapped a route in her head to get her son help that would be most direct and hopefully lack cracks and bumps. The Blue Hills ER off of Challenger Road wasn't far away, and if that were closed or overrun, she'd continue into the central section of Roanoke and the services of the multi-storied Carilion Memorial Hospital, although the memory of all the black smoke coming up from central downtown worried her.

Another sizeable aftershock hit in the middle of the suburban neighborhood, one that turned into a long, rolling motion after the initial jolt instead of the violent up and down the first big one had been. Ethan cried out in pain as the road bounced beneath them, popping cars, people, and debris in the air like they'd been unexpectedly volunteered onto a trampoline. Everything landed with a thud as screams and car alarms wailed, then the wave action began, sending anything not secured or rooted into the ground skating into motion.

"Hold on!" Mara cried out as she threaded the needle between two cars that were on a collision course from opposite driveways into the center of the street just before they smashed together. She gunned the ATV on the two-lane highway as fast as she dared to go past the wooden utility poles that waved like the Rockettes doing a fancy kick line, one pole after another rising and falling in ever-diminishing heights as the earth settled once again. Several cars had ended up in the ditch from the tumbler, their owners getting out dazed and bleeding. A few other vehicles continued along the road, but were impeded by the latest debris while the ATV was much nimbler and able to get around fallen sections of earth.

Mara slowed as she came to an intersection that had been hard hit. The chicken restaurant on the corner had crumpled to one side and the whole back side of it blazed with fire. The metal pole that stretched into the center of the intersection and its two hanging stoplights had crashed to the ground, and had created a massive crash of five cars. Two of the men involved in the wreck brandished guns at each other as they shouted epithets.

"Keep your head down, Ethan." Her fear level elevated at the sight of the weapons being waved around. Her son and she were completely exposed on the ATV, with nothing standing in the way of a stray bullet. She rolled over the grassy road divider onto the other side of the highway to get around everyone. Several people clocked the ATV's progress as she glided around the wrecks and beyond the burning building, and the avaricious look in their eyes gave her the realization that her ATV was a highly desirable vehicle to possess.

Mara wished she'd brought her Sig Sauer P365, if only so she could pull it out and show people she had a gun on her and back them off. Logan had insisted on buying her the gun last Christmas after she'd taken some time trying different models. She'd settled on the small gun that fit her hand so well with its little palm swell, but hadn't been good about practicing with it at the range. At any rate, it had been a dumb move on her part not to have brought it along with her, and she resolved not to make the mistake again, for as long as this disaster lasted.

Mara swung back across the meridian as they approached the ER. A section of the brick hospital had collapsed, revealing the guts of the facility, which was also destroyed. Mara slowed and stared at the scattering of bodies in white coats inside of the wrecked building. A few people were in the parking lot but it was clear that they were in no position to help anyone.

"Doesn't look good, mom."

"I agree. I'm going to head to the main hospital."

"Can we just go home?" His voice sounded weak. "If it's bad here, it's going to be worse in town."

"We don't have the kind of first aid you need, Ethan." Mara let the motor idle as she contemplated her choices. There were several ER rooms scattered throughout the area, but none were truly close by, and if what she'd seen so far was any indication, the damage in this area was widespread.

The back of her neck prickled, and she turned. A man hustled toward them from across the road, and there was something about the angle of his shoulders, the set of his neck, the intentionality of his stride that set all of her alarms off. "Hold on," she said to Ethan, and gunned the ATV forward as soon as his arms wrapped around her waist.

The man yelled something unflattering as they zoomed away, and Mara's grip tightened on the handlebars. Internally, her mind raced as she tried to figure out where to get help for Ethan. If he had broken the bone yesterday, it would've been just as serious, but it would have also been easily fixed. Now, finding him the right kind of help had become an odyssey without the certainty of a good outcome.

Mara slowed the ATV and looked at the gas indicator after they rounded a bend, and the man was out of sight. They'd need more gas soon if they wanted to get back home. Mara's guilt flared as she pictured the mess back at home. Her stepchildren, Caroline and Will, had been there alone for nearly seven hours, and there'd been at least two big aftershocks since then. Ethan still needed her to produce a solution quickly, but other than the ER and the hospital she couldn't think of any other options since she was fairly sure that the CVS only carried prescriptions and was staffed by pharmacists, not someone versed in first aid and basic trauma care.

Ethan moaned behind her, ratcheting up her stress even further as she racked her brain for a solution. Suddenly, she gasped out loud, and turned the ATV around, headed away from the hospital and into the suburban neighborhood where Anita Hillin lived, the long-time nurse for the high school. Mara moved along quickly, thrilled that she'd joined Anita's book club group, and knew exactly where she lived, and the best route to avoid the main streets, which felt full of danger to her after the encounters with the angry people at the traffic accident and the man who had looked like he wanted to take their ATV.

"Just five more minutes, and we'll have the help we need."

"I'm not feeling so great, mom."

"I know, honey, you've done great so far. Just a little longer."

Mara weaved along the back country road that led to a neighborhood full of older homes to the east of Roanoke. She turned onto the short street that dropped into a small valley and motored down the center of the narrow road. The houses were set back a bit, with waist-high chain-link fences that marked the property lines of houses built for returning soldiers after World War Two. Some were in sparkling shape, but others had fallen into disrepair, the sort of neighborhood her aunt would have called "mixed" with her patented sniff of dismissal, while her uncle would've flat out called it a disgrace and made a call to the mayor to do something about it.

Anita's cream-colored house with its inviting yellow door and walkway lined with annual flowers – happy daisies mixed with bright orange and yellow marigolds – was a welcome sight. Mara motored straight into the gravel driveway that ran next to the house and stopped the ATV.

"Let me make sure she's here," she told Ethan as she swung off the bike, her muscles fighting the move, stiff from both the hiking she'd done and the tension of the drive.

Anita's doorbell had never worked, so she swung open the screen and pounded on the stout wooden door. "Anita! It's Mara Padgett. My son needs your help!"

There was a long pause, then the lock turned, and the door opened. "Mara, what on earth?" Anita's hefty, tall figure filled the doorframe, her disheveled brown hair streaked with grey, her face lined with wrinkles and dotted with age spots, wearing a battered black track suit with a pink stripe running along the legs and arms that she'd probably bought at a used clothing store back in the eighties. Mara had never seen anyone more beautiful in her life.

"Anita! Thank goodness you're home. My son Ethan broke his leg in a fall, and the ER is gone."

"Gone? What do you mean, gone?"

"Half of the building had fallen down. I just didn't want to risk trying downtown. People have gone a little crazy since this morning."

"Not supposed to be earthquakes around here," Anita nodded. "It's bound to rile people up."

"Can you look at him, please?" Mara held her breath, not sure what she'd do if Anita refused her.

"Well, yes, bring him in."

Mara rushed back to the ATV, and helped Ethan inside as Anita held the door open for them. The smell of onions and peppers filled the air, as well as the smell of cat litter that needed to be changed. "Go on back to the kitchen. It's going to have the best light this time of day," said Anita.

After she got Ethan seated at the kitchen table, Mara turned to Anita. "Can I pull the ATV behind your house? I was getting some overly-interested looks on the way over to you."

"People," muttered Anita, the single word conveying her annoyance. "Go ahead, and when you come back in the front, lock the door behind you."

Careful of Anita's flower beds, Mara parked the ATV where it couldn't be seen from the street in a nook between her friend's garage and the back door. By the time she'd gotten back in, Ethan was drinking a tall glass of orange juice and had a plate of cookies by his elbow. Anita was on the floor, taking off the last of the makeshift splint, and the dead leaves they'd used littered her floor.

"I'll clean that up," Mara said as she headed to the broom closet, well-versed in where things were in the house. Armed with the broom and a dustpan, she worked around Anita and Ethan.

"Pretty good splint you made."

"How bad is it?" Ethan asked around a mouthful of cookies. He looked slightly better now that he had some food and drink in him.

"Well, you can wiggle your toes, and they were warm to the touch, so that's a good sign. From all that swelling, I'd say it is definitely cracked, probably a closed break on your tibia," Anita said as she pressed the leg with gentle fingers. "It's hard to say without an x-ray, but I think from the swelling that the break extends into the ankle, which means you'll need to stay off of it for a good six weeks, if not longer."

"Oh, man." Ethan moaned at the news.

"Can you put a cast on it?" Mara asked.

Anita shook her head. "It's not a bad break as breaks go, but I don't have anything to make a real splint." Anita huffed as she stood, her knees sending out loud clicks of protest. "Ethan needs a proper splint for the next few days until the swelling goes down. We don't want your young man getting compartment syndrome. Then after that, a plaster or fiberglass cast to keep it steady while the bone heals."

"What do you need? I'll go get it right now."

"Heaven help us when you get determined, Mara, and you are determined, I can see that fire in your eyes. I'll make you a list. I'll ask you to get some bottled water, too. The main must've broken because I've got nothing coming out of my taps."

"You don't happen to have some spare gas, do you? I'm about out. Or I can maybe get some at the store."

"No need for that. There's some right out in the garage, I keep a spare one of those red containers, should still be good, I only filled it up last month."

Five minutes later, armed with a short list, and her backpack emptied to help her carry the goods, Mara rolled out on the half-full ATV for the nearest big box store, hoping that it wouldn't be swarmed with people looking to stock up yet, and wished one more time she'd remembered to bring her gun.

CHAPTER SEVEN

Airspace above Minnesota

Logan dreamed about escaping the rough neighborhood behind Tufts University in Boston, where he'd lived for a time after college. His car, his bike, and his wallet were lost while he scrambled through dark alleys and up sand dunes but couldn't find the way out, no matter how hard he tried, yet he kept trying, driven by the need to find his family once again.

"Hey."

Logan was dragged from the dream by a light pressure on his arm, his breath coming in a sharp inhale, his leg muscles still twitching in an attempt to run. The gentle face of an older Indian woman came into focus as he turned his head, surprised that he was seated, buckled in, momentarily unable to reconcile current reality with the vividness of the dream he'd been having.

"I think we're descending," the woman said with anxiety tinging her words. Myrna, that was her name. Myrna from Mumbai, and he was on a plane that had been diverted to Minnesota. Logan pushed up the window shade. A clear blue sky shone beyond the wingtip, but below that was a solid grey mass of what appeared to be dense clouds, tinged a slightly brown color. Logan rubbed his eyes to center himself and turned to his seatmate.

"How long was I out?"

"Not long, twenty minutes or so. The captain hasn't said anything else, but I think we're getting lower."

"Sir, do you have any trash?"

It was the crew member who'd given him the cookies, her latex-gloved hands extending a bag, in a bizarre attempt at normalcy. Wordlessly he handed her his empty can and cookie wrapper debris, and she moved on down the aisle mechanically moving her head right and left, asking the same question repeatedly in a monotone.

The red buckle seatbelts sign flashed above their heads with an accompanying dinging sound, then the intercom buzzed to life. "Okay, folks, this is Captain Beresford. In a moment, we are going to ask you to take crash positions, which is your head between your knees, hands clasped behind your neck. There is a floatation device underneath your seats in case you need it. After all, we are in the land of ten thousand lakes."

"Did he just make a joke?" Myrna asked.

"The joke is me bending in half," the big man at the end of the row said ruefully. Maybe being in a life and death situation had mellowed him.

Logan secured all the fastenings on his backpack before tightening his seat belt another few inches. The cloud cover was level with the wings, the tips of them cutting through the top layer. Moments later, the view was obscured by the clouds, which had a sickly yellow tint to them, rather than the wispy grey he was used to seeing.

"Please assume your crash positions. The crew will be coming through to ensure you are in the correct position. We're going to be landing on a nice, long, straight part of the US 10 Northwest freeway, which is a bit north of St. Cloud, Minnesota, in the next five minutes. I'm signing off. We'll see you on the other side."

Logan didn't take his position right away as he watched out of the window during the descent. Deep green swaths of dense trees, intermittent fields, and in the distance, some high hills came into focus, as well as the gleam of water he assumed was the Mississippi, which looked much wider than he'd imagined it to be here in the far north, where the mighty river had its headwaters.

"Sir, close the blind and take your position!" the male crew member barked as he strode by. A child was crying, but other than that, the cabin had gone preternaturally silent as people bent over in their chairs.

Logan did as he was told. At the last minute, he reached down and grabbed his backpack and hooked one of the arm straps around his elbow, determined to hang onto it if he could. His ears popped as the plane dropped further and he listened for the whine of the wing flaps to be extended and engaged and then the solid clunk of the wheels as they locked into place, breathing a little easier as each step was successfully accomplished. Beside him, Myrna muttered prayers beneath her breath.

The peculiar gliding sensation that always happened right before a plane's wheels touched the ground was next, a held breath of anticipation before the airborne plane reconnected with earth. They hit the pavement, and the engines reversed their thrust, the rumbling of the wheels jarring as they connected with the highway until they hit something solid which threw the passengers violently against the seats in front of them, eliciting screams. There was a shriek of metal on metal as their forward momentum jolted to a halt for a moment, then continued into a clockwise spin. Logan was pushed against his right armrest as the plane swept in a shuddering arc that added the grinding sound of metal on pavement to the cacophony of noise, the plane vibrating violently before it finally came to a stop, tilted forward onto the nose, the right side of the plane significantly lower than the left.

Logan unbuckled his belt and stood hunched over below the overhead compartment, bracing himself against the seat backs against the awkward tilt of the plane and looked behind him, yellow dashing lights catching his eye as they flowed toward the middle of the plane, the automatic system in motion to guide people to the emergency exits.

The principal he knew, Jasper, jumped out of his seat into the aisle, his eyes bulging as he took in a ragged tear in the plane's body. "The engine's caught on fire. We have to get out!"

Jasper's words caused a massive panic as people screamed and shoved to get away from the area, creating a boiling mass of humanity behind him. The smell of mechanical burning filled the cabin, along with eye-stinging smoke. The passengers in the middle seats yanked hard on the emergency exit door on his side of the plane, but it didn't budge.

The crew members dashed to help them, and finally the door popped open, allowing a rush of moist air to enter the cabin. Up near the nose of the plane, the entrance hatch had been opened and the people closest to it had started using the emergency chute. Behind Logan was utter chaos as the people nearest the fire leapt over seats, uncaring if they stepped on or hit anyone. Trying to exit that way would be a poor choice.

"Go forward!" Logan yelled at the big man at the end of their row who still struggled to remove his seat belt, his face panicked as the smell of burning got stronger, along with the smell of fuel. The screams at the back of the plane became even more frantic.

The man nodded, his face a sheen of sweat as he finally got the belt undone. He heaved his bulk out of the seat and bullied his way forward. Logan grasped Myrna by the upper arm and pushed her along out of their aisle while he kept a tight hold on his backpack. "I've got you. Stay in front of me, Myrna. Follow him, right behind him."

The tiny woman nodded and allowed him to steer her into the wake of the big man who made a path forward. Others, seeing what they were doing, crowded in next to them. Logan focused on the goal of reaching the front slide as fast as possible while keeping Myrna upright in front of him. If she fell, she'd be trampled as the surge of people trying to get off pushed hard behind him, hands pushing his back and shoulders to move more quickly.

A woman further up the aisle wept as she tried to release her seat-belt while her little boy howled next to her. Logan stopped, shoved backward as hard as he could against the tide of people. "Move your hands," he ordered, unclasping it in a moment.

He let the woman wiggle out in front of him with her child clasped to her. Logan inserted himself behind her and kept moving to the chute. He could see the glare of light from the open doorway where crew members helped the passengers exit down the slide. He moved his backpack in front of him as he readied himself for his turn.

"You can't take the backpack," one of them said. He pretended like he didn't hear them, and jumped feet first onto the slide directly after the woman with her child, then made sure they all cleared the way for more people to exit. Several people had simply slumped to the ground looking dazed near the slide after their exit, including the big man who'd been in his row.

"Thank you!" the mother said distractedly as she clutched her son to her, looking around them with wide, blue eyes. "I can't believe this is all happening."

"It hasn't sunk in for me either," he admitted, as he scanned the growing crowd for Myrna. Puffs of acrid black smoke wafted between them from the engine that burned on the other side of the aircraft. In a precautionary move, he took the mother's elbow to pull her further away from the plane, which lay at an angle across the four-lane divided highway on its belly, the underside of the front end crumpled from where it had skidded the final yards to come to a stop. Up in the cockpit, he could see the figures of the pilot and copilot still working their controls.

"I want to shake our pilot's hand," he said to the woman. "That's twice he saved our life today."

She focused on him, her face worried. "We're from Dallas, and my husband is—" she broke off and swallowed before continuing the sentence. "Do you think anything's left back there?"

Logan shook his head, glad he didn't have a definitive answer. "Downtown looked bad. I'd only be guessing about the rest of it, though."

The woman let out a shaky sigh. "We're out in Addison, so maybe he'll be okay." She patted her jeans, concern filling her face. "Oh no, I left my phone on the plane! It was in Braden's diaper bag! I have to go get it. How do I get back on?"

Logan took his own phone out and showed her the blank screen he got when he tried to dial. "I don't think that's possible or advisable. It won't work, anyway. There's probably towers down, or that haze is doing something." He gestured to the low hanging cloud cover, which had deepened with the addition of the stinking black smoke from the plane. He wished he had a mask to put on, but then again, he'd just survived a devastating earthquake and an emergency plane landing, so perhaps he should just count himself lucky.

He turned from the mother and child to find Myrna and walked down a short incline in thick grass toward the train tracks which paralleled the road about fifty yards away from the plane. A number of people had seated themselves on the broad ties that supported the tracks, while others lay on the grass, their relief at being back safely on the ground evident. It was good to move his legs in a brisk walk after being cramped in the confines of a plane seat for the past few hours, and Logan stretched his arms out as well, waving them back and forth, enjoying the motion through space and the stretch around his upper shoulders under the comforting weight of his backpack, feeling grateful and free. He was alive, they'd survived the crash, and were on the sweet earth once again.

Myrna's tiny form stood up on the tracks, and she waved to him, a smile creasing her face. He waved back as he descended the slope, happy to see that she was safe, though her face changed to terror a moment before an odd whuff of sound puffed behind him, followed immediately by a searing blast of air and a huge explosion. Logan was thrown to the ground by the force of it, and a billow of fire passed over the space where he'd just been standing. He swiftly tumbled on the grass to extinguish any wayward sparks from the fiery blast, then he flipped onto his belly with his arms shielding his head as a second burst of flame erupted from the aircraft in a massive explosion. A burst of heat rolled over and past him, billowing toward the train tracks, followed by a steadier pulsing of warm air and the smell of burning rubber, fabric, and flesh.

Gagging, his ears still thrumming with the sound of the blast, Logan rolled to his knees, aware in a distant way that the tops of his hands had been singed black where they'd been exposed to the blast.

He turned and crawled back up the embankment and was confronted by an image of utter devastation. The plane burned along its entire length, including inside the cockpit where the windows had been broken out by the force of the blast. The escape slides had been turned into melted messes of plastic which sagged against the hulk of the plane. No one left aboard could have survived the two explosions that had happened so close to one another. Numerous burnt bodies of people who'd been standing or sitting closer to the plane than he had been lay scattered on the scorched earth, including the big man who'd been in his row. A few still tried to run as they burned, falling to the ground as he watched.

"No," he breathed as he forced his legs to take staggering steps to where he'd left the mother with her child. He found her about half the distance to the plane, a charred form hunched face down on the grass, knees and arms drawn in tight. Swallowing his horror, Logan nudged her incinerated body aside and revealed her child huddled on the ground where his mother had thrown him, and then tossed herself on top of him in a valiant effort to protect him.

The boy lay silently shaking, his eyes shut, but he was unburnt, his skin still pink instead of charred black. Logan gently picked him up as the little boy's eyelashes fluttered and his mouth turned down in a frown. "Hey buddy, I've got you. Let's get you a drink of water, okay?"

Logan cradled the child and hurried away from the burnt husk of the boy's mother, away from the plane where black smoke belched and hungry flames licked, back toward the train tracks where Myrna and other people had gathered. As he walked, he hummed a little song he'd sung to his kids when they were little, only half remembering the words. He reached the embankment and moved carefully down it, crooning to the child, keeping his head tucked so he couldn't see what Logan saw.

People had been burned to death on the slightly elevated tracks, the explosive gouts of flame catching those who'd been standing. The lucky ones who'd been seated, or laying lower in the gully like he had been, had survived the blast with only a few injuries. They wept as they processed the burns on their hands, faces and bodies, as well as the loss of loved ones, or the new acquaintances that they'd just made on the plane. Logan tried to hold on to hope as he looked for Myrna in the area where he'd seen her last, his steps slowing as he got closer, the heavy weight of the little boy in his arms the only thing keeping him grounded.

Myrna was lying on her side, her crisped body curled as if she was simply resting for a moment on the hard gravel and metal. Guilt struck him in an inescapable wave, knowing that if she hadn't stood to wave to him, she might have escaped becoming engulfed in flame. Logan let a long breath hiss from between his teeth in lieu of sinking to the ground and weeping. He turned away from both the plane and the tracks and kept walking until the air was clear of the dark smoke. He found a shady tree to sit under and set the boy down on the soft grass as he pulled his backpack off. The hum of insects and various bird calls made the spot an incongruous paradise, a strange juxtaposition to the flaming plane a few hundred yards away.

Logan was shocked to see that his backpack was half gone, the outer half of it seared away and he must have put out the fire when he'd rolled onto his back to extinguish the sparks on his jeans. The things in the second compartment were still there; water bottles and snacks, as well as the first aid kit. His book, rain jacket, foil blanket, the coil of rope, the flashlight and charger had all been destroyed in the explosive blast of fire. His hands shook as the adrenaline wore off and made it hard to undo the top slider on part of the pack that had been closest to him. The little boy watched him fumble with big blue eyes that were so like his mother's, it was painful for Logan to look into them. He fished out a bottle of water and took several short sips before offering it to the boy, racking his brain to remember the child's name. Braden. Braden from Addison, Texas.

"Drink some water for me Braden, and then you can have a cookie if you want to, okay?"

"'Kay." Braden's voice was faint, but it was good to hear him communicating. He drank obediently, taking the small sips that Logan gave him. Logan unwrapped a biscotti and handed it to the boy, then addressed the burns on the tops of both of his hands, first rinsing them with water, then dabbing them dry before putting on antibiotic ointment and wrapping them up in gauze.

"I want my Mommy." The boy had perhaps cried all of his tears away earlier, or was in shock, as he sounded as if he were ten years old rather than the two Logan guessed him to be.

"I know you do."

Logan was at a loss as to what else to say to the little boy, so opted for silence instead of empty words. He was utterly drained from the events of the day, particularly during the last fifteen minutes with its emotional impact of the deaths he'd witnessed, including the brave captain and crew, and even worse, the two women, and the man who'd been on his aisle, all of them killed in such a brutal way, people who in the normal course of life would have disappeared from his memory quickly as once-met strangers, but were now seared there forever. He looked at the little boy who poked at the ground with a stick and tried to see a life saved rather than death and sorrow. Logan wished to see it that way to honor the mother's sacrifice, but he couldn't manage it yet, so instead, he resolutely built a dam of composure against the flood of feelings that yearned for release. Braden had no one else to be strong for him right now, so it was up to him to hold steady until he could find the child some aid and reunite him with his family.

In the far distance, the welcome sound of first responder sirens wailed as billows of black smoke continued to rise from the carcass of the plane. Logan allowed himself a pop of hope. Perhaps emergency services could put him in touch with Mara and the kids using their radios, and they could access a database and find Braden's father and sister or some relative so he wouldn't be all alone in the suddenly upended world they'd found themselves in.

He looked down and saw Braden regarding him solemnly. He couldn't force even a hint of a smile, but managed to keep his voice even as he addressed the little boy. "Want to go meet some firemen?"

CHAPTER EIGHT

Central Virginia Seismic Zone and The Stafford Fault System

Ripley scrabbled at the debris in front of her, feeling for and grabbing chunks of what had been part of the ceiling, working to dislodge them and toss them down the stairs behind her. The work would distract her from the knowledge that she was living her worst nightmare, trapped underneath the ground in a confined dark space, the air growing worse and worse until she suffocated. Her imagination made her work faster, clawing at the debris in front of her and yanking it loose as quickly as she could manage.

"Careful, you'll bring the whole thing down on top of us." The man she'd helped out of the fallen rubble was at her left, and by the sound of his calm, even voice, had seated himself on the staircase.

"The whole thing is likely to come down on us anyway," Ripley retorted. "Don't just sit there. Help me move this."

"Just stop for a moment, and think, Ms. Baxter. Use that brilliant mind you're purported to have. If you're pulling the rubble from below, the likelihood is that the remainder on top will fall directly onto us once the support underneath it is removed. Isn't that just simple physics?"

The overly proper phrasing and slight sneer in the voice allowed her to recognize the speaker. It was the lean black man who was the Director of Homeland Security, Thaddeus, who'd been so vehement in his questioning of her at the meeting. Ripley had no idea what his last name might be, so she went with what she knew.

"Thaddeus, we are about five feet away from the entranceway to this staircase. I seem to recall that it was quite a high entrance, too, maybe twice my height, so anywhere from ten to twelve feet high. How do you propose we start at the top of that? Would you like me to stand on your shoulders?"

The silence that followed was bittersweet. As much as Ripley enjoyed being right, and it had been good to speak her mind, she wanted him to have an answer to the problem even more.

"Point taken."

"The only other thought I have is that we go back into one of the rooms off the hall behind us, and see if there's another entrance or perhaps a duct we could crawl through."

"There isn't. Those are high-level conference rooms, designed to be self-contained and secure. Not even someone as petite as yourself could move through the ventilation for it." He grunted painfully as he shifted a bit. "Ergo, your original action is the only one left to us, aside from waiting for aid to arrive."

Ripley considered the option for a long beat. Allowing skilled rescue people to do their job in a safe manner was something she naturally gravitated to, but the likelihood was high that they were all on other jobs at the moment.

A rumble vibrated everything around them, strong enough to rattle Ripley's teeth in her head and make Thaddeus cry out as his leg was jostled. The rubble shifted and fell, and more of the corridor above the stairs collapsed behind them, kicking up dust, making their space even smaller, and their air barely breathable.

Thaddeus coughed violently after the shaking stopped. "How long will those go on?"

"It's not predictable. That could be the last one for another century, or worst case they'll keep happening, each movement triggered by more movement in an inertia effect that could take years to come to a complete stop." Ripley pulled off her jacket and took off her blouse, ripping it along the back seam to make a couple of makeshift masks. "Tie this around your face. It'll help some against the dust."

She was calmer after the exchange, which had narrowed their options to just one action: moving the rubble in front of them away so they could get out. "Can you stand on one leg a while?"

"Yes." The answer was clipped, and she imagined he was in quite a bit of pain, but pushing through it.

"Good, you stand there, braced against the wall, and I'll move over a couple of feet so we're working on the same section." She paused, then acknowledged his earlier observation. "And by keeping it closer to the wall, there's less likelihood of it collapsing."

"An acceptable plan, Ms. Baxter."

"You can call me Ripley."

"I prefer the former."

They worked steadily instead of frantically, aware of each other's movements in the pitch black. As she worked, Ripley thought about her college friends who were scattered all over the United States, particularly Emerson Davies. He was a fellow geologist for the USGS who had gotten a plum job stationed outside of San Francisco. She wished she would have called Emerson from the car on the way to the White House and shared her theory of quakes being triggered by quakes with him so that he'd have been able to do something to prepare people for the Hayward fault and the San Andreas rupturing, and Cascadia too. That she believed the quakes might even continue triggering each other on into the Pacific and the so-called ring of fire, spreading outward from the initial quake in Arkansas, continuing like a perpetual motion machine around the globe, time and again until their momentum finally subdued. And if that sequence happened, the lifestyle humans around the globe had known would be disrupted for multiple decades as the remnants of society struggled to find a path forward without the infrastructure they'd all come to rely upon, especially those who'd been blessed to live in first world countries.

Sweat poured off of Ripley and with each breath her lungs struggled to expand, a sure sign they weren't getting enough air. Thaddeus was wheezing even more than she was, and occasionally let out a suppressed whimper of pain.

"You can say ow, or cuss, you know. I won't think less of you," she said wearily, needing a momentary break. Her fingers ached and were wet with what she assumed was blood from dozens of nicks and cuts. She wiped her hand across her forehead, then dried it on her slacks, as was her habit. They'd cleared a decent size opening about a foot wide and four feet deep between them.

"I, however, would think less of myself."

"So you're one of those 'I'm harder on myself than I am on others' people?"

"I wouldn't say that. I have... personal standards."

"That's just code for 'I'm difficult,'" Ripley said promptly, and was rewarded by a dry chuckle.

"Perhaps."

They continued to work for a while longer in silence. Ripley found that if she closed her eyes on purpose, it was better than straining to see something. Her panic at being enclosed had diminished with the work of moving debris, but it still hovered close beneath her focus of grabbing the next stone, the next bit of masonry, and moving it aside.

"Oh, no."

Thaddeus' voice was a low rumble. The panic she'd just been congratulating herself on tamping down spiked once again.

"What is it?"

"A body. Someone's arm. Someone who got caught in the fall. He's collapsed close to the wall." The staccato sentences fell like stones.

Ripley hoped it wasn't the President, but he had been ahead of them in that final mad dash to exit the underground corridors. It very well could be him, or one of the Secret Service men who'd been running with him.

"We have to keep digging." Ripley said. "Maybe they're just knocked out, and we can help him, too."

She didn't believe the last part was true, but stopping was out of the question. The air was definitely getting stale, just like it had the last time she'd been trapped beneath the ground five years ago. Ripley shook off the memory and accompanying fear that wanted to rob her of all hope, reached deeper into the hole she'd made for a decent grip on a piece of rubble, and tugged, removed a section, turned, and let it drop behind her to roll down the stairs. To her left, Thaddeus was doing the same thing, but his breathing sounded even more labored than her own.

"Ms. Baxter."

She stopped pulling on the particularly stubborn bit of rock she was trying to dislodge. "What?"

"We might be able to work a safe passage through. Look at knee level, between that man and the wall."

She opened her eyes and moved to his side, bending low. Having been robbed of all light for the past several hours, for a moment she didn't understand what she was looking at. A thin ray of light, no wider than the lead inside of a mechanical pencil, stabbed into their chamber, its sharp point dissipating, overwhelmed by the dark.

Ripley rocked back on her heels, considering. "If we were smart, we'd stop trying to make the tunnel we're making, and instead widen that space enough to get air, and then wait for help to arrive."

"If we wait, another quake might happen and bring the rest of the roof in on top of us."

"If we move enough rubble for a crawl space that low to the ground, this whole wall of debris might collapse, too, as you pointed out earlier." Ripley forced herself to explore options, even though her brain was sluggish from the lack of oxygen.

"I'm willing to risk that. Are you?" There was challenge in the man's words, but underlying it, she could hear the same desperation to be free that she was experiencing. She wanted to agree with Thaddeus, then attack the stack of rocks in front of her and beat it down with sheer will and determination, but years of working in geology gave her the strength to fight against that instinct.

"I'm not. Listen, this is what we're going to do. I'm going to move in front of you and pull one piece out from beside the body at a time, along the edge of where the light is coming in, and pass it to you, and make that little hole bigger and get fresh air in here. In my opinion, that is our best and safest option."

After a long pause, she heard the shuffle of him moving down a stair. "You're the expert."

Ripley began the work, grateful for the miniature shaft of light that guided her and then widened as she worked, opening into first a pencil-wide opening to one that was about as big around as a tin can. It was as if she was being a reverse archeologist, the buried artifact clawing its way back into modern life. After she'd cleared a hole large enough to look through, she was gratified to still see light beyond it.

"Hello!" she shouted through the chink. "Is anyone out there?"

There was nothing but silence. She turned back to Thaddeus. "I don't understand it. Isn't the White House normally a hive of activity? Wouldn't they have people hunting for all the important people like you?"

"I've been wondering why we didn't hear digging from the other side," he admitted. "I don't know why it's silent unless the whole building has fallen down past that one clear part. Or the whole city. We must face reality, Ms. Baxter. There's no one out there trying to help us."

"Okay, well, then we'll get ourselves out, one pile of rubble at a time." Ripley said with an effort to keep upbeat, but her heart sank as she began to carefully enlarge the new opening, her hands brushing along the dead man's body every time she pulled another piece of broken stone out.

After a while, she just shut her mind off about what shored up one side of what she hoped would become their escape tunnel and dug. After twenty minutes of digging, she swapped places with Thaddeus, letting his longer arms reach into what had shaped into a narrow triangle about nine inches across at its widest between the man and the wall that ascended four of the final five steps before the landing. He finally pulled back, wheezing.

"I can't get my arm in any further. You'll have to go in and push through to the other side." His voice was weary, and what she could see of his body in the dim light was covered in dust, streaked with blood that had seeped from his hands from dozens of cuts. He shifted uncomfortably, and she was reminded again that his leg had likely been crushed in the roof fall that she'd pulled him from earlier.

She licked her lips nervously. "That's... just nuts." The idea of wiggling like a worm into the minute space, arms extended as she tried to push her way out, bounded on one side by a dead man, made a shiver run along her entire body.

"You realize freedom is just a few feet away, Ms. Baxter. Your small frame is ideal for this."

"I'm not a piece of machinery that you can just order up for the task at hand!"

He dropped his head to his chest. When he raised his eyes, there was an intensity to them. "How fast do P waves travel, Ms. Baxter?"

"We're having a pop quiz now?" Ripley forgot to be afraid for a moment, she was so flabbergasted. "They travel between one and fourteen kilometers per second."

"So, if your theory is that these earthquakes are triggering one after another, and that they might continue, how long before the next round hits, roughly?"

"I don't... well, the diameter of the earth is twelve thousand seven hundred and something, so best guess, forty minutes, give or take ten minutes."

"By that calculation, the next tremor will hit in the next five to ten minutes. Nothing may happen, but then again, all of our hard work may be reburied, with us alongside it. Does that make you want to proceed?"

His voice was pitched as if he was talking to a recalcitrant child, and it infuriated her. Maybe he'd meant it to do just that, because Ripley plunged herself into the tight space, arms in front of her, using her initial momentum to shove rubble out of the way as if she was the front prow of a locomotive, then wiggled forward after that, still pushing. One hip was against the hard surface of the wall, the other against the long body of the poor soul who'd not made it out of the lower levels of the White House alive.

Thaddeus pushed her up the stairs from below, all propriety gone as he helped her inch up and forward, his hands on her thighs, then her calves. Ripley blinked away the dust that swarmed into her eyes as she let her fingers push ahead of her into the last two feet of rubble.

There was no room to expand her lungs in the compressed space, and Ripley panted so hard she got dizzy. She'd taken exactly one course in spelunking because it was required in college, and there had been a similar section in the caving run they'd had to execute correctly as a final. There had been an eight-foot-long wormhole with a tight bend halfway through the run, and the trick had been to move one shoulder at a time to slither around the corner along with taking tiny sips of air so that her ribs could be pressed inward by the stone. Blessing the course requirement she'd loathed at the time, Ripley duplicated those moves, singing an old Janet Jackson song in her head to keep the rhythm steady and her over-active imagination occupied. It was either do that or start screaming that she was trapped and could feel the weight of millions of pounds pressing on her from all sides, wanting to squeeze her to death.

"How's it coming?" Thaddeus' voice threaded through her rising panic that no amount of singing to herself could overcome.

"Nearly there." She said it just to say something, but then her fingers waggled in the free air, with no more debris to push away. She inched forward, one shoulder roll at a time through the narrow space she'd created until her hands were free. Not daring to pull on the fragile structure, she managed her eagerness and kept scooting with one shoulder at a time until her elbows were out, then pushed back against the pile with them using steady pressure, edges of stone scraping her torso and legs as she edged them through the wall of rubble and finally wiggled her way clear onto the floor of the hall.

"I'm out!" she called back through sobs of relief, tears pouring down her face.

"Excellent, that's excellent."

Ripley looked around the space that she'd entered. The once grand hallway was a wreck, with huge sections of the ceiling smashed onto the ornate carpet so that she could see up into the second story of the building from where she sat. Further down the hall, a portion of the floor of the room above had collapsed at an angle, forming a triangle with the hall where she stood, the furniture that had been in that room turned into a tall pile of smashed sticks, broken lamps, and torn cushions. Thick dust circled in huge wafts, the air so thick with residual debris that she couldn't see the end of the long hall that led to the outer doors of the White House. The whole right side of the passage closest to her had partially collapsed into the room beyond where the damage continued to stretch, the beautiful old paintings that had lined the walkway in that section now just canvas tatters in smashed frames. She coughed to clear her parched throat and then croaked out, "Hello?"

Only the echo of her raspy voice returned to her, along with the sound of some residual bits of the building falling somewhere in the distance. Dragging herself up to stand, she brushed off her ruined slacks and took a few paces down the hall, and tried calling again. "Anyone here?" Again, she was greeted by silence.

Ripley returned to the rubble pile she'd crawled out from beneath. "I don't think there's anyone around, and this part of the building is certainly badly damaged."

"Then they've likely evacuated with the President; it's what I would have ordered."

"You wouldn't have left people behind." She was sure of that fact to her very bones. A surge of hot anger toward whoever had presumed them dead and given the order to evacuate rose inside her. Ripley sniffed and wiped her face with her filthy blouse, breathing in the cleaner air from the interior of the White House. "I'm going to get you out of there. That's a promise."

"I'll hold you to it, Ms. Baxter." His trust in her abilities strengthened her. Ripley stood with determination, and methodically widened the gap she'd just squeezed through. She'd removed only a few chunks when the next quake hit, making her stagger backwards and fall to the floor, helpless to do anything but witness the space she'd emerged from refill and become covered with more rubble, obliterating the crawl space.

"Thaddeus!" she scrambled to kneel at the space that had disappeared as if it had been an illusion all along, and screamed his name twice more once the vibrations subsided, but only silence emanated from the other side of the fall.

She knelt in place, her hands over her face, a wave of despair threatening to render her incapable of doing anything further, but her promise to get Thaddeus out provided a buoy for her to cling to. *Use your rational mind, Ripley,* she ordered herself. Use that brilliant mind you're purported to have, as Thaddeus had said. The old West African proverb her grandmother used to say popped into her head; "When you pray, move your feet."

Ripley nodded her head in acknowledgement to her deceased grandmother's wisdom that both prayer and thinking were all well and good, but it was taking action that got things done, and she set back to work clearing the space next to the wall once again. She emptied her mind of everything except moving the next bit of rubble aside, aiming to get as deep as possible first so that she could find out if Thaddeus had lived through the last aftershock.

Ripley had only moved two or three pieces with her bloodied, bruised hands when she stopped and ran along the hall until she found a doorway. It led to an elaborately decorated conference room which had devolved into a disheveled mess, its decorations, chairs, lamps, and end tables tossed everywhere. But at the far end of the room was what she'd hoped for; a fireplace which boasted a set of real fire irons. Ripley pounced on the treasure of the poker, shovel, and tongs, and dashed back to her work.

"I love tools," she said aloud as she worked to remove the debris, the job going three times faster with the metal implements able to lever in and pull away the rubble much more easily than her human hands had done. As she worked, she did numbers in her head to keep her focus. It had been about a five yard crawl up the stairs for her to reach the hallway. With the tools she was using, she could rip through that in no time.

It occurred to her that the five feet of rubble may have been too thick for any sound to penetrate, which would account for her being unable to hear Thaddeus, and could give a bit of credence to the decision that someone had made to leave them behind, if they had called out, and gotten no response. But just thinking about hale and hearty people simply calling out and not bothering to dig brought her temper back to a boil. She let the anger fuel her as she kept going, ignoring the pain in her shoulders and arms, enlarging, and deepening the section between the dead body and the wall. She vowed that she'd find out who'd been behind the decision to leave without even trying to rescue anyone once she got Thaddeus out.

Her watch had been smashed at some point in the past several hours, so she had no idea what the exact time was, but her interior clock was telling her to hurry, that the forty minute mark when she might expect a new earthquake was fast approaching. She shoved her poker in and yanked out another hunk of rubble, then flung herself onto the floor to see how far she'd gotten. The darkness of an empty space rather than more debris had her sighing out with gratitude, but the silence from the dark was ominous. If she called and got no reply, all of her efforts would have been for nothing.

"Thaddeus!" she croaked, her throat tight.

A wet, wheezing cough came first, a gasp of air before he spoke. "Took you long enough," was the dry reply. "It's gotten rather cramped. I have about three feet surrounding me."

Ripley shut her eyes against the horror he must have endured in such a tight space, waiting, and hoping she'd come, his breath getting shorter and shorter. "Can you make your end big enough to fit your body through?"

"I haven't just been sitting and twiddling my thumbs, Ms. Baxter."

Ripley laughed, a bit of hysteria creeping in. "All right. I think we're about due for another shake."

"I'm aware."

A slight vibration ran along the corridor, electrifying her. Ripley spoke rapidly and with authority.

"I'm going to pass you a shovel and you're going to hang onto the top of it with your dominant hand, one arm extended as far as it will go so that your shoulders are parallel to the ground, your head resting on your extended shoulder. Keep your chin tucked and your eyes shut. I'm going to pull, you push however you can, and we'll get that head and a shoulder through, and then wiggle the rest of you out in the next thirty seconds, got it?"

There was a slight hesitation before he responded. "Affirmative."

Ripley laid on the floor, inserting herself under the towering twelve-foot-high pile of rubble, her hands wrapped in a firm grip around the handle of the iron shovel as she pushed the business end into the narrow tunnel she'd created, swallowing her terror as her head and shoulders once more became submerged. The shovel moved as Thaddeus grasped it and the earth trembled under her belly as tiny bits of the ceiling rained onto her legs, and she tensed.

"Ok, go!"

Ripley pulled with all her strength, screaming as she did so, a similar yell coming from Thaddeus. After an agonizing few seconds, she got her arms and head out and adjusted herself so that she sat on the floor with her feet braced against either side of the rubble and continued to pull, overcoming the resistance his body made as it scraped through the narrow aperture. The tool nearly pulled from her grasp, but then his arm emerged, then his head and shoulder. She dropped the shovel and got a grip on his upper body as the shaking began in earnest. The joint in her right shoulder popped out from the strain of dragging the man who was over twice her weight and shrieked at the fiery pain of it as she hauled him backward over the tiled floor, but didn't stop until his legs finally slithered out.

Ripley took one look at Thaddeus' pulped, bloody left leg and continued to pull the tall, lean man away from the pile that had buried them alive as more of the corridor rained around them and the ground undulated. She dragged him to the doorway of the room where she'd gotten the fire irons before she collapsed as the rest of the temblor played out. Thaddeus leaned his head against the door-frame, his hands and arms limp at his sides, his face drawn with exhaustion. His body was a mass of wounds and blood and white dust, his clothes a shredded mess, and his face and hair had been transformed by the dust so that it looked like a kabuki theatre mask, dull white with vivid streaks of red blood, the only hints of his naturally dark skin showing through where trickles of sweat, and tears had tracked. From what she could see of herself, she was in the same boat, her entire body covered in plaster and debris and scrapes, her jacket long gone, her shirt sacrificed for masks, so that all she now wore was her sports bra, ripped pants, and sneakers.

"Thank you." Thaddeus' simple words cut through her observations.

"You're quite welcome," she responded in the slightly prim tone that was an adaptation of his formal speech.

He eyed her, and then grinned, his full set of brilliant white teeth on full show. He started to roll into a laugh, but it turned into another sticky, wet cough and he winced. "Think I cracked some ribs during that final journey."

"Your leg looks bad, too." Ripley hauled herself to her feet with a moan, her shoulder on fire from being dislocated, and slid to the floor again. "You're going to have to fix my shoulder, then I'll go find us some help."

"You need to lay flat, and put your arm at a—"

"Ninety-degree angle." She interrupted him. "This isn't my first time doing this," Ripley said grimly, knowing how awful the next ten seconds were going to be.

He got a good grasp on her arm and pulled until the shoulder snapped into place while she gritted her teeth against the pain. "Okay, you got it," she panted. "I don't know about you, but until I find someone that can patch you up, I could use some pain meds. You know where they might keep those?"

"Any office desk you find intact, most likely."

Ripley nodded wearily. "I'll bring them, or a person, whichever I find first."

Her shoulder wasn't on fire anymore, but it was sore, as was the rest of her. She moved cautiously along the destroyed hall, edging between fallen sections of walls and those that still stood, detouring around the sections fallen in from the floor from above. As she did so, Ripley kept a careful ear out for any cracking sounds that would alert her that more of the structure was about to come down. She called out periodically as she walked, but it only created echoes instead of a response.

After a few minutes, she found what she assumed was a secretary's office. The desk had been upended, but within the shattered drawers was a plastic bottle of painkillers, and a package of antibacterial wet wipes as well as a couple of old masks, which she took. In the corner was a mini fridge, and she nearly squealed with delight when she discovered it was stocked not only with waters and diet sodas but also a huge hunk of left-over cake on a plate. Ripley grabbed a water bottle and sucked it down greedily, then she pulled the liner out of the trash can, figuring a little extra litter on the floor wouldn't make much difference and turned it inside out to use as a carryall for everything she'd found except for the cake.

Thaddeus was in the same position she'd left him sitting in when she made it back with her loot, which worried her until his chest rose and fell in a deep breath that ended in another thick cough. She sat opposite him and pulled out a bottle of water. "I didn't find any people yet, but would you like something to drink?"

"That sounds wonderful."

Ripley shook out several of the pills and handed those to him as well, before downing another entire bottle of water and taking several aspirins herself. She couldn't remember water ever tasting so good as the last two bottles had been.

"I'll get going and find someone," Ripley said, wiping her hands and face with one of the antiseptic wipes she'd discovered, making sure that the cuts on her hands were as clean as she could get them. She handed him the package of wipes. "You should try and clean up your leg as best you can," she suggested. "Get a head start before the EMTs get here," she added in the most optimistic tone she could muster.

He looked at her with his serious dark brown eyes. "My leg may be injured, but my ears are working perfectly well, Ms. Baxter. I heard you calling out with no responses, so I think you'll have to range quite far afield to accomplish your task. Take a few minutes to rest and have some of this cake before you proceed. The sugar will do you good."

She hesitated as she eyed the chewed skin on his leg and listened to the raspy sound of his breath. He frowned. "Ms. Baxter, it won't do me any good if you collapse while you're seeking help. Eat some cake."

"We must look like a couple of animals," she remarked after taking a final bite of the delicious vanilla cake, marveling at the fact that thick buttercream frosting and rainbow sprinkles were part of the terrible day's events.

"We look like survivors," he corrected her, then moaned as he shifted. "You didn't see any radios lying around out there, did you?"

"No, but I'll keep looking," she said. "I still don't understand why there's no one around, why people didn't stay behind to dig out that rubble."

Thaddeus spread his hands eloquently. "We're in uncharted territory."

The man really didn't look much better even after the cake and water, which worried Ripley, as she'd gotten a surge of energy from their repast. She went into the destroyed room next to them and brought him out a stack of paper and pencils. He looked at her with a single eyebrow quirked, and she explained. "I think you're like me, you do better when your mind is occupied. You can doodle, or pen orders..." she stopped short of telling him he could write out his last will.

"Ah," was all he said, but perhaps he was thinking of the unspoken part of her sentence as well. "See you soon, Ms. Baxter."

She couldn't help herself. "Really? After all we've been through, you're not going to use my first name even now?"

He gave her a grin that looked nearly feral. "Things haven't gotten that bad, yet."

Ripley shook her head and left him with the drinks she'd found and set off to find both of them some much needed aid.

CHAPTER NINE

Giles County Seismic Zone/ The Narrows, Saltville, and Holston Valley Faults

The big box store parking lot wasn't as frantically busy as Mara had feared it would be, but there were still plenty of cars parked close to the front of the store. She swung the ATV away from them over to the side nearest the gardening section, choosing a small space between the store itself and the retaining wall of the parking lot that couldn't easily be seen from the street. Carefully tucking the keys into her jeans pocket, she hurried inside through an open door by the garden department.

Plants and pots were strewn everywhere, whole huge stacks of tiles and bricks tumbled to the ground and many shelving units had toppled, turning the entry into a maze. The sliding doors into the main store had been blocked open by a large earthenware pot that she stepped over. Right next to the door an armed security guard stood with his hand on his pistol and he looked at her suspiciously, especially at the backpack.

Mara waved her list. "Just getting a few things, my son fell and broke his leg."

He pointed. "Pharmacy and first aid is that way," he said in a low rumble of a voice.

She nodded her thanks, picked up a basket, and proceeded into the dim store lit only by the available light that came in through the doorways at the front and a few blue emergency lights scattered throughout the place. Despite the destruction and lack of illumination there were plenty of people shopping, some with huge carts that they left in open areas, carrying handfuls of goods to them from forays into the tumbledown aisles. The shelving was only seven feet high and some of it had remained standing, though she could only imagine what the insides of the stores with shelves that had towered more than twenty feet in the air must look like.

Mara beelined past the front checkout lines, which had begun to get long. When she reached the Pharmacy department, she was gratified to see that a lone man in a white coat worked steadily behind the counter serving a patient line of people who waited to get their prescriptions filled. There was no pushing or shoving, probably because of the security guard who stood next to the pharmacist. Moving past them, she filled her basket with several dozen gauze rolls and pads and antiseptic ointment. The bandaging tape only came in hot pink – and if Ethan minded, that would just be too bad – and she put five rolls of it in her basket, along with three bottles of pain medication to help stock their supplies and Anita's as well, then moved on to the section she hoped would have splints. Anita had told her that she wouldn't find a traditional splint anywhere but a medical supply store, but that one normally used for plantar fasciitis would work just as well for the next few days. Mara pounced on the box, relief surging through her that she'd found one. There was a single pair of the universal crutches left at the back of a shelf, and she jubilantly grabbed them as well.

Next she went to the home improvement department for a bucket of Plaster of Paris. The eight-pound tub was awkward to carry along with the crutches, and she wished she'd grabbed a cart. Unwilling to put down any of her goods, she risked being taken for a shoplifter and placed the big bucket in her backpack, freeing her hands for the basket containing the smaller items and the crutches.

Thinking about the journey they'd be taking back to the homestead, Mara picked up a pair of bungee cords to use to bind things onto the back rack of the ATV. They had some at home, but it hadn't occurred to her to bring them. Next, she trotted to the food department to get Anita's bottled water. The shelves had been picked nearly clean, so she took eight bottles of the fancy water that had been left, fitting them into the backpack and basket as best she could, and prayed that the fold of cash she had would be enough to cover everything.

The line to check out had gotten longer, and the people more impatient. A store manager walked the long line, repeating the same sentences. "Credit cards are not working. We are cash only." "The machines are not working. We are adding by hand, so it's taking longer." She was followed by a third armed guard, who looked menacingly at anyone who tried to start an argument with her.

Several disgruntled people got out of line as they absorbed the information, many leaving their carts behind. Mara grabbed one and moved the sugary cornucopia they'd gathered of cereal, cookies, and candy to one side before gratefully putting her own items inside. She considered the inside of the cart, then moved several bars of the candy back to her section of it. Caroline and Will had been working all day and they deserved something special, as did Ethan after his ordeal. There was also a big can of coffee she'd keep if possible, which would be her treat for herself. They were running low back home, and coffee was on her list of things she hoped she'd never have to give up.

Finally, after a long wait, it was her turn at the register. The tired-looking checkout woman looked up and said, "Put your items down one at a time so I can record them." She paused, then brightened. "Oh, hey Ms. Thomas!"

The use of Mara's maiden name surprised her, and she studied the young woman's face and recognized her as one of the high school students who had volunteered in her library a few years ago. "Laura McLemore! I'm glad to see you! And I'm Ms. Padgett now. I married the principal of the high school last year."

Laura arched an expressive brow. "Wow, well, that's something else. It's nice to see a friendly face, that's for sure."

Mara sympathized. "This has got to be hard."

"You're telling me. I'm just glad the security guys came in. If they weren't here, I'm one hundred percent sure things would be a whole lot worse." She surveyed the contents of the cart. "Is someone hurt?"

"You remember Ethan, my son? He's sixteen now, and broke his leg in a fall."

"Oh, gosh. Okay, let's see what you've got." Laura used a black notebook to add items up, writing down Mara's contact information as well. Mara was a few dollars short, so she started to take out the coffee and chocolate, but Laura waved her hand. "You know what? That's okay. Just come back and give us the last ten dollars when you can. If you can't trust your high school librarian, who can you trust?" She smiled as she put the bottles of water into doubled plastic bags and handed them over.

"Thank you, Laura. I really appreciate it. Take care!"

"You too, Ms. Thomas... I mean Ms. Padgett!" She laughed and shook her head. "You know, the whole school thought he was super cute."

"Principal Padgett?"

She nodded and laughed again. "I'm glad you two are together!" Then Laura turned her head to help the next person in line.

The simple friendly exchange had been comforting, and as she unloaded her goods, Mara wondered if such moments would become commonplace or a rarity in the days ahead as everyone tried to put their lives back together. It would be nice to think that a disaster would bring people closer together, but she suspected that even if it did for a short while, situations would quickly turn from cooperation into competition if goods became scarce.

Mara stashed the smaller items into her backpack then fastened it around her waist, using the bungee cords to strap down the Plaster of Paris, the crutches, and bags of bottled water onto the ATV. Satisfied that everything was secure, she prepared to leave the store. The engine clicked over, and she'd pushed the ATV into gear when a group of older teenagers deliberately moved in front of her and arranged themselves to block her way out. Mara's nerves jumped, but kept her features neutral and her right thumb on the throttle, while she moved her left to take off the parking brake. She dealt with teenagers every day in her job and most of the time they just wanted to be heard, so she made sure to make eye contact with the one in the center who seemed to be the leader.

"Hey," she said in a neutral tone, hoping he'd sheepishly give her a chin up and keep his little gang of friends moving along after the acknowledgement.

He smirked. "Get off the bike," he said, as if the request was the most natural thing in the world, the other teens laughing and clustering more closely to her.

Even though her heart was hammering, Mara slowly tilted her head as if she was puzzled, then gunned the machine straight through the group, scattering them with cries of outrage as they were forced to jump out of the way. A hand grabbed at her backpack, and another yanked one her braids, the first almost pulling her from the machine, the second making her cry out in pain, but she gripped the seat with her knees and yanked forward hard and both of them ripped away. Mara zoomed out of the parking lot at high speed, coming close to flipping over when she hit a crack in the road that sent the ATV flying, so she geared down, breathing heavily from the encounter. She risked a look behind her, but didn't see anyone in pursuit and slowed to a more manageable pace.

She drove straight behind Anita's house once she got there. Mara was still trembling from her unexpected encounter with the teens as she climbed off, but resolved not to say anything about the upsetting encounter to either Anita or Ethan, and took several deep breaths to calm herself before she approached the back door. The last thing her son or Anita needed was a report of how dangerous things had become in just a few short hours, and that she'd had such a close call and nearly had their ATV and the goods she'd brought with her stolen from her in broad daylight. As the breaths in through her nose and out through her mouth began to work their magic, Mara climbed the back two steps to the kitchen door, knocked, and called out. "Hey, I'm back!"

Anita opened it right away, relief on her homely features. "You were gone longer than I expected, you run into some sort of trouble?"

"I brought you fancy water," Mara avoided the question. "And I scored some candy. You want some chocolate?"

"Oh, me and chocolate aren't friends anymore," Anita replied as she carefully shut and locked the door behind Mara. "I got diagnosed with diabetes last year, so I'm doing my best to stay away from sweets, so I don't have to poke myself too many times a day."

"Oh, Anita, I'm sorry, I didn't know." She swung the waters onto the counter, frowning as she considered the difficulty being dependent on insulin would bring Anita until the mess from the earthquake was cleared up. "Do you have a good supply of meds?"

"My pharmacy is just down the road. I can walk if I need to." The older woman brushed off the concern.

Mara shook her head. "Anita, there was a really long line and just one pharmacist. Do you want me to go back and get your prescription filled for you?"

"It'll keep for a few days, anyway. I have a cellar under the house, my insulin will stay cold enough down there."

Mara put a hand on her arm. "Listen, I'm happy to go to the store for you if things don't sort themselves out soon." She hesitated, then went on. "People really are getting kind of weird and aggressive. I was glad they had armed guards at the store."

"Honey, people were always weird. Catastrophes either bring out the worst or the best in them." Anita gave her a little smile. "Ethan's having a lay-down on the sofa. I'll get this splint on him, so you can scoot on home to your family. My cats are tired of hiding from all you strangers in their house."

Daylight was on the wane as they left Anita's with the promise to return in a week so she could cast his leg and Mara took a moment to hug the nurse. "I am so glad you were home."

Anita patted her on the back. "Well, honey, I'm glad you thought to bring him over. If he starts running a fever, that's normal, just keep him resting and the pain meds rolling." She looked over Mara's shoulder at Ethan. "Did you hear me? Resting with that leg elevated! No gallivanting!"

"Yes, ma'am."

Grateful that she'd lived in Roanoke for the past five years and had a good grasp of the layout of the roads, Mara drove them home along a circuitous path that avoided stores and main roads. It edged along the bottom edge of one of the mountains that circled the city, and was lined with single family farms and large patches of open fields for the most part, and no traffic lights and only a single combination gas station and general store that they used on occasion when they only needed one or two grocery items or a quick gas-up of the ATV. The place was called Bart's, the name the current owner, Vivek Patel, had inherited and kept when he purchased the store. Mara kept up a steady pace as she made her way along her chosen route, as even at the base of a solid mountain that had stood rock solid for a millennia, there were huge cracks in the road as well as mature trees fallen alongside and across it, their dying leaves fluttering forlornly in the dusty air.

As they rolled past Bart's, she lifted a hand to Vivek, who was outside of the little store, sweeping glass into piles from his shattered front window. He gave her a wave back, then continued with his chore. Further along the road, she had to detour widely upslope around a long line of fallen telephone poles, their downed forms creating what looked like a logjam on a river. Ethan moaned a bit as they crossed the rough grass at an angle that had him gripping her waist tightly to keep himself as still as possible. Mara was utterly grateful when she finally pulled into their gravel driveway and drove straight down the path to park by the kitchen door, clicking the ATV off with a sigh of relief.

"Where have you been?" Caroline banged out of the kitchen door and down two of the crooked stairs of the porch, followed closely by Will and Gretel. The dog was the only one who seemed happy Mara was home, her tail wagging so hard it moved her entire rear end as Mara petted her. Caroline crossed her arms from her higher ground on the final step and frowned. "We were about to have to go to Lloyd and Eva Crowe's house!"

"Whoa, what happened to your leg?" Will dashed to the ATV to look at the splint.

"I know, I'm sorry it took so long," Mara said, her hand raising as she walked toward Caroline to perhaps brush her cheek and soothe the frown away, but the girl dodged away, bristling even more with a huffing sound of annoyance, so instead Mara turned and helped her son to stand, then took off the bungee cords and handed him the crutches. "I'm going to get Ethan situated, and then I'll start something for our dinner."

"I already started a pot of chili on the firepit in back with a low flame," Caroline said shortly. "Will was hungry, and I had to do something with the tomatoes."

Mara felt her cheeks heat as the teen stared at her defiantly. "Thank you, that was really smart," was all she could manage.

"Yeah, well. You left us alone all day long with a huge mess."

"She had to pull me up a really steep hill, and then find help, Caroline, which wasn't easy," Ethan snapped. "Mom's had a hard day, too."

Caroline rolled her eyes. "Stick up for your mom, like you always do."

"She's your mom now, too."

"Lucky me." Caroline stomped off across the yard.

It certainly wasn't the homecoming Mara would have wanted, but at least they were home. With a tired sigh, she hoisted the backpack and put herself where she could catch Ethan if he took a misstep as he tottered forward.

"Can I try your crutches, Ethan?" Will asked, seemingly oblivious to the tension that had stirred up around him.

"They're not toys," Mara broke in before Ethan could say yes. Ethan needed the crutches, and Will tended toward being a daredevil. She could just see him playing around on them to see how high he could swing himself, then accidentally propelling himself off of the porch, breaking one of his own limbs and the crutches themselves in the process.

Will's eyes shuttered as he shrugged eloquently. "Whatever." He patted his leg for Gretel to come to him, and jumped off the porch, the dog happily following him as he moved into the yard. Mara's heart sank as her husband's children walked away from her.

"Let's get you inside," she said to Ethan.

The kids had done a good job in the kitchen; the floor was swept and clear of glass, and everything had been picked up, and the table had been cleared of all the cooking gear she'd had out earlier in the morning for her canning attempt. That effort seemed like it had happened a lifetime ago. After she got Ethan settled in his room with his leg elevated, a peanut butter sandwich, another dose of painkillers and some lukewarm water from the tap, Mara sat herself wearily at the kitchen table and allowed her head to fall into her hands. There were hundreds of chores that needed to be done, but she didn't even know where she could begin. She longed for a hot shower and a hot cup of coffee, but the coffee maker had been one of the fatalities of the earthquake, along with most of the mugs. She wanted to talk to Logan or her sister for even just a few minutes, but when she pulled out her phone and input her husband's number for the hundredth time, she was met with a black screen, not even the mechanical voice telling her the number could not be completed as dialed. Mara slumped in her seat, and tapped the phone with her finger as if the morse code of her touch could somehow reach Logan.

Before she could sink any further into her fatigue, Mara slapped the table with one hand to rouse herself into action. "Okay then, let's work on our food situation," she said out loud, then stood with a groan as her knees popped to check on the refrigerator and its contents.

It was still somewhat cool, but definitely not working, so the first order of business would be to get their generator fired up so that they could keep the food they had before it went bad. Mara went to the breaker box and turned everything to off so their circuits wouldn't blow if the power was restored, then trudged outside to the concrete slab where their home generator sat. She checked the oil, then moved the choke and flipped the red switch on before pulling the cord, and the motor immediately spun to life, running loud enough to startle the birds from the nearby bushes in an explosion of feathers and squawking, but it meant they had power, and she did a little victory dance to celebrate. Once it was running, she moved the choke back to run and snaked the extension cord that hung next to the generator around to the fridge. It's soft hum started up again and she stuck her head all the way inside just to feel the breath of air swathe her cheeks with welcome coolness.

She opened the door to the cellar, picked up the big flashlight mounted on the wall and shined it down the stairs. Mara had steeled herself to see a mess, but gasped a bit when she saw the utter shambles that covered the concrete floor of the cellar. The shelving had been built into two of the walls, and was bolted into the concrete, so those were still standing tall, but most of the jars that had been on them were smashed on the floor into a cacophony of colors and textures, pinpointed with hundreds of shards of glass and round metal tops that were all useless trash. Worse, the whole room smelled like an odd mix of sweet peaches and sauerkraut that made her belly do a flip of disgust. It would take hours to clean the sticky, goopy mess up and there were other, more pressing things she needed to do before night closed them in, so it would have to wait a little longer. She pulled another looped extension cord off of its place on the wall and made her way back to the big freezer, hoping she wasn't too late to save the meat and cooked, bagged meals they'd stored there.

Their freezer was top of the line, and had a good seal, and a cold puff of white air greeted her as she cracked it open. She checked the appliance thermometer and sighed with relief that she had talked Logan into getting the expensive investment, because the temperature inside had only climbed to seven degrees during the many hours without any electricity. The number was not perfect, but she'd caught it in time before the contents had spoiled. Mara plugged in the cord and then went back outside to connect it into the generator. She crossed the lawn, relieved to see that both Caroline and Will were by the pond and hadn't wandered off of the property so she'd have to go looking for them as the night continued to drop into their little valley. She walked to the barn to get one of the smaller gas cans they kept next to the thirty gallon ones and filled it up to keep next to the generator.

Worry settled along her spine as she looked at all the farm goods they had in the barn storage, with only a small lock on the barn door to keep people out. She couldn't even remember the last time they'd locked it, but with the barn so close to the road, their things were too vulnerable to any sort of passerby, like the teens who'd tried to take the ATV from her this afternoon. Their fuel, and the kids bikes and the animal feed, not to mention all the tools Logan kept here were all things that people might find themselves needing in the days ahead until the roads and communications and water lines could be repaired, they needed to be prudent about protecting what they had on hand. Putting down the gas can, she went outside and called to Caroline and Will.

"Kids, come here. We need to move some stuff!"

They looked at each other and she could imagine the eye rolls, but they both walked up the rise to the barn, Gretel bounding ahead of them.

Trying to avoid a long discussion, Mara plunged in as soon as they were inside the garage. "Listen, I have a good reason for moving some things, and I think you should know it. When I was getting help for Ethan, I ran into a few people who looked like they might want to take the ATV from me because their cars weren't doing well on the roads, and it happened again at the store."

"You mean they literally tried to take the ATV?" Will asked, a tinge of doubt in his normally cheerful voice, his attention fully on her.

"That's right," Mara said firmly. "Look, I'm sure things will get back to normal in a couple of days, but for now, I want to move these gas containers to the garden shed where they're closer to the house, and your bikes as well. And the dog food."

As if she knew they were talking about her, Gretel gave a sharp bark and panted, which broke the tension she was feeling from her stepchildren. Will grabbed the big bag of dog food and staggered out with it before she could give him something lighter and she was left looking at Caroline, who placed herself in front of the containers of fuel and had her patented frown pasted on her face.

"Have you tried to get a hold of dad?"

"I have, the cell phone still isn't working."

"We should try a land line. The Buchanan's are old and don't have cell phones, and they have one in their house. It's avocado green to match the floor in their kitchen." Caroline's tone left no doubt as to what she thought of the color scheme.

Mara considered the suggestion as she looked out of the barn door. The lightning bugs were out, their bright flashes showing brightly in the deepening dusk. Her need to see the kids safely into the house for the night combined with the uneasiness about their supplies decided for her.

"Okay, if the cell isn't working by tomorrow, we'll walk over to the Buchanan's house and ask if we can try theirs." To forestall any argument, she grabbed the handle of one of the gas containers and wheeled it outside.

After several trips to get the rest of the fuel and the bikes, as well as some tools she needed to put a lock onto the garden shed, Mara asked Will to hold the flashlight for her while she installed the security on the shed. The light was almost gone when she'd finished, and Mara made a mental note that to make a trip to the hardware store and get extra locks for both the shed and the house doors, as well as the barn door first thing tomorrow morning after she got them a good amount of groceries to tide them over until life returned to its normal ups and downs.

Mara took the flashlight from Will as they walked across their backyard. Caroline was sitting by the low cookfire, stirring the pot of chili she'd cooked up. The teen looked up at them expectantly. "You ready to have some food, yet?"

Mara's belly rumbled, reminding her that it had been a long time since she'd had anything to eat, but she needed to take a quick shower first. "Caroline, that smells delicious, there's some ground beef in the refrigerator, can you fry it up and add that to your chili while I take a shower, please? I think we can all use the extra dose of protein."

"Yum, beef!" Will's enthusiasm overpowered Caroline's sigh.

"Come on inside with me while I get some candles set up for us to use, and you can have the flashlight." Mara waved an encouraging hand to Caroline. "I have the generator going, of course but I only want to use it for the fridge and the freezer, at least for tonight, so we get to be old fashioned with candles tonight!"

"Whoo." Caroline said flatly, but held the flashlight for Mara as she rummaged in their candle drawer for some nice fat candles and wooden matches, and took the time to melt the bottom of the candles to stick onto some of the saucers that hadn't succumbed to the earthquake.

Mara took a few minutes to take a cool shower and rinse off the long day, marveling at the amount of dirt that came off of her skin and hair as it swirled down the drain. The cool water felt good on her tired body, taking away some of the inflammation around her knees and ankles. Mara was grateful that the water was still flowing, and made another mental note to check on the well pump in case their city water stopped working. She sighed at the sheer number of things she needed to remember as she toweled off and changed into a loose t-shirt and jeans, the clean fabrics feeling like a bit of heaven against her skin.

She stopped on the way outside to dinner to check on Ethan, the candle flickering on his pale face and the thick eyelashes that twitched a bit as he dreamed. She felt his forehead, and noted the heat of it, and his flushed cheeks, and opted to let him sleep for the time being since she could always bring him some supper later. She left the door open so she could hear him if he called to her and walked out of the screen door of the kitchen, noticing that it now sat awkwardly in the door frame. That was going to have to be something Logan addressed, she knew nothing about fixing doors, and he loved working with wood.

Mara continued outside and joined the kids by the flickering fire, the aroma of the chili even more enticing than it had been earlier. She pulled up a campfire chair and served herself a bowl of the simmering meal with gratitude. The first mouthful was bliss, even if the kids liked their chili a little more fiery than she did. Caroline had also brought out the last half loaf of bread and a Coleman lantern so they could see to eat their food. It would probably be good to get another lantern or two, as well as the fuel for them, Mara thought as she added yet another item to her ever-growing list of necessary things.

A peaceful silence descended as they ate, the quiet of the countryside even deeper than it normally was without the residual noise of occasional cars going by. Mara had expected that the stars would be out, the high accompaniment to the lightning bugs that zipped and zoomed around the garden in their intricate dance, but the dust kicked up from the earthquakes and their aftershocks still drifted between them and the night sky, dimming their brilliance.

After they'd finished, Mara let out a long breath and felt some of her tension ease. "That was great. Stay here a moment, I got something at the store for you both when I was there today, along with extra coffee for you and me, Caroline. That's one thing I for sure don't want to run out of."

She walked inside, noticing how her muscles had gotten stiff after sitting still for only a short time. She'd be wise to take some ibuprofen before she went to sleep tonight, or she'd wake up in knots from all of the walking and hiking and lifting that she'd done today, aside from the just plain worry putting her shoulders into knots. Mara pulled out two of the candy bars she'd bought at the store from her backpack, and carried them back out to the fire.

"Here you go, a little thank you for holding down our homestead while I found Ethan." She handed the kids the treats and was glad to see a bit of joy light up their faces as they took the bars.

Heartened that they seemed happy with her contribution, Mara outlined a general plan for the next day as the fire simmered into ashy logs that kept a few hot spots. "It might be days or even weeks before we get services back, and while we are prepared for emergencies, I'd like to get to the store early to replenish some canned goods, and things like bread and cereal and butter. We have fresh vegetables, and the frozen meals and plenty of meat, and our eggs of course, but we lost nearly everything that was in jars in the cellar. I didn't look too closely, but I'm sure our packaged goods are fine, and anything like peanut butter that was in plastic. Now, here's a little bad news. I don't want to run the generator any more than we have to so we can save our fuel, so it'll be cold showers for the next little bit."

She smiled at the groans. "Just be glad it's summertime, those cool showers might actually feel good."

"I'll come with you to the store tomorrow," Caroline unexpectedly volunteered. "If you're worried about the ATV, we can put the panniers on the mountain bikes and ride those. Will can stay home and keep Ethan company."

"Yeah, I'll get him to play some card games with me!" Will said.

"That sounds great," Mara said, as she was overcome by a huge yawn. "I want to get there when the store opens, so we should leave at six-thirty, okay?" She scooped Ethan a bowl of the chili and took a couple of slices of bread to go with it. "Let's just leave the dishes to soak in the sink, I'll do them in the morning."

"I'll take care of the fire!" Will said. "I know how!" Mara was tempted to stay and watch him do it, but her exhaustion was getting the better of her.

"Thanks, Will. Caroline, can you get the rest of the food and put it up in the fridge? I don't want to waste a bite of what you made."

Mara pulled a thick candle from their emergency drawer and lit it. She'd need to get more camping lanterns tomorrow if she could, as well as the hardware for the locks, and maybe purchase another thirty gallon container of gasoline as well. Putting Ethan's meal on a tray, she walked to his room, the candlelight casting odd dancing shadows on the wall. She gently woke Ethan and took his temperature. "It's a little high, but Anita said that would be normal. It's chili for dinner."

"I'm not hungry right now, mom."

Mara was worried that her normally ravenous son would refuse one of his favorite meals, but she smiled and nodded. "Okay, take a couple more aspirin, and I'll make you another sandwich. I can wrap it and leave it on your nightstand in case you get hungry in the middle of the night. I don't want you getting up unless it's absolutely necessary."

After making sure Ethan's needs were met, Mara took the candle and dragged herself up the stairs to her bedroom, shucked her clothes, and gratefully put on one of Logan's oversized cotton t-shirts. The bed called to her, but she had one more thing to do.

Kneeling in front of the wall safe Logan had installed, she opened it, and pulled out her gun, checked to see that it was loaded, and that the safety was on. She carried it with her and slumped onto the bed that had slid into an odd diagonal into the center of the floor and put the gun under Logan's pillow. Mara laid back and struggled to stay awake long enough to continue the mental list of what they needed to accomplish on the morrow, but didn't add a single item before sleep took her.

CHAPTER TEN

The New Madrid Fault

Deb hadn't been as busy as she'd expected at St Jude's hospital working as a volunteer nurse, although halfway through the day her twisted ankle wasn't happy that she had used it so much. Very few people came from the outside seeking help, which she guessed meant that the destruction of the downtown area of Memphis had been too sudden and profound for there to be many survivors. Deb's main job became ferrying the people they continued to pull from the rubble in the fallen sections of the campus, bringing them to the smaller care unit that had survived, then giving them first aid and a bit of comfort until they could be seen as the doctors conducted their triage.

Most of the people who had been extracted from the wreckage at the hospital had been crushed too badly to save, but the ones who could be helped were rushed into the last remaining medical wing to be attended to. It had been the big multi-story buildings on St. Jude's western campus, the ones that faced the river which had collapsed, their tall structures unable to stand against the long, rolling vibrations that had continued throughout the day. Deb fought back hourly tears as the small, limp bodies of the patients who'd been housed there were extricated from beneath fallen beams and walls by a cadre of firefighters who'd managed to make it through the streets to the hospital, along with the parents who had been with them, as well as hospital staff, identifiable by their scrubs and doctor's white coats. She wanted to scream at the injustice of it all, that the young innocents who had already been in a fight for their lives had been struck down in such an outrageous, brutal fashion.

Orderlies took the people who'd not survived in a different direction than where Deb wheeled her patients. Yet everyone who dug or waited to be of service clung to the hope that they'd find more who had survived the quake, and every time a living person was discovered, it was a celebration, no matter how serious their injuries were. Deb's emotions had been pulled up and down so many times in the past hours that she was exhausted. She could only imagine what it was like for the regular staff to be working in the pile of concrete and glass that used to be a major wing of the hospital. They knew those people they'd pulled out by name, or by sight, and many of them would've been good friends. At least for her they were anonymous victims, without the extra burden of seeing the person you ate lunch with yesterday broken and crushed. She wiped away her tears again and again, then girded herself with the professional manner she'd used as a shield for years as an ER nurse, and kept working despite her aches and pains, pausing only to grab a drink of water from the bottle she carried and refilled from the trickles that still ran in the bathroom sink.

Later in the day, as fewer and fewer living persons were discovered, Deb took the time to seek out Jenny and her little girl, Mattie, who she'd helped rescue from the influx of the Mississippi river after the initial quake and the first few aftershocks. She found them in an open space that was normally used as a waiting room, but which had been reconfigured to hold beds for those who had been less severely injured. Some smart hospital staffer had brought in tables and chairs from the cafeteria, and some board games and toys, as well as a box of donated clothing to put in the area that currently held about thirty people. Deb found Jenny and Mattie had carved out a small space in the corner of the room, seated on the floor, playing with some big blocks.

"Hey, how are you holding up?"

"Mattie's doing great. She just had a couple of scratches, and they got my ribs taped up nice and tight," Jenny replied. "They said I broke four of them, but not badly, and as long as I don't overexert myself for the next week or so, they'll heal right up."

"That's great news." Deb slid down the wall to sit next to Jenny, glad to take a load off of her aching ankle.

"They gave me some pain meds and said we could stay in the hospital until the air outside gets better. Then they let us have some packaged sandwiches, and coffee and water around noon," Jenny told her. "An hour ago, they just opened up the vending machine and said we could have any of the chips and cookies we wanted. But it didn't look like they had much food besides that. You want a cookie?" Jenny held open the little packet of mini chocolate chip cookies.

Deb's stomach growled at the sugary scent of the snack, so she took a couple and munched them gratefully. "Thanks. I haven't had time to think about eating since I volunteered. It's a bad habit of mine. Once I start on a shift, I just keep going with my head down like a bulldog with a bone."

"I hear that. It's the same with me when I'm cleaning someone's house for them, especially those deep cleaning jobs where you're wrist-deep in grime." Jenny shared a knowing smile with Deb. "Sure does feel good when you stop, though."

She glanced over at Mattie, who was still engrossed playing with a big blocks set, and brought her voice down to a whisper. "Have you looked outside? I know the hospital staff said we could stay for a while, but that ash is getting worse, not better. I don't think a person could go out there without a respirator or at least a good mask, so I don't know how we'll get home. Can you imagine how much of the city must be on fire for it to look that way?"

"I haven't looked, but it's probably made up of a lot of particulates and dust that swirled in there as well, and that would need to settle instead of smoke, which can be blown away by a breeze." Deb fought down the bump of fear that Jenny had given her with the information of the air becoming worse, as she'd been considering the idea of leaving this hospital to go to St. Francis, the hospital where she normally worked. She was worried for her co-workers and could only hope that her hospital's location some twelve miles away from the epicenter had resulted in less damage and death than it had here.

"I'll find out about the food situation, though, and for now, we can be glad the hospital has a generator and that we're in air conditioning, that's for sure." Deb promised Jenny, then asked the question she'd been thinking about on and off. "Tell me, how did you end up on Poplar street? Do you live downtown?"

"No, we're up north, but I'm a single mother, so Mattie stays with my Mama a few days a week while I do my job cleaning houses and apartments for people. I was only a block away from dropping her off when the street just disappeared under all that water, and I couldn't do anything to get us out of it. I saw my Mama's building just collapse, right in front of us." Her eyes teared up at the memory, and she held Deb's hands with both of hers. "I couldn't save her or Mattie and me. You were like an angel sent from heaven, and that's the living truth, so help me. If it hadn't been for you..." her voice trailed off as she broke down.

Deb patted her on the back, moved by the woman's gratitude, but wanted to protest that she wasn't any kind of hero. She'd just been late going for a run with her friends, or she'd never have survived the first wave of the quake, nor would she have been positioned right there as the car containing the pair had floated by. It was a miracle of sorts, she supposed, that she'd been there, but it hadn't felt anything close to miraculous at the time.

"I'm just glad I was able to help you both."

"You know people have been saying that was a nine point seven magnitude earthquake, and it's not the only one, too."

"What?"

"There's a man who heard bits of news on his transistor radio before it died, that these quakes are happening all over the USA, and even across the world, and that they're not stopping. Can you believe that?"

"I don't know what to think. Although, these tremors keep

happening, and that doesn't seem right to me. I thought earthquakes were more one-and-done."

As if she'd called it to life by speaking about it, another shake rumbled through the building. Jenny snatched Mattie up to hold her close as the blocks the girl had built into a tower collapsed under a series of back-and-forth vibrations that bounced the tables violently, toppling some people to their hands and knees, cries of panic and screams filling the air along with the loud grind of earth moving. It lasted for a full thirty seconds before easing off and stopping. A few who'd been pushed past their emotional limits sat with their heads in their hands, weeping.

Deb hurried over to an older lady who was having a hard time rising from the floor. She picked up the chair she'd been sitting in when it tipped over, and helped the woman to sit back down as she went into what she thought of as her nurse's patter that she spoke in a calm, competent way. "Is this your water bottle? Have a nice sip. There you go." She fished a packet of tissues she always carried and handed her a couple. Deb scanned the room, walking the perimeter to ascertain if anyone had been hurt, but no one had been re-injured, except Jenny, who was holding her ribs, fighting back tears.

Deb moved to her and bent to help Jenny settle into the corner, where she could sit up and be a bit more supported. "You're going to have to be careful not to grab up Mattie like that," she scolded her. "You'll set your healing back."

She was surprised when Jenny let out a dry chuckle. "You don't have kids, do you?" Jenny panted the words a bit as she dealt with her hurt ribs.

"Well, no."

"You might as well tell me to not feed her, as to not reach for my child when the earth is heaving around like that." The response was from the heart, and Deb found herself agreeing with Jenny.

"Yeah, okay, I get that. My sister's the same with her son, Ethan. She'd fight to the death to protect him, even if both of her arms had been chopped off. Forget I said it, all right?" She patted Jenny's knee and then focused Mattie's attention on the blocks so Jenny could continue to lean back. "Can you build your tower up again for me?"

"Yep." Mattie got back to work. Deb stood, her knees cracking, and her ankle resuming its throbs of protest despite the tight wrap she'd put on it. "I'm going to find out about the food, and I'll come back and let you know. You just rest if you can."

Deb chewed on the conversation they'd been having about the quakes as she went in search of the Filipino nurse who'd been acting as a greeter that morning. Could it really be possible there had been multiple quakes all across the United States? She'd felt earthquakes rumble underneath her feet living in Memphis for the past few years, but none had been strong enough to even warrant her moving into a doorway, they'd just been little ones that the newscasters on television turned into a quasi-joke as they talked about milk containers being moved over a whole inch in their refrigerator. Deb was absolutely sure no one was joking about earthquakes anywhere at the moment as she walked into the atrium and found the nurse she was looking for resting her head on her arms by the front desk.

Deb's stride hitched to a stop as she took in the changes to the outside landscape through the big atrium windows. The air outside looked thick enough to eat, a dark sepia brown in color, with large white ash flakes drifting slowly down to add to the pile of white on the ground. In place of the black Mississippi waters she'd waded through to get to St Jude's, there was a coating of ash, making it appear as if they'd somehow gotten a slightly soiled white Christmas in July.

She pulled her gaze away from the mesmerizing sweep of the ash coming down and approached the Filipino woman, touching her gently on the arm to get her attention. "Hi, remember me? I'm Deb Varden, ER nurse from St. Francis. I came in earlier with a mom and her daughter."

The nurse looked her up and down as she stretched and straightened the top of her scrubs before recognition bloomed. "Sure, sure. Thanks for volunteering."

Deb pointed at the windows. "I think I should thank you for giving me a place to shelter."

The woman let out a deep breath as she contemplated the atmosphere outside. "I've been watching it, and that ash that's coming down has gotten much worse over the past hour. We haven't had any new cases come in for a while." The short woman tutted with dismay then continued, "The dispatcher said the ambulances can't get through the streets, so they've been carrying anyone they can find on stretchers."

Deb flashed on images from an old World War Two documentary of the Blitz in London, and the way the injured had been carried through destroyed streets strewn with rubble and nodded her understanding. "Listen, some of the people in the waiting room with superficial injuries were wondering if the hospital might be giving them some dinner soon."

The woman was shaking her head before Deb could finish the sentence. "I checked earlier. Our cafeteria kitchen was wiped out in the aftershocks. They're welcome to what is in the vending machines we opened up, but that's all we've got."

"Should we maybe radio another hospital for supplies, since we have a group of people taking shelter until the air clears?" Deb said the words carefully, not wanting to be offensive, and suspecting that the woman was probably way ahead of her.

"Yeah, yeah. We did that early on, and found out that the VA has their kitchen up and running strong, but the problem is the same as it is for the first responders. Too much wreckage between us and the VA for a vehicle to get through. So if you wanted to go home, or..." she drifted off when Deb shook her head. "Anyway, you don't have to stay and continue to work is all I'm saying, since we don't have new patients coming in from the outside." Her face drooped and her voice sounded bleak. "I think we're down to trying to save our own injured at this point, those that *can* be saved at any rate."

Silence dropped over them as they both contemplated the swirl of dust and debris that had turned the late afternoon into a dim twilight. The flood of water she'd had to navigate to get to St. Jude's may have receded a bit, but she dreaded the death and destruction she'd see in the leftover muck of it once she left the sanctuary of the hospital. It was one thing to face and fight death in the confines of an ER, but quite another to have it all around and be helpless to do anything constructive. Deb was hungry and tired after being on her feet for the past eight hours, and would love nothing better than to find a free bed or even just two chairs pushed together and rest, but there was something in her that wouldn't let her stop trying to help.

"I'm willing to bring in some supplies walking if you want to organize that," Deb said. "Maybe a few others could go, and we could at least feed the doctors and the nurses as they're working. I just think we might need masks or even respirators to walk out there. Do you have those?"

The woman's eyebrows arched up to hide behind her bangs, but then she nodded as her decision was made. "If you're willing to do that, I'll take you up on it. The VA is only about a mile or so away. I can get some others, and we can use our N95 masks." She looked critically at Deb, then pulled a power bar from her pocket and handed it to her as she offered her chair. "Have a seat, eat this, and get a bit of rest, and I'll organize it. We'll leave in the next hour. I'm Maritza, by the way."

"I'll be ready." Deb took the moment to eat the bar and sit on the cushioned surface of the chair, but her mind refused to let her rest. She pulled out her phone to try calling Mara again, but there was still no service available, and she tucked it back into her sports top as she contemplated the thick fall of ash outside. Moving through that, even with a mask, was going to take a lot of effort, and the VA hospital was only a couple of blocks away from her apartment. Maybe it would be smart to get her personal items from the locker room and bring them with her so she could break off and go home. Deb rubbed her face with her hands as she discarded the selfish notion immediately after it had drifted into her tired brain. If by some stroke of luck her building was still standing, she wouldn't just bail on her own plan to haul food back to St. Jude's. There was no need to collect her things. Instead, in imitation of Maritza, she opted to put her head on her arms on the desk in front of her, just to rest her eyes for a moment.

A nanosecond later, Deb was shaken awake, her brain spinning a bit as she was pulled from deep sleep back into the present. Maritza stood next to her with a bottle of water in her hand. "Good, you got in a nap." She handed her the water. "You should have a good drink before we head out," she said in her efficient manner. "This is Tom, and the other one is also Tom." Maritza gestured to the two burly men who stood by her side, one taller than the other but both with wide shoulders. "They volunteered to come with us."

Deb willed herself to pull out of her groggy lethargy, and nodded at the two men, noting that they each carried bulging pillowcases tied together with a long length of rubber tubing in their massive hands. "What's in there?"

"First aid supplies for the VA." Maritza spoke up. "I told them we were coming, and they said they can't access their basement storage, and were running low on bandages, antibiotics, gloves, and masks."

"Good trade." As Deb's comment flowed out, she had a sense of wonder at how quickly reality had changed in the major metropolitan city where she'd lived for nearly a decade. In only a few hours, they'd been reduced to trading for supplies as if they were medieval villagers.

"Yeah." The shorter Tom spoke up. "We jury-rigged these carryalls so Other Tom and I can each carry two sets over our shoulders. You ladies will take one pair."

"Then we'll use them to carry food back with us if we need to," added Other Tom with a grin that showed off perfect veneers. "I'm hoping they've got a cart or something that will work instead, but hey, we're ready for anything."

Maritza stuck a thumb at them. "Their idea, and a pretty good one, I have to say."

The men high-fived each other in a moment of levity before Maritza pulled out her clipboard and waved them over to look at it. "I've drawn a rough map of where we're headed. Not that I'm expecting trouble, but who knows what it's like out there, and it's best if we're all on the same page." Maritza said pragmatically. "It's pretty simple. We'll take a left once we're out the door, and then angle down Alabama to Pauline, as best we can. I've radioed ahead that we're on our way, so they're expecting us before dark." She glanced outside. "Not that its going to look that different than it does now."

Deb swallowed as she masked up and mentally prepared herself for the trudge ahead. They'd be walking within a block of her apartment building, so she'd find out if it still stood. If it had fallen and all her things had been destroyed, she didn't know what she would do, or where she would go, but at least she'd have the facts and could move on from there.

"Everybody ready? Deb? Tom and Tom?" Maritza got their acknowledgements before she shouldered her bags and walked to the glass doors of St. Jude. They all paused for a moment to tighten the seals on their masks, and then followed her outside into the swampy heat and murk of Memphis.

CHAPTER ELEVEN

US Army Reserve, Brainerd, MN

Out of the two hundred and fifty-seven passengers and six crew members aboard Logan's flight, ninety-nine people had survived the explosions after the plane made its successful emergency landing. After the first responders had screamed in from a nearby town, the firefighters had moved everyone back and pumped water from the river to put out the remaining spots of fire as ambulances arrived, and had given first aid to all who needed it, then transported a few burn victims away.

Another fire unit and a group from the coroner's office brought body bags, respectfully putting the people into them, then carried their grim burdens on stretchers to a large truck. Logan stopped one team as they headed to the train tracks to collect the dead and pointed at Myrna's body so that they could identify her properly. "Her name was Myrna Goenka, and she was from Atlanta." He wanted to tell them more, that her voice and hands were gentle, that she loved history, and had toured the Civil War battlefields with her husband, but had kept quiet as they gathered her while he monitored Braden.

As well-equipped as the ambulances had been, none had carried diapers in their emergency supplies, so Logan fashioned one for Braden using a towel and some safety pins, which seemed to puzzle but not bother the little boy. He was content enough to play in the grass back by the trees where they'd sheltered to get away from the hustle and bustle as long as Logan stayed near him.

There were about sixty survivors who had gotten away from the crash landing and the horrific aftermath with only a few superficial cuts and bruises. The EMTs had given them power bars, water, and foil blankets and told them to wait until the military came to fetch them from an Army Reserve unit that was located forty miles north of their current position between the highway and the railroad tracks.

Forty miles north was forty miles in the wrong direction from Mara and his kids. Logan clenched his fist and bit back his protest at the orders they'd been given. He saw little choice except to comply for the time being, especially as it had fallen to him to get Braden into competent hands. After that was accomplished, he could make some strides to make his way home to Virginia as fast as he could get there. He'd seen that Braden's mom had printed his name on the label on his pants when he'd changed him into his Macgyvered diaper, and had learned that the child's full name was Braden Frye.

As he eyed the little boy, who was pulling up fistfuls of grass and sprinkling them over his head, Logan's heart went out to the inno-cent child whose life had been completely upended. The best thing he could do for the child was to convey his knowledge of Braden's name and that his mother had said that they were from Addison, Texas, so someone could take the steps necessary to get Braden reconnected with his real family.

"What a day," remarked Jasper as he walked up to Logan, with about as much inflection as someone referring to a day that had been slightly busier than normal. The man stood too close to him, and just started talking as if he were sure Logan would be interested in what he had to say. "Is your phone working yet? I dropped mine somewhere."

"No service, yet. The first responders said their radios were working in a limited range, but that reception was spotty."

Jasper removed his glasses to wipe them down and did his trademark bounce on his toes, then continued to chatter away as if they were in the lobby area of the convention hall like they'd been yesterday, unaffected by the tragedy that surrounded him. "Did they know anything about these earthquakes, how widespread they are? I've been talking to a few people, and heard all of the USA has been affected, maybe even the entire world." The little man's eyes gleamed as if he were eager to learn some bad news to spread gossip about. "I mean, I'd almost pay money to hear that New York was taken out, so that I don't have to pay my ex-wife any more alimony." He laughed as if what he'd said was funny.

Logan was taken aback by the man's callousness and his ghoulish curiosity. They certainly weren't traits Jasper had exhibited in the time he'd spent with him, but then he didn't really know the man aside from participating in educator conferences with him. "I haven't heard any specifics about cities that were hit. Just that the earthquakes seem to be widespread, but they weren't as bad in this area, compared to other places, like Memphis and Dallas," Logan said.

"Oh, man, Dallas. I could only see a little from the aisle seat, but to me it looked like the whole downtown was just getting swallowed up by the earth." Jasper widened his eyes and mimed that his head was blowing up. "Mind blown. I mean, I thought things like that only happened in the movies."

"Join the club." Logan was tired of talking to the irritating little man and his seemingly incessant drive to talk about negative things.

"You'll be okay, though, I bet."

"What?"

"Well, you know all that homesteading stuff, right? Like you were teaching those loser kids? Fending for yourself off of the grid. So even if this whole planet has gone belly-up for the rest of us, you'd be good, lighting your fires, and gathering food from the forest, right?" His tone had a nasty edge to it, a taunting bully.

"I've learned a lot, made a lot of mistakes along the way, but yes, I know how to do those things, you're right." Logan used his technique of removing the steam from aggressive bullies by simply agreeing with them, hoping the little man would be mollified and go away.

"Does that include hunting animals with your bare hands?" Jasper made a little growling sound and pretended like he was pouncing on an animal. "You're going to be the big cheese now, the way the situation looks, in demand! The BMOC." He chuckled, a braying sort of laugh that had nothing at all to do with humor or shared amusement.

"Sure." Logan was just plain worn out from the horrible events of the day and had no patience left to endure chatter, so he'd responded with the flattest tone he could muster. He turned his back on Jasper and laid down on the metal blanket he'd been given in what he hoped was a clear signal he wasn't up for any more speculation and a moment later, Jasper's shadow crossed him as he walked away, giving Logan some relief.

Braden toddled over, solemnly sprinkled a handful of grass on Logan's chest, then laid down next to him, then snuggled his little body next to Logan's and laid his head on his arm. "Nap," he said wisely, and in moments was asleep, his lips forming a little O as he breathed in and out.

The absolute trust the child had in Logan broke his heart. In just a few hours, he was most likely going to have to leave him behind in the care of child services so that they could start the process of finding Braden's family, but he'd sure miss the little guy. He'd just have to trust that the authorities could find his relatives and that the boy would thrive after his own brief sojourn in the child's life was over. He flung an arm over his eyes and focused on lowering his heartbeat, willing himself to find a space of tranquility and calm, like he did in a deer hunting blind, and as he calmed to a doze, he swung his free arm protectively over Braden.

The transport vehicles from an army reserve unit pulled up about an hour later. Logan folded the blanket he'd been lying on, and collected two more from where people had just left them discarded on the ground, and put them all into the remaining pocket of his burnt backpack. He offered Braden a sip of water and another cookie as an after-nap snack, then secured him safely in his arms as the survivors formed a ragged circle near the trucks.

The young reservists who helped them onto the trucks didn't rush anyone, but simply assisted those who needed it to get into the trucks and seated on the long benches that lined the back and both sides of the transport vehicles. When it was Logan's turn, he hopped easily up into the truck and then swung around to take Braden from the young men as they lifted the boy up. Logan walked back into the dim interior to sit in his place on a bench. Braden's eyes were wide as he took in yet another new thing and his bottom lip trembled as he dropped his cookie, and looked around wildly in the dim space.

"I want my mommy!" He wailed and tried to wiggle out of Logan's arms. Logan caught him back into his lap and soothed him as best he could, patting him on the back and murmuring nonsense words into his ear, but the child had clearly reached his limit, and was in a full-on meltdown. There were a few sympathetic looks from his fellow passengers on the truck, but quite a few disgruntled ones as well.

An older woman stuck her face near Braden's and gave him a little poke on the arm. When the little boy looked at her, his blue eyes awash in tears, she used a sickly sweet voice. "You'll see your mommy soon, but only if you stop crying."

"Back off!" Logan snapped the words, then glared at the woman until she moved away, muttering audibly about how young parents these days spared the rod far too often and it resulted in bad manners and selfish behavior.

He rocked the little boy back and forth, continuing to say soothing words until the child finally wore himself out. Braden put his head on Logan's shoulder, and with a final hiccup, fell asleep. The closing of the gate on the truck startled him to wakefulness briefly, but then he drifted off again as the truck rolled out, creating a pleasant breeze that blew into the back of the truck as it bounced on the uneven road at a slow speed. Logan looked out over the heads of the other passengers at the receding husk of the burnt out plane that had carried them until it disappeared behind a rolling hill, his view becoming simply a cracked and broken road running through a sea of vibrant green, with a dingy sky hovering above.

An hour later they rolled into a gated compound of the army reserve unit. It had a couple of large parking lots along with a long stretch of grass about the size of half of a football field. At the bottom of the field, a big army tent stood, while a series of smaller four man tents were in the process of being erected in straight lines running perpendicular to it. At the front of it all was a one story brick administrative building that had a line of ordinary people snaked in front of it. Stepping down from the truck, the passengers from his flight were directed to get into the line in front of the admin building.

As they walked across the small patch of grass, a line of school buses with more people pulled in. Logan's gut churned as the yellow buses crawled to a halt behind their transport and began disgorging more tired-looking, confused people. The only reason he could come up with for more refugees being funneled to the small base would be that more planes than just his own had been diverted to a tiny area of Minnesota. His unease was evidently shared by others as people from his plane whispered to each other as they clocked the new arrivals piling in behind them. Logan turned his attention to keeping Braden occupied with playing "I spy," until they got through the doors of the building and the single line became three, each leading to a young man with a roll book seated behind a folding plastic table.

When it was Logan's time to step forward, he told the reservist his name, home address and Mara's contact information, as well as his own cell number.

Logan glanced at the reservist's name patch. "How many flights is your unit taking in, Private Ingersoll?"

Private Ingersoll shoved up his thick glasses as he considered the question. "They didn't tell us that, but they told us to prep for between five hundred and a thousand people. Some are landing at the airfield, but others on the roads." Ingersoll looked a bit worried as he shoved his glasses back into place for a second time. "I think we're planning on using the high school gym for showers tomorrow, and maybe a couple of churches can put folks up if we get too many more after you guys are processed. The local PTA for the grade school across the street is pulling together a buncha hot dishes for your dinner." His Minnesota accent had a friendly quality to it.

"Well, your efforts are sure appreciated," Logan told him.

The reservist smiled. "You betcha. And is this your son?" He pointed his pencil at Braden, who had seated himself on Logan's feet and was busy picking at something on the linoleum floor.

"No, Braden's mom went to see the angels after our plane ride," Logan responded carefully. "His name is Braden Frye. He's about two years old, and he lives in Addison, Texas. His mom told me her husband and other child are there."

Ingersoll got an uncomfortable look on his face and squirmed in his chair as he wrote down the information about Braden. "That's different. I'm not sure what to do about that. I'll have to ask my sergeant." He wiped the back of his neck as he looked past Logan at the long line of people stringing behind him, clearly uncertain of the best path forward, and torn between getting the information and continuing his job of processing people into the makeshift shelter.

Logan smiled pleasantly. "You're busy. I promise I'll come back up and talk to you after we get settled, and put Braden into a clean diaper, if that's acceptable. He's been with me all afternoon and we're getting along okay."

"I guess that's fine." Private Ingersoll pointed behind him to another table located in the long hall that bisected the low building. "Go over there, and you'll get a bunk or tent assignment and some personal goods. I'm pretty sure the Red Cross is set up with them, and they probably have diapers."

With a final smile for the earnest soldier, Logan moved to the indicated table, manned by more reservists. There he gave his name again, along with Braden's, and they were given a tent number, two blankets and two pillows, and a single plastic bag. They waved him to a row of folding tables lining one side of the hallway that had big bins filled with travel size personal supplies as well as some single servings of granola bars and water. A couple of stout women helped people fill their bags, while they also kept a watchful eye for anyone who might take more than their fair share.

Logan got himself personal toiletries, bottled water and bars, and a ten-pack of diapers and travel packet of baby wipes as well. The final four tables in the long row held piles of clothes to pick through, and he found a rain jacket as well as a plaid long-sleeved shirt and two pairs of socks for himself. They had a few children's toys and clothes as well, so he picked out some adjustable overalls for Braden as well as two t-shirts that looked like they'd be a decent fit, as well as a pair of socks and a little black and brown stuffed dog.

"Doggie." Braden said as he clasped the toy close to him. "Whuff."

"Whuff? Is that your dog's name?"

Braden nodded. "Whuff."

"Well, let's find our tent, and we'll make up a bed for him."

Logan put the little boy down once they got back outside and began walking the tidy row of tents, and found theirs. Entering, he found four cots stacked by the door, so he set up two of them side by side and placed the blankets and pillows on them, tucking the little dog into one of them as if he were napping, which earned him a smile from Braden. He got him changed out of his sooty, grass stained clothes and into a fresh diaper and some of his new things, then tucked the boy's old clothes into the plastic bag, which he placed under the boy's cot.

He looked at the kid, who met his gaze with unblinking trust, and wavered in his earlier determination to get Braden hooked into the system as soon as he could. So much had happened so quickly, perhaps it would be better to take a breath and not rush into anything. If he went back to talk to Private Ingersoll, it might mean Braden would be taken away before he had a good grasp on the overall situation they'd found themselves in. Logan considered the tidy tents, with the long mess tent at the end of them, and the way the reservists were focused on making the refugees as comfortable as possible. While the army reserve base appeared to be calm and relatively coordinated, the events Braden had experienced had been traumatizing enough without him adding to the child's distress. He made up his mind and squatted down so he was eye level with the boy. "You want to go get some dinner, buddy?"

The little boy nodded, so Logan changed out of his soot-smeared, filthy jacket and dress shirt into the red plaid shirt and picked up his backpack and slung it back on, unwilling to leave anything of value behind in the unsecured tent. Observing Logan as he picked up the backpack, Braden imitated him and gathered Whuff and hugged him tight to carry along as well, and they headed back out into the early evening, huge mosquitos buzzing around them as they walked.

"Hey Logan!" A familiar voice called out from one of the tents.

Logan ducked his head down to see that it was Jasper Collins, the little principal that he'd been at the conference with in Dallas. "Hey there, Jasper," he said, pasting a smile on his face, and taking another step toward the mess.

"I see that you still have your little hanger-on there," Jasper said, bouncing out of his tent. He pinched Braden's cheek hard and wrinkled his nose when the boy gave a shriek at the imposition. "Noisy," he commented, then looked Logan up and down, utterly uncaring that Logan was glaring at him. "So, you busy helping the staff here put up the tents, or are you already pulling a Paul Bunyan and chopping wood for a fire, something manly like that?"

The taunting tone was hard to ignore, but Logan did his best. "The soldiers are doing a fine job pulling things together, they don't need my help."

"Just seems like you'd be in your element with all your do-it-yourself wisdom, like I said before. Ready to take charge, not just acting like a nursemaid to a kid."

"The CO of this camp seems to have things well in hand. Now, if you'll excuse us, I have a hungry boy here." Logan swung Braden up onto his hip as he strode quickly away from the annoying man.

They followed the crowd of two hundred or so people to the mess hall and got in line for dinner. The atmosphere was subdued, with few smiles and few words other than thanks as people accepted the plates that were handed to them. By the time it was their turn to be served, all that was left of the promised hot meals from the PTA was spaghetti in a runny red sauce, along with two meatballs apiece and a hunk of garlic bread.

Logan looked out over the mess hall full of shellshocked people, and noticed that most were sitting in twos and threes, forming little islands at the long tables lined with benches, with very little interaction going on between groups. He followed suit and got them settled at the far end of a table, with a good amount of space between them and the next people. Logan cut up Braden's food for him, as memories of doing the same thing for both Caroline and Will when they'd been toddlers flashed through his mind.

A fit-looking couple in their early thirties hovered across the table from them with their trays. "Can we join you?" the man asked.

"Sure," Logan said around a bite of his pasta. Braden picked up a portion of a meatball and popped it in his mouth, then pretended to feed Whuff one as well.

The two slid into their seats with tentative smiles. "I'm Joe, and this is my wife, Sandra, from New York. We were on our way to Colorado for our vacation."

"We were going for some fourteeners," Sandra explained. "Those are mountains that are fourteen thousand feet or more. We like to hike the big ones."

"Logan Pagett, and this is Braden. We were in Dallas, headed for Atlanta."

A bit of silence followed as they all tucked into their food. Eventually, Joe spoke up again. "We were mid-flight when we got diverted, landed on the municipal strip not far from town. We haven't gotten much information about what's going on, have you?"

Logan shook his head. "I'm hoping someone will tell us something soon."

"I see you've got your backpack there. Are you planning on leaving?" Joe's questions had been asked in a conversational tone, but as Logan wasn't sure what he was planning on doing until he knew more specifics about the current situation, he opted to keep his response vague.

"Just a habit, and those tents aren't secured is all."

Sandra looked worried. "I guess we don't really have anything but the clothes we were wearing when we deplaned. They wouldn't let us have our suitcases. Did they let you have yours?"

"I'm guessing that's standard procedure for emergency landings." He evaded answering her directly, unwilling to share the too-recent crash landing trauma, especially around his little companion. He looked at Braden, who was just pushing his spaghetti around on his plate, making a mess. "Hey buddy, let's get you cleaned up, shall we?" He looked at the couple. "Did you find the bathrooms?"

Joe shook his head. "I don't think they got to erecting any extra ones yet. We just used the ones inside the building to freshen up."

"Sounds good, thanks." Logan gave them his best professional smile and piled Braden's plate and his own onto his tray to bus them to the area by the kitchen. Just inside the cooking area was a bowl full of oranges and apples, and he signaled the tired-looking cook and pointed at them. When the man gave a wave to go ahead, he reached a long arm in to snag an orange in case Braden got hungry later, and tucked it in his backpack.

After a stop in the bathroom to do a quick rinse of their faces and brushing of teeth from the toiletries they'd been handed earlier on, Logan headed toward the intake area as he'd promised the young reservist, but they were swamped with yet another batch of refugees. Logan took Braden's hand and plodded back to their tent at the child's pace. They'd have time enough in the morning to get Braden sorted out.

Worn to his very bones, Logan got the little boy tucked in, and when he fussed a bit, pulled the cot over so they were next to each other with no space. The boy calmed down after Logan made sure his toy dog was securely on one side, and that he was within arm's reach on the other. Before he fell asleep, Logan sent up a prayer for the good health and well-being of those he loved, and an extra thought for those he'd met today that wouldn't see another tomorrow.

At some point after midnight, he woke to the sound of people coming into the tent. He sat up quickly, his adrenaline popping and his instincts on high alert to defend their space. A person dimly visible in the wash of light that emanated from the main building turned to him, stopping two waist-high shapes from entering.

"Sorry, so sorry to wake you," a female voice whispered. "They assigned me and my two sons to this tent, though."

"Mama," a piping voice said, "I wanna lie down." "I'm hungry," the other boy spoke up, almost on top of the first boy's complaint.

"No worries," Logan replied, his heartbeat slowing to normal after being startled awake. "Here, I'll help you with the cots."

He had them set up on the other side of the tent in just a few minutes. "I'm Logan, and the little boy with me is Braden," he told them.

"I'm Gayle, and my twins are Darien and Demarias," she told him. "We're from Wichita, Kansas, and I thought we'd be in Chicago, and that by now I'd have them dropped off to their father for two weeks, but..." Her voice trailed off.

"We're all in that same boat," Logan replied. "I guess we'll find out more tomorrow." He dipped into his backpack and pulled out the orange he'd gotten from the kitchens earlier, along with two granola bars, and pressed them into Gayle's hands. "Here you go, something to tide you over until the mess tent opens tomorrow."

"You're very kind, thank you." The boys echoed their mother in quiet voices, thanking him.

He went back to his own cot and checked on Braden, who continued to sleep soundly. It took him a long time to fall back asleep even after the new residents stopped munching and rustling around and settled in. His mind churned on the events of the day and gnawed on how Mara would manage the homestead on her own. Both Ethan and Caroline were old enough to be a big help, and Will was good about completing his chores, but blending their families was something that was still in process. He could only hope that the shared crisis was bringing them together so that things would run smoothly.

His other worry was the little boy who had become his responsibility. Tomorrow, he'd have to make sure Braden's family was contacted somehow. If he was being honest, there was a part of him that didn't want to let Braden go into a system without some way of knowing what was to become of him. He'd grown quite attached to him over the past day, and at the very least, he wanted the family to know how brave the boy's mother had been, and ensure that her final act of saving her son from the explosion that destroyed their plane was known.

The next morning, the sun rose, but the air remained hazy. Logan got Braden up early and changed him, moving as silently as possible so as not to wake the woman and her twins. Once again, Braden insisted on bringing Whuff with him, clinging to the little toy. They stood in line for the bathrooms so he could get himself cleaned up, then they headed back to the mess tent for some breakfast. The weary-looking men serving on the line gave them each small scoops of scrambled eggs, two packages of saltine crackers and a few grapes each, as well as a half cup of weak coffee and waters. Logan sat them down at the end of a table, as he had the night before. The lack of food supplies was concerning, and he wasn't in the mood for any chatting until he'd had the bit of caffeine that had been offered.

"Cracker," Braden said, nibbling it enthusiastically. "And scram." He had a good appetite this morning, eating everything on his plate, including the grapes that Logan cut in half for him so he wouldn't choke.

"Braden," he began, then stopped as the little boy looked up at him with those big blue eyes that were the echo of his mother's. Logan had planned to explain that Braden might go to a new place where there would probably be other children to play with, but the words died in his throat as the boy gave him a wholly trusting gaze. Instead, he smiled, and said, "Good job on your breakfast. Wait right here for me for a moment, okay?"

Unnerved by his growing reluctance to move Braden into whatever system had been set up to reunify people, Logan resorted to the thing that worked for him when he was agitated or distressed; he took some sort of action to help another person. He moved to where the Reservist was serving up the half-cups of coffee. "I had a woman with her sons assigned to my tent. Is it okay if I take her a cup of coffee? They sounded pretty beat up when they came in."

The man looked surreptitiously to his right and then handed him the cup with a wink, along with packets of cream and sugar, waving him on so that no one noticed. Logan wanted to repeat that he really was taking it to his tent mate, as the man clearly thought he was just getting a second helping for himself. However, if he was being completely honest, he was a little tempted to down the caffeine, but he carried through with his original impulse and brought the coffee back for Gayle.

She was still sleeping, so he put a hand on her arm to wake her.

She woke with a start, and it was his turn to apologize. "Hey, sorry to wake you, but it looked like the canteen was getting low on breakfast food already, and I know you missed out on dinner last night. You probably want to get the boys in there sooner rather than later." He held out the cup of coffee to her. "Something to help you get started on your day."

The woman brushed her curly black hair back from her eyes, then rubbed them, a soft smile on her generous lips. "You are a thoughtful man, thank you." She inhaled deeply, and then dumped both packets of sugar into the cup, swirled it, then took a sip. "That is nigh-on the worst coffee I've ever tasted," she declared, then added, "and I don't care one bit, I needed the dose!"

"I thought the same thing. It took a bit of willpower to bring it to you instead of drinking it myself," he admitted. "But then I thought that I probably didn't want a grumpy roommate for the rest of the day, either."

"A practical man, as well as a considerate one. Where were you when I was looking for husbands?"

Logan chuckled at her easy humor, the first time he'd relaxed enough to laugh since he'd gotten on the plane yesterday morning. "Want me to take your boys to the restroom while you enjoy those marginally passible reconstituted coffee crystals?"

"No, I can manage, but thanks." Gayle downed the rest of the cup, and then woke her twins up with some difficulty, but when she told them they'd miss breakfast if they didn't get their behinds moving, they responded by rolling out and stretching. Logan guessed the boys were around Will's age, seven or eight. Both had lost their baby fat, and their long, awkward limbs promised that they'd be tall men someday. They shared their mother's round facial features, but both boys were quiet and shy as opposed to her take-charge extroverted personality.

"Darien, Demarius, this is Mr. Logan. He's our tent mate," she said. "And that's Braden, his son." She gave her boys a little push forward, and they both extended their hands and shook his one after the other and smiled at Braden.

Logan's conscience gave him a twist at her assumption, goading him that he needed to get the little boy squared away onto a path that would reunite him with his real father. "I'm just Braden's caretaker," he corrected her, making sure to choose his words carefully around the tentful of kids. "He needed someone else after our plane went down yesterday."

Her brow crinkled with concern, but her gaze held steady as she looked at the boy and then at him, and gave him a slight nod of understanding. "Well, I suppose we should get ourselves moving."

"The bathrooms are in the main building where they checked us in," he told them. "I'll see you around."

"Thanks again for the coffee, Logan. It made my morning better. Let's go, boys."

The tent was quiet after they all left, and Logan took a minute to sit and watch Braden as he played with Whuff on his cot, wholly engaged in the activity. He'd forgotten how magical toddlers could be as it had been years since his own kids had been that age, and his job entailed working with teens who were sometimes the complete opposite of magical, especially if things had escalated so far as to be in the principal's office. Logan pinched his nose between his eyes, staving off the headache that was threatening to build, and dug into his backpack to pull out the pain medication from his meager stores.

His fingers brushed metal, and Logan pulled out his multi-tool from the corner of the backpack where it had lodged with a grin, then shook his head at his delighted reaction to finding something so small. It was the fact that it had belonged to him, and it registered with Logan that his life would eternally be divided into two utterly distinct sections, just as it had been when his first child had been born and he'd entered the new territory of being a parent. However, the division wasn't anywhere near as joyful as meeting his daughter for the first time and crossing into daddyhood. The dividing line in the present would be his life before the earthquake and then after it. He'd need to find a way to adapt to a new reality, and carting around a toddler that wasn't his just couldn't be part of that, no matter how much he'd grown to care for Braden in the past few hours. Perhaps it was a trauma response, this strong bonding he had with the boy, but the truth was he needed to get Braden into whatever funnel it was that would return him to his relatives, and the sooner he started that process, the better both Braden and he would be for it.

"C'mon buddy, let's go talk to some people about finding your dad," he said.

"Da?" The boy looked confused rather than excited by the prospect. "Mama?" he asked in a brighter tone.

Logan's heart broke for the little boy. "Your Mama was very brave. She saved you because she loved you so much. And we're going to find your family, because they love you too, okay?"

The boy looked and sounded doubtful as he echoed Logan's last word. "'Kay." He reached up his arms to be picked up. Logan scooped up Whuff as well so that the boy would have something to hold on to, then bent under the tent flap and started the walk to the main brick building through the cool morning air. The sky was overcast in a combination of dingy grey and sickly yellow that prevented the sun from shining through, and there was a fine layer of dust coating the grass and concrete as he cut between the rows of tents that had been set up. Many of the flaps were still closed, while the ones that had been opened revealed exhausted people sitting on their cots staring blankly as he went by. A long line snaked into the back hall of the main building, with people waiting to use the restrooms. Most of them moved slowly as if they were on autopilot, although a few were animated enough to look annoyed at the inconvenience of having only six bathroom stalls to service so many. If he were organizing things, he'd coordinate with a nearby school to use those locker rooms and showers.

He gripped Braden close to him as he approached the folding tables at the front of the facility. He'd hoped Private Ingersoll would be back on duty, and he wasn't disappointed. The young man had dark circles under his eyes, but he was sharp enough to remember Logan and Braden.

"Good morning," he said. "I missed you last night."

The simple comment made Logan's defenses rise. "You were pretty busy, and I just thought it'd be better for Braden if he had a meal and some rest." He tacked on a friendly smile when he finished speaking, even though his heart was contracting painfully at the realization Braden was going to be passed on to more strangers, and that the likelihood was high he'd never see him again after that was set into motion. The little boy wriggled against Logan's reflexive tightening of his arms, so he put Braden down, monitoring him as he waited for the young man to give him some next steps to take.

The private gave him a quick nod, then pulled out a notebook from his pocket and waved it in the air before he opened it and found some penciled notes. "So, I talked to my sergeant last night, and he says that we wouldn't handle any lost or separated children, that would be FEMA and the Red Cross, and a thing called the reunification strike team if they show up at some point, or Save the Children, but we don't have a branch of that in Brainerd." He rattled off the information, then tucked the notebook away.

"So, I should go talk to the Red Cross people that were in the hallway last night?" Logan reminded himself that the young man was doing his best and kept his voice even and his expression neutral instead of snapping at him to give him a better plan of action for the small human that toddled across the floor with his toy dog.

Private Ingersoll rubbed his hands over his face, and glanced over at the other Private who manned the front area with him. He was busy calming down a red-faced man who was on the verge of yelling, his arms waving wildly as he tried to convey his demands. "Yes, they should be back later today. In the meantime, I guess you should just keep taking care of him. He seems pretty happy." He looked at Braden. "You know my sister has a kid that age, and she's a single mom. I can't even imagine what she's going through down in Minneapolis."

"What do you mean?"

The kid looked abashed and shook his head. "I think our staff sergeant will be making some sort of announcement to all you refugees soon, but the earthquakes from yesterday were bad. Really bad."

"We flew out of Dallas, and I saw what happened there, and we heard about Memphis. Are there more cities that were impacted?"

Private Ingersoll nodded, his speech pattern speeding up as he leaned forward to keep their conversation confidential. "Oh, you betcha. We got a briefing at o-six-hundred and our CO told us that every state has been affected by ongoing earthquakes except Minnesota, and maybe Iowa, I don't know why, but that's why all the planes that were in the air yesterday morning were diverted here to land. The CO said that New York, Boston, and DC were hit hard, and those West Coast cities were obliterated, you know, San Francisco and LA, and I guess Portland had a huge tsunami sweep over it because of some fault line out in the Pacific ocean." He paused to take a breath, then looked again at Braden with sadness etched on his face. "So, depending on where his relatives were located, could be he's an orphan."

The deluge of information rocked Logan back on his heels as he struggled to take in the awful news. If what he'd seen happening to Dallas had been repeated across the United States, the loss of life would be in the hundreds of thousands, perhaps even into millions of people dead or injured in a single day. The secondary destruction would be just as bad as the initial tremors had been, with collapsing dams, electricity wiped out, the pipes carrying water and waste broken, the roads damaged, and bridges wiped out. Suddenly, his idea of finding some transportation and getting home in a day or two had been rendered into nothing more than a pipe dream. Realistically, it could take weeks or even months to make his way a thousand miles or more from the middle of Minnesota back to their homestead in Virginia.

Braden sensed his dismay and reacted to it. The little boy's face crumpled into a long wail. "Mommy!" he cried out, loud and long, disrupting all the activity in the foyer with the intensity of his outburst. Logan scooped him up, and with a nod of thanks to Private Ingersoll, he pushed down on the metal bar that accessed the front of the Army Reserve building and shouldered the door open as Braden arched and screamed in his arms. Happily, there was a playground at the school located across the street from the base, and he hurried over to it, intent on finding Braden a distraction.

The playground sported old-fashioned swings and a jungle gym and slides made of metal, which he hadn't seen on a playground in his neck of the woods for a long time. It was nostalgic to see the kind of equipment he'd used as a kid, with only the potentially lethal merry-go-round and see-saws missing. Swings and a slide would certainly do the trick for Braden, though, as his squirming calmed when he swiveled his head to look at where they were going.

Braden pointed. "Swing!"

"Yeah, I like to swing too, let's do some swinging." Logan sat on one, the supple seat wrapping his behind, and he set Braden on his lap as he pushed back and started the motion to get them going, one arm firmly wrapped around the boy. His memories flashed to the hundreds of times he'd swung with both Caroline and Will, until they got too old to be held, and demanded he push them—higher, Daddy, higher!—for hours on end instead.

He let the metronomic gliding soothe him as it did Braden, the feel of the air on his face and body as they moved back and forth, the little chuckles Braden was letting out leading to his own laughter as they got higher and higher. For a few moments, Logan let his worries drop away as he simply enjoyed the present. If the sky had been clear blue with puffy white clouds, it would have hit perfection, but the air was still a dingy yellow-brown and the overcast thicker than it had been earlier. His momentary bubble of happiness disappeared as he contemplated the air around them while his logical mind dissected how it must have gotten its odd color from the debris and dust from hundreds of structures collapsing, of once-solid earth being heaved into the air by the inexplicable earthquakes. Earthquakes which had erupted everywhere except for this state and Iowa, if Private Ingersoll could be believed, and Logan had no reason to doubt him. It certainly gave a whole new meaning to the words "a stable environment in which to raise a child."

The information Logan had been given changed the equation he'd been considering how he might get himself home again. He was fairly sure that plenty of rivers, including the Mississippi, would need to be crossed, perhaps without the use of a bridge. If the highways and streets had collapsed as he'd witnessed in Dallas, then driving a car or truck would probably be a bad choice, as they weren't maneuverable enough to get past a myriad of obstacles. A motorcycle might do better, or an ATV, or failing any of those, a sturdy bike. Camping out wouldn't be an issue for him, but foraging and hunting for food might become difficult, if the dust in the air continued to rain down ash poisoning everything, so he'd have to carry his own rations and water supplies as best he could.

Logan lowered his cheek, so it rested on Braden's head as unwanted tears clogged the back of his throat. He gave himself a few more moments to listen to the delighted chuckles Braden let loose as they flew back and forth through the air while he worked his way to a final decision. The boy may have captured his heart, but it didn't make a lick of sense to cart a toddler along on such a long journey across a multitude of states that had been impacted by disaster, especially if the government wasn't able to restore the infrastructure at a quick enough pace. People lost their veneer of civilized behavior when they were pushed into a corner by circumstances beyond their control. He'd had a firsthand view of that kind of stress-induced bad behavior, first as a teacher and then even more of it as he'd risen through the ranks to become a high school principal. It didn't matter if people were normally decent, disaster didn't bring out the best in a lot of folks, and there'd be plenty who'd take quick advantage of the chaos the earthquakes had brought. It also didn't matter how protective he'd become about Braden, it would be immoral of him to bring a toddler that wasn't even his own on a cross-country journey that was likely to be fraught with dangers and hardships.

His reluctant decision finally made, Logan put his feet down to slow the swing to a stop, the scrape of them harsh to his ears. His voice cracked as he put Braden down. "Let's go on the slide for a little bit, and then I'll take you to meet some new nice people."

CHAPTER TWELVE

The Blacksburg-Pembroke Fault
Day Two

Mara had passed out quickly the night before, but she'd been roused from her sleep multiple times despite her exhaustion. Twice due to shakers that had rattled the house and another two times to check on Ethan. She'd spent time wiping his face with a cool cloth and murmuring him back to sleep as he fought the fever Anita Hillin had said to expect. Each time she'd dragged herself up the stairs back to her bedroom, she told herself she would sleep in for a bit to make up for the lost rest, but she'd woken before dawn at five, as was her habit. Mara rubbed her grainy, sore eyes and lay with her arms and legs spread wide atop the tousled bed sheets for a moment, staring at the ceiling fan and wished it was running, that it was a normal day and that her absent husband was just out of sight in the bathroom, or in the kitchen making coffee instead of lost somewhere beyond her current reach.

She churned about the chores that needed to be done before she and Caroline biked over to the hardware and grocery stores as early as possible. Perhaps the pharmacy, as well, after she checked on their remaining stock of first aid supplies. She should've taken care of that several weeks ago, but had pushed off the task, first busy with the end of school craziness, and then... she had no good reason that she hadn't gotten it done. It had been pure procrastination about a low-priority item on her to-do list that she'd consistently pushed off, leaving her flat-footed in a disaster without the supplies they might need to stay healthy. Mara clenched her fists in the bedsheets as the circling negativity threatened to pin her in a chokehold comprised of her own shortcomings. No matter how tired she was, the chickens, goats, and Gretel depended on her to be fed and watered, the garden and the fish pond needed tending. She'd have to pull out some meat from the freezer to make dinner for her family, as well as determine what they could salvage from their cellar and clean up the sticky mess. None of it would get done unless she got out of bed.

"Three, two, one." Mara chanted aloud, an old countdown trick she'd used since college to get rolling when she was stuck. Mara swung her legs to the floor on 'one' and moved to the bathroom to take a cold rinse, but all that emerged from the showerhead was a trickle that turned into a dribble, and then nothing.

"Fine," she said aloud as she yanked her thick hair into a ponytail, pulled on a pair of jeans, a sports bra, and an old college t-shirt as well as thick socks and her work boots. "Fine!" she exclaimed again as her irritation with the inconvenience of no running water became underpinned by the concern that getting clean water had become an issue much more quickly than she'd expected. She should have started a load of laundry last night while the water was still running, and filled the big pots as well, but she hadn't done it. Mara tsk'd as she berated herself for the uncompleted tasks, the self-recrimination growing inside of her. She stopped at the bedroom door, and took a deep breath through her nose, and let it hiss out of her teeth to calm herself.

"Stop 'shoulding' on yourself," she said in a low, firm voice. "You did the best you could yesterday, and you'll do the same today, Mara Padgett. Pull yourself together."

She inhaled and exhaled several more times, then opened the door. Before she took a single step, she threw her hands in the air.

"Oh, for Pete's sake!" She retrieved her P365 from underneath the pillow of the bed, checked the safety, and then went to her closet to get out her gun belt and holster with its mag pouch, and strapped it on, securing the weapon, then untucked her t-shirt so that it didn't show. After a brief inner tussle, she pulled her bed together as well, a little island of tidiness despite the bed's odd position in the middle of the room where it had slid during the first big quake.

Mara descended the stairs and checked on Ethan. Her son was awkwardly positioned sideways on the bed, his good leg twisted over the broken one, but he slept soundly. Caroline's bedroom door was closed, so she left her be, promising herself that if Caroline wasn't up by six, she'd wake her. She opened Will's door a crack to let Gretel squeeze out, the dog's tail wagging in thanks before she did a long stretch to greet the day as she moved with Mara into the kitchen. Mara unlocked the kitchen door and let the dog go outside to do her business, then stood in the doorframe for a moment, breathing in deeply, coughing as granular dust tickled the back of her throat instead of the clean air she was used to experiencing. She wiped her mouth, listening to the somewhat muted sounds of bugs and birds waking in the early morning, the warm press of a July summer day on her skin making her glad that the inside of the old wooden farmhouse remained relatively cool.

She pulled out both a large and a medium size cookpot as well as their fancy French Press which she placed into the sink wrapped in a towel as opposed to simply setting it on the counter as a precaution against another earthquake. The sun was just peeking over the surrounding mountains, lightening the landscape enough to confirm her earlier suspicion that the air was still full of dust. Mara grabbed an N95 mask to put on, and her sturdy canvas and leather gardening gloves, then picked up the keys to the shed, promising herself a big cup of strong coffee as a reward for the work she was about to do.

Moving outside with the pots, her skin went instantly sticky from the humidity and heat, even though it was early dawn. The sky was obscured with a thick layer of sludgy-looking cloud cover and eddies of dust moved in the light breeze that did nothing to cool the air. Moving to the well, Mara regarded the old-fashioned hand pump she'd previously considered as just a quaint, decorative addition to the yard. They habitually used a nearby hose attached to the currently useless electric pump. With no other resource at hand to get water, she pulled on her work gloves, grasped the curved metal handle and began the motion that would first prime, then activate it. Twenty deep, knee-bending, double-handed pumps later, she was covered in sweat, but the first drips of water trickled, then poured in a steady stream from their fifty-foot well. Mara filled the medium pot, then the big one, then hauled them one at a time to their outdoor cook fire. She scraped the coals and ash back to the edges of the pit and refilled it with kindling and small logs, then used the ferrous rod and striker they kept in a box nearby to get the fire going, pushing the old ash and coals back into the ring it once it caught and placed the two pots onto the metal grate to boil.

Mara brought four stacked buckets from the shed to the primed pump, which gushed water immediately when she worked the mechanism, and filled each of them. The first went to the goat pen, where she was greeted by enthusiastic head butts by their three brown and white lop-eared Nubian goats. She refilled their alfalfa pellets, then turned them out into their fenced off section of yard to crop a bit of forage.

The next bucket was for the hens, the agreeable flock hopping from their makeshift roosts in the tree branches they'd set up for them in lieu of their destroyed house, clucking greetings as she did a quick cleanup of the penned area, dumped their old water, and gave them fresh, then readjusted the fencing to include a new area of grass so they could scratch and find bugs to eat, as well as a nice scattering of grain in the run. "I'll bring you girls a cabbage to peck on later," she promised as she left the egg collecting for Will to do later.

The third and fourth buckets of water went to the garden, tipped a half bucket at a time onto their Three Sisters mounds. She fingered the slightly wilted leaves and drooping tassels on the corn, frowning at the way they looked. The broad squash leaves curled slightly, with a bit of yellow on the tip. They'd both been coated in a light veil of dust and were unhappy about it. Only the sunflowers remained unaffected, their bright cheery faces turned to the east, hoping for the sun.

After she'd watered the rest of the plants with continued trips to fill her buckets at the gushing pump, the water getting colder and crisper with each fill, she went back to check on the status of her hot water at the firepit. The medium pot had just hit the boiling point, so she pulled it from the grate and pushed the big pot closer to the center before she carried the pot inside and set it on the stove. She pulled out a bowlful of the hot water and dipped a kitchen towel in it to wash her face, arms, and hands, the heated liquid feeling like a blessing.

As Mara spooned coffee into the French press and added her boiled water to it and a stir with a long wooden spoon, she had time to think about how much she normally took for granted in terms of the easy accessibility of clean water. On a normal day, making the coffee would have been a simple matter of turning on the tap, filling the pot and turning on the machine, and watering the plants a simple twist to turn on the soaker hose. While carrying buckets of water to the chickens and the goats remained the same, filling them would have been much easier with the water pulled from the well automatically, and she would've had a nice shower to start her day.

Still, she was grateful for what they did have; the clean water well, the hand pump, the outdoor firepit with ample firewood, the sturdy pots and buckets she'd pulled from storage. Mara considered that most people in town wouldn't have access to any of those things, and a new worry piled onto the heap she already carried. Their homestead wasn't perfectly loaded with what they'd need to survive the next few days or weeks until repair crews got everything back to normal, but they certainly had resources that others would find themselves wanting, coveting, hunting. She drummed her fingers on the table as she considered their flimsy privacy fence, and the way the house stood in plain sight of the road with its generous windows giving easy access to anyone who wanted to break them. She was glad she'd taken the precautions last night of attaching locks and moving a few things out of the easily accessible barn, but more would need to be done.

Plunging down the French press, the smell of the coffee wafting to meet her, Mara forced away the worries to have a clear moment just for her as she poured the liquid into one of their three remaining mugs. She lifted it to her lips, letting her breath sigh out in delighted anticipation of her first sip of her favorite beverage, straight and strong, just the way she liked it.

"Is there coffee?" Caroline's sleepy voice immediately behind her made Mara jump, the coffee slopping over the edge of her mug and spilling onto her shirt in an aromatic hot splash. Jumping up, she stripped it off to rinse it in the cold water of the pump, but paused to take a big gulp of the coffee that still remained in her cup, scalding her mouth in the process, but unwilling to go another moment without the beverage she'd worked so hard for. It also gave her time to snatch her temper back from the edge where it danced.

Swallowing the mouthful, Mara pointed to the French press. "Help yourself, but if you take the last of it, make me another cup, will you?" She was proud that her voice sounded calm and that she'd not yelled even a little bit, then she caught Caroline's startled expression.

"What?"

Caroline pointed at Mara's gun belt. "Why are you wearing that?"

"Just being cautious."

"While you make coffee?" The question came with the arched eyebrow that Caroline used when she wanted to convey she thought someone's actions were uncalled for or downright stupid.

"As a matter of fact, yes. And I'll be wearing it when we go into town in," Mara checked her watch. "Twenty minutes. Will you be ready?"

"I said I would be."

The sulky teen replaced the snooty one in the blink of an eye. Mara wasn't sure which version of Caroline she found more trying, but she only nodded to acknowledge the answer, then strode out to rinse her shirt before the stain could set, putting the shirt over a camp chair to dry. She'd need to string some clothes line before they did a batch of laundry in one of the old washtubs stored in the barn, so another two items got added to her mental list—clothesline and clothespins.

Mara took a moment to top off the generator with more fuel and pull the big pot of hot water off of the campfire and smother the fire with the surrounding ash so that it would be both safe and easy to get going again to make the soup. She hefted the massive pot onto the stove with a grunt, noting that Caroline had made a fresh French press of coffee, and had left out a half of a peanut butter and jelly sandwich for her breakfast.

Her stomach rumbled at the smell of the food, and she yearned for more coffee, so she took five minutes to have both for a quick breakfast while making a list for Will when he woke up, then headed upstairs. As she pulled a fresh, loose t-shirt on, Mara got the clear message that she'd accomplished a lot of small chores since she'd gotten up, the clenched muscles in her back and shoulders a testament to the unaccustomed activities of pumping, lifting, and carrying multiple buckets of water. Prudently, she dumped some painkillers in her hand to take before they headed out. If she kept ahead of the inflammation, she'd be okay to keep going for the rest of the day.

Mara checked on Ethan one last time, and found him awake, and a bit flushed. "Hey, how are you feeling?"

He gave a see-saw motion with his hand. "Been better," he admitted, which let Mara know her stoic son was probably at least a seven on the pain scale of one to ten.

"Okay, let's get you some meds and some food. There's coffee if you want some, too."

"I'll get those for him, Mara." Will spoke from the door frame, his shock of dark hair standing nearly straight up. "I know you want to go to the store early."

"Thank you Will, that would be a big help."

The boy waved the paper that contained the list she'd made for him. "I've got this, no problemo!"

Mara pulled her phone from her pocket and handed it to Ethan. "I don't know when cell service will come back, but try Logan and your aunt a couple of times while I'm gone, okay?"

"Sure thing, mom." He groaned a bit as he shifted his weight. "See you when you get back. I'm sure nurse Will can take good care of me." He gave a wink to the young boy who still loitered in the doorway.

"Hey! It's doctor Will to you, mister!" The boy teased back. "And I'm charging you with card games later."

Mara smiled at the exchange and gave her stepson a nod. "I know you'll do a great job, Doc! There's a pot of hot water on the stove, you can use that to wash yourselves or any dishes you create." With a final caress of her son's cheek, Mara moved on to the hall closet to get out the big backpack she planned to use to carry groceries and supplies. She filled it with a couple of gallon jugs of goat's milk from the refrigerator, making sure the lids were screwed on tight, then tested it for weight. It pulled on her shoulders, but she could manage it for the fifteen-minute bike ride to their local market. Remembering the cash-only requirement at the big box store from yesterday, she raided Logan's cash stash, wrinkling her nose at the sight of so few bills remaining in the empty coffee canister. Counting it confirmed her suspicion. They had less than a hundred dollars in cash left.

Caroline trooped in from outside. "I got the panniers on the bikes," she announced. "Why are you taking our goat milk?"

"We have enough, and someone might need it," Mara replied.

"You should keep it for trading," Caroline said, as if it were the most obvious thing in the world.

Mara hesitated. The teen had a point, but she went with her initial impulse and zippered the backpack. Their neighbors were experiencing the same hardships as they were, and with two goats producing, they had more than enough for their own needs. It wouldn't do any harm to be generous, at least for one day.

"Let's just see how it goes," she said to mollify Caroline, who gave her an eloquent shrug in response. Mara reminded herself that at least Caroline was willing to help out, and that was what mattered. She handed her a backpack from the closet.

"I said I put the panniers on," Caroline pushed it away as she spoke. "We don't need backpacks as well."

Mara closed her eyes and stuffed the sigh that wanted to escape deep inside of her. She opened them to find her stepdaughter with her arms crossed the way she did when she prepped for a fight. The teen's dark brown hair waved around her shoulders in unruly waves, her chin tilted upward with defiance, but the normally clear skin was dotted with acne around her chin and forehead and there were dark circles under her dark grey eyes. Instead of seeing an obstacle, Mara recognized someone who was as deeply worried about things as herself, and opted to level with Caroline.

"I'd like to get as many supplies as we can," she began. "We're low on first aid things, too, and there's going to be a lot of people who wake up today to the realization that what we all thought of as normal—so normal we didn't even think about it, like running water and electricity at the flip of a switch—isn't coming back on right away."

There was a pause as Caroline chewed on her lip, working her way through what Mara had said. "So," she began slowly. "You want to get as much as we can for us before other people grab it up."

"I do."

Caroline took the backpack from her and slung it across her shoulders. "Makes sense. We should go, then."

Mara considered the exchange a small victory in the ever-evolving dance creating a blended family required and handed her a mask as well. "The air is still pretty bad. We need to wear these."

The teen hesitated as she took the mask. "Do you think people are going to want our stuff? If they get desperate, I mean? Like our chickens and the goats?"

Hesitant to heap more worries on the girl, but unwilling to lie to her, Mara opted for the simple truth. "We have to consider the possibility of that, yes."

"Then we should go to the hardware store and get what we need to fix our fence and put up a gate of some sort."

Caroline had responded in a practical tone, as if she were an adult. But Mara had seen fear flash in her eyes before she spoke. She took the risk and put a hand on the girl's shoulder. "I'm sorry if that frightens you. It does me, too. It's kind of just you and me who need to do things with Ethan laid up."

"And my dad not here." Caroline finished the thought in grim tones as she looked at Mara, a faint frown creasing her face, as if whatever she saw there disappointed her, and as she did so, the fleeting sense of camaraderie Mara had momentarily experienced with her evaporated. "I'll bring the bike chains so we can lock them up while we're in the store."

They wheeled the bikes along the graveled drive together in silence, both of them taking in the landscape of the fallen fence, the absent gate, the ease with which someone with a bit of determination could take what was theirs. Mara frowned as she viewed her homestead with new eyes, ones that understood it to be a vulnerable place, rather than a safe, homey one, and regretted her decision to tell Caroline her concerns. She stopped and turned to her stepdaughter.

"I will figure things out, I want you to know that."

"Okay."

The short answer that came complete with an eye roll crawled under Mara's skin, an irritant that not only undermined her confidence, but cut straight to the shaky foundation of her relationship with her stepdaughter. If Caroline didn't believe Mara could get them through the current growing emergency, she'd eventually think she had a better idea, and would likely do something that would get her in trouble, or worse, cause her to be hurt. Mara cut the wheels of her bike in front of Caroline's as they reached the intersection of the county road, noticing that there were new cracks and upheavals in the surface of it that hadn't been there the day before from the smaller earthquakes the night before. *The road looks like my relationship with my stepdaughter*. It was something she couldn't afford to let get worse.

The teen aggressively angled her bike wheel to move around Mara with an impatient huff of breath. "Shouldn't we be getting going?"

Mara edged in front of her so that she couldn't move forward, getting the girl's full, if annoyed, attention. "Caroline, your dad married me because he loved me, but also because he respected me and my intelligence. I'm a librarian. If I don't know something, I will research and figure it out. While I don't expect love from you, I do expect you to respect that anything I choose for us to do has been carefully considered and for you to follow my lead over these next few days so we all move in the same direction at the same time, okay?"

The set of Caroline's jaw tensed as they locked eyes, but she gave an abrupt nod. "I understand."

"That doesn't mean that I don't want your input, but the final decisions will be mine until your dad gets back."

Caroline eyed her suspiciously as she gave a deep sigh. "Adults all say things like they 'want your input,' but they never mean them."

"I'm looking forward to proving you wrong. So, are we agreed on the chain of command?"

"Ugh. Okay, fine."

The bike ride to the small family-owned combination grocery store and nursery Mara preferred over the big brand-name market took half an hour longer than she'd expected because of the need to constantly dismount and walk their bikes around trees and the downed telephone wires that lay across the road as well as navigating the bumpy, cracked surface in the few open spots which could easily blow out a tire if they weren't cautious. There had been many fully grown trees lining the road, and now the long limbs with their dying leaves spread like a sacrifice across it. It was a hot and sticky business as the temperature and humidity rose, and Mara also found wearing the necessary mask confining and uncomfortable.

At last the small store came into sight, and they coasted down the small incline to the graveled parking lot. It was empty of cars, but there were two ATVs parked to the side. Brushing the sweat from her forehead as they wheeled their bikes the last few steps, Mara considered that perhaps she'd been too cautious by not using theirs to come to the store. Caroline's sideways glance at them told her that the teen had the same thought. The store had a short line of people wearing backpacks just like they were in front of it, but everyone appeared to be calm, lacking the desperate edge she'd experienced at the big box store the day before.

They locked their bikes to the chain-link fence on the edge of the property and joined the line to get inside. Mr. Larcher was nattily dressed in a crisp white shirt and green bow tie and he greeted them with a wave. He looked like one fourth of a barbershop quartet with his tidy little mustache and white hair, only lacking the straw boater hat to complete his ensemble. Most barbershop quartet singers didn't wear a thick belt with a gun strapped on either side of their body, however.

"Hello Mara, Caroline," he said in his light, clear voice with its thick mountain accent. "We're letting five in the store at a time, should only be a few minutes until it's your turn."

Mara took off her backpack and pulled out the two gallon containers. "I thought you might know of someone who could use some milk," she said. "Our goats are producing plenty."

Mr. Larcher squinted. "Well, that's kind of you. If you'd give that to Mrs. Larcher inside, she'll know who that might be. If not, we'd be happy to take it in trade if the Missus gives the go-head." He got a twinkle in his eye, ducked his head lower, and whispered conspiratorially, "I'm just the hired gun, you see. She's the one who makes all the rules."

Caroline's eyes were boring a hole through her back, but to the girl's credit she refrained from uttering the words, "I told you so."

"Have you had any trouble at the store?" Mara asked as they edged closer to the door.

"Well, nature-wise, that first shaker gave us some damage inside with considerable breakage, and we lost the main window, too." He gestured at the empty frame. "I'm just glad we have a gravel parking lot, not concrete. It kind of went with the roll, if you take my meaning. The Missus was after me to change it to concrete a couple years ago, but I said it could wait." He paused with impeccable comedic timing. "Of course I'm still waiting for her to acknowledge it, and like to die before that actually happens." He gave a little heh-heh to let them know he was joking.

"So, no trouble outside of nature?" Mara pressed him a bit, eager to understand why Mr. Larcher had felt the need to openly carry his two pistols and keep the flow of people controlled.

He touched his pistols as he inclined his head. "Late last night, some folks came by after we closed, thinking to take advantage of the broken window and help themselves. They didn't count on me keeping watch, I guess." He gestured to the ATVs. "There were four of them, they came in on those, but left running on their own two feet, except for the one whose leg I shot. He hobbled." He shook his head. "I know nearly everybody that comes in our store, but I didn't recognize them, so I'm waiting to see who comes back to reclaim those machines, so I can give 'em a piece of my mind." He looked away as another pair of people walked into the lot, carrying backpacks. "Y'all go on in, and tell the Missus about your goat's milk. Could be she'll want to arrange something."

The inside of the store was dim, but did nothing to conceal what Mr. Larcher had labeled "considerable breakage." The floor was clean and swept, but the normally neatly packed shelves that rose to the height of Mara's head barely had any food on them, and the low hum of a generator was only needed to power half of the refrigerated section as the other side was empty. Mrs. Larcher hunched on a stool at the counter, helping another customer check out with a battery-run calculator in her gnarled hand.

"That'll be twenty-one dollars and twenty-three cents, but let's just say twenty even for my sanity's sake," she said, as she recorded the sale in a college-ruled notebook.

The customer handed over a twenty and left. Mara stepped up and put the two gallon containers on the counter. "Mrs. Larcher, your husband said you might want to trade for the goat's milk, but I'm fine if you just have someone you think needs it."

The woman tilted her head, the steel-grey helmet of hair moving as one unit. "Well, aren't you thoughtful of your neighbors. That's nice to see. Old Mrs. Hayden might surely appreciate one of these, but if you have more, we'll arrange to do a bit of a trade for the next week or so until our calamity resolves itself." She touched the containers, which were still cool, and dewed with condensation. "You got refrigeration?"

"We do."

"That's good. More than many have, that's for sure. Well, pop those in the refrigerated section while you take a look around, don't know if we'll have much stock left after today, but if things stretch out, me and the Mister were thinking of starting up a swapping place, so bear that in mind, maybe check back in on Monday."

For a moment, Mara blanked, not able to remember what day it was. Surely an eternity had passed since the first quake, but it had only been yesterday, Friday morning, that her entire world had been literally and figuratively upended, so today was Saturday. Day Two, her mind filled in, as if she'd suddenly gained an interior narrator. Mara shook her head slightly to clear it.

"I'll do that."

"We're limiting everyone to two of anything," Mrs. Larcher said in her crisp, no-nonsense voice.

Mara waved acknowledgement, slid the milk into the cooler, then joined Caroline, who eyed the cereal choices mournfully, rolling the cart back and forth in gloomy despair. "There's none of the good kind left," she complained. "Just the boring ones." Mara took note that the teen had placed two large plastic bottles of sugary soda into the cart, but let it go.

"Well, pick out a couple of boxes of the least boring ones. I'll grab some butter and bread," Mara said as she took the little cart from her and pushed on. She acknowledged a kinship to Caroline's disgust with what was on offer when she reached the space where the milk and butter should be and found it completely empty except for the faux butter tubs she'd come to loathe. Still, something was better than nothing, and she certainly didn't want to add churning butter to her chore list, so she added one to her cart, as well as a packet of sliced American cheese. Moving on, she found two loaves of the sourdough bread Ethan liked and added them to her basket as well as canned beans and a lone package of corn tortillas and a jar of bay leaves. She checked the small first aid section of the store, but it had been stripped bare. Mara wrinkled her nose, then went back to the tinned goods and slung some canned meat into her cart. She'd never liked the stuff, but if they somehow lost their generator, she'd be glad they had it.

Caroline approached and dropped two boxes of admittedly boring cereal into the basket, but also slid a box of the crackers she liked as well as a package of double chunk chocolate chip cookies in with a defiant motion to which Mara said nothing at all. They made their way back to Mrs. Larcher. She added up their bill on her calculator with rapidity. "Eighteen fifty, lets round that down to eighteen, then five dollars off for the goat's milk leaves you with thirteen dollars even please."

Mara fished out fourteen dollars and pressed it into the elderly woman's palm. "Let's round that number up instead, and I'll see you Monday morning." She gave Mrs. Larcher a wave as she exited and gave another one to Mr. Larcher.

"Don't be a stranger," he said, as he always did whenever she shopped with them.

Mara smiled broadly beneath her mask. "See you on Monday, Mr. Larcher."

Her spirits buoyed as she pushed the cart over to the metal corral and pulled out the contents of it to divvy into their backpacks. The pleasant encounters with both of the Larcher's at the store, the lack of drama doing the shopping with Caroline, and a final small bit of normalcy with the shopkeeper's standard farewell had acted like a balm for her soul and spirits. A surge of hope bloomed within her chest that the earthquakes were over, and that sometime in the next few days, her husband would return home. She turned to Caroline and chuckled. "Hey. Pick a number between one and ten."

The girl's eyes smiled even as she shook her head in mock annoyance. "Really?"

Mara laughed again as her spirits continued to rise. "Yep! It's for where we shop next." It was a game that their father played with both Will and Caroline when there was a choice to be made, with one answer assigned to a number between one and five, and another for those between six and ten. As much as they sighed about the game, often calling it lame and a total hassle, Mara was sure that the kids secretly liked it, and Caroline's playful moan confirmed it.

"Totally so lame. Two," Caroline answered.

"Hardware store first it is then," Mara said. "And then the drugstore for first aid supplies, and then home to start our soup and fix that fence."

Game plan firmly in place, they rolled onto the street that turned just past the Larcher's store, creating a T-junction, and discovered a nearly smooth, untrammeled patch of road before them. It curved gently around a large hill covered with a spreading green stand of mixed pines, cedars, white ash, and pin oak, with bits of brilliant green grass and wildflowers spreading in the open spaces. Taking the sight of the unsullied stretch as a sign that things were indeed on the upswing, Mara whooped with delight, pedaling faster as she let go of the handlebars and extended her arms out on either side of her as if she was flying. She turned her head to see Caroline doing the same, laughing along with her in a moment of pure fun, soaring on the smooth surface of the thoroughfare. Suddenly, with no warning at all, not even the whisper of a rumble or precursor tremble, the road beneath them bucked savagely and instead of pretending to fly, Mara found herself doing it literally hurled through the air, her joy turned to terror in an instant as her bike toppled away and the road fell from beneath her.

CHAPTER THIRTEEN

The Blacksburg-Pembroke Fault
Day Two

Caroline's scream echoed in her head as Mara tumbled through the air, adding to the rumble of the quake, the groans of the trees being uprooted, and the tumble of rock breaking free as the hillside next to the road began to slide as one piece into the valley below. Dust and debris burst into the air along with her and the bike, and everything slowed, giving her time to see with terrible clarity each tiny facet of earth and rock that had been thrown so violently upward.

An endless, extended moment as she fell gave her the frightening, odd impression that the trees were actually walking down the hill rather than simply tipping over, most of them staying upright as they quivered and shook, looking exactly like she'd imagined the Ents in Tolkien's works. Through it all, her stepdaughter's scream grew louder, until Mara finally hit the ground with a smack, sliding down the pitched slope that had been formed by the creep of the earth to cover the road they'd just been riding on.

The landing was hard, but her backpack took the worst of the blow, and the impact had the effect of throwing her into real time. A new sound entered her consciousness, the terrible grinding of the hill as it slid as one broken piece, the trees, flowers, and grass picked up roots and all as it all disintegrated beneath her.

"Caroline!" Mara screamed the girl's name as she whipped her head around to locate her, then gasped. Her stepdaughter was somehow still upright, her hands gripping the handlebars of her bike, feet on the ground on either side of it as she and the bike rode the hillside like a crazy earth surfer. Despite the shudder and roll, Mara got to her feet and scrambled toward her stepdaughter, ignoring the terrible ache in her back.

"I'm coming!" Mara called out to her as she continued her mad dash sideways on the crumbling hill to reach Caroline, but her feet slipped on the nearly liquid soil as she dodged around the trees that tumbled past her, losing their verticality as the shaking continued, slapping to the ground like pick up sticks tossed from a child's hand.

Her voice penetrated Caroline's frozen state, and she swiveled her head to look at Mara, pure panic etched there. Mara gestured wildly. "Let go of the bike, go up, head up!" It was the only thing she could think of to do, to continue to climb as the hill dropped. It was either that, or be swallowed by the earth as it folded down into itself.

Caroline either heard her, or understood the gesture, as she jumped off the bike, threw herself upwards and scrambled with hands and feet to ascend the slippery slope. Mara's back screamed in agony as she tried to do the same thing a moment later, but she'd stayed in one place too long, and the crumbling earth had buried her legs to her knees in those few seconds. Kicking furiously, she tried to dislodge them, but by then even more earth had tumbled around her, covering her thighs. Frantic, Mara clawed at the earth above her, seeking a handhold to pull herself free, but there was nothing stable to grasp, the loose dirt crumbling beneath her grasp. Helpless to do anything else, she pushed the cascade away from her chest and face as it descended, but every moment, more of her torso was buried.

A small tree slid by her, and Mara feebly grasped onto a branch, hoping the momentum of it would pull her loose, but it ripped from her and continued its downhill slide, the branches sweeping over her, painfully raking her skin with bark and limb, the trunk sliding only inches from her side. A sudden rush of earth on her other side had her flinching away, her arm sweeping out to bat away whatever object was there. It met the warm grasp of another human, and she turned, her chest contracting in fear as the ground pressed more tightly around her entire torso and discovered Caroline was next to her.

"Slide down, don't try to go up, slide with it, Mara!" Caroline yelled as she tightened her grasp on Mara's arm, gripping it above her elbows, and pulling her along. "It's the only way out!"

Unable to turn in her tight sarcophagus of dirt, only her shoulders, arms, and head above the surface, Mara nodded her understanding and pushed back from the still-falling mountain. It was definitely looser behind her. She arched her back to get out over the hump of earth while Caroline maintained her hold, pulling her out.

The pressure on her spine was excruciating, causing her breath to come in short gasps of searing heat as she tried to slide backwards down the slope instead of fighting her way up it, even though it exposed her face to more of the falling rubble. She strained to extricate herself before more of the mountain top slid onto her and buried her alive. Caroline helped her by reaching around and grasping Mara's other hand, pulling her downslope, her body weight adding to Mara's efforts to pull out of the encasing loose soil and debris. Her pinned feet had lost all feeling except for a persistent thrum beneath them that Mara imagined was an action of the quake itself, its preternatural heartbeat making it seem like a living, malevolent thing intent on swallowing her whole.

She got her elbows free, the extra leverage adding to her ability to struggle free from the earthen trap. The rate of the earth cascade had lessened as well, with only a few smaller trees sliding down, along with occasional rocks as the moving mountain eased to a halt. Mara bent backwards at nearly a ninety-degree angle, her muscles straining to pull out the rest of the way.

"I'm going to dig underneath your back and make the hole bigger," panted Caroline. "Brace yourself on your arms."

The dirt loosened around Mara's hips as the teen worked to tear away the loose soil with her hands. Mara writhed in the hole trying to help the process of making it bigger, eager to get her legs free before another quake hit or a last-minute tree or boulder tumbled while she was unable to move away from it. Finally, the earth crumbled enough that she was able to wiggle out, using the strength of her arms and shoulders to extricate herself from her near-entombment within the side of the mountain.

As soon as Mara was free, she reached out and pulled Caroline to her in a tight hug, sobbing her thanks as she did so. For a brief moment, Caroline's arms tightened around her in return, the teen's face resting buried in her shoulder, then she backed away. "Let's go," she said, her voice trembling. "I just want to get home."

Caroline was covered in dirt and debris, brown pine needles and leaves caught in her hair, making the slender girl look like some sort of Elven creature that had popped out of a long sleep in the depths of the earth, tear tracks marking the only clear passage on her face, her mask torn off at some point during the last minutes of terror. Mara was sure she looked ten times worse.

"Yes, let's get home." Mara took the first tentative step on the loose soil of the newly formed hillside, but then stopped as her back sang in an agony of pain, making her gasp, then cough in huge spasms, gagging and spitting up dirt that she'd swallowed during the past few minutes. She'd lost her mask just as Caroline had done, so they were both unprotected from the swirl of dust that lingered in the air. By some fluke or perhaps good construction, both still wore their backpacks.

"I don't know where we are," admitted Caroline, as she supported Mara by the elbow. "The road we were on was totally wiped out, and I got turned around during that..." She paused, then picked a descriptor. "Earthfall." She sounded downcast and ashamed of herself.

"Caroline, you just saved my life and survived the earthfall." Mara repeated her use of the word, thinking it an apt description. "That's two incredible things you did in the past five minutes, so don't be hard on yourself about losing your sense of direction. We'll figure out where we are in a minute. Do you still have that soda in your backpack?"

Caroline looked nonplussed at the question, then brightened, and pulled the backpack off to yank out a misshapen but intact plastic bottle of cola. She twisted the top off, held it away from her as the cola fizzed up from the shaking it had gotten, and once it stopped, she drank, her throat bobbing, then handed the bottle to Mara, who also took a long pull. She'd never in her life drunk anything as delicious as that first drink of soda pop. Between the two of them, they polished off nearly half the bottle.

Caroline belched and giggled. "Excuse me," she intoned quite formally, then giggled again. "I don't know why I'm laughing," she said, and promptly burst into tears a moment later. Mara almost followed suit with tears of her own in a sympathetic response to the girl, but restrained herself, merely lightly laying a hand on Caroline's back until the sobs subsided.

"Okay, I'm better." Caroline's voice was still shaky, but as she wiped her nose with her arm, leaving a new muddy trail, Mara was glad to see that her eyes were steady.

Mara considered for a moment. "I think we should treat where we're walking as if we were on a snowy slope freshly fallen. We'll just go slow, and cut across sideways until we see something familiar." She didn't mention how badly her back was banged up from her fall, hoping that the slow movement would keep the muscles from inflaming further and making it impossible for her to walk at all.

With Caroline downslope of Mara to give her a bit of support if she slipped, they inched their way across the fallen mountainside, stepping over downed trees and around huge boulders. Mara broke out into a cold sweat as she imagined what would have happened to her if one of those had rolled over her while she'd been trapped. Her head would have been crushed into her shoulders, her neck snapped, and her life ended in a moment. Mara shook off the horrible images and instead focused on putting one foot forward, and then the other, even though every step was painful. Nothing mattered except getting home.

They made their way slowly across the fall, Caroline moving ahead a few times to see if she recognized anything while Mara caught her breath. The day was hot and close, making the ordeal even more difficult, perspiration creating muddy trails of dirt over their bodies, but they persisted for at least an hour before Mara stumbled over a tree limb and collapsed.

"I just need to sit for a minute," she lied as she rolled over to lie on her side, the position that was the most comfortable. The pain in her back hadn't improved with the exercise, and Mara worried that she'd done serious damage to her spine, unsure about how much further she could go on the loose, slippery soil. Caroline lowered herself to the ground, and they took off the backpacks and ate crumbled cookies with squished cheese slices along with more of the soda in weary silence. Between the grey sky above and the gloom of the earthfall, there was a homogenous quality to everything. Nothing looked familiar or different, just a continuous wreck of fallen trees and loose dirt. They might be circling the mountaintop, Mara supposed, walking but getting nowhere. Worry wormed its way through her bit by bit even as she fought to be grateful she wasn't buried alive and that she had something to eat and drink to keep her strength up.

Caroline startled, and put her hand to the ground seconds before Mara felt it tremble. Caroline looked at her, her eyes wide. "Do you hear that?"

It was a rumbling sound, but at a higher pitch than the earthquakes had emitted. It got stronger and louder, as did the vibration on the loose earth where they were sitting. Caroline stood, her body turning like an antenna until she stopped, centered on where the sound came from. Mara struggled to get to her feet to join her stepdaughter, but she'd stayed down too long. Her back seized along the spine as if a vice gripped her, making any sort of movement impossible. She was as trapped as she had been in the mountain of dirt, rendered helpless by her injury.

"I think it's people on ATVs," said Caroline, her face alight with hope.

"Caroline don't—" Mara broke off as the girl suddenly darted forward, arms waving frantically, her feet churning through foot-deep debris as she charged recklessly down the newly formed hill, yelling for someone to stop as she did so. Left behind, Mara doubled her efforts to get to her feet, rocking back and forth to get the momentum to roll up, but it only left her exhausted and out of breath. She settled for taking her Sig Sauer P356 from its holster, taking time to brush off the dirt that had covered it and waited for Caroline to come back.

Mara's mind spun with possibilities, all of them bad as she waited for Caroline to call out, or return, her anxiety growing along with the continuing silence until she yanked her gun from its holster. It felt awkward in her hand, but she had to be ready to fight. She lined her sight on a leaning tree that had only partway been twisted out of the soil, the roots still stubbornly clinging to where it had grown. Taking careful aim, she squeezed the trigger, gratified to hear the snap of the gun and then the reverberation bouncing back. The puff of a bit of bark flying off of the tree had been about two feet away from where she'd expected it to fly, but at least she'd hit it. The gun worked and there were ten more rounds in her magazine if she needed them.

"Mara!" Caroline's voice sounded frightened, and she cursed herself for having fired the shot that no doubt had stirred up the girl's anxieties.

"Here!" she called back in a shout just above a croak. "I'm okay!"

"Ms. Padgett?" It was a male voice, vaguely familiar. "Don't go shooting me. Me and Eva is just downslope with Caroline. Can you come join us?"

Mara placed the voice, and with it came the mental picture of the neighbor who lived closest to the homestead, a tall, wiry man in his thirties who never went outside without wearing a beat-up brown baseball cap so old it had holes on top of its holes. "Lloyd Crowe, is that you?"

"As sure as a bear does its business in the woods!" came back the cheery answer. "Your Caroline says you got yourself in a bit of a pickle, and we'd like to help."

Mara tried once more to push herself to her feet, but found the action to be beyond her abilities. "I've twisted my back," she called. "I could use some of that help, please."

The grunting that came from below her signaled that Lloyd was on his way up before the man himself finally heaved into view. He looked very like a skinny spider, his arms and legs spread akimbo, scrambling along the crumbling slope in a series of zigs and zags. Following behind him was his wife, Eva Crowe, a lean woman with blonde hair, shorn high and tight in a man's crew cut with a two-inch high bristle top, wearing overalls over a pink t-shirt, her gold hoop earrings flapping against her wide jaw as she followed her husband's path.

Mara tucked her gun back into her holster and waited, saving her energy until they reached her level and put elbows to knees, leaning upslope like a pair of mismatched salt and pepper shakers. The breath that puffed out had the distinctive odor of the applejack moonshine they made behind their house in the middle of their orchard. It was an open secret that the only "crops" the Crowes grew on their homestead were the apples they kept to brew the moonshine, and peaches for the brandy they made in small batches for tonier tastes. They sold both out of the back of their truck, using one of the US highway rest stops as an easy exchange point. They'd leave the mason jars full of shine or peach brandy in the open back of the truck and go inside for a while, and whoever was buying would take it, and leave a brown bag of money in its place. Mara hadn't had much to do with the Crowes in the time she'd been living at the homestead, but Logan and the kids had gotten along with them for years.

"Eva, Lloyd. Sure is good to see you," she said, grunting as another spasm hit her back.

"Well, you are bunged up for sure," Eva remarked, her head at a slight tilt, her grin with its blindingly white veneers on display. She turned to her husband. "You think you can carry her down?"

"Oh, you don't have to do that," Mara said hastily. "If you can just help me up, I've been walking."

"I might could do," Lloyd answered Eva as if Mara hadn't spoken at all. He regarded her with a keen eye, no doubt considering how much she might weigh.

"I'm okay to walk, really."

"I'll take that backpack, carry that, if you can get her." Eva talked right over the top of her.

"Stop!" Mara's shout made them blink and rear back a little. "I can walk on my own, just need you to help get me up," she repeated in a softer tone, lifting her arms a bit as she did so, even if the action made her wince at the zap of pain the tiny movement created.

"Your funeral," Lloyd remarked, hefting himself to get on one side of her while Eva took the other. Without another word, they lifted her to her feet with exceptional strength in the firm grip of their hands.

"We're going to traverse the hill, three steps one way, then three steps the other, down thataway." Lloyd pointed his free hand to the right. "Logan's daughter is there watching our ATVs for us."

"I nearly ran her over," remarked Eva as they started their wandering course down the hill. "She came bursting out of that deadfall like the hounds were after her."

Mara nodded, keeping her teeth tightly clenched against the pain that pulsed up her spine and into her neck at each step, refusing to let the Crowes know how much it cost her to descend the hillside on her own two feet. Anything was better than being hauled on Lloyd's back like some creature he'd shot in the woods, that was for sure. They reached the end of the earthfall after only a few minutes, Mara grateful to be standing on level ground again, and even more grateful to see Caroline smile at her.

"Let's get you two back home," Lloyd said. "Little girl, you climb on in back of me, and Eva, you can take gimpy." He laughed as if to indicate he didn't mean anything by the comment, but it was cutting all the same. There was an edge to Lloyd, a sharp bit of metal under the good old boy exterior, and it showed in his backhanded compliments and sideways remarks. Mara didn't like the lingering way he watched Caroline get on the back of his ATV, but kept her mouth shut as the teen was behaving as if nothing was out of the ordinary, smiling at Lloyd as he gestured for her to climb on first. She'd grown up with them as neighbors nearly all her life, Mara reasoned. She was probably just being overprotective.

"Hang on to me, we're going cross-country," Eva said with another grin. "I bet it's going to hurt you some, but it'll be over in about ten minutes, so hang in there, okay?"

The pair rolled out, grinding over the deadfall until they mounted an incline to pop onto the country road they both lived off of. They edged from the countryside next to the Buchanan's home, making Mara blink in surprise. They were the older couple who had a land-line she'd wanted to try to use at some point. Mara's relief that they were almost home turned to concern as she took in the condition of the house as they rumbled past. The windows of the place were broken, and the porch sagged with the roof of it broken in half, the tumbled bricks supporting one side scattered on the scrubby lawn. There was no sign of any movement from within the house, adding to her worry.

"Have you checked on the Buchanan's by any chance?" She shouted in Eva's ear over the noise of the ATV.

The woman shook her head, then shouted back. "Nope, we've been too busy trying to pick up. The dang earthquake destroyed both our stills, and don't even get me started about the state of our store-house. Hardly a bottle of anything we put up is left, not shine, not peaches."

"Same." Mara puffed out her cheeks and blew out, thinking of all the work at home, her heart quailing at the sheer volume of daily chores on top of making the homestead safer. She yearned for a book that would give her step by step directions, as she had no idea how they'd manage since she was now injured, as well as her son. Caroline and Will couldn't be expected to take on all the chores that needed to be done, that was for sure.

They roared up to the house along the gravel drive. Will banged out the door to greet them, waving both of his hands in greeting, his eyes growing round when he saw the muddy, bedraggled state that Caroline and Mara were in. Gretel followed him out, but stopped short of coming down the crooked steps of the porch when she scented strangers, her ears pricking forward, then giving three sharp barks and standing her ground in front of the door as she'd been trained.

"Did you feel that last one?" Will demanded as the Crowes cut their engines and swung easily from their machines, while Caroline and Mara slowly eased themselves off. "Me and Ethan was playing cards in his room, on his bed, and bounced us both in the air and the bed too, all at once while we were sitting there." He spoke excitedly, as if it had been a fun amusement ride, then turned to Mara in the next beat. "Ethan says he's okay, it didn't hurt his leg any, I guess because we went with the bed, you know?"

"Ethan's laid up?" Lloyd asked with interest.

"Yeah, he broke his leg yesterday!" Will said excitedly. "He gets to use crutches!"

"Well, goodness gracious," Eva said in a slow drawl. "I hope your daddy can take care of all y'all while Ethan and your stepmomma heal." Will darted a quick glance at his sister, then at Mara, who gave the slightest shake of her head.

"Uh-huh," Will said. The conversation ground to a halt.

Eva's head jerked slightly to the side in the long pause as if she were listening for something before she turned to Mara with an extra-wide smile. "If you want, we can help you get into the house."

"Actually, I'm headed out back to our old pump before I do anything else," Mara said, tired of the neighborly chitchat and feeling the need to get painkillers into her system soon. "I need to get this mud off of me." She turned to Will. "Did the chickens have any eggs?"

"Not a one," he said dolefully. "I think the earthquake upset them."

"How about the goats, then? I'd like to offer our neighbors something as a thank you."

"Yeah, both Fiona and Hermione did fine. I got them milked before that shaker happened." Will ran distinctly grubby looking hands through his hair. "Want me to go get them a gallon?"

Lloyd put up his hands. "No offense, but we don't consume goat's milk. No need to recompense us, neither. Happy to help out our neighbors in time of need, aren't we, Eva?"

Eva nodded, her bright blue eyes dancing around the yard. "Your place is looking much better than ours does." She turned to Lloyd. "I told you we should have us some kids so they can help out like that one there does." She chuckled as she pointed at Will, but there was an underlying edge to her words, as if it were a longstanding argument between them.

He brushed a dismissive hand her way. "Oh, don't get started on that again. You know my brothers will come do for us if we ask." His chuckle had no humor in it.

Eva continued her appraisal of their homestead. "Are those bees?" She asked. "Over by your pond?"

Will answered her. "They are. The hives tipped, but I got them up again and then braced them with some bricks." He looked proud of himself as he spoke.

"Smart fella," remarked Lloyd. He also took a long slow look around the yard, at the drooping but still lush garden, the makeshift coop with its healthy flock, and the goats, his lingering glance creating a small dot of concern in the center of Mara's chest that grew when he saw him raise an eyebrow at his wife. Suddenly she wanted the two neighbors gone, as much as she was grateful to them for the rescue.

"Well, we'll have to share our jam with you when the pawpaw's come on," she said a bit too cheerfully. "I truly appreciate you helping us get home." She turned to Caroline. "You and I are too filthy for words. Let's go get cleaned up."

Caroline had been lingering back, uncharacteristically quiet through the whole exchange. Abruptly, she spoke to the Crowes. "You don't have a landline, do you?"

"Phone, you mean?" Lloyd verified, then went on when Caroline nodded. "We used to, but it hasn't worked in a long time. I think the Buchanan's have one though. Why, you trying to reach someone?"

Mara interrupted before Caroline could say more. "My sister in Memphis, we haven't been able to get a hold of her since yesterday."

"Oh, well, I hear all of Memphis is just plain gone, nothing left at all," Lloyd said.

"Lloyd." Eva scolded. "She just said her sister was there." She turned to Mara. "We'll say some prayers she got out safe from there, honey."

Mara had to brace herself on the ATV to stay upright, the bad news rippling through her body. "How'd you get your information?"

"I have a ham radio we've been listening to. I gotta say, our signal's been intermittent at best, and it's getting worse all the time. I guess because of all the dust, but we heard these earthquakes are happening all over the United States, maybe even the world."

Eva was nodding her head as her husband spoke. "Memphis wasn't the only place hit. There's millions dead. Dallas and St Louis and Kansas City and Minneapolis were wiped out. Then all of them big cities on both the coasts, and DC were hit bad, and then more all along the mountain ranges, too."

"And tsunamis, off of Oregon," added Lloyd, his little brown eyes taking on a shine of excitement as if he was thrilled to impart the information.

He opened his mouth to say more, but Mara had had enough of the Crowes, who were oblivious to the impact they were having on both Will and Caroline with the deluge of terrible news, the kid's faces turning pale and their mouths gaping open.

"Well," Mara said, using the pitch of voice she usually saved for recalcitrant teenagers at school. "We'll just have to hope all the people in those places have nice neighbors like yourselves." She mustered a smile. "We sure do appreciate you!"

Caroline choked back a sob as she dashed around the corner of the house, while Will sank to sit on the step of the porch, Gretel nudging closer to him as the dog sensed his upset. Mustering her strength, Mara let go of the handlebars of Eva's ATV and stepped over to her stepson, laying a protective hand on his shoulder, forcing herself to walk with apparent ease so that the pair would have no more excuse to linger.

Eva took the hint. "We'd best be getting back to picking up our house, Lloyd."

"Sure, sure, we'll do that. We'll come back on over in the next day or two to check on you."

"No need. We'll be fine, but thank you. You take care!" Mara said in an overly-bright tone.

Eva and Lloyd shared a look between them, then mounted up, gunned their engines, waved in unison, then rolled up the driveway to the main road. Mara's shoulders loosened slightly once they were out of sight. She spoke firmly to Will, whose gaze was locked on some sort of middle ground in the distance while his fingers twitched nervously. Behind them, Gretel gave a little whine.

"Don't pay attention to them, Will. We don't know if any of that was true. I'm going to find your sister, and get cleaned up. Why don't you see if you can make us some sandwiches?"

Mara pulled off her backpack, and hauled out what had been a loaf of bread, now squashed beyond identification save for the wrapper surrounding it. The boy gave her such a look of disbelief that she was forced to laugh. "On second thought, maybe I'll be making some bread pudding to go with dinner."

"Yeah," Will responded with a tiny chuckle. "Or stuffing. How'd it get so squished?"

Flashing on the terrible toss and fall, and subsequent near-burial, Mara decided Will had heard enough traumatizing news in the last ten minutes. "Must've happened when I fell off my bike," she said lightly. "It broke my fall, so it's like, hero bread!"

He laughed at that, even if it did have a slightly hollow tone. "Don't worry, Mara. I'll find something to make for lunch." He stood to go inside, sparing a glance up the driveway. "How come you didn't want me to let the Crowes know my dad wasn't home?"

Mara told her next lie. "Because I expect him to be back at any minute. No need to worry them about it, is there?"

"Mm-hmm." He sounded doubtful about her explanation, but patted his leg for Gretel to follow him into the house.

With a bone-deep groan, Mara stood up. Her bruised back was stiff, but she managed a shuffle as she made her way to the pump, where she found Caroline washing the last of the mud and grime off of herself and her clothing.

"I'm nearly done," Caroline said brusquely, scrubbing her legs with her hands as the gush of the pump lessened to a trickle.

Her stepdaughter's nose was reddened, and her eyes were swollen. Mara's heart swelled in sympathy. "You can't believe what the Crowes said…" she began gently.

Caroline stood abruptly, water streaming off of her, her face turning red and her vocal volume rising. "They have no reason to lie,

Mara! I know dad was in Dallas when that earthquake hit, and that's why the phone cut off, so don't you try to lie about it!"

The tears had started again, huge drops cascading down her face. Caroline swiped them viciously away, then continued. "I wish you were gone, not my dad! Why did it have to be him? I should've just left you to be swallowed up on that hill!" The last words were a strangled whisper as her fear and grief overtook her. With a final look of pure anguish that gutted Mara, her stepdaughter dashed into the house, leaving her utterly alone.

CHAPTER FOURTEEN

Central Virginia Seismic Zone and The Stafford Fault System
DAY TWO

Ripley startled from her doze with a gasp, bolting upright from the cushioned wingback chair that she'd scavenged from the anteroom outside of the Oval Office. Poised on the balls of her feet, she held her breath, listening hard. She'd heard something, a mechanical burst of some sort, the tail end of it still echoing in her ears. Ripley tilted her head to listen more closely while she blinked against the yellow flicker of candlelight that was overly bright to her gloom-accustomed eyes. The fat-bottomed candelabra wavered into focus, its five candles burning well in their ornate metal holder. They'd taken the precaution of putting it on a metal tray on the floor, since the shudders and shakes had continued throughout the previous day. By the look of them, she hadn't been sleeping for very long, as they weren't burned even half-way down yet.

Perhaps Thaddeus had called out, and she'd misheard it. She moved to where the man lay on his makeshift nest of curtains and cushions from various couches and chairs. Squinting, she couldn't tell in the wavering light if he was still breathing, so she knelt and put a tentative hand on his chest, waiting for the gentle rise of it to calm her racing heart. The pause before he breathed was overly long, but at last it came without the wet rasp she'd been worried about earlier, and she relaxed a bit, easing back from him. The Director of Homeland Security was in a deep sleep, so whatever noise had roused her hadn't come from Thaddeus.

Ripley moved the platter with its candlelight closer to look at the man's leg, propped on three fancy ivory damask silk pillows she'd purloined from the couch of the President's chief of staff. Jerry, that had been his name, the man with the bushy eyebrows and widow's peak who'd had her called in to advise President Blake Ordway on the New Madrid earthquake. Since Jerry was the one who had gotten her into this mess, she hadn't been bothered in the slightest to take things from his office, including an intact bottle of single malt scotch from his lower desk drawer. Thaddeus in his usual prim way had been a little huffy about the liquor at first, but as his pain had subsided with the painkillers she'd found, they'd used the alcohol to clean his ravaged upper right leg that had been macerated by a chunk of falling ceiling, and his objections had evaporated. Later, they'd both had a swallow of it to help them go to sleep on the floor in the sturdy arch between the hall and an inner conference room.

The bleeding of his upper thigh had slowed, with only a few dark splotches showing through the tan wrap of ace bandage she'd used to bind the flesh together as best she could. She'd have to hunt for another such item to change out the dressing if help didn't find them in a few hours, as well as real food and drink instead of the paltry snacks she'd found in assorted drawers. Thaddeus had been adamant that they stay put for at least twenty-four hours, his faith in protocols and procedures unwavering. Ripley had chafed at the idea of simply sitting still in what was clearly an unsafe building, but he'd told her in a stern voice that she was free to do as she pleased, but that he would obey the chain of command rules, that they'd been set up for emergencies exactly like this one. When she'd raised the option of leaving a second time hours later, after she'd found no one else left in the building, he'd only commented that in his experience, it was the ones who wandered away from a crash site area who most commonly died. She'd left it alone after that, too tired from her exertions of the day to argue further with the grumpy, stubborn man.

A hissing noise had her whipping around, peering down the hall. After a final check of Thaddeus, and adjusting her mask, Ripley plucked a single candle from the holder and stepped cautiously into the passage, holding it high. Using a candle instead of electricity to illuminate her way made Ripley feel like she should by rights be wearing long skirts and a corset, but she was grateful to have the oasis of light in whatever form it came in. The hall looked the same as it had when she'd fallen asleep, a messy tumble of broken furniture, fallen ceiling, one fifteen foot section engulfed by a sloped pile of wall and roof that had caved in from the floor above, however many hours ago that had been. It was strange, not knowing what time it was with a quick glance at a watch or a phone, another discomfort to add to the pile of them that had heaped up since the first quake had occurred.

Ripley dissected the noise that had woken her. It had been a man-made purposeful sort of sound; she was sure of it, a clicking hiss that was quite different from the steady patter of plaster and lath succumbing to gravity that she'd become accustomed to hearing over the past hours. It had definitely been mechanical, like the brief burst of a radio not quite tuned to a channel. She made her way past the slide, so as to not wake Thaddeus before she called out.

"Hello?" she called softly, then listened intently.

The short-lived hissing came again from further along the hall, and she followed it, gingerly placing her feet around the obstacles of broken things that littered it. A small tremor vibrated against the soles of her shoes, and she froze, ready to dart back to the relatively safe double doorway she and Thaddeus had set up camp in, but it subsided after a few waves of motion. Somewhere from the depths of the White House, things crashed, but only dust stirred in this section. Stifling a cough from the thickened air, she listened intently for the next burst of sound. It came from behind a closed door just steps away, past a tangle of cotton sheets and wood, a bed that had partially fallen through from the floor above, the mattress preventing its further fall through the broken ceiling. Ripley gave the precarious thing a wide berth to reach the door. Ripley tried to push it open, first with her free hand, and then with her shoulder, bracing her feet as she shoved the door inward, sweat popping on her brow as she met tough resistance.

There was a scraping sound as whatever had blocked the doorway moved back by her efforts inch by inch until she had enough room for her head to pass through the crack, the candle once more held high and in front of her, hot wax dripping onto her fingers. Ripley startled when the static came again, loud, and clear now that she was next to it, definitely something mechanical, but she couldn't see anything beyond the ring of light cast by her flame.

A heavy file cabinet had fallen against the door, preventing further entry as it was wedged against a desk, but she could wiggle in if she could get it opened three more inches. Letting wax drip onto the floor by her feet, Ripley stood the candle upright and let it mold into place before taking a deep breath and putting her all into a final go at the door with both hands and a bit of a running start.

There was a scraping crash as the file cabinet tipped back the other way, jarred loose by her efforts, and further metallic banging as the thing came to a rest. Panting, her hands and wrists aching, Ripley took a moment to catch her breath before entering.

"Ms. Baxter, is that you?" Thaddeus' voice floated down the hall.

"It is," she responded. "Checking something out."

A grunt of acknowledgement had her smiling. The man was the most taciturn person she'd ever met, but the forced closeness of the past hours had revealed his quiet humor and intelligence, as well as his bravery. Ripley found herself liking the man despite his acerbic manner, and suspected perhaps he liked her too, although she doubted he'd ever tell her so, or even use her first name, for that matter.

Ripley picked up her candle and edged into the room. It was a small office, no more than ten feet square, jammed with filing cabinets taller than she was, all of which had fallen atop each other in a hodgepodge of open drawers and spilling paper. Leave it to a government building to still be housing papers this way rather than neatly collected onto a thumb drive. Ripley's way forward was impeded by a crossing pair of fallen cabinets, so she paused, hoping to hear the hissing again so she could make her way precisely to whatever had made the sound.

Long minutes passed as Ripley leaned in the doorframe and waited, using the time to melt another puddle of wax to set her taper into so she'd have both hands free when the time came to follow the sound. A staticky hiss emanated from the floor area in the middle of the room. Ripley cautiously climbed through the X-shape of the file cabinets, moving one foot and one hand at a time so they wouldn't tumble awkwardly and injure or pin a part of her in some fashion. She edged around a large printer with its side collapsed inward, her feet skidding in something like fine sand.

"Probably the toner," she said aloud, glad that she'd left her candle beyond the metal cabinets, as the stuff was highly flammable.

The light was dim, so she bent low to the floor, her feet crunching over the spilt mess, peering in a grid until a lighter area emerged from the gloom like a pale jellyfish in a dark sea. Moving toward it, she was confused by what she was looking at. Eventually, she extended her arm and touched the lighter area. It was cold, but pliant, with a smooth texture, until she reached short tendrils of hair as the shape curved and narrowed.

Ripley gasped and snatched her fingers back from the dead person's hand, someone who'd been dead long enough for rigor mortis to have come and gone, head and body crushed beneath a pair of filing cabinets. She took a deep breath to gather herself, then she touched it again, feeling beneath the hand, curled the fingers back from the object it grasped, an oblong box. Ripley pulled it out from their grasp, and moved back through the obstacle course of the room to her candle, hoping she was right about what she had in her hand.

Her soul leapt with a surge of delight as she shoved the object into the light.. It was a walkie-talkie, one that still had its juice. She pressed on the talk button eagerly. "Hello? Can anyone hear me?"

Releasing it, her heart quickened its beat as she stared at the device, willing it to make that clicking hiss that signaled someone was on the other end.

"This is a secure channel for emergencies only. Please desist from using it."

Ripley let out the breath she'd been holding and spoke rapidly. "I'm Ripley Baxter, I'm with Thaddeus, the Director of Homeland Security. We were trapped in the White House, and he needs medical assistance!" She released the button, biting her lip as she waited for a response.

"Come again?"

The voice on the other end sounded noticeably young. Ripley forced herself to slow down and speak in a measured way. "We were advising the President this morning when the first quake hit. I'm Ripley Baxter and he is the Director of Homeland Security. He's been injured," she added, before releasing the button.

The pause was even longer this time. "We'll need confirmation of that," the voice said sternly. "Put the director on."

"I'll get him," Ripley replied eagerly.

Holding the walkie like it was a bar of precious gold, she clambered out of the chamber, not bothering to take the candle, as she could see the glow of their own set down the hall. Moving fast through the obstacle course of debris, she reached Thaddeus and thrust the walkie at him jubilantly.

"They need confirmation it's you!"

"Who does?"

Ripley jiggled, giddy with excitement. "I don't know, but they said it was a secure channel!"

He frowned. "Ms. Baxter, this could literally be anyone. Did you reveal our location?"

It was like being dashed with a bucket of cold water. "I did," she said slowly, her excitement draining.

"I'll get to the bottom of it." Thaddeus held out his hand for the walkie, working the switch with his capable fingers. "Who is this?" He demanded, his bass voice snapping with authority.

"Who is this?" The voice came back. "This is a secure channel. We're not playing games."

"Neither am I. Use the correct code response for Zero Alpha Delta Seven."

There was a long gap. "Uh. I'm going to go get my CO," the voice finally said. "Stay on this channel."

Thaddeus pursed his lips in thought as he let the device fall into his lap. "I believe whomever this is, that they are not a government sanctioned organization," he said at last. "They would have either responded with the correct code, or would have said he was getting his sergeant or captain."

"I've heard the term CO used before," Ripley countered.

"On TV?" he asked with asperity. "In the movies?" He shifted his leg off of his pillows. "I think you have put us in a precarious position, Ms. Baxter."

"I was getting us help!" she protested. "You can't know for sure that those are some... bad guys or something on the other end of the line!"

He arched an eyebrow. "I don't ascribe to good or bad guys in general. There are far too many grey areas within each definition unless one is utterly naïve." He looked at her as if he were daring her to argue the point. Ripley clamped her mouth shut and crossed her arms. "But do I believe people become opportunistic during times of crisis? Why yes, I do. And that's who I think we have here. A militia perhaps, they've proliferated over the past few years, or just a group with access to a walkie. And I, in my position, might be a valuable target if said group was so inclined to take advantage of the situation."

His energy seemed to run out after his speech. Thaddeus grimaced in pain, his attention drifting off as he adjusted his leg again. The dark spots on the bandages spread as he did so, the blood welling to the surface.

"Stop moving around," she snapped at him, her mind racing to produce multiple solutions for their growing problems.

"Becoming angry with me won't diffuse this situation," he said, holding up the walkie talkie.

"Can't we use that thing to call someone else?" she demanded.

"Certainly, there are anywhere from 22 to 256 different channels on one of these, depending on the unit. Finding one that is active and in use, one not used by the so-called 'bad guys' will take some time, however." He sniffed the air, wrinkling his nose. Ripley caught the scent of smoke as well and whipped her head around to see where it was coming from.

"There." Thaddeus pointed down the hall where she'd gotten the walkie talkie.

Ripley gasped. Fire filled the doorway of the room she'd left just minutes ago with pieces of flaming paper wafting from it like freed birds. One perched on a splintered chair, which promptly caught on fire, another greedily hopped its way into the bedsheets, flame erupting, then climbing the cloth to the floor above, the conflagration growing in size, lighting the hallway with licks of red and gold. It would almost be beautiful in another setting.

"My candle," she breathed as the pieces clicked together. She'd left it behind when she'd dashed to him with the walkie talkie. It must have fallen amidst all of that paper. And the spilt toner from the large office copier.

"We need to move now!" She cried out, her fear lending her strength. She got behind Thaddeus and hauled him upright while he gripped the side of the doorframe to help, for once not arguing with her.

"Lean on me," she said, and moved them away from the fire as fast as the man could hop, his weight pressing painfully on her shoulder every other step they took. Ripley didn't bother to look back, she just hauled Thaddeus along, heading toward the section of the building she knew best, the Oval Office and its surrounding rooms.

A small pop and a momentary lessening of the air pressure around them was the only warning they got. An explosion and accompanying concussive blast of heat ripped through the hallway, followed by a curling boil of fire. Ripley was shoved to the side and onto her face, with the heavy weight of Thaddeus landing on top of her as it billowed over them.

"Crawl!"

She could tell from his contorted face that Thaddeus had screamed the word, but all Ripley caught was the faintest whisper, her hearing robbed by the blast. They slithered like worms along the corridor, heedless of the debris they bumped over, keeping low, where the air might still be breathable, the hungry flames that ignited all around them greedily wanting to steal it from them, the heat becoming intolerable in the narrow confines of the hall.

They squirmed along, Ripley using her hand as a guide to keep them close to the wall, seeking a side passage away from the main gout of flames. Finally she found one and they moved into it, lending them momentary relief, but the inferno pursued them, the debris in the halls acting as perfect fodder helping the fire to grow. As they crawled, her fingers detected the indentation of a door which pushed easily inward at her touch..

"Here!" Anything to get out of the direct sear of the fire. She tugged Thaddeus to follow her as they slithered into a cool, tiled place, the door closing behind them. Dim light from a high transom revealed toilets and sinks. Thaddeus moaned, patting ineffectually at his back, where a bit of spark had caught. She patted the ember out with her hands, noting that his tattered black jacket was hot to the touch, and parts of it smoldered.

Ripley staggered to her feet, turned on a tap, but nothing came out. She went to the nearest toilet and yanked off the top of the tank, dipped her hands into the water reservoir there and dropped water on his back, returning several times until she was sure there were no more hot spots. Ripley took a moment and splashed the tank water on her face, licked the drips that were on her lips, shrugged, then drank the slightly musty water, the liquid cooling the smoky burn inside her throat.

"The water seems good. Do you want some?" She couldn't tell how loudly she was speaking through the ringing in her ears from the blast.

Hearing no response, she moved closer. Thaddeus lay on his belly on the floor, unmoving. Alarm zipped through her, and with an effort she turned him over, propping his head and chest on her lap. She laid her now-cool hands on his cheeks and forehead, noted they were overly hot. He flinched away from the touch, but still didn't respond, his eyelids quivering as though he was trying to open them but failing.

Gently she put him down again, got paper towels from the dispenser, wet them in the tank, and returned, making a cool compress for him, pressing it onto his neck, his forehead, the inside of his wrists. Her worry grew as he continued to be unresponsive.

"Thaddeus, are you with me?" She spoke gently, encouragingly, to the man, but only received a moan in return which might have simply been air in his lungs, not a conscious response at all. The dim light of the bathroom made it hard to see his leg, but when she put her hand there, it came away bright red and sticky with his blood. Bearing down on the tears of frustration and fear that wanted to flow, Ripley got more paper towels, pressing them to his bleeding leg.

Outside of their tiled cocoon, the roar of the flames continued, and a curl of smoke wiggled in under the door. She touched it gingerly, snatching her fingers back at the heat. Ripley stripped off her jacket and soaked it in a toilet bowl then pressed it to the traitorous crack, hoping to keep their air clear within their little space. She didn't dare try to climb up and break open the transom window to get fresh air, for fear of feeding the flames in the hall. The paper towels were nearly gone, but she wet two more of them, placing one over Thaddeus' nose and mouth, and holding one to her own as a preventative measure in case the smoke from the fire got in past her flimsy barricade.

With nothing left to do that she could think of to make their situation any safer or better, Ripley eased her back against the cool of the tiled wall, Thaddeus' head and shoulders still resting on her lap, the damp paper towel covering the lower half of his face. His eyelids had stilled, but his slow breaths, one for every two of hers, gave her hope. Hope that Thaddeus would survive his wounds, hope that they would escape the fire, that they would somehow find their way to wherever the President was located, and that in time, the world would turn itself right again.

CHAPTER FIFTEEN

The New Madrid Fault
Day Two

Their first trip to trade aid supplies for food to feed the people sheltering at St. Jude's hospital had ended in utter frustration for Deb, Maritza and the two Toms. What had looked easy to navigate on the post-it note that Maritza had drawn up early in the day had become anything but easy out on the streets of Memphis. Most of the downtown buildings had collapsed in the tremors after the initial one, obstructing pathways, which was bad enough, but the river had also been cast from its course multiple times, covering everything with a slimy black mud containing waste and corpses.

The path Deb had taken with Jenny and Mattie to get to St Jude's was no longer passible. The Danny Thomas Boulevard overpass that spanned the I40 had dropped onto the freeway beneath it, making their hospital into a veritable island from every direction except north. Disappointed, the group had been forced back only a few hours after they'd stepped through the doors to make the attempt. As they'd returned, one of the Toms had slipped in the Mississippi mud, a jutting bit of rebar puncturing his shoulder, which had nearly gone through to the other side of his body. He was in a bed in the makeshift ICU, bandaged and on antibiotics.

When they'd returned empty-handed, Maritza had gotten on the radio with her counterpart at the VA, and agreed to try to triangulate a meet to exchange supplies at a northerly halfway point between them in the morning on the following day, and then she'd made the disappointing announcement to the people jammed in the waiting room that there was no new food or water coming that day. Deb's stomach had churned as she saw Jenny trying to explain to her daughter why she was going to have to go to sleep hungry.

The people who'd been counting on them for food had been gracious about the setback, with hardly any grumbling, which to Deb's mind almost made their failure worse. Hospital staff had rummaged through lockers and vending machines, everyone gathering what they could find to share a scant meal. A sizable trembler had sent another section of the hospital crashing to the ground, and it had somehow stopped their water from flowing, leaving only whatever sodas and bottled water that remained to wash, tend to the wounded, and drink.

Deb caught Maritza's eye after they'd eaten. "I'm going out with you again tomorrow."

"I appreciate it. Tom is in too, and I'll see who I can round up." She rubbed her forehead, where deep creases showed. "It's hard to ask anyone to do it though. The doctors and nurses that are here have been working around the clock since yesterday. I've instigated sleep shifts, but four hours isn't going to do much good for the kind of expedition we're taking on." She looked critically at Deb. "Speaking of sleeping, you need to find yourself a quiet spot and get some."

Deb nodded wearily. "I think I'll try to bed down in one of the pews of the chapel."

"Good idea. We're leaving at dawn, or whatever passes for it tomorrow. Around six, best guess. I'd love to have lunch available for our doctors, nurses, and patients tomorrow."

Impulsively, Deb gave the little Filipino woman a hug, even

though she was not normally a hugger. "You're one in a million, Maritza."

"You, too." The woman shoved a bottle of water at her. "I noticed you didn't take any earlier. This is for you."

Deb mulled over the sentiment of being one in a million as she stretched out lengthwise on a pew in the tiny chapel off the main hall. The wooden bench supported her back and the slight curve of the hard wood let her slide into a relatively comfortable position. Deb didn't think she was any kind of hero, that was for sure. In fact, she'd failed in her mission to get the food for people. With a disappointed sigh, she pillowed her head on her arms and whispered the short prayer she always said when things became overwhelming, and she needed a sense of peace. "Grant me the serenity to accept the things I cannot change, courage to change the things I can, and the wisdom to know the difference."

Her thirst woke her from a deep sleep, and sitting up, she took a long drink from the water Maritza had pressed on her the night before. Soft snoring informed her that others had sought out the chapel as a resting place as well. For a moment she laid still, hoping to recapture the blissful respite of sleep, but her brain was already spinning about the day in front of her, so despite her grainy eyes, Deb slid out of the pew and stretched, her joints popping and aching muscles protesting at the movement. She winced as she took the first tentative step on her sore ankle, sitting again to re-wrap it with stronger tension before she stepped out of the chapel and limped along the quiet hall of the hospital. Deb was careful not to disturb those who'd camped out along its length on gurneys normally used to transport patients from place to place within the hospital.

Making her way to the staff showers, she tried the faucets with the vague hope that the water would be running again, but not even a drip came out of them. She used a splash from her bottle to wipe off her face, and wet wipes to clean her hands, arms, and torso. Grey dirt came off of her skin, even the parts that had been covered by the green scrubs with the cheery little unicorns she'd been wearing for the past twenty-four hours.

Deb dug into the linen cupboard and pulled out a fresh pair of scrubs, a bit too large, but by cuffing the trousers, and pulling the drawstring tightly, Deb was satisfied they'd not fall down at an inopportune time. She dug through the lost and found once more, producing two more pairs of socks, and took the time to clean and re-bandage her feet and her ankle before putting on the clean socks. She downed a couple of painkillers with the last of her water, and with a glance to see that her plastic bag of possessions still lay atop the lockers, moved out of the locker room.

Both Toms were at the front doors, along with a third young man, whose slender features were drawn and pale, and Maritza.

"I'm just here to send you off, and to man the front desk until you come back," the injured Tom said. He gestured to the young man, who sported a tidy goatee. "This is Giles. His daughter is one of our patients here."

"Hello," the man said, his British accent thick, reminiscent of the way Hagrid of the Harry Potter movies spoke. "Here to help."

The man didn't look like he was capable of lifting an empty pillow case, let alone two pairs of bedsheets tied together and stuffed full of first aid supplies, but Giles hefted the bundles and placed them on his shoulders with no assistance. "Awkward, but manageable," he commented.

"We're heading north first, then east," Maritza said. "Hopefully, that will get us away from the river surge and we can make better time. We're meeting a group from the VA at Junior's Barbeque up on Jackson. There's an orderly at the other hospital who heard the place is still standing, and that the grill out back is functional."

The shorter Tom who was going with them smiled, revealing a sizeable gap between his two front teeth. "That place does good chicken. It's maybe a mile and a half from here. I run over there sometimes for my lunch when we're not busy."

Deb flinched. It had taken them over an hour to go a half-mile yesterday, which meant chances were high this was going to be a three-hour journey each way with no guarantee that the other team would make it. It could be yet another trip that ended in failure. Maritza seemed to read her mind, her face turning grim. "We'd best get started. I have granola bars for all of you, but we have to share a single water bottle between us."

They stepped into the early morning, the air heavy with dull yellowish- grey dust that was only slightly lighter than the night sky had been. Tightening her mask, Deb took her place in the straggling line of the four volunteers, walking just in front of Tom, who brought up the rear. The first hundred yards or so were easy, as someone had cleared a foot-wide path through the mud and debris past the statue of St. Jude until it intersected with the road.

Looking up just before she took the first carefully placed step into the thick mud left behind by the river, Deb turned her head to survey the landscape of what had been downtown Memphis. She sucked in air to steady herself, wholly unused to seeing into the far distance. Her view was of a flattened landscape, devoid of the tall, proud buildings that used to make up the vibrant skyline of her chosen city. All the bridges that used to span the Mississippi were gone, and the big, splashy pyramid had been stripped of its shiny windows, displaying empty ribs on half of it, the other half fallen away. The very bottom parts of a few of the buildings still stood a story or two high here and there, but anything taller was nothing more than blackened girders, tilting at odd angles, reminding Deb of the horrible images that had come out of the fall of the twin towers on 9/11. Flames still licked upward within the remains of the destroyed city, but there was no sound of sirens coming to put them out. The silence was so profound, it was like they'd stepped into a silent movie, and it gave her a shiver up her spine.

Sweeping her glance north, where they were headed, all Deb could see were more flattened buildings with coils of smoke rising as the interiors continued to burn. Here and there, stone churches dotted the landscape, steeples gone, but the walls of the main build- ings still standing, as well as a few low-rise apartment buildings, as if they were the islands of some tiny archipelago rising above the vast- ness of the sea.

"Oh, my." Giles had done the same thing she had, stopping in his tracks. "I didn't realize..." his words trailed off.

Maritza waved her hand at them, shouting to be heard through her mask. "Come on, let's get moving." Her tiny form marched forward, carrying her share of the supplies, her determined movement pulling them along behind her.

Besides the destruction of the physical buildings and roads, they had to contend with the smell of decay that had built over the past day. The rising reek of broken sewer lines, rotting debris left behind by the river, and the scent of bodies beginning their inevitable decay made Deb glad she was wearing a mask. The dead were scattered everywhere, heaped with the rubble of the buildings they'd once lived or worked in, mangled bodies strewn in between broken walls and furnishings, some with hands outflung as if in their last moments they'd cried out for someone to hold them. After the first fifteen minutes of her stomach rolling at the sight of them, Deb opted to keep her sanity and to walk staring only a foot or two in front of her as a protective measure which also worked to help her keep her balance as they maneuvered precariously among the ruins.

Maritza stopped every once in a while to confer with Tom about their path, not moving forward until he concurred with her bearings. Deb let the weight of the makeshift bags she carried drop and rolled her shoulders in a futile effort to ease their ache every time she could. At one of the stops, after they'd been inching their way along for nearly two hours, Giles moved closer to her.

"How many people lived in Memphis?"

"Around six hundred thousand," Deb responded.

"How many do you think survived?"

Deb spoke slowly. "Not many in the center of the city, looks like, maybe a few hundred here, and I think most of them found their way to St. Jude's." It was hard to say the words aloud, as if saying them confirmed her dark suspicions and turned them from possibility to certainty. Deb tried to lighten the bleak outlook by adding, "Maybe the people and buildings on the outskirts of town, further away from the epicenter here by the river, did better."

Giles frowned. "Wouldn't they be coming to help if they had? And... If so many are gone... who's going to be working to get the water system or the electrical grid up again?"

Tom turned and pointed at him. "I was wondering the same

thing. And how come we haven't seen any Red Cross or FEMA people? Or Army or National guard?" The burly man shook his head. "I think this thing is bigger than we realize, or else they'd have been here helping by now."

"Less talking, more walking." Maritza broke in, her voice stern.

The conversation haunted Deb as they trudged on, her spirits sinking lower and lower as they passed destroyed buildings, most crumbled beyond recognition, and no other living people besides themselves. They were just little ants crawling over the corpse of the city, taking on a futile task that wouldn't matter in the long run when the resources ran out. Deb swallowed against the sob that wanted to rise in her throat, the leaden dry lump that was her tongue, but didn't want to stop the group just to get a sip of water from their communal bottle, so she remained thirsty, each step becoming harder and harder to take as sweat poured down her body in the rising heat of a Memphis summer.

The walking went on forever, with no end in sight. Bit by bit, despair inched into her core, making the trudge even more difficult as her sense of purpose waned. Her weak ankle turned on a piece of hidden rubble as she lost focus. Deb stumbled as she tried to gain her balance, then tripped on a section of tumbled brick, falling to her knees in the sludge, slicing both of them open on the rough edges that cut through the thin material of her scrubs, blood coursing down her legs as she struggled and failed to stand.

"Man down!" Tom called out from behind her. The line stopped. Tom moved over to help her stand, holding her elbow as she readjusted the weight she carried, making sure she got her balance. His deep brown eyes looked at her with concern as she swayed.

Maritza came back to her, forced the water bottle in her hand. "Drink, Deb."

She tried to make a joke as she handed the water back after taking a few small sips. "Are we there, yet?"

Tom obliged her with a deep chuckle as he nodded. "I think we only have a few more blocks to go, less maybe, you gotta hang in there."

Maritza knelt and looked at her knees. "I think you're best off just letting those bleed for a while, clean anything out. We can fix you up when we get to the BBQ place." Her face was sheened with sweat as well, pale beneath her normal dusky skin, but determination still emanated from her tiny frame.

The flow of blood had already soaked into her socks, so a little more wouldn't make a difference. Deb didn't want to let Maritza or this little team down, so she forced herself to nod. "Okay, let's go."

A few minutes later, Giles turned to look at her. "You all right?"

She wanted to lie and put on a positive face for the man, but didn't have the strength to do anything but shrug. "As well as anyone can be, considering."

"Honest answer, that is." He added something else to the sentence, but his accent was so thick under the mask she couldn't understand him. Deb twitched in irritation, and nearly asked him to repeat himself, but she was too tired to actually care what he'd said.

She tried to damp down the negativity that was once more growing in her by thinking about her sister, but that soon devolved into a searing burst of jealousy that Mara was currently living high on the hog with her well-stocked homestead with her extremely competent husband who seemingly always knew how to do everything.

"Oh, for heaven's sake!" Deb exclaimed, letting her bundles fall to the ground to give herself a body shake to force the insane and negative thoughts that weren't serving her at all to leave.

Everyone turned to look at her. "Just loosening my muscles," she lied with a blush, then picked up her load again and looked forward so she wouldn't have to see them looking at her.

"Pull yourself together, Deb," she muttered as she continued to step forward. Only one thing reliably worked for her when her emotions turned and churned in a gloomy turmoil, and that was to purposefully be nice to someone else and focus on them instead of circling her inner pit of despair. Deb increased her pace, so that she was nearly even with Giles. "Thank you for joining us. It's a big help to have another set of shoulders."

"I'd do anything for the staff at St. Jude hospital," he replied. Deb was surprised that she now found him fairly easy to understand since she'd made the effort to shove aside her stinking thinking, and filed away that information for future use.

"They've done wonders for my Ellie," he continued. "The hospital, they care for her for free, it's amazing. So I decided if I could lend a hand, give something back, I would." He struggled to scramble over a chest-high wall that Maritza had deemed the best way through a series of downed apartment buildings, so she held his load while he did so. Once he'd crossed over, Giles took them back, commenting, "I must say, I don't think I'm the best candidate to haul things cross country."

"None of us are," Deb replied dryly as he held her bundles while she navigated the same broken section of wall by straddling it and rolling over the top.

"We Brits have a saying from World War Two," Giles remarked once they were moving forward again. "We're just muddling through."

Deb smiled as she repeated the phrase, the anger and despair that had been trying to take the heart of her dissipate. "I like that, not too much pressure. Kind of like a saying one of my roommates in college used to say, 'You don't have to do it perfectly, just do it.'" The conversation lulled as they walked a few more steps in pleasant harmony. "How old is your daughter?" Deb finally asked.

"She'll be six in August. Next month." He caught his breath and looked behind them as if he could see his daughter in the haze. "She's a fighter, so I had to turn into one as well."

The man's simple statement struck Deb to her core, and she chewed on it as they marched onward, the streets seeming to match her rising spirits as they became easier to navigate the further from the river they got. Turning into a fighter was something she'd experienced firsthand. It was necessary for her to be strong for her baby sister when their parents had been killed, strong as she worked her way through college and nursing school, paying for it with lots of waitressing jobs. Just because her old enemy, self-doubt, had raised its ugly head didn't define her this time any more than it had the countless other times she'd doubted her abilities. Heartened by the realization that things had been hard before, but she'd gotten through them, Deb kept moving forward. It had been nearly three hours since they started out from the hospital. Surely they must be close to their goal by now.

Maritza's voice filtered back to her a few minutes later. "I see the restaurant!"

"Thank goodness," Tom muttered from behind her. "I hope that something's cooking on the grill!"

The single-story beige-painted brick building was standing, although three of its four windows on this side had broken and the sign had fallen off the side of it. A curl of smoke came from the rear of the building, and they made their way around to find a pair of wiry Black men turning meat on an open-air cooker, both wearing red and white checked aprons and hair nets.

"Is that chicken I smell?" Tom called from behind her.

The two men turned, looking a little guarded, their tongs extended as if they might fight the group off with them. The older of the pair spoke. "Who are you?"

"We're from St. Jude's," explained Maritza. "We're meeting a team from the VA hospital here to exchange supplies. One of their orderlies said you might still have your doors open."

"They have to be open," quipped the younger of the pair. "That earthquake ripped our door clean off its hinges, along with the other side of our building!" To Deb's utter surprise, he laughed and thumped the older man on the chest.

"You laugh about anything," grumbled the older man, but then laughed right along with him. "Only thing that didn't fall down during that last quake was that woodpile." He pointed to the huge pile of neatly stacked logs that formed a pristine triangle rising a good eight feet in the air. "My son knows how to stack! Welcome to Junior's Barbeque. Now, who's hungry?"

"Our freezer went out, so we're cookin' up everything we had before it goes bad!" said the younger one. "Pop's not happy unless he's feeding people, so you'd be doing both of us a favor!"

He gestured to a stack of chairs that had been pulled from the inside of the restaurant, along with a couple of red-topped Formica tables that sat in the shade of the half-destroyed restaurant. Deb happily let her burden drop and sat with the others. In moments, there was a slab of chicken and several slices of white bread sitting in front of her, along with ketchup and containers of barbeque sauce.

"You want a coke or a sprite?" The younger of the two asked her. He had a long red burn mark up the side of his arm. "It's warm, but it's wet and sweet."

"Coke, please, but let me take care of that for you first." Deb pointed to the burn.

He waved her off. "It's nothing. Part of being a grill master."

"It'll take less than a minute."

Before he protested further, Deb pulled the supplies she needed to clean, treat, and bind the burn from a bundle she'd been hauling. She handed him a couple of gauze bandages and a tube of antiseptic cream so he could take care of changing it later. Since she had the supplies out, she tended to the jagged cuts on her knees, wincing when the antiseptic wipes hit the ripped skin, but feeling better once they were bandaged.

Deb set to eating her meal. The chicken was falling off the bone and the sauce they provided was sweet and smokey, just the way she liked it.

"Want another piece? We got plenty." The older of the two asked.

"It's delicious, and yes, I would." He placed the meat on her plate, still sizzling from the cooker. Her mouth started watering all over again from the sight and the aroma of the perfectly cooked chicken. "Which one of you is Junior?" Mara asked in reference to the name of the restaurant.

The man laughed. "We're both Junior. My granddaddy was also a Junior, he started this place, and that's my son, Eloisus Zachariah Bartholomew Junior the third" He gave her a wink. "You can see why we just went with the Junior part. And that also makes me, Junior, Senior."

His laughter was contagious. Deb had to put down her chicken so she wouldn't choke to let the joyful sound bubble out of her. It chased back the last vestiges of the gloom of the morning like a sunbeam bursting through after a heavy storm, the shared laughter thrusting against the horrors inflicted on the people and places of her beloved city. Food, companionship, laughter, and people helping each other because they could, restored her.

While their team waited hopefully for the other team from the VA to arrive, they helped the two men clear the wreckage from their building, rehanging plastic sheeting from the fallen freezer section to help keep the dust out from the little triangular section formed by the remaining corner of the building where the two men had made a place to sleep for themselves and store the non-refrigerated food. They put items in neat rows inside of upturned tables whose lips would help contain the precious supplies if another quake hit. Another quake rolled through as they worked, much smaller than the initial ones, so they were able to keep their feet during the minute of shaking and rolling. The protective sheeting worked fairly well to repel the billowing dust that was created after a nearby building that had only partially collapsed finally fell all the way as the shaker subsided.

Deb stood out on the corner with the two Juniors, keeping a lookout for the team from the VA while Maritza, Tom, and Giles slept for a few minutes in the protected area of the restaurant. Deb's weariness had fled with the good meal and good company and a second Coke.

"I've never been so glad this place is on a corner off away from other buildings," remarked the younger Junior after the long silence that had followed the fall of the building across the street.

"And that your granddaddy built it to last," added Junior Senior. "He set all these bricks by hand, along with my uncles in the late fifties, when this place was just starting to grow. My daddy was a saxophone player by night and grilled up lunches by day." He grinned as he settled into the rhythm of the story. "Now, daddy wasn't much one for breakfast, as sometimes he'd be out until four in the morning swinging down on Beale and other spots. Why, he even knew Elvis, although he never made music with him. But he'd rouse himself every day at ten, and be ready to open for lunch at eleven, all week long, except Sunday." He turned to his son. "And it was my job, just like it is yours to come in two hours ahead of time to get the meat to cooking and prep the potatoes for the fries in the summers when I was off school, then stay and take people's orders and ring them up at the cash register." The man shook his head at the memory. "My sisters would take the food to people, get their drinks and whatnot, and our aunties would bake the cakes and the pies we sold by the slice in those days, too. Just baked 'em up at home, then brought them in."

"What a wonderful heritage," Deb said appreciatively.

The older man brushed the brick with a calloused hand. "I guess it's at an end, though. I bet there's not a hundred souls left in this part of town, maybe less." He shook his head mournfully as he looked out over the devastation. "This store was our everything, and now I got nothing to pass on to my son."

"Don't be that way, pop. We can cook and we know how to run a restaurant. We'll find a new place to start again, you and me." He put an arm around his father's shoulder and hugged him close.

The love between them clear, the warm spread of it bright enough to make her smile, but in the next moment she gasped with a sharp stab of missing her own family, her sister and nephew, and their expanded blended family, the bite of jealousy she'd had a few hours ago long gone, transformed into longing to see them again. Deb let out a long, controlled breath to manage the sudden physical pain of missing them, but the tidal pull of it was so strong she had to turn away to brush away tears and sat abruptly on the doorstep of the restaurant as the feeling left her legs.

Deb buried her face in her hands as she made the effort to work her way through the burst of feeling and clear it away, but before she accomplished compartmentalizing it, the older man noticed her distress. "Hey now," he said, patting her arm kindly.

She let out a strangled half sob, half laugh as her tears fell more quickly. "That's exactly how I comfort my patients."

"Physician, heal thyself," the older man quoted with deep kindness in his voice.

"I don't even know what that looks like anymore. I certainly can't heal this." Deb waved a hand at the destruction all around them. The despair she'd stuffed away threatened to engulf her once more.

"Seems to me you're the sort of person who will figure something out," he replied. "Just got to give it some time. Let the answers bubble up for you. My answers bubble up when I'm mixing my barbeque sauce," he added in a confidential tone. "Just something about putting those ingredients together makes me relax, and then, as I'm mixing, there it comes, the answer I needed." He pointed to his son. "That one there, he goes for runs, that's what does it for him."

Deb nodded as she rubbed her sweaty palms on her scrubs, then stuck out her legs and waggled her feet that were encased in the running shoes she'd put on yesterday morning and a thousand years ago. "I like to run, too, and you're right, it does clear my head. But I don't know that there's a straight bit of clear land to run on anymore. At least not around here." She bit her lip as she surveyed the landscape. There'd be no good, smooth runs on this ground for a long time.

"Well, then find a place that has them. It's not good to keep your emotions all bottled up like that. Bottles is good for sauces, but not much else, you want my opinion."

"You have good ones, both sauces and opinions."

The conversation faded again as they stood watch at the intersection. The grey skies continued to block the sun, and the crackle of burning fires in the distance was the only sound besides the breathing of the two men next to her. She'd never known it to be so quiet here in the city, without the traffic and hustle of people going about their lives, the rumble of aircraft overhead, the steady flow of the river sweeping by to join the gulf waters. There weren't even any dogs barking or birds singing.

In the lull that required no action from her other than to wait and watch, Deb let her thoughts roll freely. It had served her to keep her feelings compartmentalized during the brunt of the disaster so she could focus on the patients she'd been helping, but now they rolled and sloshed making her head ache, all division gone. She was happy to be doing a service for Maritza and the staff at St. Jude's, but simultaneously worried for her friends at her own hospital, St. Vincent's, twelve miles from here, to the south and east. Deb looked in the direction of the place, and wanted to be there, but it wasn't as strong as the yearning she had to go even further east, to see her sister and her nephew.

"How far do you think it is from here to Roanoke, Virginia?" She asked abruptly.

"I went to college about three hours south of there, at ETSU, for a couple of years." The younger man looked at his father. "What you think, maybe six hundred miles or so?"

"About that, yep. Take the I40 to the 81, be the most direct route."

"Six hundred miles, wow. I guess I forget how long Tennessee is," Deb said, her impulse to just get up from her seat and start walking fading as she contemplated the distance.

"You have people there?" Junior Senior asked her.

"My sister and her son, and she just married a man who has a couple of kids last year. They have a homestead outside of Roanoke."

"A homestead? You mean with chickens and ducks and the like?"

"Yes, that's right. My sister loves to garden, and they have a big one, and a pond and goats, too. An old farmhouse that creaks something terrible." Deb laughed at the memory of trying to sleep on her sister's big couch, but waking up every five minutes thinking someone was sneaking up on her. It had been terrible at the time, but now she'd give just about anything to be camping out on that big sofa right now.

Junior Senior nudged his son. "Look at her face. What is that face telling you?"

"That she wants to go to Roanoke and be with her sister."

The blunt statement had her nodding before he even finished his sentence. "Busted. Am I so transparent?"

The younger man laughed. "Well, I would love for you to join my weekly poker night, so I could take all your money from you. That's all I'm going to say."

Deb gave him a good-natured push on his shoulder when a movement about three blocks away caught her eye. She caught her breath and pointed to the group of people who were coming closer. "I think that's them!" She waited a few minutes longer until it became obvious that six people in hospital scrubs were headed for the restaurant, two pairs of them carrying what appeared to be stretchers between them.

A surge of energy swept through her, and she waved vigorously. The figure in the front, who was not carrying a stretcher, waved back. Deb hurried inside to wake her companions, while the two Juniors moved to put more chicken on the grill.

An hour later, the group from the VA leaned back in their chairs, clasping their stomachs. "That's got to be the best meal I've ever eaten," declared Spencer, a tall man with ginger hair and large, dark-framed glasses. He had been the person Maritza had coordinated with for the exchange.

"Told you," said a short orderly. "I come here at least once a week to get my fix."

They'd all exchanged information as the group had eaten, and Tom had gotten seconds, cobbled together from the bits and pieces put together from the infrequent radio communications Maritza and Spencer had gotten over the past twenty-four hours. The VA group confirmed that Memphis wasn't the only place that had been devastated by earthquakes, that they'd happened nationwide, all close together, which would account for the lack of any government help.

"I think we're going to be on our own for a long time," Spencer said, his face grim. "It kills me to say it, but I predict there's going to be a lot more suffering for those of us who survived as we run out of supplies."

A hush fell over all of them as they considered his proclamation. Finally, Junior spoke up. "Well, I think we'll find a way to pull through, like y'all did today with your exchange. There's plenty of good people that will do the right thing by each other." His father beamed at him after he finished talking, and several of the others nodded their heads thoughtfully.

"Do you think they went global, too?" Giles worried. "I have family scattered all through Europe."

Spencer answered him. "It seems like each earthquake triggered another, from here all the way out to both coasts. I suppose it's possible they continued all around the world. What's that thing called, the ring of fire, it circles the Pacific ocean?"

Maritza paced, glancing at her watch and the sky. She cleared her throat authoritatively. "As much as I'd like to stay, I think we ought to be making our way back now. It's nearly noon, and our people are going to be mighty hungry and thirsty."

"You want to try to meet like this again in a couple of days, Maritza?" Spencer looked over at the two Juniors. "Will you still be here, and open?"

The two men exchanged a glance, then the son spoke. "We have family scattered through Memphis, and we're hoping they show up here as they can make it, so yes. Can't guarantee another meal, though."

"We have frozen chicken in our freezers, and our generator is still running. We'll bring you a batch, and anything else you need to keep cooking," the man responded, rubbing his hands together. "There are lots of sodas and waters, too, we'll bring you those." He turned to Maritza. "The VA got its big monthly delivery of restaurant supplies the day before the quake, thank goodness."

Maritza brightened. "You know, we got a delivery that day, too. Our kitchens were buried in the initial quake, but I can organize a team to see if we can't dig those out. Our hospital supply room is well stocked, and that part of the building is still standing, so we can bring more first aid for the VA, no problem." She turned to the Juniors. "I'm going to bring you two first aid things too, and masks to use," Maritza added. "And maybe, if you think it might help, one of our nurses could come here and stay, create a sort of emergency outpost." Her gaze drifted to Deb.

"That'd be good." The Juniors eyed Deb expectantly.

Deb looked at the small circle of people who'd been strangers only a day ago, but she'd become as emotionally tied to them as if she'd known them for decades. They were her kind of people, the type who nearly always put caring for others ahead of their own needs. It was a core value for all of them, which made what she had to say feel selfish, but Deb needed to speak the truth.

"I wish I could say I'd come back and be your outpost nurse," she said reluctantly. "But I can't guarantee it. I need to find out what's happening at St. Vincent's, and if they need me..."

The hospital staffers from both St. Jude's and the VA all uttered a hum of acknowledgement after she let her words drift off, affirming her need to be with the people she normally worked with, giving her a sense of relief that they understood, and didn't hold her refusal against her, even if they didn't like the answer.

"Well, we'll find someone," Maritza said, her voice crisp, but Deb thought there was a tone of disappointment beneath the efficiency.

"I volunteer as Tribute!" Tom said, making them all laugh, and breaking the slight tension that had developed from Deb's refusal of the job.

"You're just in it for the meals," said Maritza.

"Darn tootin'!" he said promptly, provoking another round of laughter.

The momentary bright spot was soon lost to exchanging bundles, and the grim reality of the hours of slogging it was going to take getting back to St. Jude's, this time carrying even more weight, each of them responsible to lift and carry half of a stretcher with over a hundred pounds of meals and water tightly bound onto it.

Spencer eyed the four of them thoughtfully. "Next time, use six people like we did, that way you can trade off."

Maritza put her hands on her hips and faced him. "Like I didn't already think of that."

Spencer flung his hands up in mock defense.. "Just trying to be helpful. Don't hurt me!" It was a funny statement coming from the man who was nearly twice Maritza's height and size, and everyone laughed, the camaraderie palpable as they waved goodbye to the group from the VA, who then trundled off with the bundles of first aid gear they'd brought for them.

Deb was partnered with Giles to carry one of the stretchers, and she was glad she'd taken the time to get to know him on the way to the restaurant. It would take a lot of coordination with the Brit to manage the weight and the length of it around hundreds of obstacles and uneven ground, but at least they knew the path back to the hospital, and each thing they carried was going to make someone's life a little better, which provided a lift to her spirits, just as the meal and companionship had done.

Junior Senior pulled her aside just before she set out to leave. "I feel it in my bones that you're not coming back here, and as much as I've enjoyed your company, I want you to know I'd be sorry if you did," he said softly. "You need to go to your people." His eyes carried the weight of long years of wisdom as he gazed at her. "I don't just mean the people at St. Vincent's, either. I mean your people."

Her heart beat faster as she imagined the hundreds of miles between herself and her sister, but the elderly man had also reawakened the burn inside of her chest to be with Mara again, an inexorable pull to find her family. Her mouth dried, but she was impelled to tell him the truth, this wonderful man who she was likely never to see again.

"Thank you. You're right." The simple statement was nearly too much for her to bear, carrying as it did so much hope and fear mixed. Her mouth quirked even as her eyes filled with tears one more time. "Bet they need good chicken and fish in Roanoke too," she said. "Just a little trip along the I40 and the 81, and ask around for the Padgett family. I'd love to see you again."

His eyes twinkled, and he put a hand lightly on her back. "If it comes to that, we'll surely consider it, Deb. And Junior and I will hold a good thought for you on your journey. Don't look back, you hear?"

Deb's heart expanded at his kindly meant words, and she gave him a hearty hug that was reciprocated, and another with his lanky son before she moved to pick up her stretcher. "I've hugged more people in the last twelve hours than I have for a year," she remarked to Giles as she tightened her mask.

"Disasters change you," he said. "I used to be a cold fish, before my Essie got sick. Now I'm woefully squidgy with nearly everyone. I'll take the front for the first bit, and then we can switch off, yeah?"

"Sounds good." Deb grasped the two handles of the old-fashioned stretcher, rising in unison with Giles, stifling a groan as the weight pulled on her shoulders and back. Her ankle gave a twinge, reminding her that it wasn't enjoying all the exercise she was giving it, but she stepped forward on it all the same, a first step into an uncertain future, but one she was compelled to take.

CHAPTER SIXTEEN

US Army Reserve, Brainerd, MN
Day Two

The time they'd spent outside playing on the swings and the slide had calmed Braden while it had given Logan space to steel himself to do the right thing by the boy. By the time Logan had changed the boy's diaper and gotten them each a peanut butter and jelly sandwich and a Dixie cup full of what the Private in charge of the line in the kitchen tent had optimistically called "orange juice," but was clearly thinly reconstituted Tang, Logan had equipped himself with all the reasons Braden was better off being left in relative safety in the care of child protective services.

He repeated the list he'd come up with in his head as they emerged from the mess tent, Logan contentedly walking at the meandering toddler's pace past the long line of about a hundred tents set up in three neat rows, pausing any time Braden discovered a bug or an interesting patch of dirt. He was in no rush to let the boy go, even though he was resolved to do it, and the child's elastic ability to find joy playing with a roly-poly, his infectious chuckles as its tiny legs crawled over his hand and his mischievous glance at Logan before he 'fed' the bug to his stuffed toy dog Whuff lightened Logan's heart even as the knowledge that he was spending his last few minutes with Braden slowly crushed it.

The leisurely pace also gave him the time to observe the transformation the Brainerd National Guard base had undergone in detail. A relative calm had settled over the camp after the influx of multiple planeloads of refugees had filed in, and their food, shelter, and clothing needs had been met with alacrity. Each of the hundred or so tents the servicemen had erected held between four and six people each. The mess tent, which had been running noticeably low on food the day before, had a pile of supplies beside it that were being ferried in by a line of servicemen, and the promised outhouses and portable showers had been delivered and erected along the fence. To his eye, the CO in charge of the army reserve outpost had done an outstanding job of marshaling his resources and men to accommodate what Private Ingersoll had called "the refugees." It took a deft hand to create order out of chaos when you were dealing with four or five hundred confused and frightened people with only a handful of part-time soldiers to help.

There was a waft of permanence to the tidy operation that pricked at him, however, and one thing the camp definitely lacked was good information on what was going on, both with plans for the refugees and with the world at large. No one he'd talked to knew much, only rumors that the earthquakes had been widespread, and all the soldiers had remained irritatingly tight-lipped when he'd asked them over the course of the past few hours if they were aware of how the plane survivors were going to be moved to their homes. Private Ingersoll had said the CO would talk to them soon, but the day was wearing on with no forward movement.

Braden had crouched again in the shadow of one of the tents, picking at the ground. He stood and held his hand out to Logan. "Yours."

"You've got something for me?" Logan smiled at Braden as he bent his knees to crouch on the toddler's level.

Braden nodded, extending his hand toward him. "Issa rock," he said helpfully.

Logan let the little boy tip the flattened black rock that was the same size and shape of a bottlecap into his big palm. "Well, look at that. Thank you, Braden."

The little boy smiled his sweet grin, then toddled forward and gave Logan an exaggerated kiss on the side of his face, saying, "Mwah!" Logan felt the damp wetness the child had left behind with his voluntary kiss, and came dangerously close to bursting into tears, but managed to swallow them down as he stood, tucking the rock into his pocket.

They'd reached the shadow of the brick building where the Red Cross had set out their tables, the place that Private Ingersoll had told him the Child Services people would be. Taking a deep breath to steady himself, he picked Braden up along with Whuff to carry them inside. Passing by the tubs of personal goods on offer, he picked up an individual package of tissues emblazoned with the ubiquitous red cross symbol, shoving it in his pocket with his free hand, figuring he was going to need them all too soon.

A short Korean woman with dark hair, deep laugh lines, and kind-looking features waggled her fingers at Braden as they approached. "Hi," she said in a soft voice. "I'm Cathy. How can I help you today?"

There was a long pause as Logan hunted to find the right words to start the necessary conversation, all the spit drying up in his mouth at once as a tension headache bloomed tight across his fore-head and embedded itself in his temples. Braden looked at him with a solemn expression, as if sensing his distress, a little crease forming between his brows.

"Hi Cathy. I'm Logan Padgett. And this is Braden," he said finally, in what he considered to be his professional voice that was neutral in every way. "Braden Frye. His mommy was on my flight yesterday, but she passed, and I've been taking care of him since then."

The woman's eyes crinkled with compassion. "I see. Well, in a case of extreme serendipity, you're in luck. I'm a volunteer at the Children's Home as well as helping out the Red Cross. The home has been put in charge of any displaced children by the CO of this base."

As the seconds ticked down to when he'd have to let Braden go, Logan suddenly disliked the words displaced and serendipity, and wanted to be anywhere than here talking to Cathy, the volunteer wonder from the Children's Home. He tightened his grip on Braden, who promptly stuck his thumb in his mouth and leaned his head on Logan's shoulder, the display of trust nearly unmanning him.

Cathy read Logan's indrawn breath accurately as she looked between Braden and himself. "It looks like you've been doing a good job with him."

"He's a great kid," Logan managed. His carefully modulated professional tones flew out the window as he choked on the words.

"A great kid with a great doggie," she said, then addressed Braden. "What's your doggie's name?" she asked sweetly.

Braden buried his head in Logan's chest, hiding his face, but as both adults patiently waited, he finally said, "Whuff."

"Whuff. I like that. And what's your mommy's name, Braden?"

He looked totally confused. "Mommy," he replied, then looked around as if she might materialize from the dark of the hallway.

"Does Mommy have another name?" Cathy asked gently.

Braden squirmed, becoming more agitated. "Mommy!"

"Can't you find that out from the plane manifest?" Logan butted in, his temper flaring at her demands of the boy.

"It's our procedure," she told him, using a calming tone he recognized, having employed it many times on frantic parents of high schoolers who were absolutely sure their darling child could never have done the thing they'd been caught red-handed doing. "I need to find out if he's verbal or nonverbal, so we know what kind of unit to place him into."

The woman was doing her job. He should at least be polite to her and help her put Braden in the best place possible. "Braden's verbal. He knows the names of lots of things."

"Can he tell us his address?"

Logan was at a loss. While Braden was a bright kid, he doubted if a two-year-old could produce that kind of information. His own kids hadn't known their address until they were in kindergarten and had to do a show and tell with a poster about where they lived. He was about to tell the woman exactly that when Braden shut his eyes and spoke rapidly.

"Four, four, four one Chespeek." The boy whispered.

"He's from Addison, Texas, by Dallas," Logan filled in as Cathy wrote the address down, tucking his chin to look at Braden directly. "Is that your house, Braden? Four, four, four one Chesapeake?"

"Brown house," Braden nodded. "Big tree."

"Wow, good job, buddy!"

"You are one smart boy," Cathy added. "Or did Whuff tell you?" She reached out and tickled Braden, making him giggle. Logan was impressed by her, in spite of himself, and how she was creating an easy bond with Braden.

"I wish our computers were working," Cathy said with a sigh as she copied what she'd written into a second record book. She pulled out her cell phone, pushed it a few times, then waved it in the air. "These aren't working either, so we can't check the address on the internet. I tend to believe him, it seems specific."

"His parents taught him well," Logan said with a pang.

Cathy smiled, the lines around her eyes and mouth deepening. "They sure did." She turned to Braden again. "Would you like to go play with some other kids?"

Braden looked at Logan as if he was asking his permission. Logan's heart melted out of his body and flowed into the floor, leaving a Braden-sized hollow that would forever be empty. He cleared his throat and made himself smile. "It's okay, you can go play with the other kids, buddy."

"'Kay." Braden said to Cathy.

"We're using the kindergarten rooms over at the school across the street for a few days," she said to Logan. "We have four other kids over there who've been... left to their own devices. And those of us volunteering are bringing our own kids in to keep them company. My oldest and youngest are there. They're four and eight. Our six-year-old wanted to hang out with his daddy."

"Uh-huh." His breath had become short, and he had to fight to maintain his outward appearance of calm.

"You know, you seem pretty attached," said Cathy matter-of-factly as she studied his face. "Why don't you just hold on to him a little longer?"

Answers flew through his head, the ones he'd prepped to gird himself for this moment. Because yes, I am attached to this boy, and I don't want to get any more attached. Because everybody has told me it's safe here. Because I can't drag a toddler thousands of miles cross-country to my home, through terrible hardship and danger. Because he deserves someone to find his relatives for him. Because he doesn't belong to me.

"I think this is best," he managed to blurt out. "Listen, his M-o-m was incredibly brave," Logan added, spelling the word so as not to upset Braden. "She literally saved his life by sacrificing herself. Can you put that in your notes? Both Braden when he's ready and his D-a-d deserve to know that."

Cathy's face softened. "I will absolutely do that." She reached her arms to Braden. "Do you and Whuff want to come with me and play?"

"Yus." Braden's sturdy little arms slipped from around his neck, his chunky legs unwrapped from Logan's torso, and he went to her easily, taking his sweet, solid warmth with him. A shudder ran down Logan's spine as Cathy settled the boy on her hip with practiced ease, his heart snapping painfully as he took in his final memories of Braden. He was suddenly aware he wouldn't be visiting Braden across the street because he couldn't say goodbye a second time to his little buddy. Once was hard enough.

"I can tell this is difficult for you," she said, studying Logan. "You're doing the right thing for him. We'll be keeping Braden over there. We decided it's safer for the kids to keep them with just a few caregivers in one place rather than over here with so many unknowns. The kindergarten classes are nice and big with running water, they face the playground and we've set up cots. He'll be there for several more days, best guess, until the system gets back up and running and we can start the search for his relatives. If you end up wanting to visit, just come over. I'll put your name on the list, just in case."

"Sure." Logan was barely keeping his emotions in check. It took everything in him to give a casual smile to Braden as Cathy walked away with the boy, the far door of the armory limning them in a golden light. "Have fun," he called to Braden. "Bye." His voice choked on the last word, and he held his breath so he wouldn't break down further, his carefully erected defenses shattering as Braden was taken away. Logan blindly turned down the narrow, dark hall and marched outside, back to his tent and opened the flap, letting out a grateful, relieved sigh at the absence of Gayle and her two boys. Collapsing onto his cot, eyes streaming with tears, he let his held breath out in a long breath that turned into a moan as he attempted to release the deep sadness that filled him. He focused on Cathy's words that turning him over really had been the right thing to do for Braden. He'd fulfilled a private obligation and gotten the boy to safety with professionals; it was time to focus on getting back to his own sons and daughter, and his wife.

Logan pulled out the Red Cross tissues, blew his nose and wiped his eyes, then clasped his arms around the emptiness of his chest and hugged himself hard to recenter. He focused on the grounding pressure and thought about the next steps he needed to take to get home, blocking everything else out but that goal.

Though it took a few moments, his breathing slowed and his chest relaxed as he worked through the problem logically. Supplies and something to carry them in came first, then transportation and a good map that could guide him through the thousand or so miles he'd need to traverse to get home. The starting point was his current backpack. Logan sat up and reached under the cot to pull it out. It hung limply in his hands, a battle-scarred, fire-scorched object that was missing half of itself. He should just toss it and see if perhaps Private Ingersoll could provide him with a new backpack. The problem was he didn't want to replace it, even as decrepit as it was. The pack had served him well, it had survived the crash and its aftermath, and it had saved his life during the explosion of the plane. It didn't seem right to simply throw it in the trash.

"I'm being sentimental over an object," he said aloud to the empty tent, shaking his head at his own folly. "And I know it's because I'm displacing my feelings about Braden, but knowing why I'm doing it isn't stopping it."

"And I'm guessing you're talking to yourself." Gayle's penetrating

voice sounded from outside the tent. "Sorry to disturb your conference with me, myself, and I, but can the boys and I come in?"

Logan's skin heated in an all-over blush he hadn't experienced
since middle school when he'd tried to ask Rebel Baumgartner to the
eighth-grade dance. "Come on in," he said, even though he'd prefer to
be alone.

Gayle looked apologetic as she ushered her twin boys into the
shared space. "I promise I didn't listen in on purpose, it was just a
timing thing." She scooted the boys onto their respective cots. "Go
lie down for a few minutes and rest. Momma's going to do the same,
and take your shoes off before you get mud in your bed."

The tone of a mom fussing over her kids was a familiar one for
Logan, and the buzz of it helped him climb out of the hole of embar-
rassment and slight resentment at their intrusion he'd fallen into.
"Did you get some lunch?" He asked more to have something to say
instead of any real interest.

She nodded and then yawned, not bothering to cover her mouth
as she did so, displaying an impressive array of fillings. "We did, and
they announced that the man in charge is going to be addressing
people in the mess hall at two o'clock today. Thought I'd get some
rest, then see what he has to say."

"I'm going to get there early," Logan said. "The mess isn't big
enough to hold everyone at once."

"I really need to grab a nap after what we went through last
night." Gayle said. "Can you save me a seat?"

As pleasant as his tent mate was, the combination of giving up
Braden, his growing headache, and being caught giving himself a pep
talk pushed him to the verge of telling her no, that he didn't want to
be responsible for anyone else. Then he looked at her hopeful expression and couldn't bring himself to turn her down. It was just seat-
saving, after all. "Sure."

"Where's Braden?" she asked.

"He's in good hands," Logan said shortly.

"Ah." Gayle left it at that, giving him the impression she didn't
actually care one way or another as she stretched out on her cot.
Although Logan was tired in body and soul, he was too restless to lie

down, so after stowing his backpack, he popped out of the tent, and moved to where the temporary showers had been erected and joined the short line to use the facilities.

A soldier stood by the showers, handing out small bits of soap and a coarse hand towel to each person in line. "Shampoo's in the stall. Please limit your shower to three minutes or less."

No stranger to fast, cool showers after years of camping out, Logan made the most of the thin, cold stream that emitted from the overhead showerhead, efficiently shedding the accumulated dust and sweat from the past two days off of his body. When he was done, he rubbed himself vigorously with the small towel before changing into his clothes. He carried his boots with him to put them on outside of the cubicle, sitting on a flimsy metal chair, then threw the towel in a waiting bin.

He looked at his watch. There was still another hour and a half before the meeting in the mess, so with no other viable choice, he went back to his assigned tent, tiptoeing so as not to wake Gayle and the boys. He pulled out his backpack to assess what he had, taking the things out one at a time and laying them in tidy rows on what used to be Braden's cot.

The lineup looked pitifully small to him once it was spread out. Three water bottles, a few snacks, a small first aid kit, his multi tool and some emergency foil blankets, along with simple toiletries made up the entirety of its contents. He also had what he was wearing, jeans, his hiking boots, a short and long-sleeved shirt. Under his bed were a sports jacket and a rain jacket he'd gotten from the Red Cross. He stripped the pillow of its thin cotton pillow case and added that to his pile, then re-inserted everything into the backpack.

He folded Braden's extra shirt and the remainder of his diapers to give back to the tables out front, and took a moment to rest his hand on top of the pile, patting it gently as another wave of sadness washed over him. The entire process had taken less than ten minutes. Once more he was left with nothing but idle time on his hands. His tension regathering, he tiptoed out of the tent, taking the remaining bits that had belonged to Braden with him.

He deposited the items on the long table inside the main building, leaving them with a final tap of his finger. His heart didn't hurt any less, but he'd at least checked off a mental item on his list of things to be done before he left the camp. He perused the tables to see if there were any pain relievers on hand, but that bin was empty. Instead, he snagged a blue baseball cap sporting a Minnesota twins logo that was in good condition along with a few power bars. Cathy was nowhere to be seen, so perhaps she'd stayed with Braden to transition him into his new space.

He took a moment to check in with Private Ingersoll, who was manning the quiet lobby on his own, doodling in a notebook that he hastily tucked away when he saw Logan approach.

"Mr. Padgett," he said by way of greeting.

"Private. It's finally quiet, I see."

"Just had a few in a camper van at oh-ten-hundred," the young man replied, then yawned widely. "Pardon me, haven't been getting a lot of shut-eye the past thirty-six hours."

"I think that goes for all of us. You don't happen to have any pain meds, do you?"

"No, but check with first aid. They're tucked in that little hall beyond the bathrooms on the left."

"Great, also, is there a supply room with backpacks and the like? I'd love to pull together some supplies for myself."

The young man shook his head emphatically. "The gear is only for enlisted personnel." Then he yawned again. "Man. Sorry!" He rubbed his face vigorously with his hands.

"Did someone come and relieve you?"

"Oh, you betcha. I got to go home for a few hours last night. Say, my aunt sent me back with some snickerdoodles, would you like one?" The young man fished in the satchel at his feet and came up with a plastic bag jammed with golden-brown cookies.

"It so happens I have a rule to never turn down snickerdoodles," Logan replied, taking one and biting into it. "Does your aunt win prizes for these at the state fair?" He asked once his mouth recovered from the bomb of delicious, sugary cinnamon flavor.

The boy grinned and nodded so fast his glasses nearly slid off of his nose. He pushed them back into place with a decisive finger. "Oh, for sure! You mean the Great Minnesota Get Together. She's won for these and her blueberry jelly, don'tcha know." He grinned, his northern accent getting thicker as he spoke.

"Well, you can tell her they're the best I've tasted," said Logan, finishing the cookie off. He fiercely squelched the drifting thought that Braden would have loved the treat. It was time to check one more thing off of his list.

"I was able to connect with the Child Service representative earlier, so there's a free cot in my tent if you have need of it." A pang of regret ripped through him as soon as he completed his sentence, and he half-way wanted to turn around, burst through the doors, run across the street, and reclaim the boy.

Private Ingersoll must have read his expression and spoke with quiet sincerity. "Yes, I saw Miss Cathy taking your little fella over to the school earlier," he said. "She was my second-grade teacher, he's in good hands, fer sure."

Logan nodded to the young man, glad of the confirmation. In just a few days, Braden would have forgotten all about Logan, and would be happy playing with other children until his father or some other relative could come for him. Logan changed the subject. "I hear your CO is addressing us in the mess soon?"

"Yep, he's probably in there already. Captain Johnson is an early bird."

"Good to know. Thank you for the cookie, Private."

Logan stopped by the first aid room, but the door was shut and locked. He opted to pace the long way along the perimeter fence instead of straight through the camp to give his legs a bit more of a stretch, his stiff muscles reminding him he'd spent most of the past thirty-six hours sitting or walking only short distances. The lack of exercise was likely a big part of the reason he was feeling on edge and confined. Of course he was free to leave the facility at any point, and had done so earlier with Braden, but the way the camp was enclosed by a high chain-link fence topped with curls of razor wire, with only one egress through the main building, gave it a prison-like feel that was becoming more irritating by the hour.

He walked into the mess tent through the back door, helped tote in a few boxes of food, and scored a cup of weak coffee from the cook before entering the main section, where the CO was talking to some people near the center of the space. Logan tucked himself in a quiet spot at the side of the tent to observe the man that had put such good order into the camp. The CO was speaking to a group of three intent young men and one woman, all with three gold bars on the sleeve of their uniforms. Sergeants, then, the ones in charge of making his orders happen. The sergeant's attitudes were respectful of their CO, snapping salutes as he finished talking. Logan waited until they'd dispersed, then moved over to the short, stocky man to introduce himself.

"Captain Johnson, I'm Logan Padgett. I wanted to thank you for your organization and hospitality." He extended his hand.

"You're the one with the little boy," the man said as he shook Logan's with a solid grip. "One of my Privates filled me in," he added.

"Ingersoll," Logan guessed.

"He's a good soldier," the Captain confirmed. "Will you be sticking around to hear what I have to say?"

"I am. I need to get back to my wife and kids in Virginia."

The man's dark grey eyes held Logan's for a moment as he tightened his lips. "That might prove difficult," he said. "I've been in contact with the acting President, and it will be months before even a few bridges are put back up over the major rivers, and she was saying it would be even longer before we make the roads passable for vehicular traffic."

Logan reeled at several bits of the information he'd just been given. "Acting President?"

The CO frowned. "I'll be telling everyone in just a few minutes, but word is that both the President and the VP were killed in the initial earthquakes, Ordway in DC, and Arkoosh out in California. The Speaker of the House, Janet Givens, is the acting President who will be confirmed once those deaths are established."

"So it's true, these earthquakes were everywhere?"

"Global catastrophe," the short man said. "Millions and millions were killed in the USA and abroad. More will fall in the days ahead from disease and lack of basic services." He shook his head. "I can surely say I never wanted to be part of a world that was so upended, but we'll do what we can with the resources we have. Now if you'll excuse me, I'd like to get a cup of that very weak coffee before I have to tell the refugees all that news and more."

Stunned, Logan returned to his out of the way seat at the edge of the room, his back to the tent wall, facing outward as was his preference. He traced the pattern of wood on the surface of the old picnic table with his finger as he let the information sink in. Bridges out, roads impassable, global catastrophe, and the acting President were all phrases he'd never imagined that he'd have to embrace. Captain Johnson had used the right word, 'upended,' as that was exactly Logan's impression as well. Downing the last of his coffee, Logan confirmed his earlier idea that returning home as fast as possible would be his single goal. He couldn't do anything about the infrastructure or politics - they were beyond his purview - so the focus would be where it should be, on his family.

The mess hall had nearly filled as Logan pulled out of his contemplation. Joe and Sandra, the couple from the night before, were just winding their way over to him, and he scooted along the bench to make room, saving a seat for Gayle as he'd promised.

"Did you hear the news?" Sandra asked, her eyes wide. "This state and Iowa are the only ones unaffected by the earthquake. Every other state has had catastrophic damage, either from the earthquakes or by tsunamis." Her lip trembled. "New York City was decimated, and Queens is under water, our home is gone." Joe rubbed her back in small circles. "So many friends and relatives..." she covered her face with her hands and sobbed.

"I'm so sorry," Logan said.

Joe nodded, his jaw pulsing with restrained emotion. "We must have been spared for a reason, right?"

Logan wasn't sure he agreed with that sentiment, but didn't disparage the man's belief. Everyone needed all the hope and belief they could muster now and in the days to come. A soldier moved past them, clearing the way for Captain Johnson, who carried a battery-powered microphone in his hand. "Looks like we're about to hear a bunch of news," Logan commented, calling the couple's attention to the Captain.

There was a rush of motion from his left as Gayle squeezed in next to him. "I figured you'd be by an exit," she said as the CO tapped the mike to see if it was on. Her thigh pressed against his, and she gave a little wiggle, forcing him to move further down the bench so that he was only partially seated. He swallowed his irritation and focused on the man he'd come to listen to.

"I'm Captain Johnson, and I first want to tell you that anyone is welcome at our camp for as long as they need to stay, and our supplies hold out. We have a global catastrophe on our hands, and unless you live in Minnesota or Iowa, or near the four corners region in the Southwest, most of you will not have homes to go back to, or cities that have infrastructure."

He waited for the gasps and muffled shrieks to subside. "If you do decide to stay, we'll put you to work in some capacity, as I cannot continue to ask the young men and women under my command to bust their humps the way they've been doing for the past thirty-six hours. While you'll keep civilian status, if you're under my roof, you will be under my rules."

More vocalizations, many with an undertone of dislike, including Gayle, who muttered. "I don't want none of that, not for me, not for my boys."

"For those of you who wish to leave," the man continued, "We'll allocate two trucks a day to take you for the first sixty miles, which will get you close to St. Cloud."

"Why not all the way to the Cities?" someone shouted from the crowd.

"The Cities—Minneapolis and St. Paul for those of you uninitiated in speaking Minnesotan—" he paused at the light laughter, but then his face grew grim. "The Cities have their own issues. They were inundated by the Mississippi river, which flowed backward for over twelve hours after the initial massive quake along the New Madrid fault line. The bluffs contained some of it, but the downriver areas were overcome, with St. Paul suffering damage that it will take months to rectify."

He let the crowd mutter for a few seconds, dissipating the tension in the room, and Logan gave him props for the way he handled them. "The other reason we cannot take you any further is that we don't know when we'll get more gas supplies for our vehicles, and, frankly, we cannot tell you what conditions are like in most of the USA. The government was able to get the word out to your planes to land you safely, but our communication has been intermittent and is diminishing due to the dust that has blanketed most of the globe. It could lead to a year or more without full sunlight or working communications, which depend on satellites that are beyond our reach above that silica-based cloud."

The gathered refugees became deathly still like the calm in the center of a hurricane, with anxiety and anger swirling darkly around the perimeter, ready to break through at any moment. Reading the fear bubbling in the crowd of people who'd passed through their initial stages of shock, Logan's shoulders knotted, and he had to focus to loosen his tight grip on the underside of the bench. He set his hands lightly and precisely on the table in preparation to fight or get out fast when the outburst of violence that was brewing broke out.

"Be ready to go if things get ugly," he said to Gayle. He said the same thing to Joe as he indicated the kitchen area, just to their left. "That way is best." Joe nodded and whispered to his wife, her eyes widening, but she also gave a bob of her head in acknowledgement.

Captain Johnson looked at the floor, then glanced around the room at the soldiers who rimmed the edges of the tent, spaced evenly apart. So the Captain had expected outbursts and had prepped for violence. Logan would have gone a different route himself, perhaps limited the size of the crowd to minimize the chance of conflict, even if it meant repeating the same information in multiple sessions.

"I'm going to ask you to remain calm and civilized," the Captain continued. "Think about what you want to do, stay or go, and report to Sergeant Blaine before we serve dinner at eighteen hundred—six pm." He gestured to a tall Black woman dressed in an impeccable uniform holding a clipboard, who obligingly raised her hand. "Sergeant Blaine will take your information and assign the seats on our vehicles out. First come, first served. She'll also create initial lists of chores for those of you who are staying." He looked around the hushed room with a steely eye. "I do expect all of you to choose one way or another by tonight."

Grumbling filled the tent, and bodies stirred, the beginning of a seethe of unhappy, upset people. "One final thing." The Captain stopped the talk and movement as he spoke, his face set. "President Blake Ordway is missing and presumed dead, and his VP Aaron Arkoosh has been confirmed a casualty of the earthquakes out in California." He raised his voice, the microphone whining feedback as gasps of disbelief rang out. "There is still a chain of command, and we will follow the orders of the former Speaker of the house, and now acting President, Janet Givens and her staff as we receive them in an orderly fashion. Thank you for your attention." A moment of shocked silence was followed by more outcry as the Captain double timed his way out of the tent through the main doors.

"I've heard enough," Gayle said. "I'm going to check on my boys." She turned to Logan and rapped out an order. "You see any of those so-and-so's who are about to cause a whole bunch of trouble coming in the direction of our tent, you head them off." She hustled out as a rising tide of dismay turned into angry and profane words, political divides becoming instantly apparent at the final bit of information about the acting President as some found it to be great news, others disastrous. A few tables away, a shoving match broke out and the reservists nearby waded in. The motion of it churned up the crowd, with more people standing and shouting. One man overturned a table while others shoved their way to the main exit.

"Who's that guy to tell us what we have to do?" A belligerent voice rang out, louder than the rest.

"He's the one in charge, dummy," someone yelled back.

"Who's calling me a dummy?"

A well-built young man stood on a table and waved his arms. "That guy's right, we're free citizens. We don't have to take his orders, we provide his paycheck!"

"He's just trying to keep us safe," a woman in the crowd countered.

"Everyone calm down," a reservist squawked, his arms flapping.

His words had a reverse effect to what he'd hoped. "You can't tell us what to do!" Voices rang out from throughout the tent.

"As long as you're staying here, you do!" Another young man, looking jittery, shouted, his young face reddening.

"We should go," Logan said quietly to Sandra and Joe. He guided them out through the kitchen. The cooks who'd been prepping the evening meal swarmed by them to join their comrades to quell the growing fray inside the mess as the trio headed out the back flap of the big tent and into the heat of the overcast summer day.

By unspoken accord, they stayed close together as they walked along the fence, not speaking until they were well away from the tent and the increased sounds of yelling emanating from it.

"I didn't see any of that crazy coming," Joe said shakily while Sandra kept glancing over her shoulder. They both were white-faced from the shock of the past few minutes. "I've never been in a meeting like that." He looked over at Logan. "I work in commercial real estate, and it's pretty calm most of the time."

"The reservists will handle it in just a few minutes," Logan assured them.

"You want to go back to our tent, honey?" Joe asked Sandra, his voice solicitous.

"No, I don't like that pair of gigantic men in there with us," she responded quickly, then blew out a breath with her hand on her belly. "Can we come to your tent instead? Just for a little while until things settle again." Loud shouts and a sharp scream blasted from the mess tent as a burst of people hurried from it and Sandra looked genuinely frightened.

"Let's at least head in that direction," Logan said diplomatically. "I'll ask Gayle if she's okay with it when we get there."

Logan eased the flap of his tent up. Gayle sat between Darien and Demarius, an arm slung around each of their shoulders. "Sorry. Are you having a private family meeting?"

"Just finishing. Come on in."

"Joe and Sandra are here too. Is it okay if they hang for a while?"

"Just the people I wanted to see." Gayle moved to her own bed while her boys stayed on their own, watching her intently. Logan sensed an odd vibe in the air as he eased down along with Joe and Sandra.

"Sorry to intrude," Sandra flapped her hands as she settled. "It's just we have these two buffalo-sized men assigned to our tent, and they haven't bathed, or..."

"She's sensitive to smells," Joe supplied.

Gayle eyed Sandra speculatively, then arched an eyebrow. "I bet you are, same thing happened to me when I was pregnant with these two. How far along are you?"

Sandra flushed, her hand going to her belly. "We just passed the three-month mark last week. It's why we were headed out to hike while we could. You know, after the dicey part of pregnancy was past, but before I get too big to do anything. We figured once the baby gets here, hiking fourteeners will be off the table for a while."

"She had zero morning sickness!" Joe announced proudly. "She's going to be a terrific mom."

Seeing their hopeful, shiny faces as they talked about their baby, Logan smiled. "Congratulations," he said, meaning it. He kept his personal reservations to himself about what bringing a child into the new world six months post disaster might be like. The pair were clearly in love and devoted to each other. If anyone could pull off having a baby after a world-wide disaster, it would be people like Sandra and Joe.

Gayle had no such compunction as she frowned, her tone taking on a scolding quality. "So are you staying, or do you plan on getting somewhere else before you're big as a house, and not able to walk ten steps without wanting to lean up against something?"

The pair exchanged looks. "Our relatives were mostly in Boston and New York. I don't know if they..." Joe trailed off. "Maybe it would be better to stay, honey."

"Stay here in a tent?" Sandra said doubtfully. "Joe, it's fine now, but in six months it'll be December. I don't think I want to experience Minnesota in winter in a tent."

"Well, me either. Me and my boys are headed back to Wichita first thing tomorrow morning," Gayle announced firmly. "And we

STACEY UPTON & MIKE KRAUS

wanted to ask if you'd travel with us," she said to Logan. "You're a capable sort of fella, seem a decent man, and we'd be much obliged to have your company and your help."

Her twins looked up at him and spoke in unison, "Please come!" Their chorus added to the punch of their mother's plea, but it felt to Logan as if they'd been coached to do so.

Logan was unhappy about being blindsided by the out-of-the-blue request, and his gut twisted in protest that she might try to trip him into making some sort of commitment. "I'm not headed as far south as Wichita. That would add a good three hundred miles or more to my journey," he said firmly.

Undaunted, Gayle kept up her full court press. "You could go that way, though. I know geography. Roanoke's a straight shot across from there, practically, and likely easier travel too. It avoids all those big cities they say have collapsed like Chicago and Cincinnati."

Her boys flinched when she mentioned Chicago, but a glance from their mother kept their mouths shut as she continued. "Logan don't tell me 'no' in a knee jerk reaction. If you think on it a moment, traveling in a group just makes sense, and we really do need you."

Gayle shifted her attention to Joe and Sandra before Logan could respond. "I wanted to offer for you two to join us as well if there's nowhere else for you to go. I have a nice three-bedroom house with a big backyard if you need a place to stay for a while, or if it's... gone, I got a patch of land with water on it we can use out in Maize. And I have several midwife friends to call on for when your time comes."

Gayle stopped talking, spread her hands out like she was offering them a generous platter of food, and then dropped them into her lap as Joe and Sandra gazed at each other in a sort of silent communication. Sandra was twisting her fingers, Joe rubbed his knee, but neither seemed capable of saying what they thought.

"You're right. Safety in numbers is a good idea," Logan finally broke the silence, keeping his voice as level as possible, even though his anger bubbled at her pushy tactics to cushion her own journey by enrolling others to go with her, the headache knotting around his skull and pulsing down his neck into his shoulders. "But I'm not going to chaperone you and your boys, Gayle. You'll need to find someone else. I plan to travel fast and light, and on a diagonal, which is the shortest distance between two points."

Gayle continued to press. "We wouldn't burden you. My boys are sturdy. They'll walk as long as you say they need to every day, and I will too. I don't know anything about living off of the land, or camping, but I'm a good worker, and if you tell any of us to do something, we'll do it."

"You're not going to talk me into it, Gayle. That's enough." Logan stood, needing to escape the confines of the tent before his head exploded.

"I thought you were a good man," she replied, her clear disappointment cutting deeply into Logan, where her pushiness had failed.

"What?"

"Um, Sandra and I are going to think about it," Joe said quickly, and gave his wife a hand to stand, pushing her in front of him to leave. He turned to Gayle. "I appreciate your offer. We'll let you know in an hour." They hurried out of the tent.

Gayle brushed a hand at Logan as if she was done with him, and her voice was frigid. "Well, you said no. I guess you can just go do what you're going to do."

The woman was treating him like he was some sort of disappointing toy that hadn't worked properly or to her liking. "My being good or bad doesn't have anything to do with my decision! You're doing what's right for your boys. I'm going to do what's right for my kids, too."

Logan strode out of the tent, intent on walking off his boiling temper outside of the confines of the encampment. He didn't get ten steps before his way was blocked by Jasper Collins, who slapped a hand on his chest to stop him, and bounced on his toes with his cheesy grin. "I was just coming to find you, my homesteading friend who knows oh-so-much about oh-so-many-things. I'm collecting a group of people to travel with over to the upper peninsula of Michigan, where I have a bit of land that has water on it. It'd only be a little out of your way, and there'd be some good money in it for you at the end, or a spot to plop if you need it, you know, if your family didn't survive this." The obtuse man actually chuckled after he said the words.

Logan blew past anger and went straight to fury at the intimation that his family was dead. He shook his head in vehement disagreement, the movement of it creating severe nausea from the full-blown migraine that had taken root. "I'm not a guide for you to hire," he managed to say, before he scooted past the man.

Jasper grasped his arm to stop him, then poked Logan in the belly and chuckled. "You gotta think bigger, my backwoods friend."

"We're not friends, Jasper." Logan replied through gritted teeth. "Now please get out of my way." He moved to get around Jasper a second time, but impossibly, the man stepped in his path again.

"Not so fast, not so fast. I'm talking good money, and no more than a week or two or three of your time." The man bounced as he made his points. "I already have some beefy muscle for our group, and a couple of women who can do the cooking and the cleaning for us. I need a handy guy, and that is you. You're a valuable commodity, Logan, with that brain full of how to make shelters and fires and whatnot, and me and some others are willing to pay top dollar. Be a good man and say yes." The cheesy grin came back, as if Jasper was sure he'd sealed the deal as he wagged a playful finger. "I won't take no for an—"

Jasper's words were cut short as Logan stepped back and punched him square in the face.

CHAPTER SEVENTEEN

The Blacksburg-Pembroke Fault
Day Two

Mara and Will had prepared their evening meal for the family outside over the firepit, Will taking particular joy in turning their squashed loaves of bread into what he called 'toasty sticks.' He'd rolled the decimated loaves out, then salted and spun the resulting dough around green sticks he'd cut to toast above the fire while Mara had made a soup filled with bounty from their garden, as well as some hearty skillet herb omelets with the last of the eggs. Mara's back screamed at her as she pulled the heavy pot off of the heat, but the aroma of the soup was enticing, filled as it was with diced tomatoes, peppers, celery, zucchini, onions, and potatoes, the broth seasoned with fresh garlic, oregano, and thyme.

Caroline had shown up when the cooking was nearly done, taken one look at their progress, then gone to set the table inside in complete silence. She'd eaten with them in silence as well, disappearing into her room immediately after clearing her bowl and plate to the kitchen sink. Her continuing anger at Mara had been deadly to the spirits of everyone, the unease she created spreading to all of them no matter how many pleasant subjects Mara tried to bring up to diffuse it. Will had eyed his sister throughout the meal, but hadn't needled or teased her, and even Ethan had caught the unhappy mood, as glad as he'd initially been to get up from his bed for the hour, he was quick to navigate his way back to his room after he'd eaten, refusing any sort of help as he used the new crutches.

Depressed by the feud she'd wanted no part of, and every bone in her body aching, Mara did all the washing up and evening chores on her own, instead of asking for help from the clearly furious girl or her brother, who'd also disappeared into his own room. Mara dragged her way through them, not finishing putting up the goats and chickens until it was almost full dark. Using the Coleman lantern, she went in to check on her son with a glass of clean water for him and found Ethan straining to read a book by candlelight, propped up with extra pillows.

"You take your pain meds?"

"Yes, mom." He focused on his book.

"Okay then, I'll leave you to it." Mara brushed back a curl. "Tomorrow you're going to take a bath whether you want to or not. Maybe first thing, while we change these sheets." Everything she touched had a gritty feel, a result of the dusty air outside.

"At least it'll be something to do. I feel like a jerk just laying here all day."

"You're healing, that's your job, to get healthy as fast as possible. Then I promise I'll make you work until you weep for me to relent."

He handed her back the cell phone. "I think it's dead. I tried to call Aunt Deb and Logan like you asked, but there was never a signal." He eyed her critically. "You need a bath yourself, mom."

"Tomorrow. I'll wash myself along with the sheets, and we'll rig a line in the cellar for them to dry." She smiled at an old memory. "My aunt Helen used to dry everything on clotheslines, she used these old-fashioned wooden pegs. We hung them outside in summer, though. If we did that now, we'd have grimier sheets than we had before."

"You think the dirty air is going to last a long time?"

She rubbed her eyes tiredly. "I have zero answers, son. I'm basically making all of this up as I go along."

Ethan looked away and made a little sound in the back of his throat, the way he always did when he wanted to say something, but wasn't sure how to proceed. Mara folded her hands in her lap as Ethan sorted out his thoughts.

"You know how you just told me the truth, just then?" He finally said softly and waited for her to nod before he continued. "You need to do that with Caroline for sure, and probably Will, too. You're trying to be all perfect and pulled together in front of them, I get that. Maybe in normal circumstances, that might be a good idea. But it's not now. You need to trust them like you trust me. They deserve that."

It was a long speech from her normally taciturn son, a considered one that forced her to both see him as someone on the cusp of manhood, no longer her little boy, and to listen to him. He'd passed beyond needing her for everything when he went into high school three years ago, and now the rest of him was catching up and he was becoming his own man with his own ideas and take on the world. Tears welled at the loss of those younger days as she met his sincere gaze. He slipped it away from her again, glancing at the book where he held his place with his fingertips.

"Okay," she said softly, then smoothed the bed cover before taking up her lantern. "Okay. I'll try that."

"You should probably start now," he added when she was nearly out of his room. "That dinner was pretty uncomfortable."

"Yep, it was."

She'd almost closed the door all the way when Ethan spoke again. "And mom?" She leaned back in. "I love you."

"I love you too, Ethan. See you in the morning."

She rested against his door after it clicked shut, eyeing Caroline's door just across the hall. She saw a glimmer of flickering candlelight underneath it, evidence that the girl was still awake.

"Oh, boy." Mara muttered. What she really wanted to do was to crawl upstairs to bed and sleep for hours on end, but Ethan was right, the anger needed to be addressed and not allowed to fester and grow. She tapped softly. "Caroline, it's me. Can we talk for a moment?"

The light beneath the door wavered. Maybe the kid was just going to blow out her candle and keep quiet in the dark so that she'd be forced to slink away like a rejected door-to-door salesman. Not that there were such things anymore, but the metaphor was right, especially that complete rejection part. Mara dug her fingers into her hair, rubbing her scalp where the beginning of a headache grew, then tapped again, her courage barely bobbing on the surface. "Caroline?"

The door yanked open suddenly, startling her, the hand holding the lantern jerking and sending wild shadows dancing up and down the narrow hallway. Caroline stood in the partially open space, her hand still on the knob as if she might shut it again in an instant, her gawky, slender body blocking the entry to her room. "What?"

In for a penny, in for a pound. The old saying echoed in Mara's head as she steadied the lantern and took in Caroline's defiant glare, the crossed arms defensively guarding her heart, the tender skin under the eyes still swollen as if she'd had another bout of crying since dinner, opened her mouth and let the truth drop out. "I'm scared, too."

Caroline stared at her a long beat before she stated flatly, "You're the adult, you're not allowed to be scared."

The blunt assessment bubbled a short laugh from Mara. "Heh. Yeah, well, that trope needs to be rewritten." Bafflement crossed Caroline's features. "Sorry, that was librarian-speak, a trope is a well-defined expectation for a genre, one that readers expect."

"I know what a trope is. What do you want, Mara?" The slight emphasis on her name gave it a derogatory slant, as if the girl hated the sound of it.

"For you and me to be on the same page. As much as I'd love to be the all-knowing adult in the room, the truth is, I have no idea what tomorrow is going to look like, or how exactly we're going to deal with it. I can't fight with you on top of that and expect to get anything done."

As if underscoring her words, the house unexpectedly shook and jolted, causing them both to grab the doorframe at the same time, the lantern swinging wildly, casting the light to and fro like they were in some sort of old horror movie as the roll shook the house. Caroline stopped the sway of the lamp as the trembler finally eased to a stop, and as her hand passed the invisible boundary that had separated them to do so, Mara reached out to push back an errant tumbling curl from Caroline's face, just as she would have done for Ethan. Caroline startled backwards from the near-touch, her own hand rising from the Coleman to bat Mara's hand away.

"I don't want to be mothered by you! I'm almost sixteen!"

Weariness battled with annoyance as Mara dug into the last remaining dregs of her patience so as to not just turn and leave the girl to her ill temper. "Well, then, what do you want?"

"I already told you, I want my dad."

Mara matched her intensity. "So do I, Caroline. More than just about anything. But we don't get to have him, at least for the next day or so, maybe longer than that, so what else?"

Caroline let out a huff of impatience. "I get that you're like, a city person and you don't know how to do much on the homestead, and I get you think you can read about something in a book and know how to do it, but as far as I can tell, that doesn't get us very far on the survival road."

The words hurt, but to be fair, there was some truth to them. Mara's jaw hurt from clamping her teeth together to stop herself from protesting or explaining herself. "Okay, that's fair," she managed around her clenched jaw. "What's your point?"

"So maybe, you should ask us about stuff to do with the homestead, instead of making declarations and running around like you're some sort of one-person army. Include us. Or at least me. Dad taught us a lot of stuff while we were growing up."

"Just what do you think I've done that was so wrong, Caroline?"

Caroline broke eye contact as she snapped her mouth shut, eyes shifting left the way Ethan's did when a thought had captured him. Mara's energy and patience dribbled away as they stood there in silence, a slight trembling of the earth vibrating against her feet as a reminder that anything could happen at any moment, exhausting her even further. She forced herself to wait it out and see what the girl was thinking, just as she had done for Ethan. Mara shifted her body weight to ease the tension in her back, the movement pulling Caroline from her distant reverie.

She started slowly. "Look, I don't exactly hate you, okay? I just... you don't keep your word, Mara, I can't trust you. We didn't go to the Buchanan's like you promised me we would do yesterday to try the landline, then you were all weird when the neighbors who had just rescued you wanted to help you just a little bit more. You were really rude to Eva and Lloyd after they dropped us off. We might need their help in the next few days or weeks, you know? It was a dumb move."

Shocked silent by Caroline's assessment when all she'd been doing was trying to protect them, Mara braced herself on the door as Caroline went on, the words tumbling out of her faster and faster as she counted on her fingers all the ways that Mara had messed up. "We lost two of our bikes, we didn't get what we needed at the hardware store or the pharmacy, we didn't start fixing the fence line, and you used the last of the eggs for dinner instead of saving them for breakfast. The hens are off their feed, one of our bee hives swarmed and left, and you didn't bank the fire after you finished cooking the soup, so it burned to ash, so we'll have to start it again."

Mara didn't care for being verbally slapped over and over again, or for the seven fingers Caroline waved in her face as proof of her incompetence. "I'm doing the best I know how."

She took a breath to enumerate what she had accomplished, but Caroline bowled over her. "Exactly. It's not good enough, Mara. You have to do better. We all have to do better, or we're not going to make it through this earthquake thing, or its aftermath. It scares me to be partnered with someone who doesn't know what they're doing." The last words dribbled out slowly as if the girl had been reluctant to say them, or perhaps the brutal truth of them frightened her. Caroline stopped talking as she scrubbed her nose with the back of her hand, then re-crossed her arms, challenging Mara to refute what she'd said.

Mara swallowed and counted to ten as she considered the best way to move forward after the drubbing she'd just received. "Okay, what do you think we should do first tomorrow? Besides the regular morning chores and rebuilding the fire, heating water, and having very strong coffee, because that is a must for me."

Caroline seemed startled that she was actually being consulted, and she eyed Mara suspiciously. "Well, I think we need to pull some meat from the freezer for our evening meal, because we'll need the protein, especially if the hens have stopped laying because they're freaked out. Then you make a list for the pharmacy and the hardware store, and I'll use the ATV to go to those stores, then after that, I'll go to the Buchanan's and see if we can use their phone, while Will goes to the Larcher's store again on his bike to buy some not-squashed or broken food to get us through the next few days." She put a hand up before Mara could protest.

"I know you don't want Will going there by himself, but your back needs rest, just like Ethan has to let his leg heal. You're going to put yourself completely out of commission if you keep trying to do stuff, and then we'll be in even worse shape than we are now. Will has been to the Larcher's a hundred times on his own. He can do it."

Caroline was making excellent points, Mara had to admit. As much as it went against the grain to let Logan's children out of her sight, dividing up what they had to do, at least for tomorrow, made sense. "And what am I doing while you two are out doing those things?"

"Gardening and cleaning the cellar," Caroline answered promptly. "Ethan would probably jump at the chance to help you do some of that before Mr. Athlete loses his mind lying in bed for another day. The last thing I want is a crabby-patty stepbrother to deal with." She smiled a little and added, "He's okay for a stepbrother most of the time, though."

The girl had her father's knack for softening hard realities, Mara realized. The thought of her husband made the tough conversation slightly more bearable. This was his daughter, someone he trusted and loved. As his wife, she needed to find a way to trust her and love her, even if Caroline never returned the favor. "I'm glad to hear you think so. I think Ethan likes you, too."

"Ethan just tolerates all of us mere mortals, you know that, right?"

Mara chuckled at the wry assessment. "He can be a little superior sometimes, that's true. It's to cover up that he's a big softie underneath it all."

There was a lull in the conversation, and Mara thought they'd probably accomplished all they could tonight. "Well, good night, Caroline."

"So, are we going to go with my plan tomorrow morning?" The challenge was back in her voice, but the implied need for Mara to agree with her was something to build on.

"As much as I want to cave to this wave of almost-good feeling between us and just say yes, I need to sleep on it," Mara said. "But I have to admit they are sound ideas, and I'm glad we had a talk."

Caroline nodded. "That's fair, I guess." The sulky tone was back, as if it had never left.

"Good night."

She'd taken several steps away from the door when Caroline softly called out, "Hey." Mara swung the lantern around, hissing as her back protested the movement. Caroline continued, "I'll make the coffee in the morning. You sleep in if you can. I don't want a crabby-patty for a stepmom either." The girl quirked an eyebrow and gave Mara a little smile before she shut her door.

"Okay, that was progress," Mara said to herself as she slowly ascended the stairs, mentally shaking her head at the girl's last words. "Uncomfortable progress, but better is better."

CHAPTER EIGHTEEN

The New Madrid Fault
Day Two

Step, step, pause. Step, step, pause. Re-grip handles, start again. Deb and her stretcher partner Giles had found a rhythm that worked as they carried their load over the rough and tumbled boneyard that used to be Memphis. During especially difficult passages, they'd put down their stretcher, move to help Tom and Maritza heave theirs over a wall or a wide tumble of building, the four of them pushing and shoving until the precious burden cleared the obstacle, then returning, carefully stepping around the waxy-skinned bodies that were starting to bloat in the heat of midday to pick up Deb and Giles' stretcher full of food and water and navigate it together over the same terrible terrain. The group of four did it all mostly without speaking, except for occasional directional comments when something got stuck on the edge of a building or smashed piece of furniture that they responded to with grunts, all their energy needed for the lifting and walking.

At least there was no blinding sun to add to their misery, as the heavy overcast of ash and debris had gotten discernably thicker since they'd first stepped out into a new reality of greyed skies some eight hours ago, but the humidity was still going strong, creating rivulets of sweat that continuously dripped to the broken ground. Deb had been used to the climate of Memphis, inured to sweating when outside, even welcoming the healthy gloss of it on her arms and legs as she did her daily runs in the days before yesterday, but her most recent sweating was an entirely new category, a combination of slow, soaking wet that became dripping streams. The unceasing dampness of their bodies attracted the floating dirt in the air, coating all of them with a fine silica so that they all resembled inhuman walking statues slowly making their way back to St. Jude's hospital, feet slipping in the sticky mud and decaying water plants left behind from the river's overflow.

There were more tremors, too, ones that had them dropping to hands and knees to ride them out. Some were sharp snaps that tossed rubble into the air like the first kernels of popcorn in a pan while others were a slow roll, lifting entire sections of the city in a single wave, making solid earth look like a liquid ocean filled with litter bobbing on four-foot waves that undulated unopposed across the landscape. After each of them, more bits of buildings fell, forcing them to walk as far away from any standing structures as possible, even if it sent them more than a block off course, as the tremors were entirely unpredictable and dangerous.

"I see it!" Maritza's voice was hoarse and muffled by her mask. The little force of nature waved an arm and pointed to the miraculously still-standing wing of the hospital they'd been aiming for. "Maybe a quarter mile to go."

"Thank all the pretty stars in heaven," remarked Giles, wiping his arm across his forehead as they placed their stretcher down to guzzle water, making a momentary pink streak in his dull grey coating of dust.

"You can say that again," Deb said after she swallowed her own long drink, tucking her half-full water bottle back under a strap. "No, don't!" she said sharply as the man playfully opened his mouth to repeat the sentence, shaking a finger at him.

He grinned, white teeth remarkably bright in his dirty face, the movement making cracks along the dusty coating around his mouth and eyes, reminding Deb of the historical pictures she'd seen of coal miners just emerged from the deep shafts captured from the turn of the last century. There was a sharp crack from behind Deb, and a whoosh of air passed near her, puffing the strands of hair to flap in front of her. The smile was ripped from Giles' face in an instant as bright red blood burst into bloom on his left cheek. He clapped his hand to the space where the side of his face had been, staring with incomprehension as it came away soaked in blood.

"What?" He was dazed, looking to Deb for some sort of explanation as he sank to his knees.

"Shooter." Deb tried to shout, but couldn't make her voice work right away, the single word coming out like a whispered order from a mother to a child to hush rather than an urgent warning. "Shooter!" she tried again, this time the word bursting out loud and clear as more shots popped around her. "Run! Run!"

Maritza and Tom turned around at her screams, mouths gaping as they looked behind her. She whipped around to see three men with their guns pointed directly at her, appearing and disappearing as they maneuvered around the same obstacles she'd recently cleared with Giles. She ducked as more bullets winged past her, Giles doing the same as the shots ricocheted off of broken concrete and slammed into destroyed cars with a ratta-tat-tat.

Deb's initial confusion bloomed into understanding as garbled shouts behind her demanded they leave the stretcher with its food behind.

"They want the supplies," Deb shouted to Giles. "Can you pick up your end?"

Giles nodded, the remaining piece of his cheek flapping loosely where it hung off of his face. Tears poured out of him, his eyes bugging in abject terror as he turned and picked up his two handles, surging forward, while Deb stumbled to keep up with his sudden jerky move. They crouched and trotted forward in a fast bent-kneed walk, her thigh muscles bunching and her calves cramping with each step.

She kept going, ignoring the pain, all the while expecting to feel a bullet slam into her at any moment as they hustled as fast as they could toward St. Jude's, Giles leaving a spattered trail of blood as he went. Deb was forced to keep her eyes on the ground in front of her to keep her footing, making her spine crawl with the knowledge that the men were right behind her, unburdened, and closing fast.

There had been a brief lull in the firing then another crack, louder and closer, hit the pile of food they were carrying. With a cry of fear, Giles dropped his end, whipping around as he stumbled and fell hard on his hip.

"Are you hit?"

He shook his head, but pointed behind her and Deb whirled. The men were only a few yards away, grinning as they closed in, focused on the prize of a pile of food and water, guns ready to take her down. Bending, she grabbed a piece of rubble and hurled it at them, but missed, merely halting them for a moment. Furious, weeping in fear and anger, Deb scrabbled for more to throw as they advanced ever closer.

The sound of a gunshot firing from behind her made Deb flinch, then Maritza's voice bellowed, "Back off!"

The woman stood erect, a pistol in her hand, a steely look in her eye. Behind Maritza, Tom continued moving to the hospital, dragging their bundle like a travois, muscles bunching in his neck as he powered forward on his own, the bottom handles bumping and clattering behind him. Maritza marched forward, a pink and purple snub-nosed revolver steady in her hand as she seemed to glide effortlessly through the rubble, her focus wholly on the people who'd attacked them.

"These supplies are for sick children! How dare you try to take it?" Her fury was evident with every word, every step. The men who were the object of her fury backed away several feet.

"We'll take what we want to take!" One of them snarled, lifting his gun to point at Maritza.

Deb whipped out her half-empty water bottle and threw it at him while his attention was on Maritza, smacking him dead center in the face, throwing off his aim, the bullet zinging into the air. He swiveled toward her, rage contorting his face into a rictus smile as he aimed the black pistol directly at her. Deb bent and yanked another water bottle and threw it just as Maritza fired, the sound loud in Deb's ears as her friend stepped next to her.

In a moment, Deb had three more bottles wiggled from beneath the straps holding them to the stretcher, throwing them at the three men as Maritza fired her weapon a third time, hitting one of them who went down clutching his arm with a scream, his gun flying from his grasp. One of the other men dropped his pistol as he bent to his companion, leaving only one still firing at them.

"You want food? Here's food!" Deb screamed, throwing package after package straight at him as fast as she could, causing him to throw up his arm to shield his face and body from her relentless barrage. "Eat it!"

"Grab those!" the man who was down yelled at his companions, his voice cracking into a higher register. He was just a teenager, as was the one who'd bent to him who was scrambling to gather the food packages, stuffing them into the front of his shirt as the final remaining gunman backed away a few steps after Deb's next water bottle missile caught him in the neck. Maritza took careful aim and fired at his feet, backing him up still further.

"You've only got two more bullets in that little thing. How're you going to use them?" The lead man challenged Maritza, waving his Glock at her. "I still got plenty of nines." He was older than the other two, but not by much perhaps a year or two into his twenties, a thin fuzz of scrubby beard marking his chin, his skin covered in dirt, just as theirs was.

"You sure about that?" Giles called out to him, the words coming out slurred from his ruined face.

"Seventeen plus one," the man bragged as he took a swaggering step forward. "Plenty."

"You don't want to steal from the kids in that hospital." Maritza sounded sure of herself. "You're going to take what your friend has in his shirt, and go."

"I want all of it." He stepped closer, his gun aimed at Giles, who'd staggered to his feet. "You'd best leave it and get your man some help."

235

Deb had one more water bottle in her hand and raised it. He turned to her, his voice pitching up a notch in aggravation. "I swear if you throw that those at me, I am going to kill you. In fact," he took another step closer, lifting the Glock as he did so, "I—"

His next words were lost as Maritza fired a bullet into his heart, hitting the center mass of his thin frame precisely. He staggered back, the gun dropping from his hand as he looked down at the spreading blood that pulsed from his body with a bewildered look on his face, sinking to his knees. His companions cried out as he crumpled without another word to the broken ground.

"Go," Maritza ordered Deb and Giles, her voice choked, but keeping her focus on the men. "I'm right behind you."

Nausea rising in her gut, and freezing cold at her core, her arms shaking and hands numb, Deb picked up her end of the stretcher and did her best to run with it, following in Giles' footsteps as they traversed the final stretch to the hospital. They hit the final hundred yards that someone had thought to clear of rubble and was able to lift her head from the ground. Ahead, four people in scrubs and masks ran out to help Tom bring in his load over the last fifty yards as he collapsed to his knees, utterly spent. Three more hospital workers followed them, charging toward Giles and herself.

Tears coursed down Deb's cheeks along with the ever-present stream of sweat, her nose running as well, but she forced her legs to keep moving at a jog, her fear and weariness washing away as the gap between herself, and the hospital closed. Despite her tears, a huge grin formed in recognition of what they'd accomplished. Deb looked back to be sure Maritza was close, reassured that she was right behind them, still holding her purple and pink gun at the ready as she followed, her stride lengthening when she hit the cleared section.

Three bright flashes caught Deb's eye a microsecond before the sound of the three gunshots echoed across the plaza. She ducked instinctively, stumbling on her weak ankle as she did so, the stretcher falling along with her. Her knee barked in pain as she landed on it with the full weight of her body. Deb rolled to her feet, hopping as her knee threatened to give way again, facing back the way they'd just come. Maritza was sprawled on the ground and the youngest teen was standing mere feet away from her, the gun still aimed at Maritza's back, his shirt bulging with the food packages he'd gathered just minutes before.

"You killed my brother!" He shouted thickly, his reedy, high-pitched voice shaking with emotion. "You hurt my cousin!" He sobbed, then dropped his gun arm and stumbled away.

"Maritza!" Deb called out as she hobbled back, but the woman laid utterly still, arms and legs akimbo, a dark splotch spreading from beneath her.

Deb reached the little Filipino and saw that two out of the three bullets had struck Maritza in the back, two tidy holes, one low by her kidneys, one dead center of her back through her spine. Reaching into the calm that she always accessed when working with trauma patients, Deb let the rest of the world fall away and focused only on her patient as she gently turned Maritza over, prepared for the worst from her long experience in the ER as her friend's limbs flopped without resistance.

The large exit wound through the vaporized kidneys was responsible for the red tide pouring from the woman's body. The other bullet must have lodged in her spine, for there was no sign of it having penetrated. Maritza's eyes were wide open, staring, and as Deb gently removed her mask, her breath caught. Maritza had been smiling when her life was taken from her. Deb used her fingers to close the woman's eyes gently, stroked back the dark curling hair from Maritza's still-sweating forehead and murmured softly as she often did to the recently departed, sure that somehow the last vestiges of spirit lingered for a while after death.

"We did it, the food is here, your plan worked, Maritza, you can rest. We're going to feed the doctors and your nurses and the all the children today and in the days to come because of you. Well done."

Grief and exhaustion formed a cocoon around her, muffling feeling and experience. Deb was aware that others came and lifted the lifeless body so they could take it inside, that vague voices murmured beyond her comprehension to hear them, that there was a touch on the shoulder, encouragement to stand and come with them, but she remained rooted where she was, all of her strength evaporated. Deb was sure that the staff would clean Maritza's body and give her a proper sendoff and she knelt, staring at the empty space where Maritza had fallen. The little pink and purple Ruger, with its single remaining bullet, lay to one side where lifeless fingers had let it fall, and Deb picked it up. She held it in her hands for a long moment before she stood, her movements shaky on her injured ankle and knee, then wiped the splatter of blood from the little gun before she tucked it into the back of her dusty, blood-soaked scrubs, and limped the final paces into the hospital.

The next few hours passed in a blur as Jenny, the woman she'd rescued from her floating car just the day before, helped her strip off her destroyed scrubs and slipped her shoes off of her feet. Jenny helped her take a cold sponge bath, and even washed her hair for her as Deb slipped in and out of an exhausted haze that fell into an occasional doze, punctuated by Jenny pushing beverages into her hand, forcing her to continue to replenish her fluids, and then laid her on the floor with a pillow and a blanket, holding her until Deb drifted away again.

Deb might have slept for hours or only minutes, she wasn't quite sure, but when she swarmed back to consciousness, she found four-year-old Mattie looking at her with grave eyes, the child gently stroking her arm with fingers as light as butterfly feet. "Are you waked up?" the little girl asked in a whisper. Deb managed to nod, and Mattie vanished, coming back a few moments later with her mom.

"Hey, Deb. You're looking better." Jenny said, as she helped her to sit against the wall. "I heard Coke is your drink of choice, here you go." She handed her an entire can, and even though it was warm, Deb drank thirstily, nearly polishing off the whole container before letting it drop from her lips.

"I'd be belching up a storm if I did that," Jenny said after a moment.

It pulled a weak smile from Deb as she pointed at herself. "World-class chugger, right here. A skill set that was very valuable in college."

Jenny smiled back, then hesitated. "Want me to fill you in?" After

Deb nodded, she turned to Mattie. "Honey, can you go find our friend a sandwich from the cart, please?" She pointed to a nurse who stood with a cart a few feet away. Mattie nodded and scampered off.

Deb's stomach growled at the idea of food. "How long have I been out?"

"Four hours or so. Everyone's been busy. Tom, not the one that went with you this time, but the other one who took the rebar through his shoulder, he kind of took charge. I guess he and Maritza were a couple, so everyone agreed to what he said without question."

"You could do worse for a leader," Deb agreed, thinking about his positive, can-do attitude from their first expedition. "I didn't know they were together."

"It was one of those well-kept secrets, I guess."

"So what does Other Tom have people doing?"

"The biggest thing is that he sent a bunch of orderlies and patient parents over to the pyramid, to where that huge sporting goods place was, and they dug around to pull out guns and ammo and other survival gear like MREs. That group just got back a while ago with a whole lot of stuff and went back for more. Your Tom told him about Maritza's plan to dig out the kitchens here to salvage supplies, so there are people doing that, but someone just told me it may be buried under too much heavy rubble to get to it."

"Is Giles okay?"

"Yes, one of the doctors is a reconstructive facial specialist, so he's in good hands. He'll probably come out of it with just a minimal scar, is what I heard. Tom is okay too, except he was suffering from severe dehydration and exhaustion like you."

Jenny stopped her litany and looked at Deb with concern. "I saw you were limping when you came in, but no one's seen to anything like that for you. I just told them I'd take care of you and got out of the way. I wrapped a bandage around your knee, but I don't know if I did it right."

"I really appreciate it."

"You had this." Jenny pulled the pink and purple gun from her waistband. "I didn't know what you wanted to do with it."

"I should probably ask Tom about it," Deb said thoughtfully, tucking it behind her as Mattie approached, bearing a sandwich and another wrapped bag.

"They had brownies," the little girl said, nearly reverentially as she handed the packages over. "I got two!"

Deb smiled at her breathless excitement. "Thank you, Mattie. You know, I don't think I could eat two whole brownies, could you eat one for me? If it's okay with your Mom?"

"I sure can! Right mom?"

"As long as I get a bite!"

The three ate their food together in companionable silence. Deb considered what her next moves needed to be in light of what had happened, although it was a struggle to think about anything, as images of Maritza fallen beneath a bullet continued to flash. She'd not ever considered that looters would try to attack them, willing and able to kill, and it scared her to the bone to go back out among them. She still yearned to get to Saint Francis hospital and her friends, and there was still her strong pull to head to Roanoke and leave Memphis entirely. Deb licked her fingers of the last vestiges of chocolate as she let her thoughts spin down into plans. There would be time to grieve Maritza privately later, but for the moment, Deb was most worried about Junior Senior and his son, who didn't have any sort of protection that she'd noticed, and they'd popped to the top of her concerns list.

"Is it still daylight out?" She asked Jenny, having lost all track of time.

"It is, it's maybe six o'clock, so another three hours of daylight left."

"Good, can you help me find the Tom who's in charge?" She groaned as she forced her stiffened limbs to move, scooping up the gun as she did so and noticing she just had on socks and no shoes. Jenny followed her line of sight.

"Your shoes were covered with—" she broke off, looking at her daughter. "Lots of things, so I cleaned them as best I could. They're over with our stuff in the corner."

They walked to the waiting room area where the people who'd made their way to the hospital in the early hours of the disaster had been placed. Jenny and Mattie had claimed a small section for themselves, equipping it with blankets and pillows and a little pile of toys.

Jenny handed Deb her running shoes, which she promptly put back on, even if they were still a bit damp. "Thank you for doing all that for me," Deb told Jenny. "And for finding me real clothes instead of scrubs." She indicated the jeans and blue t-shirt she wore, along with a pair of bright pink socks.

"Sure, they were in a closet of donations. I just guessed at the sizes. Oh, here's a hair tie, too." Jenny pulled a scrunchie from her pocket.

"Mommy, that's your scrunchie!"

"And now it's Deb's," her mother responded evenly with a special smile for Deb.

"Thanks." Deb pulled her long brown hair off her neck and into a looped up ponytail, the tidy action of the motion steeling her resolve. "Listen, I think I'm going to the hospital where I work, and then on from there back to Roanoke, where my sister lives sooner rather than later."

Jenny gave her hand a squeeze and nodded her understanding. "I figured you might. Thank you for all you've done for us. Mattie and I are going to stay here for a while, and help as we can."

Deb nodded, then bent to Mattie. "Thanks again for my brownie, Mattie, and for watching over me while I slept."

The little girl nodded, looked at her with her big blue eyes, then reached her arms up and hugged Deb around the neck. "Bye."

"I think Tom is probably at the front desk," Jenny told her. "Be safe out there; we'll be praying for you."

Deb walked slowly, letting the aches ease out as she went to the front atrium. Tom was indeed there, manning the post where Deb had first met Maritza. Her eyes hazed with unshed tears as she approached, and Tom saw her.

"Tom, I'm so sorry about Maritza," Deb said. "She saved our lives out there."

"She was the best," he said, then narrowed his gaze. "You've got ideas popping in that head of yours, I can tell."

"I want to go warn the Juniors, or maybe even take people to help them guard their place," she told him, and then explained the situation she thought the father and son might find themselves in. "I don't know if you can reach Spencer at the VA anymore," she concluded, "but they need to be warned about what happened to us and that there's a significant danger for them when they come out to meet us on Monday. What do you think?"

Tom grimaced as he held up a radio. "This thing is barely working, it's just gotten to where it's static on all the channels. I think it has something to do with the dust, blocking the signal or something. I agree with you, though, about warning them both and providing protection if they'll take it."

"Then we'd need to go to the VA hospital, too. How many guns did you get from the sporting goods store at the pyramid?"

He gave what passed for a smile. "Lots. And ammo, too. After what happened, I knew we had to get some right away..." his words drifted off as he glanced out of the doors in the direction where Maritza had fallen. "I didn't know it was possible to miss someone so much."

Deb pulled Maritza's gun out of her waistband. "I picked this up, did you want to have it?"

He took it from her, weighed it in the palm of his hand. "Her Ruger LCR. She named it, 'Honey,'" he smiled a bit with remembrance. "Maritza was a dead shot, you know? She took me a few times to the range she liked to use, would just annihilate me. Maritza'd hit a cluster of center mass, every time. She'd say, 'Tom, if I'm going to be working at a hospital in the middle of a big city in the south by the front doors, I'm going to be packing!'" He did a good imitation of her incisive speech pattern, then inhaled sharply as he pinched the bridge of his nose. Deb looked away, not wanting to intrude on his grief.

"So, do you know how to shoot?" Tom asked when he could speak again.

"Yes. I don't go to the range as much as when I was in nursing school, trying to blow off steam, but I can shoot."

"Then I think she'd want you to have Honey," Tom said after a long minute. "It takes thirty-eights, and we got a bunch of that from that store. You take it, and keep yourself safe. Maritza would like that. She liked you, called you a hum-zinger, which was good in her book."

Deb nodded and took the gun back from him. "I want to leave as soon as possible, with a couple of guns for the Juniors and some for the VA, too. I don't think they have a sporting goods store anywhere around them. It's summertime, so we've still got a good three hours or so of light left."

"Then what? Are you coming back?"

"No, going on."

"Maritza said she figured you wouldn't stay, not that she was happy about that." He spread his arms wide and shrugged. "If we can't keep you, let's get you loaded up right."

Half an hour later, Deb, Other Tom, and four more men were ready to move out. Each carried a brand new, sturdy backpack filled with extra masks, flashlights, waters, compact first aid kits, MREs, ammunition and an array of handguns, as well as a couple of Mossberg Patriot rifles each, one slung over each shoulder. They all wore sturdy hiking boots and socks. Deb had been further outfitted with a rain jacket and tarp, a multi-tool, a fire striker ferro rod, and extra MREs by Tom.

He patiently showed her how to use the ferro rod, using some old charts as the fire starter in the sink of the nurse's locker room, making her do it over and over again. Deb failed miserably for her first seven tries, but got it to spark and light on the eighth. "I'm no camper," she admitted.

"You said you were going cross-country, so you're going to have to turn into one if the rest of the USA is like Memphis. Let me show you how to load and put on a pack so your shoulders aren't crying after an hour."

Deb staggered a bit the first time she stood up under the weight of the pack, but quickly learned how to put it on so that she was mainly carrying the weight on her hips. She added her little plastic bag of extras and more socks that she'd been holding on to since she'd first arrived, and tied her running shoes front to back with a clove hitch in the laces to attach them to the back of her pack under Tom's watchful eye.

"You can tie knots, but you've never camped?"

"We learned knots, me, and my sister, to earn a girl scout badge. It stuck with me." Deb finished attaching the shoes with a bungee cord to make sure they didn't bounce around. Honey had been reloaded and was belted onto her waist, while the extra ammo for the Ruger was tucked into an easily accessible side pocket.

Deb hefted the bag a second time, tightened the hip belt, adjusted the shoulder straps, and snapped the sternum strap together, obtaining Tom's approval. "Ready," she said as she swung her two rifles onto her shoulders and taking a few practice steps with the load. The hiking boots were like fifty pound weights on each foot compared to her running shoes, but their durability and stability would be far more useful on her trek.

Other Tom saw them off, handing a radio to Tom at the last moment. "Just in case we can get them working again." He gave a paper map to Deb. "Thought a map of metro Memphis might be helpful, since nothing looks the same anymore."

The group stepped into the gloom of late afternoon, the dust in the air still swirling and gathering into an ever-thickening cloud cover. Deb paused once to look back and wave a hand at whoever might be watching from the big windows, then paced with the rest of the crew. She kept a sharp lookout for any movement beyond their own, especially after they passed the place where they'd been ambushed before, but didn't see another living soul.

With Tom leading the way, they made good time back across the wasteland of Memphis, but even so, the mile and a half journey took them nearly two hours to complete. The delicious aroma of barbequing meat reached them long before the sight of the restaurant did, making Deb grumble. "It's like they have a neon sign or a loudspeaker, 'Please come take my food,'" she groused.

"You didn't say that last time we were here," Tom said, falling back to walk with her.

"That was before people tried to rob us and shot Maritza. I can't believe it devolved into that behavior so fast."

He waved a hand at the decimated landscape. "The stores are gone, electricity gone, running water gone. The law is gone. People will survive any way they can, is the way I see it."

"Tom," she started and then stopped, what she needed to say weighing heavily on her. "You do know the hospital is going to run out of supplies eventually, right?"

"Yeah, I know, so does Other Tom. We'll figure something out, or maybe things will get better, you never know."

"Do me a favor, and keep an eye out for Jenny and her little girl, and Giles too?"

"I will, you can count on me. But only after I have another serving of that man's barbeque." He indicated Junior, who'd come out to the front of the store, and was warily watching the approaching group. "Junior! It's Tom from St. Jude's. We're back with some supplies that it looks like you're going to need!"

Junior waved a hand, and ducked back into the half store, coming back out a moment later with his father. They waited until the group got closer. Junior Senior frowned when he spotted Deb, and called out to her, "I told you I didn't want to see you 'round here no more!"

"Extenuating circumstances," she replied, happy to see him again, even though it had only been a few hours.

"Well, you are loaded for bear," he commented. "What do you want with all those weapons?"

"Some of them are for you, and you're getting two of these guys as permanent company, along with Tom."

"What we'd do to rate such service?"

Deb studied the dark grey sky, the destroyed landscape, the cracks in the cement before she answered. "You cared," she said. "You care about people. It matters, now more than ever."

Junior Senior nodded slowly. "I hear that. Can you stay for a bite to eat?"

"I'm going on with the other two to warn Spencer at the VA about the looters that attacked us, and then I'm going to do what you said I should do."

"Good. You're going to go to your family. That's good, well, all right then." He cupped her cheek with his warm hand, and she leaned into it, smiling back at him. Junior Senior thought for a moment, held up a finger for her. "I got something for you before you go, hold on a sec." Junior Senior whispered something in his son's ear. Junior grinned and ducked inside, coming back out with a folded piece of notebook paper. He solemnly handed it to his dad, who carefully placed it in Deb's hand.

"What's this?"

"That is my daddy's recipe for his special barbeque sauce, the one you so enjoyed earlier today." Junior Senior said with a twinkle in his eye. "We only share it with family." He folded her hands over the paper, then pulled them to his heart. "We are family now."

Deb sniffed hard, then nodded as tears popped into her eyes. "Yes, I feel that, too. Thank you for everything." She carefully tucked the paper inside of her blouse, then stood on tiptoe to give the man a kiss on the cheek. "Bye for now," she whispered to him.

"Bye for now."

Deb took a final look back at the two Juniors who stood together on the edge of their restaurant to wave farewell, then turned to the men who waited for her a few steps away. Deb moved past them to lead the way. "The VA's about a mile south, but we have some downed freeways to deal with, so let's get going. I think we can make it before dark." She touched the piece of paper that sat next to her heart and stepped forward into the waning day.

CHAPTER NINETEEN

The Blacksburg-Pembroke Fault
Day Three

It had rained sometime in the night, cooling the air, although the oddly colored, dust-filled overcast had persisted. Mara welcomed the sight of the darkened soil and glistening garden from the window of her bedroom, and took the time to do a few stretches to ease her back before getting dressed for what she intended to be a productive day. She'd awoken after a solid seven hours of sleep with a renewed sense of purpose that was solidified when the delicious aroma of freshly brewed coffee welcomed her to the big farm kitchen. Caroline saluted her with a cup and poured her some from the French press.

Mara closed her eyes and inhaled the steam before taking her first heavenly sip. "I may have to hug you for this," she teased Caroline.

"We're not there, yet." The teen told her flatly, although there was a slight upward tilt to her lips.

"I think most of your ideas from last night were excellent," Mara said. "I also think we should write down what we need to do on a daily basis, maybe have morning and evening meetings, at breakfast and then after dinner. What do you think?"

"I know you love a list."

"Guilty as charged."

"Then, yes, let's do that. What do you mean, *most* of my ideas were excellent, though?"

"I just have a couple of changes. Shall we roust the boys and have our first meeting over Will's sugar bomb that pretends to be cereal?"

After gently shaking the two boys awake, Mara left them to get dressed and went out to her garden. She picked a few dozen ripe strawberries to add to their breakfast, taking a moment to look over the entirety of the garden, and then back at the sky. If the thickening layer of cloud cover persisted for more than a few weeks, the things that needed full sun - which was most of her garden - wouldn't survive. Pensive, she took the time to brew more coffee as the kids made their way to the kitchen table.

"Yum!" Will exclaimed as he sat down to his bowl of cereal and splashed a healthy amount of goat's milk onto his serving. Gretel had followed him into the kitchen, and promptly went to her own food and water, her tail wagging agreeably. Mara picked up a strawberry and popped it in her mouth as she placed a yellow legal pad on the table, along with a pen.

"Welcome to the first Padgett/Varden breakfast meeting," she said, raising her coffee cup in a salute.

Ethan raised an eyebrow at her as he raised his mug also, and a moment later, Will joined in with a wave of his spoon and Caroline with her own cup of coffee. A wash of love for all of them saturated Mara as they began their meal, followed by the surety that she'd do anything it took to get them through the crisis, keep them all safe until Logan got back to them. Taking a deep breath against the quiver of nerves in her belly at what she needed to say, Mara took a final, fortifying sip of coffee and cleared her throat.

"I'm going to share some concerns with you, things I've kept to myself for the past couple of days, things that you may find scary. I know I do," she began, stopping again as Will's big brown eyes rounded and he stopped his spoon half-way to his mouth, the thick goat's milk dripping back into the bowl.

"Go on, mom," Ethan prompted.

"Yeah, no going back now," Caroline added, leaning back in her chair, gripping her coffee cup tightly. "Let's hear the doom and gloom."

"Okay. First, these earthquakes that may be global,"

"Yeah, that's what Eva and Lloyd said yesterday!" Will spoke with some excitement.

"I'm going to get to our neighbors in a moment," Mara said, with a glance at Caroline, who scowled at her. "These earthquakes have done more than just destroy things; they seem to have broken the electricity and sewage and water systems, and it may take a long time to get those back, especially if the earthquakes keep going the way they have the past few days."

"But we're okay. We have the well, and our generator and candles and stuff," Will popped in again.

"But not everybody has those things," Ethan told him gently.

"She's trying to say people are going to want to take our stuff," Caroline interjected abruptly. "We're going to have to make our place stronger to keep them out."

"Oh, wow. Okay, cool." Will nodded a bunch of times, his eyes getting even bigger.

"He can handle it, Mara, so can I. What else?"

"I think we'd be smart to expect to have to live off-grid for months, and to do that, we're going to need more supplies. I'll start a list and then, as Caroline suggested last night, we can divvy up the chores so we can get it all done. We're behind right now. I worry that a lot of people will want the same things we do, so the sooner we get the supplies, the better."

"Months?" Ethan's jaw had dropped. "Mom, come on."

Mara shook her head and put down her pen. "You saw what it was like just on day one, Ethan, how quickly the people became angry and combative, like outside of the ER just down the road. The scope of the disaster is big, and I'm not going to let us be caught short-handed. There will be things none of us know how to do, or get, too. But I know where there's a big library and I have the keys for it, so we can learn as we go."

"You mean the high school library?" Caroline asked.

"Exactly. But that's for later. For now, our priorities are securing our property and shoring up our supplies."

"That doesn't seem too hard," Will said. "I thought you said you were scared."

It was time for the part of the family meeting she'd been dreading. Mara gripped the edge of the table to steady herself. "There are two things that scare me, Will. The first thing is the cloud cover that's building out there out of the debris and dirt kicked up by the earthquake. It's blocking out the sun, and it's gotten thicker every day. Even the rain we had last night didn't clear it. If that doesn't disperse in the next few weeks, our crops will die, and it will become like wintertime very quickly. We need to prepare for that as soon as we can."

"Dang," he said, his face turning a bit pale.

"What's the second thing?" Caroline demanded.

Mara hesitated and then plunged ahead. "Our neighbors, Eva and Lloyd. I don't trust them."

"No way!" Will dropped his spoon in his bowl.

"Oh, come on!" Caroline threw her hands up. "They helped us! They're fine! You're being so weird."

"Let mom talk!"

Gretel barked sharply at the rise in tension and raised voices. Mara hushed the dog with a hand command, then cut in over the top of them. "I got a bad feeling from them when they dropped us off. I didn't like how they looked at our homestead, it was like they wanted it for themselves, with the kind of comments they were making. Caroline, I also didn't like the way Lloyd was looking at you, or the fact that he never used your name most of the time when he spoke to you or Will, and Eva didn't either." The words tumbled out, and she put her coffee cup down firmly and sat on her fingers to to hide that her hands were shaking.

"Mara! The way Lloyd was looking at me? Come on! He wasn't doing that."

"Mom, that seems a bit extreme."

Mara raised her voice over the protestations. "Maybe it is extreme. I am willing, so very willing to be wrong about it." She stopped, then continued in a more reasonable tone. "Can you, at least for these next few days, while we pull our place together, keep an eye out, and just call me if you see them again? Don't interact with them, okay?" The three of them just stared at her. "Okay?!"

"Sure, mom."

"Okay," Will said more reluctantly.

"Whatever," Caroline added after holding out for a few seconds more. "We're probably going to be too busy around here, anyway."

First hurdle cleared. Spared the need to argue the point further, Mara plowed forward. "On to what we should accomplish as fast as possible. Caroline suggested last night that she goes to the hardware store and the pharmacy this morning on the ATV, and Will, that you go to Larcher's for things like more canned goods like beans, bread, butter, and cereal on your bike, I'll make lists for both, then you can look and see if you want to make any more additions or corrections to my ideas." She looked to Caroline as she finished, who gave a slight bob of her head that she approved. "Will, we'll need to trade some goat's milk for it, so can you milk the goats as soon as we're done?"

"Cool, can I get some candy too?"

Having had a couple of years to become acquainted with Will's insatiable sweet tooth, Mara nodded. "Yes, you can get yourself a treat. Next, I think we should harvest our garden soon and put it up, which means we need to find lots of jars, anywhere we can, but we have to clean the cellar first."

"I can see if there's some at the hardware store," Caroline said.

"That's another thing. We don't have a lot of cash on hand, so if you have some stashed away, I'd ask you to contribute it so we can buy what we need." Mara rose and got the cigar box they used for their cash stash, and put it in the center of the table. "Just put it in this, and write down what you added, so we can keep track, okay?"

The kids nodded their assents, so Mara went on. "I'm going to move your dad's truck in front of our gate to block it, and then Caroline, Will, and I will strengthen the fence line by the road this afternoon. Ethan, please clean the guns from the gun safe like Logan showed you, so that we're sure they're in good working order, and then later we'll do a little target practice out back."

"Whoa! Me too?" Will wiggled in his seat, arms raised high in a victory dance, when Mara nodded at him.

Caroline was startled. "Dad said that Will had to be ten to start shooting. That's how old I was."

"Under any other circumstances, I'd agree, but I want him to be able to handle himself if it comes to that. And Will, you're going to listen to everything we say about gun safety, right?"

"Totally! Oh boy!"

Ethan was looking off, as if he'd had a thought. "We could make a secret entrance back behind the pond, where the woods start," he said. "That way, we can leave the truck up front, and drain the truck's gas to use for our generator, and people wouldn't see us coming and going."

"Great idea. Caroline, is there a good spot for that?"

"I might know one, but I need to go look." Caroline stood and then stopped. "That is, if our meeting is done?"

"Yes, I think that's plenty for this morning," Mara said. "I'll have those lists for you in say, a half hour, so you can be at the stores when they open."

"I'm on the goats!" Will dashed out with Gretel close behind him, the screen door banging as they passed through it. Caroline put her brother's bowl and her mug in the sink and went out immediately afterward. Mara sagged back into her chair with relief. Ethan regarded her, then drained his coffee cup. "Good going, Mom."

A bit of tension left her shoulders at his compliment. "Thanks, I imagined that would be harder, somehow."

"They want this to work as much as you do."

"What? Us making our homestead safe or making us a family?"

Ethan shrugged elaborately as he grabbed his crutches and wobbled to a stand. "I think we have to start out with the first one, and let the second come as it does."

"It's already been a year." She couldn't help it, the disgruntled words popped out.

"Patience, my young Padawan," Ethan quoted wryly. "Now, what does a guy have to do to get a bath around here?" He sniffed his pit and wrinkled his nose. "I am seriously rank."

Mara laughed at the Star Wars reference. "They wash the dishes in that small pot of warm water while their mother makes a bigger pot of warm water on the fire in the backyard. Strip your bed, too, we'll do the sheets after we all have a wash."

The early part of the morning passed quickly as Mara started the big pot to heat, topped off the generator, and plucked a big head of cabbage for the chickens. She took it to their enclosure and called for them to come out. "I know I promised this to you yesterday, girls, but things went a little south, here you go." She chuckled when the flock scurried to it and started pecking happily. "And if you start laying eggs again, there'll be some blackberries in your future," she said as she left the enclosure.

Will was busy milking the goats in preparation for his trip to the store when she walked past toward the porch where Caroline was waiting for her, petting Gretel. "Guess we're going to have to do something about that, too," Mara said, indicating the slanted surface, and the way the end boards had crumpled against the brick of the house's foundation. "Did you find a place to put our secret entrance?"

"Yeah, there's a narrow gap in the fence there already, we just might need to clear some scrub and put in a gate we can close, something that we can fit the ATV through. We'd be a bit on the Buchanan property to get out to the road, but I don't think they'd mind. You didn't tell me what you changed about my ideas, yet." Caroline dumped the last part of the sentence into her report with challenge in her voice. "Did you think I wouldn't remember?"

"Right. I'm going to go over the Buchanan's, not you."

"Why?"

Mara was tempted to take the easy "I'm-the-parent" route by telling her that was just the way it was going to be, but instead told Caroline the truth, although she was fairly sure she'd be mocked for having yet another bad feeling. "When we drove by yesterday, I got the feeling they weren't... there."

"You think they're dead in there, and you don't want me to see their bodies." The girl's perspicacity took her aback. "They are pretty old," Caroline went on thoughtfully, "and I can see how that might happen, like with a fall, or a heart attack or something." She stood, wiping off the seat of her jeans. "Fair enough, do you have my list?"

Mara was just able to stop herself from goggling at Caroline's easy acceptance of her explanation. "I will in about five minutes. The water should be hot enough to wash. Can you manage to bring in the big pot on your own?"

In lieu of response, Caroline merely lifted her arms into a bent strongman pose and moved off to do as she'd been asked. Mara went inside to get washcloths and towels ready, as well as gathering a few plastic bowls that had survived the quake and would work for everyone to use as old-fashioned wash basins, then sat at the table again to do the lists for the kids.

After they'd all washed and stripped their beds, Will and Caroline had been given cash, two jugs of fresh goat's milk had been loaded into the panniers of Will's bike, and Caroline was set up on the ATV with a big box and extra bungee cords to strap the things she'd hopefully bring back. "Wear your masks the whole time. There's no need to rush over those broken roads," Mara said as she stood with arms crossed with a deep, cold pit of worry swirling in her chest, "You'll be the first in line, I bet, just navigate your way there as best you can, and be careful."

"Ok!" Will called out cheerfully, hopping on his bike and zooming up the driveway, his eight-year-old legs churning, spewing gravel as he went.

"He'll be fine," Caroline reiterated as she started the ATV. "See you in a couple of hours, tops."

Mara tucked her worry into a small compartment, rubbed the small of her back where an ache was already setting up shop, and turned to her son. "Would you rather sit on a stool and pick blackberries, or sit on a chair and help me clean the cellar?"

"Blackberries," he said promptly. "You going to make a crumble?' He asked hopefully.

"If the oats survived the cellar, then yes. After you're done with the blackberries, check in with me. If I find enough jars, we'll start putting up what we can: tomatoes first, then potatoes, then the zucchini. And wear a mask, this air isn't getting any clearer. And gloves, some of those blackberry thorns are enormous."

Armed with buckets to haul out trash and thick gloves, Mara swung open the door to the cellar. Gretel was next to her, poised on the step. "No, you can't go down there, girl. Go watch." The dog obediently trotted off to her post by the back door to do her job while Mara propped the cellar door open to get as much light as she could without wasting battery life on the flashlight or adding more requirements to their generator by using the fluorescents.

The cellar floor was covered with debris, and her boots made a sucking sound as she maneuvered through the goo to string the paracord she'd gotten from Logan's go-bag on hooks for an indoor laundry line, then got to work cleaning up the smashed glass and wasted food. It was a nasty, sticky business, but she had some victories along the way, the best being two whole cases of unbroken Mason jars tucked safely in a corner. While most of the canned goods were dented, they were unbreeched, and the plastic bins containing oats, rye flour, wheat flour, and sugar were in good shape, with only a portion of their contents spilled and spoiled.

Their boxes of power bars had come through unscathed as well but their honey was a total loss, however, as were the multiple jars of peaches, tomatoes, pickles, and other unidentifiable fruits and vegetables that had fallen and smashed to the ground. She shoveled up the glass and debris, mopped, and cleaned, hauling the full buckets out to their dumpster as she made her way from one side of the cellar to the other. Once the floor was clean, she brought down the boiled sheets and hung them to dry, then stepped back to look at what they had left.

It was a sad sight to see all the empty wall space. The two cases of Mason jars were a plus, but they needed at least five times that many to get them through even a partial winter if the grocery stores remained out of commission. She plucked out a single jar, and measured a cup of rye flour into it from the measuring cup that hung from the side of the wooden shelving, blessing the strong construction that had held the set of shelves that held their grains in place.

She set the jar on a step to take up with her after she completed a final project.

Mara disassembled the metal shelving that had collapsed in the quake until it was only one level high, and placed it around three of the four walls in a single level, something that wouldn't topple if they had more quakes. In the last corner, she used a cordless drill to secure a double-thick plastic tarp into the concrete, then put two wooden pallets on top of that and stepped back, satisfied. Filled with dirt, they'd become an indoor container for easily grown lettuce, spinach, and radishes to eat once she fixed the broken grow light that was in the shed. If they used the lamp only a few hours a day, the pull on the generator wouldn't be too much, and they'd have a backup for fresh vegetables in case the cloud cover really did persist, bringing on an early and continuing winter.

A shudder ran through her as she recalled descriptions from a history book of the year that summer had never come in the early nineteen hundreds after the eruption of a volcano somewhere. The suffering had been terrible for people back then as crops failed, livestock died, and famine swept over many lands. But then they weren't prepared for it, and the Padgett family would be. Picking up her tools, and the Mason jar with the rye flour, she ascended the stairs to start the next project of the day, making a sourdough starter so that they could have fresh bread next week. The Buchanan's had an outdoor brick oven that had hopefully not completely fallen over, and they wouldn't mind her using it if she shared some loaves or goat's milk. *If they're alive.* The words floated up unbidden, and her stomach churned at the idea of visiting the ghostly-looking house, but it would have to be done. Mara mixed a half cup of water with her rye flour, covered it lightly with a cloth on top of the refrigerator, and went outside to check on Ethan before she took that visit on.

"So. Many. Berries." He held up a huge basketful. "Were the oats okay?"

"They were, so you'll get your crumble. What a great harvest. We'll do some blackberry jam as well, I think. Our sugar stores stayed intact."

"Will's going to be happy to hear that. Where to next?"

"Is your leg holding up?"

"I'm sitting down, mom." He only sounded mildly annoyed. Being outside was a much happier place for her lanky, athletic boy than locked down in bed.

"Okay, I'll take these in. The tomatoes need picking next; you'll probably need a bushel basket, but that just means more tomato sauce." Mara looked past the fence line where the blackberry bushes grew with such jubilant abundance to the Buchanan land beyond. "Maybe I'll bring some of these berries to the Buchanan's."

"Do you think you should go there alone?" Ethan, as always, was sensitive to her emotions.

"Sure. It won't take more than a few minutes. I'll find out if Bonnie has any canning supplies she can spare. She was a prolific canner, if I remember."

Mara took the main road to walk to her neighbor's house with a basket of fresh berries swinging at her side, although it would have been a shorter journey through the adjoining backs of their properties. Creeping up to their house from the rear had felt wrong somehow, like it would have made her into an interloper rather than a neighbor. She'd made up her mind to tell them they'd planned a back entrance to their own home and ask if they'd mind the family cutting along the side of the fence for a hundred yards or so. Of course, Bonnie and Ed would be all right with it; they were generous people, and had welcomed her when she'd come to the homestead a year ago. Mara's steps slowed as she approached the old farmhouse. It looked as if it was listing even further than it had yesterday, more of the bricks tumbled off of the left side which had once proudly supported the porch the Buchanan's had liked to sit on and watch the world go by of an evening, commenting on the fireflies and the world in general, a sweet tea in hand, genially agreeing with each other as they had done for the past fifty years. The white clapboards seemed duller too, as if the house had been long abandoned.

She tentatively stepped onto the porch, feeling her booted feet slide to the right as she did so, the once-sturdy boards creaking in protest. Mara opened the screen door and knocked on the main door, making the cheerful "Welcome Friend" sign bang along with her firm knocks. Her unease grew when there was no response. "I need to check," Mara said aloud to herself as she walked around the wrap-around porch, then descended the three wide steps to access the backyard, pushing open the little picket fence door, carefully latching it behind her.

The Buchanan's liked to let their chickens roam the back to keep down the bugs, but she didn't see any of the birds, and made a mental note to check on the coop. The rear of the house was also collapsing on the left. Perhaps there was a sinkhole beneath that side that had never been properly identified. She looked at the rear windows, hoping to see the flutter of a curtain, anything that said life remained within, but all was unmoving and silent, the grey sky above reflecting the oppressiveness. Mara ascended the concrete steps that led to the back door. The Buchanan's told her when she first moved in with Logan after their marriage that they hadn't locked their back door in all the years they'd owned the house, continuing the proud Buchanan tradition of never meeting strangers, just friends they hadn't met yet.

The knob turned easily in her hand, and Mara eased the door open a few inches. "Hello?"

A lone cricket in the house chirped a few times in reply, but after that it was silent except for a distant buzzing she couldn't identify. She stepped further in and tried again, more loudly. "Bonnie? Ed?"

The avocado green kitchen with its patterned linoleum floor had been partially picked up, but the smashed glasses and dishes were still in the sink, and a broken chair still leaned against the refrigerator, as if they'd been interrupted in their cleanup after the quake had happened. The phone that Caroline had been so insistent on trying to use dangled from its coiled cord, swinging a bit as she moved to it to see if there was a dial tone, but it was as deadly silent as the rest of the house, so Mara carefully hung it up again.

Bonnie would never leave her house in disarray, not even if they'd been called away to be somewhere else in a hurry. A cast-iron skillet was still on the front burner of the stove, filled with a decaying substance that might have once been bacon. Mara sniffed the air, but couldn't detect any smell of gas, although one of the knobs was turned to the on position, so she snapped it off. There was a whiff of something else that her nose caught though, a moldering sweetness like a sack of oranges gone bad that stuck in her throat making it hard to swallow. Her gaze fell on the back of the kitchen door, the place where Bonnie kept her bright blue and yellow apron, but the hook was empty. Bonnie loved that apron, but she'd never wear it outside of her home, so maybe they'd been hurt and were elsewhere in the house.

Mara placed her basket of blackberries on the counter and moved into the disheveled living room avoiding fallen furniture, the cloying scent becoming stronger as she reached the beautiful stairs that climbed through the center of the house to the upper bedrooms, complete with a carved walnut balustrade that had been polished to a high shine by loving hands. Mara started up the wooden stair on tiptoe, as if she was afraid of waking some monster, but the smell that she was following faded after only a few steps. She turned back around to go to the back side of the grand staircase where a narrow door led to the Buchanan's cellar.

The door was closed, but the buzzing was louder, and the smell of moldy oranges was stronger, strong enough to make Mara raise her hand over her already masked face as she opened the cellar door. The reek hit her with full force as soon as she did so, as did a cloud of buzzing flies that had somehow found their way to a feeding source and place to lay their eggs. She flapped them away from her as the horror grew inside of her, forcing herself to look down the stairs once the flies had zipped away. The light from the kitchen and the living room windows filtered down them, becoming less powerful with every step, but still able to illuminate what lay at the bottom of the stairs; the bloated, dead bodies of Ed and Bonnie Buchanan, their limbs entangled in a final wild embrace, both still wearing their pajamas. Ed had one slipper missing, his long foot a white oval in the surrounding dimness, while Bonnie's nightdress had hiked up around her thighs. Both of their faces were turned to the open door, sunken and waxy, as if they'd tried at the last minute to shout for help.

Mara turned away, ripped off her mask and threw up her breakfast, a violent involuntary heave that left her shuddering and popping with sweat when she was done.

Mara didn't want to look at the bodies again, didn't want to verify the other thing that had been revealed in that brief horrific frozen moment when she'd looked at them from the top of the stairs, but she had to do it. Steeling herself, Mara turned back to the open door and forced herself to look at the faces of her neighbors, and confirmed the horrible reality. Both Bonnie and Ed had neat holes drilled in the center of their foreheads, blackened scorch marks standing out against the waxy white of their skin. Holes that could only have been put there with a gun.

CHAPTER TWENTY

US Army Reserve Base, Brainerd MN
Day Three

They'd put Logan in what passed for a holding cell at the army reserve until Captain Johnson could be appraised of the situation and make his command decision. The makeshift brig was a windowless broom closet outfitted with a metal cot in the interior of the main building, the strong smell an overly enthusiastic use of antiseptic floor wash making the time he spent there one that he'd always remember as pine-scented. It had a door that locked rather than bars, but Logan chafed that he'd been locked up at all.

He'd only punched Jasper the one time, but the little man had staggered backwards, tripped over his own feet, and fallen heavily, his hands to his face as a red gush covered his fingers, howling as if he was being torn apart by wolves. Logan had felt badly about his loss of control for a good five seconds, enough that he'd maybe been about to apologize and give Jasper a hand up off the ground when his arm had been grabbed and he'd been yanked around by a large, balding man with a grin that revealed a lack of dental devotion who'd socked him hard in the belly. His breath had whooshed out of him, but even as he gasped for air, the man's fist came up for his chin, so he dodged it, and then dived at the man, hitting him as fast as his own fists could move in the ribs and down by the kidneys, where you could do some serious damage if you knew what you were doing. It had been like hitting a sofa, hard in some places, soft in others, all the while sucking in air to get oxygen back into his body from the man's first blow.

More people had flung themselves into the brawl after that, hands and feet flying. He'd been knocked into a tent, collapsing it under his weight, causing the people inside to bellow with terror and scramble out of the thing, adding their voices to the ever-growing cacophony. There'd been hands on his shoulders, perhaps someone trying to restrain him, so he'd bent over and flipped them over his back before whirling around to meet the next opponent.

"Logan! Logan!" Someone had shouted his name over and over, a woman's voice that might have been Gayle, then the ground had come up and hit him for a final time, his head bouncing on the soft grass and mud of the field where the refugee tents had been set up. He'd had a brief glimpse of overcast sky before a man's face, turned puce with rage, filled his view. It was the balding man again, but the grin was gone, replaced by a grim determination etched on his features, that said, clear as anything, "I'm gonna kill you."

He'd rolled away, but had caught up against tent pegs, the sharp metal ends digging painfully into his skin, rolled back the other way and scissored his legs to dump the behemoth to the ground before he could beat him to a pulp with those giant fists, but had failed to get a good purchase, merely making him stagger sideways instead. He'd had a random notion that the man might be one of the "buffalo-sized" ones from Sandra and Joe's tent that she'd mentioned, which was followed by a moment of perfect understanding of why she'd find their company objectionable when the Buffalo's fists wrapped around his sturdy plaid shirt and hauled him to his feet, presumably to give him his own punch in the face which might indeed, knock his block off, when bodies and arms had roughly interceded, pulling them apart and bringing the fight to a stuttering finish.

The sight of the giant clutching his ribs, walking partly bent over when he'd left the field of battle had provided him a hot surge of pleasure, but it hadn't made his own body feel any better. He for sure had at least one cracked rib and there'd been blood in his urine when he'd peed into the pan the unit doctor had given him, so something was damaged internally. He also had a massive black eye, although he had no memory of any blows landing there, and his hands were a pulped mess. The doctor had administered some good pain meds for the ribs and general discomfort, which had made his migraine go away, so there was that, and he'd gotten a fairly good amount of sleep as well in the tiny room by himself.

It was coming up on midday, and aside from a poker-faced Private bringing him a breakfast of eggs, toast, and coffee, along with a little paper cup holding the pain meds he'd been prescribed, there'd been no forward motion in getting out of the camp and headed toward home. Moodily he laid on the cot and counted the cracks in the wall again, as he waited to see what was going to happen next. He hadn't lost his temper like that since he'd been in the Marine Corps and had gotten caught in an altercation between some locals and his buddies on a rare night of leave, and had become incensed when his best friend Walton had been hit over the head with a pool cue for no good reason. That night had also ended with him in a brig, a serious one with bars and a vindictive captain on the other side of them, the beginning of the end of his unstoried military career.

"Fighting other people is not a good idea," he said aloud to himself, squashing the memory of his intense satisfaction when the bridge of Jasper's nose had snapped beneath the power of his fist.

The door unlocking had him swinging his feet to the ground. Captain Johnson stood in the doorway, his face serious. "Mr. Padgett, I'd like you to get off my base," he said in a calm voice. "I assume you'd like the same thing."

"Yes, sir."

"You have five minutes to get your personal possessions out of your tent; there's a truck headed to St. Cloud in ten."

Logan stood, then swayed a bit, bracing himself against the wall. The Captain gave him a curious look. "Do you need further medical attention?"

"No. Nope, I am good." Logan waited to push off the wall until he was sure he could keep his feet and walk in a straight line.

"Mr. Padgett, I tried to put you on a different transport than the one being used by Mr. Collins and his friends, but that wasn't possible, as I want them off my base as well. That truck is my property. Don't disrespect my property again, am I clear?"

"You are." Logan gave a brisk nod of his head, and then wished he hadn't. It throbbed and his vision swam once again. "Captain, could I trouble you for some more pain meds by any chance?"

"I'll have Private Ingersoll meet you at the truck."

"I appreciate that."

The man gave him a once over and shook his head. "I'm sure you do. You look like ten miles of bad road, Mr. Padgett."

"Yeah, but how does the other guy look?" Logan quipped.

Logan thought that he'd perhaps gone too far, but then the Captain gave a little shrug. "Five miles of bad road and a bad attitude. Best of luck to you."

"You too, sir."

Logan made his way into the gloomy morning, keeping his head down to avoid meeting anyone's eye and getting embroiled in conversation or explanation or an exciting blow-by-blow of the fight. He was more than ready to leave this place, which had gathered far too many painful memories, both physical and psychological. Gayle's cot and those of her sons were empty, as was the bed that Braden had used, the sight of it striking a pang into his heart. Logan stuffed his jacket, raincoat, and the blue baseball cap into his decrepit backpack, which was already packed with his few remaining possessions, then stripped the sheet, rolled the blanket, and placed the pillow on top of it as the other occupants had done. With a final glance to make sure he hadn't missed any possessions, Logan ducked back out of the temporary lodging and hurried to the main doors so he wouldn't miss his ride.

His head pounded, his eyesight in his blackened eye was blurry and he couldn't catch a full breath without his ribs feeling like they were on fire, but Logan's spirits lifted as he walked away from the encampment and visualized getting back to Mara and the kids, his imagination leapfrogging over what might be a long and dangerous journey to the moment when he walked down their graveled driveway, at long last only steps away from his two-story white farmhouse with its broad, welcoming porch and big garden, the stunning vista of the Blue Ridge Mountains rolling and green in the distance. Logan would hear Gretel barking, and then the slam of the screen door as first Will and then Caroline ran out to meet him, then would come the feel of their arms around them, being able to hold their warm solid bodies as close as he could, then he'd look up and see his beautiful Mara as she descended the stairs, her long blonde hair pulled into a braid, the quiet special smile that was just for him on her face, while Ethan stood behind her, tall and handsome, then all of them embracing in a group hug while Gretel joyfully bounced and barked around them.

Sustained by the image that he'd firmly placed into his mind, Logan walked through the long hallway into the main area where Private Ingersoll stood waiting for him, his hands behind his back and a quirky smile on his face. The young man handed him a small pill bottle, and then with a grand gesture, swung a sturdy, grey and blue camouflage army backpack around from behind him and extended it to Logan with a broad smile.

"The meds are from the Captain, the backpack is from me."

Taken aback, Logan's mouth gaped open. The private grinned and pushed up his glasses. "There's some waters and a bag of snickerdoodles in there from my aunt, she made extra when I told her you were travelling a long way back to your family."

"Private, thank you. I don't know what to say, except that having it will make a huge difference on my journey."

The young man flushed a bright red. "You don't have to say anything. I'm glad to let you have it and Godspeed to you, Mr. Padgett." He pushed the bag gently into his hands, and then briskly moved to open the door for him. "I hope you have a safe and easy trip ahead of you."

Logan extended his hand and shook Private Ingersoll's. "It'll be much better now, with some good gear, and your aunt's cookies. You thank her for me, will you?"

"You betcha!"

A troop truck like the one that had brought him to the camp three days previously was loading passengers in front of the building, two soldiers helping the last few people in line into the back of it, the engine already running. He strode over to the truck, but Logan's step hitched when joyful laughter burbled from across the street, pulling his gaze to the playground where Braden happily ran in circles, his chubby little arms flapping as if he were trying to fly while Cathy chased behind him, laughing as well. There were other young children playing in the schoolyard, swinging, and sliding, but he only had eyes for Braden, his little feet galloping along as he laughed and tossed his head back to see if Cathy was gaining on him. Logan's heart swelled so fast he thought it might choke him as he soaked in the last few moments of seeing the boy, pinning them in them in his brain so he'd never forget this instant in time.

"Sir?" The voice intruded into the crystalline moment, shattering it. "We're leaving, if you want a ride to St. Cloud."

"Sure, yes." Logan tore his eyes away from the little boy who'd won his heart so completely and stepped up into the truck, taking the last seat on the bench, the sound of Braden's laughter still audible.

"Godspeed, little buddy," he murmured, echoing what Private Ingersoll had said to him.

The soldiers swung the back gate into place and locked it in, then banged on the side of the truck. The vehicle popped into gear with a loud grind of gears, and rolled forward, bouncing as it hit the uneven pavement of the road on its big tires. The other people in the vehicle all swayed and bounced and let out a surprised "oh," as they grabbed onto the wooden slats behind them, or the bench at their knees. Logan placed the new backpack behind his legs, not wanting to change his possessions over from his old one in the close confines with thirty other people watching him. The army reserve base and the school across from it got smaller and smaller until he couldn't see them anymore from the back of the open truck, his sight growing blurry from more than the breeze and his wounded eye.

Once they had completely disappeared, he wiped his eyes with his shirt sleeve and huffed out his breath to try to ease the dull ache that had settled deep in his core. To distract himself, he looked around the interior. Nearly immediately he spotted the Buffalo, who was glowering at him from the other side of the truck. Next to the man, who did indeed look like five miles of bad road with a bad attitude was Jasper, his glasses taped with the same white surgical tape at the nosepiece as the doctor had used on the bridge of his nose. The man's little legs didn't quite touch the ground, so they swung like pendulums with the movement of their bumpy progress down the road as he sat on the bench wedged between the Buffalo and another large man who was nearly his twin except for the shock of unruly curly hair springing from his head.

A hand waving from the far end belonged to Sandra, happily grinning at him. Joe was beside her, a protective arm around her shoulders. Logan gave them both a chin-up in greeting, and then a second one to Gayle, who was seated next to them with her boys on either side of her. The woman gave him an inquisitive tilt of her head and an arched eyebrow that worked perfectly to silently communicate her questions, "Did you change your mind? Are you coming with us?"

Logan chuckled inwardly at the woman's persistence, no longer able to find irritation or anger with her as he shook his head no with what he hoped was a regretful look on his face. Gayle got the message and spread her hands in the universal gesture of "I had to try." Logan supposed he was regretful as the rolling plains of middle Minnesota blurred with the speed of the truck into a wash of gold and green and grey, long stretches of open farmland dotted with occasional grain silos. While he had no real connection to Gayle and her boys or Sandra and Joe, they'd been through some trauma together, which had been bonding to a degree. He didn't wish to see any harm come to any of them, and having company on the road was always a plus, especially with the journey ahead being a huge enigma, so he was giving up a certain amount of safety by going his own way.

In a way, all the people who'd been at the army reserve base had all been eased into the global disaster, even considering the horrific ordeal of the rough and tumble plane landing and subsequent explosion that he'd been through. They'd had three days of food, water, and shelter provided to them, along with clothes, showers, and human compassion from both the townspeople and the soldiers at the base. Others across the United States, likely thousands of them, had gotten no such respite, people like his sister-in-law, Deb, who'd been located in one of the cities they'd been told had been obliterated by the initial round of earthquakes. He sent a prayer her way that she'd somehow survived the quake and would be able to get to the homestead as well.

The people on the truck were certainly better off than those poor souls in Dallas who'd been in the buildings as they'd collapsed, or on the bridges as they fell, the hundreds of thousands who'd perished in mere minutes, their last moments on earth full of terror as the ground opened and ate them alive or they were crushed to death by concrete and steel. Logan shook his head and wondered if Braden's father had been a downtown worker, or if he'd been spared that horrific moment of knowing he was going to die.

Thinking about Braden was like poking a sore tooth and it sent a sharp bolt of regret through him every time he did it, causing him to let out a little moan as he put his head into his hands. The older woman sitting next to him gave him an odd look as his elbows bumped into her side. Logan pulled them in and sat up straight as the truck roared along the bumpy highway, the edges of the road blurring with the speed of the trip, Logan stuck his hands in his pockets, wincing a bit as the cloth tugged at the sore knuckles, but wanting to keep himself as contained as possible in the tight quarters.

Logan's fingers brushed something round and smooth at the bottom of the pocket. Not able to understand what it was, he pulled it out, and saw it was a rounded, flat rock in the shape of a bottlecap, the rock that Braden had given to him yesterday. Every moment of the interchange was seared into Logan's mind, the way Braden's little hand had extended to him, the sweet smile on his face as he gave it to him, saying, "Yours," then the "mwah" of the kiss so freely given immediately afterwards.

He held the rock as if he held the child, cradled in his hand, all the memories of their short time together flooding in, overwhelming him. On top of it came the memory of Gayle's voice, telling him that

Roanoke was a straight shot from Wichita, that it might be a better route than the solo diagonal he'd planned. Then the final thing, not a memory, but a realization.

Dallas was a straight shot to the south from Wichita. He could take Braden home.

He clutched the rock in his fist and leapt to his feet shouting, "Stop the truck!" His voice was loud and demanding, causing the woman beside him to shrink away from him with a gasp.

"What are you up to now?" Jasper snarled, his tone stuffed and nasally from the wrapping on his nose. "Trying to ruin our trip out of here?"

"Stop the truck!" Logan braced himself on the side and roof of the truck as it bounced over another big crack, his feet nearly going out from underneath him.

"Sit down!" several people called out, others told him to shut up.

He yelled even more loudly the third time, his cracked ribs protesting at the effort he made. "Stop the truck!" The third time, he also met Joe's eyes. The man was puzzled, but turned and banged on the panel behind him repeatedly until the slot opened. Joe said something that Logan couldn't hear, but the truck slowed as it pulled to the side of the road.

There were groans as it rolled to a stop.

"For crying out loud," complained Jasper to everyone, and then continued to the people sitting across from him, "What a troublemaker. He hit me in the face, you know. For no reason!"

"You provoked him," said Gayle, loudly. "So don't go painting it like it was something it wasn't."

"You weren't even there."

"I was right there, little man!"

A soldier came around to the back and craned his neck to look at Logan. "What's the problem, is someone sick?"

"No, I just... I need to go back," Logan said, his heart beating wildly, snatching up his backpack, and clambering over the tailgate. "I forgot something." He landed with his knees bent and slung the backpack over his shoulder.

"Well, you can get another one of whatever it is in St. Cloud, mister, it's at least fifteen miles back to camp, maybe twenty." The soldier looked like he was half inclined to force him to get back into the vehicle.

Logan smiled at the man, the surety of what he needed to do filling him. "No, I can't. It's a person, you see."

"Well, we're taking these people on to St. Cloud."

"That's fine, I understand." Logan called back into the truck, "Gayle!"

She appeared a moment later. "Yes, Logan?"

"I'll find you on the road. Just head south the way you planned. I'll catch up."

A grin spread across her face, as she clapped her hands together. "I'll hold you to that, for sure! But what are you going back for?"

"I'm gonna get my little buddy," Logan said, and grinned.

READ THE NEXT BOOK IN THE SERIES

Nowhere to Turn Book 2

Available Here
books.to/KcKMO

Made in United States
Troutdale, OR
10/13/2024

23708975R00159